THE KIRKLAND SISTERS

Cordelia, a brilliant young architect, and Julia, a glamorous and gifted actress, had shared little but a troubled past, growing up in the shadow of a powerful and demanding father, world-famous architect Adam Kirkland.

And then came handsome, charismatic Tony Bain: Adam's protégé and the only man who could rival him in stature, passion and genius. In an intensely romantic triangle of forbidden dreams and desires, Tony becomes husband to one sister and lover to the other . . . until a bitter legal battle uncovers a shattering family secret that pits sister against sister and love against loyalty. . . .

Adam's Daughters

More Bestsellers from SIGNET

Adam's Daughters

Elizabeth Villars

A SIGNET BOOK

NEW AMERICAN LIBRARY

Copyright © 1984 by Elizabeth Villars

All rights reserved. For information address
Doubleday & Company, Inc.,
245 Park Avenue,
New York, New York 10167.

This is an authorized reprint of a hardcover book published by
Doubleday & Company, Inc.

SIGNET TRADEMARK REG. U.S. PAT. OFF. AND
FOREIGN COUNTRIES
REGISTERED TRADEMARK—MARCA REGISTRADA
HECHO EN CHICAGO, U.S.A.

SIGNET, SIGNET CLASSIC, MENTOR, PLUME, MERIDIAN
and NAL BOOKS are published by New American Library,
1633 Broadway, New York, New York 10019

First Signet Printing, August, 1985

1 2 3 4 5 6 7 8 9

PRINTED IN THE UNITED STATES OF AMERICA

*For Adam's Mother
and my good and enduring friend Jane*

I am indebted to many people for the time and help they gave me in the research of this book. The aid and expertise are theirs. The debt and responsibility for any oversights or errors are mine. I would like to thank especially Susan Betkowski, Richard Brodman, Helen Dimos, Mary Beth Evans, Pearl Hanig, William S. Hanway, Stephen Kay, Mark J. Schwartz III, E. Russell Snyder, and Amanda Tobier. I am also grateful to the Information Exchange of the Urban Center and David J. Bauer of the New York Public Library for their generosity with materials and to my editor Susan Schwartz for her continuing reassurance and encouragement.

E.V.

Contents

BOOK ONE
Cordelia's Story   11

BOOK TWO
Julia's Story   175

BOOK THREE
Tony's Story   263

BOOK ONE

Cordelia's Story

1

By the time I arrived at each successive stage of life my sister Julia had already left her mark on it. Not an unusual story for a younger sister, except that Julia's fingerprints were large and clearly defined, like those of a thief begging to be caught. I suppose I always knew we'd have to face each other someday, but I never thought we'd have to do it like this, in full view of everyone. Or maybe I always knew it would happen like this. Julia is nothing if not dramatic. She can't resist the grand gesture. Or the grand entrance.

There were sixteen of us in the conference room that morning—all men except for me—and every one of them looked up when Julia Kirkland walked through the door. The political types stopped whispering in each other's ears and pricked up their own as if waiting for her to deliver her first line. The money men—including Graham Fowler—stopped counting the minutes on their gold Rolexes as if they were dollars and began speculating on which seat she'd take. And the architects, a group rarely cited for their unity of opinion in aesthetic matters, regarded her with unanimous and undisguised approval. I couldn't blame them. As a sister, I might feel some envy. As an architect, I knew only admiration. Besides me, Tony, a better architect than I and a long-standing fan of Julia's, let out an almost inaudible sigh. Then he pretended to look at his watch as if he'd been expressing impatience rather than adoration.

Julia's hair, framing her classical oval face, was as thick and lustrous as the gold brocade curtain that rose on her performance each night. Her violet eyes flashed with enough passion and light to carry to the third balcony. Her figure was the stuff of a million male fantasies, her carriage the result of proper upbringing and rigorous professional training.

She crossed the room to the empty chair at the head of the conference table. Every eye followed. With good reason. Thousands of theatergoers paid upward of thirty dollars a ticket for a view of my sister. We were getting it for free.

Sean Wellihan followed her into the room. His entrance was, to put it mildly, anticlimactic. Don't misunderstand me. There's nothing wrong with Sean's appearance. In fact, before he became a successful playwright and the darling of international hostesses, Sean was an actor, and he still looks every inch the matinee idol. The fault lay with neither Sean nor his entrance but with his audience. Julia had them in the palm of her hand.

He moved to pull Julia's chair out for her, but the man from the mayor's office and another from the governor's beat him to it. She looked from one to the other. Her smile was dazzling, sincere, practiced. Julia had never learned to stop smiling because, unlike me, she'd never had to wear braces. She sat and folded her smooth expressive hands on the table before her.

Her glance swept the room, embracing each of the men in it. She did not even look at me.

"Now that we're all here," Robison began and smiled back at Julia as if to reassure her that her arrival had been well worth the wait. Robison was from a federal agency that had offered to mediate between Artists for a Cultural Tradition (ACT) and Fowler Developments, Inc., between a group of publicity-seeking theatrical reactionaries and Graham Fowler's plans for a magnificent—if I do say so myself—new hotel and theater complex that would revitalize the seedy slum that Broadway has become. In other words, between Julia and me. Robison and his group had offered to mediate, and his voice, as he called us all to order, was like cough syrup, the thick sweet kind usually prescribed for children. I knew the voice annoyed Tony, but then almost everything about Robison annoyed Tony. "You can't get him to commit himself on anything," Tony had complained, but Graham who was more easygoing if not less demanding than Tony had just laughed and said that's what government men were all about. And Graham should know. He's been buying and selling them all his life.

Robison turned to give our side a dose of the medication. "Ready, Mr. Fowler?" Graham nodded. His slender face was blank, even a little bored. Not an errant twitch of muscle or an inadvertent blink of eye gave away the fact that he had almost three hundred million dollars riding on this meeting.

"Mr. Bain?" Robison went on canvassing. Tony said he was ready, and I recognized the impatience in his voice. He used to sound the same way when he was waiting for me to finish dressing. If I'd bothered him that way, Julia must have driven him mad.

"Mrs. Bain?" Robison asked in the same sticky voice.

"Kirkland," I corrected him. My tone was sharper than it should have been, and Graham glanced at me, the ghost of a smile flickering over his thin lips. The look was reassuring and strangely intimate in that impersonal setting, but Graham, despite the impression he gave in public, wasn't afraid of intimacy. Graham wasn't afraid of anything.

On my other side Tony concentrated on the blueprints spread out before him on the table. I noticed as he bent over them that his hair, as black and thick and straight as mine, grazed the collar of his shirt. He'd always needed someone to remind him to get a haircut.

"Perhaps we might recap the issue briefly," Robison said, "just to make sure we all understand each other."

On my right Tony's long thin fingers beat an impatient tattoo on the table. On my left Graham folded his well-manicured hands as if he had all the time in the world, though, in fact, his time was worth at least as much as Tony's and probably a great deal more.

"After all, the goal of this meeting is better understanding," Robison went on. Tony's fingers were still beating on the table, but he glanced at Julia, then quickly away. "Now Mr. Fowler's plan for a forty-story hotel . . ."

". . . with a theater and working and living space for artists," Graham's attorney interrupted.

"With a theater and working and living space," Robison repeated, "designed by Kirkland and Bain Associates"—Robison paused for what I can only describe as an oily smile at Tony and me—"has been pronounced acceptable by the City Planning Commission, a special review board of the American Institute of Architects, and . . ."

"Those findings are merely recommendations and not legally binding," the lawyer for ACT interrupted.

"We're not opposed to the building," Sean Wellihan said. I noticed that Julia's eyes held Tony's for a moment, but she still wouldn't look at me. "We're only against building it on the site of the Sarah Siddons Theater."

"The new Sarah Siddons Theater in the Fowler complex . . ."

"I should think it would be called the Graham Fowler," Julia said. Her voice, throaty, promising, distinctively her own, was a powerful weapon. All eyes turned to her again.

"I'd be happy to name the new theater the Julia Kirkland, if Miss Kirkland prefers," Graham said.

"Miss Kirkland," Julia answered, "prefers the old Sarah Siddons Theater."

"The new Sarah Siddons will be twice as large," Graham's attorney took over again. "With modern air-conditioned dressing rooms and proper plumbing."

"Unlike attorneys," Sean snapped, "artists do not live by showers alone. We don't want a theater that's twice as big. One of the many advantages of the Sarah Siddons is its intimacy. It also has perfect acoustics and sight lines. And if we're going to talk about excellence of design"—Sean flashed his leading man smile at me; it was as powerful a weapon as Julia's voice—"the Sarah Siddons . . ."

". . . does not have landmark status," Graham's attorney interrupted. "The Advisory Council on Historic Preservation . . ."

"Mr. Fowler has many friends on the Advisory Council," the lawyer for ACT countered.

"Are you suggesting . . ." Graham's lawyer demanded, but Robison's syrupy voice flowed between them, urging the understanding of issues rather than the involvement of personalities.

Tony's fingers continued to drum on the table. Graham, despite the implied accusation of bribery and graft, remained impassive. I looked at the model of the Fowler Building, which we'd brought in addition to the blueprints and elevations. You couldn't expect a layman to read a plan, but surely even Sean Wellihan ought to be able to appreciate the building when he looked at the model. And Julia must have understood it too. Julia was as much Adam Kirkland's daughter as I was. She'd grown up listening to his tirades about honest and dishonest, moral and immoral buildings. She'd been dragged through muddy construction sites from the time she was old enough to walk. And she'd been there the morning Papa's fertile mind had given birth to Inter-American House, that revolutionary skyscraper that had changed our lives and architectural history.

The model of the Fowler Building standing on the table between Julia and me now wasn't as good as that, but it came close. In fact, the Fowler Building, incorporating the Fowler Palace Hotel and the new Sarah Siddons Theater—a hexagonal tower of varying heights that derived its startling shape not from fashion or whim but from its mixed function and relation to its neighbors in the theatrical district—was probably the best work Tony and I had ever done. Funny about that. After the divorce I'd sworn I'd never work with Tony again. The practical problems were too great,

18

the emotional dangers overwhelming. But Tony had given me no choice. Just as his personal excesses had driven me to a separation, so his professional ones had forced me into a partnership. I'd been furious at the time, but I was grateful now. The work we'd done since then, especially the Fowler Building, was better than anything we'd done before or separately. In fact, Graham's building just went to prove what I'd told Julia years ago. Tony and I were perfectly suited as colleagues and entirely mismated as husband and wife. At the time she'd disagreed—or at least pretended to—but she'd been proved wrong.

Robison was still droning on about environmental studies and urban preservation laws, and this time it was Julia who cut him off. "If you destroy the Sarah Siddons Theater, you destroy the mainstream of American theatrical history." Her voice was soft as a whisper, but it captured the attention of the entire room. "Nine Pulitzer Prize winning plays opened at the Sarah Siddons and four plays by Eugene O'Neill. Arthur Miller, Tennessee Williams, and Lillian Hellman made history there. As did Katharine Cornell, Alfred Lunt and Lynn Fontanne, all the Barrymores, and"—Julia looked at me for the first time—"Judith St. John."

Mother had made history there, all right. She'd starred in five plays at the Sarah Siddons, including the one she'd been in the winter of the plane crash.

"And Miss Kirkland has also made theatrical history at the Sarah Siddons," Sean added. Julia had made her Broadway debut there. It wasn't a night I was likely to forget. I could still remember that she'd been sick that afternoon—I wondered if she still got sick to her stomach before opening nights—and that she'd grown hysterical when someone had begun whistling in the dressing room. For an intelligent woman Julia was inordinately superstitious. I remember the way Papa had looked sitting there in the orchestra that night as he used to for Mother, and the flowers Tony and I had sent, and the party after it. I especially remember the party afterward. "A dual celebration," Papa had said. No, Julia's first Broadway opening was not one I'd be likely to forget.

"No one is questioning the importance of the theater's past," Graham's lawyer said. "Or Miss Kirkland's achievements. What we're talking about here is the city's future. Mr. Fowler is going to bring a great many jobs to New York. They may not be the kind of jobs Miss Kirkland or Mr. Wellihan want, but they're the kind of jobs the people of this city need. When I think of what Mr. Fowler has offered to do for this city . . ."

"And what this city has offered to do for Mr. Fowler," Sean interrupted. "Namely a twenty-one and a half million dollar urban development grant." I was surprised and noticed that Tony was too. He'd said once that Sean's financial sense didn't go beyond signing the check at Sardi's, but then Tony had misjudged Sean in more ways than one.

"That's a federal grant," Graham's attorney said.

"But let's not forget the millions in city tax credits," Sean added.

"In return for thousands of city jobs," Graham's lawyer repeated.

It was all repetition, as Graham had predicted. Everyone talked. They passed the blueprints, examined the model, nodded sagely, and talked some more. They talked about urban development and the future of the cities, about twelve hundred new hotel rooms and twenty-five hundred new jobs, about cleaning up blight and revitalizing Broadway. They talked about the new theater in which the sight lines and acoustics would be just as good, if not better, than the old. I know because two designers in the firm spent four months working them out. They talked about what would happen to the future Eugene O'Neills and Arthur Millers without small theaters in which to try out their serious dramas. They talked about compromise and conciliation, two words which had never carried much weight in our family. And then at ten minutes after twelve, when they'd been talking for almost three hours and looked as if they'd go on talking for another three, Julia stood. Her eyes were exactly like Mother's, indefinite blue-violet with infinite possibilities. I have the same eyes, even down to the almond shape, but don't seem to get the same mileage out of them. Julia's swept the table and came to rest on Graham. He stared back at her, his gray eyes steely beneath smooth brows, his face still impassive, perhaps the only impassive face in the room. "I don't care how splendid your building is or how big your theater or how many jobs you're trying to bribe us with, Mr. Fowler. The Sarah Siddons must not be destroyed. And if I have to lay my body in front of your bulldozers, I'll see that it isn't."

Needless to say, Julia knew a good exit line when she heard one. She swept out of the room carrying Sean and the other representatives of ACT in her wake.

"Bravo!" Graham said quietly, but his fingers brushed my back lightly, surreptitiously, as if to reassure me without embarrassing me.

It was still raining when we reached the street, a bleak, chilling drizzle indigenous to New York in March, but Graham's limousine was waiting in front of the building. "Lunch?" he asked, his hand firm on my elbow.

"I don't have much time."

"Then we won't have much lunch. Care to join us?" he asked Tony. Of the three of us, Graham was the only one untroubled by the tangle of our lives, but then Graham was troubled by little in life. Tony refused, as I knew he would.

Graham's limousine pulled away from the curb, and I glanced out the tinted rear window at my former husband. He stood among the hurrying midday crowd, as proud and unbending as one of his own buildings. He'd forgotten his umbrella again, and the wet stains on his trench coat were spreading like a cloak over his wide shoulders. Beneath the dark hair, plastered to his forehead, he gazed through horn-rimmed glasses at the line of occupied taxis crawling up the avenue. I thought that he was likely to get soaked and chilled and sick as well, then reminded myself that Tony was a big boy—and no longer my responsibility.

I turned from the rear window and caught my own reflection in the top of the small chrome and mirrored bar Graham had flipped open. The eyes were, as I've said, similar to the ones I'd faced across the conference table that morning, but while Julia's had flashed violet, mine were a nice safe blue. Perhaps it was the dark hair, thick as Julia's blond mane, but bone straight that made them look so much less dramatic. My nose was longer than Julia's, but fortunately straight; my mouth wider, but unfortunately neither so full nor so sensual. The same could be said of our figures. Papa used to joke that he'd fathered each of us as an architectural exercise. Julia was an exploration of the possibilities of the curve, I of the potential of the angle.

I turned away from my own reflection and took the short drink Graham handed me. The limousine turned onto Fifty-second Street and began inching east. In New York at this time of day Graham's driver headed for "21" as instinctively as a homing pigeon headed for the roost. "21" was more than a restaurant to Graham. It was a private club where his table was always waiting, his preferences in food and drink always remembered and his power always recognized.

"I don't think your partner likes me," Graham said as if the fact amused rather than troubled him.

"He designed a magnificent building for you."

Graham took my free hand in his. His hands were large and strong, a little like Papa's. Tony's hands were like mine, long, slender, and perpetually ink-stained. We even have the same bump on the second finger, the result of hours spent over a drafting board. "I thought that was *your* gift to me."

"We both designed it. It is beautiful, isn't it?"

"So they tell me."

I pulled my hand from his. "I wish you wouldn't joke about it."

He took my hand again. "I'm not joking, Cordelia. One skyscraper looks just like another to me."

"And all you're interested in is filling the envelope with as much rentable space as possible."

"Exactly." His long aristocratic face creased in a grin. "I'm interested in picking up another two or two and a half million a year, and the City of New York kindly gave me permission to—until your sister and her group stepped in."

"If all you care about is filling the envelope, why did you give us the commission? You could have gotten another building by another architect for less."

"Because I was after you."

"I'm serious."

"So am I," he answered without a trace of solemnity. "I'm interested in you, and the shortest way to your heart is through a T square. But I'm also interested in making as much money per square foot as possible. I take risks, Cordelia—that's my business—and I like to get paid for those risks. It just so happens you can help me do that."

"You think the public will pay more for good architecture?" I was hopeful by instinct but dubious by experience.

He laughed. "I don't think the public knows what good architecture is. And if it does, it doesn't care. Only 20 percent of the buildings under construction in this country are designed by architects. The rest just happen. So much for what the public will pay for good architecture. But they will pay for cachet. And Adam Kirkland had cachet."

"Papa had genius," I corrected.

Graham rubbed the bump on my second finger with his thumb. For a man of impregnable reserve, he could be surprisingly physical. "Whichever, the name 'Kirkland,' even the name 'Kirkland and Bain'"—Graham's smile was teasing but not unkind—"still means something. So the public will pay a hundred and fifty or two hundred a night to sleep in a hotel designed by Kirkland and Bain and almost as much to eat and drink in its bars and restaurants. In other words, much as I hate to disillusion you, Cordelia, I'm paying for your name rather than your genius." His thumb had moved to the inside of my wrist, as if the light caresses might soften the words.

"You're a cynic. You could probably stand before the Pyramids unmoved."

His fingers tangled in mine. "The Pyramids were nothing more than a WPA project. They had to keep the people employed while the Nile flooded. And I'm not a cynic, merely a realist. That's another reason I gave Kirkland and Bain the commission. There are architects who try to find economically feasible solutions to problems and architects who don't give a damn. I can't tell you whether the building is beautiful, but I know you'll finish close to schedule and the mechanical systems and operating costs will be efficient. That's one of the things I love about you."

Actually it was Tony who usually kept me and the designs to budget, but I didn't think I ought to mention that now. "And all this time I thought you were after my body."

He laughed, and the smooth, high forehead creased in deep furrows. I remembered the first time Tony and I had met Graham Fowler. I'd said he was handsome, despite the receding hairline. Tony had said he was bald, or at least on the way. Graham was almost as tall as Tony, slender and always impeccably dressed. I'd said he was aristocratic looking. Tony had said he was dry. "Arid," he'd added as an afterthought. Tony, I knew now, had been as wrong about Graham as about everything else.

"There are certain attractions there," Graham said. "I thought I made that clear this morning, but"—his finger traced the outline of my mouth—"if I didn't, we can forget the restaurant and go back to my place for lunch."

He had made that clear this morning. Graham's public image, aloof and impassive, was deceptive. He was a man of deep feeling, and despite the fact that he was fifty-six, or perhaps because of it, he was skillful and considerate at showing that feeling. At another time I would have preferred his apartment to the restaurant and him to lunch, but not after this morning's meeting. And Graham sensed that as instinctively and accurately as he did everything else about me. He didn't tell the driver to head uptown, but he did tell me not to worry. "It's only a building," he said.

"It could mean millions to you," I answered.

"It's not my millions you're worried about, Cordelia." I didn't say anything, and he laughed again. "And that's another thing I love about you."

At two-thirty of a weekday afternoon Park Avenue in the forties and fifties is lined with limousines. Graham's jockeyed among them for a position in front of Inter-American House. The rain had stopped, and the few rays of sunshine that cut through the clouds glanced off the dark glass of the building like slivers of ice.

"Even you have to admit," I said to Graham, "that's an extraordinary building."

His only answer was a smile. Graham knew better than to argue with me about Inter-American House. As far as I was concerned, it was more than a building. It was a member of the family, perhaps the only member of the family with which I was still on loving terms. I'd been present at its conception and had come of age in the shadow of its influence on American architecture. And it had all started with my unwanted breakfast. That and Papa's genius.

There's a lot of talk outside the profession about napkin sketches. The public likes to think that inspiration strikes like a thunderbolt and all we architects have to do is pick up a pen and translate that inspiration into form on the linen napkin of some posh expense-account restaurant. Most of us within the profession are familiar with a longer and more arduous creative process. Yet like every myth, that one is based on a kernel of truth. Inspiration does occasionally strike while lunching with a prospective client or performing some mundane function of everyday life. And buildings, even great buildings, do sometimes grow from these impulsive sketches on whatever material is at hand. In fact, the two most famous napkin sketches in modern architectural lore were not done on napkins at all. Saarinen carved his design for the MIT auditorium from half a grapefruit, and Papa created Inter-American House from my uneaten breakfast.

We were all at the table that winter morning, which means that Mother must have been in rehearsal. When she was performing, she rarely came down to breakfast, and Julia and I would go into her room to say good-bye before we left for school. But she was there that morning, her straw-colored hair held back with a pale satin ribbon that matched her dressing gown, her face, scrubbed free of makeup, radiant in the early morning sun streaming through the windows. Papa loved to have Mother across the table from him in the morning, though he wasn't paying much attention to her that particular morning. His eyes had that glazed look, like two prize amber marbles sunk in his broad face. Even at the tender ages of eight and six, Julia and I knew the significance of that look: do not disturb. Every now and then he ran a distracted hand through his hair, which was still jet black at the time. Gradually, as if he weren't seeing at all, Papa's eyes moved to my plate. Eggs were not my favorite food, and I'd used two pieces of toast to construct a wall shielding the sight of this particular uneaten egg from Mother. When Papa's eyes focused on the food and I saw the light flicker in them, I recognized the spark of creation rather than disapproval. Without a word, he pulled the plate toward him and rearranged the two half slices of bread to a more generous angle.

"That's it, Judith!" he shouted. In those days there was a great deal of shouting in the house, since Papa demanded attention and Mother demanded an audience and Julia demanded her way.

Mother stood and walked around the table to Papa's chair. "You see it, don't you? You see the space." Mother said she did see it, and then just to make sure she did, Papa took a pen from the pocket of his dressing gown and the blank paper Mother produced from a sideboard because she was still fighting the losing battle of the place mats, and began to draw.

I know now that Papa wasn't an especially good draftsman—maybe that was why he insisted artful sketching merely masked inferior designs—but he was a dramatic one, and soon he'd covered several sheets of paper with bold sketches. Meanwhile he kept mumbling about how his vision went beyond Lever House and the Seagram Building. And he'd been right. Those two glass boxes had begun the revolution that changed Park Avenue in the 1950s and ultimately every city in the world, but Inter-American House had carried the movement to its most daring and elegant conclusion. And perhaps the most amazing part of it all, I thought as I stepped from Graham's limousine, was how close the final result was to those first brave sketches. The twin towers, sheathed in skins of glistening dark glass, reaching back from the street to meet seamlessly, formed one of the most civilized public spaces in the city. These days every skyscraper boasts a public plaza, but in the midfifties when Papa designed Inter-American House, the idea of open—and, to the developer, wasted—space was a revolution rather than a cliché. Papa not only gave the urban dweller a place to stop and savor the city, he gave the office worker a sense of light and air and freedom.

Papa had broken half the rules in the book—and managed to create a whole new set of them. By building that piazza he'd thrown away hundreds of thousands of dollars in rental space. Then he'd turned around and put a parking lot underground to make up some of the revenue and add an unusual urban amenity. Below that he'd constructed a system of drives and tunnels for truck deliveries, making the streets around Inter-American House the least congested in midtown Manhattan. On the flat roof, mandatory to the International Style of which Papa was a leading proponent, he'd landscaped gardens, which brought the public pleasure and the building's owners still more unexpected revenue. On the ground floor of one of the towers he'd carved a huge space for the most stylish restaurant in town. Every inch of rentable office space was within twenty feet of a window, and—another innovative amenity at the time—centrally air-conditioned. Moreover, the tinted glass counteracted the worst effects of the sun, which wreaked havoc on the more conventional glass boxes.

No dream had been too impossible for Papa to attempt, no detail too small for him to oversee. He'd designed the light fixtures in the lobby, the faucets in the lavatories, the lettering on the mailboxes. Inter-

American House delighted the eye and nurtured the spirit. It made life more pleasant for those who worked in it and money for its owners. Even after all these years and all those bad imitations, my heart still lurched as I stood at the foot of it and gazed up at what Papa had wrought.

I was still looking up at the building, wondering if I'd ever do anything as good, but Graham, leaning out of the open window of his limousine, was looking up at me. "I wish that just once," he said, his hand on mine on the open window, "you'd look at me the way you do at that building. Will I see you tonight?" he went on before I could answer.

"I have a dinner appointment with a client."

"After dinner then?"

"I'll try."

"I'll send the car for you."

I told him not to bother. "It won't be hard to find a cab at that hour." That was the truth, but only part of the truth. The dinner was with a client and Tony, and I could picture the sardonic expression on his face when he saw Graham's limousine waiting for me. He wouldn't say anything, only smile that superior smile that makes his jaw a little too square and his mouth, which is usually a nice mouth, thin and a little cruel.

I was halfway past the newsstand in the lobby of Inter-American House when I saw it. The headline was hard to miss. Two words screamed in bold black print:

JULIA JAILED

Even without the accompanying photograph, I would have known which Julia they meant. For the American public, there was only one Julia: my sister. I bought the paper and studied the picture. A policeman was holding her arm as if he were escorting her to an opening night rather than a paddy wagon, and Julia was smiling for the camera, which loved her as well as any man ever had.

In the elevator on the way up to my office I skimmed the article. Julia and Wellihan had gone from the meeting straight to the Sarah Siddons Theater. There they were joined by other members of ACT, whose names read like a Who's Who of the American theater. The demonstration soon flowed from the sidewalk in front of the closed theater out onto the street, effectively stopping what little traffic movement there was in the theater district on a matinee afternoon. Of the twenty-seven screaming protestors who'd been arrested and carried off in paddy wagons, there were many character actors and several stars, but Julia was the leading lady. And she'd dressed for the part, as only Julia would, in the luxuriant mink that she wore in the ad asking what became a legend most. In the photograph, as in the ad, Julia's face answered the question.

I folded the paper so that the headline was hidden and tucked it under my arm, but as I walked through the reception area, down the hall, and into my outer office, the half dozen people who greeted me couldn't keep their eyes from the tabloid.

"You've seen it?" Tony was waiting for me in my office. He was sprawled in one of the black leather client's chairs with his feet on the black table with tubular steel legs that serves as a desk. The table was clear—no papers, no mementos—except for Tony's big cordovan shoes that looked dull and scuffed, as if he'd been walking in the rain.

"I've seen it. What worries me is how many other people will see it. Nobody cared about the Sarah Siddons until we announced we were going to build on the site. Now all of a sudden, it's a cause célèbre—thanks to Julia."

"I called Albert Fitler."

Albert Fitler was a lawyer, not Graham's corporate lawyer or ACT's representative but the lawyer who took care of all the family's personal matters—all, that is, except Tony's and my divorce. Fitler had referred each of us to another attorney for that.

"Why did you do that?"

"To get her out of jail, of course. Post bail or do whatever has to be done."

"For God's sake, Tony." I pushed his feet off my desk. "It's only a publicity stunt. They're not going to keep her there."

"Aren't you being a little hard on Julia?"

"Yes, well, some of us are hard on Julia and some soft." He looked away from me at that. "Anyway, she's probably out of jail by now. Today's Wednesday, and Julia wouldn't miss a performance—even for the Sarah Siddons. Or should I say another performance? She certainly gave a marvelous one this morning."

"She meant everything she said this morning." He fished around in his jacket pocket and produced a package of cigarettes.

"I thought you'd stopped smoking."

"I have," he said and lighted one. "She loves that theater."

"Which side are you on these days?"

He stubbed out the cigarette. "For Christ's sake, Cordelia, you know which side I'm on. It's my building too. Or has Fowler convinced you it's entirely his?

32

Another one of those money boys who thinks architects are just idiots with T squares. Another one of those who-needs-an-architect—''

The intercom on my desk buzzed then, and it was just as well that it did, because I knew what Tony was going to say, and he knew what I'd answer, and there wasn't much point in going on with any of it.

Tony said to forget it, and my secretary said that Albert Fitler was on the phone, and Fitler said, as I'd predicted, that Julia had already been released and was probably halfway through the first act of the play in which she was currently starring. I hung up the phone and repeated the news to Tony. He took off his glasses and rubbed his eyes, usually a sign that he was trying to hide something. Relief that Julia was all right? Annoyance that I'd been right? Or only exhaustion?

He put on his glasses before he looked at me again. I was always sorry when Tony put on his glasses because his eyes were huge and dark and had the kind of softness that is usually associated with sincerity, though in Tony's case it's merely myopia. Still, no matter what the cause, I liked Tony's eyes, and when we'd been married, I'd always liked the way they'd looked in the morning before he hid them behind the 20/20 protection of his glasses.

"I'm going uptown later this afternoon to take a look at the Sutton Place construction. Do you want to come along?''

It was a peculiar invitation, because the luxury condominiums overlooking the East River were Tony's commission and his design, and even if they hadn't been, no site required two architects inspecting. Papa would have said I was wasting the firm's time, but I said I'd like to go along. It had been some time since

Tony and I had wandered a construction site together.

"I'll be going around six," he said. "Do you think you can stand a plain old taxi? I hadn't planned to order a limo." The jibe was directed as much at Graham as at me.

"I can if you can get one at that hour," I answered, but my barb was off target. Tony had always been good at getting cabs. For one thing he was tall, for another he was agile, and for a third he was just plain lucky—or so he used to insist in the old days.

There's a peculiar intimacy to a building in progress when the workmen have left for the day and the steel and concrete skeleton soars silently into the dusk. Tony must have felt it even more strongly than I because it was his building and had come from his heart and mind, but I sensed it too, and for a few minutes we picked our way wordlessly among the naked bones of what was essentially a dream. I didn't have on the practical low-heeled shoes I usually wear for on-site inspections, and I twisted my heel once and stumbled. Tony caught me before I fell and held me for a fraction of a second longer than he had to. Then he dropped his arms and turned away with an abrupt movement, as if there'd been something embarrassing in our contact.

"What were you thinking of then?" I asked, though I knew I shouldn't have.

"What do you think I was thinking of?"

It had been a long day, but the morning was still vivid in my mind. "Julia?" What I really meant was how much he'd rather be here with Julia than with me.

He started to say something, then changed his mind

34

and walked away. I should have let it go, but I was never good at letting things go. I followed him across the site, and when I almost tripped again, he didn't help me. "I'm sorry. I shouldn't have asked."

He looked at me from behind the armor of his glasses for a long time before he answered. "I was thinking of my first design job. The day we drove out to the country to look at the site. You tripped then too."

Now I was the one who turned away. Suddenly I noticed the chill in the air and the dampness that had returned. I buttoned the collar of my coat and put my hands in my pockets. Tony asked if I was cold, but I shook my head and tried to concentrate on his building rather than on him.

"I had no idea you were this far along. I thought we still had a design team working on the project."

"We do."

"But the foundation is laid and all the ironwork is up."

Tony pretended to be examining the end plate of a pretensioned concrete beam. "We're using the fast-track system."

"I thought we agreed not to." My voice sounded shrill, like the horn on the other side of the wooden construction wall.

He looked up from the beam. "We never agreed on anything, Cordelia. You made up your mind and assumed I'd go along."

"Papa always said fast-tracking was the sign of a shoddy building and a second-rate architect."

"Maybe it was then, but times change." I heard the implication behind the words.

"I suppose that's a reference to Bryant Park Tower," I shouted over the sound of another horn.

"It wasn't, but it could have been. If Adam hadn't been so headstrong, he would have seen what was coming. And if you weren't so stubborn now, you'd admit we can't afford not to use fast-tracking. In this financial market no one can wait until all the designs and specs are in to begin construction."

"Since when are you so concerned about financial markets?"

"Since the day I graduated from architecture school and realized I'd rather see my buildings in reality than on paper! Or maybe just since I've been spending so much time listening to your friend Fowler. And speaking of that high priest of the bottom line, you'd better get used to fast-tracking. He's decided it's the only way to go from now on."

"Graham won't cut corners. He wants the best building we can give him." I tried not to think of our conversation that morning in Graham's limo.

"Christ, Cordelia, Fowler wouldn't know a good building if Inter-American House fell on him. He says so himself."

"That's an act."

"Then it's a damn good one. He certainly convinced me."

"The same way Julia did?"

"What does Julia have to do with it?" he shouted.

"What does Graham have to do with it?" I screamed back.

We were both silent for a moment, and I heard Tony take two or three deep breaths. He did that when he was trying to control his temper, and it infuriated me. "Nothing," he said in a tight voice that made me even angrier. "We were talking about fast-tracking. And if you're not satisfied with the way I'm handling my end of things, take it up at the next partners' meeting."

He stomped out into the street and hailed a cab, and for a moment I thought he was going to leave me there, but he opened the door and stood waiting for me to get in. When I did, he slammed the door behind me. I rolled down the window quickly. "Aren't you coming to dinner? They're important clients."

"You take care of them," he said. "You're the expert in architect-client relations. You and Fowler." He turned abruptly and moved off into the gathering dusk. As the taxi passed him, I saw his strong profile, set in anger. He didn't even turn to glance at me.

2

The summer I turned nineteen Anthony Bain literally fell into my life—mine and Julia's. I was halfway through Radcliffe, Julia had finished her first run in an off-off-Broadway play, and we'd just settled into the house on Nantucket.

Each year Papa swore he wasn't coming back to the island. Slapdash cottages were spreading over the moors like wildflowers, boutiques turned a once-quiet Main Street into a teeming mall, and every ferry brought another onslaught of voracious tourists. "I didn't come thirty miles out to sea," he'd rant as he pounded back and forth across the deck, "to live cheek by jowl with my fellowman and be accosted in the Athenaeum by hungry divorcees who have seen my picture on the cover of *Time*! I'll sell the house, and we'll go someplace really distant. Better yet, I'll leave it to the gulls and terns and wild roses." But we all knew he'd never abandon the house he'd built on that wind-torn bluff. It was as much a part of him as Julia and I. More important, it was as much a part of him as Mother, because he'd really built it for her.

To us the house was a beloved object, but to the rest of the island it was an oddity. Adam's Bunker they called it, though the official name in the architecture books and monographs was Windswept. The natives had a point, because from a distance where the paved road ended and our dirt one began, it wasn't a house at all but a pillbox sitting not on a bluff but in it. Tangled brush and wildflowers covered the roof, and the concrete blended into the sand. In fact, from a distance the house would have been invisible were it not for the long horizontal stripes running around the three visible sides. Only as one drew closer did those stripes become the cool glass walls of the house suspended between concrete slabs of floor and ceiling. At once, window, wall, and reflecting plane, the glass changed color with the turning of the seasons, the time of day, and the position of the viewer. There was a fourth glass wall too, one that could be seen only from within the house. That glass wall was our window not on the dune but into it. There the colors changed not with the time of day or the seasons of the year but with the ages of the earth as they had been etched in the muted tones and subtle striations of the sand.

In architectural circles Windswept had become a landmark. Admirers photographed it, analyzed it, and made pilgrimages to pay homage to it. And the natives scratched their heads and muttered that there was no accounting for taste. "Oh, you mean Adam's Bunker," they'd say when some eager tourist would ask directions to Windswept. "Go south, then east toward Tom Never's Head and then when the road ends, keep on going. But you'll probably miss it anyway, if you don't look close."

Some of them did miss it, but others persevered. They came in jeeps with four-wheel drive and on foot through the soft sand and wildflowers. They came alone and in groups, to worship and gawk and intrude, to ask questions Papa refused to answer and make comments he pretended not to hear. And Tony Bain was just another of them. No, that's not true. From the very beginning Tony was special. All three of us sensed that.

We were on the deck that afternoon, Julia stretched on her stomach with the top of her string bikini untied, and Papa in a deck chair which he'd turned to the sea. With his mane of white hair, proud profile, and great barrel chest, he made a bold ship's figurehead. I'd seen him sit that way for hours, seemingly in a trance. Then suddenly he'd stand, stride across the dune, and disappear into his studio, where the drafting table stood waiting for him. Within moments a building would spring full-blown from his strong hands. Churches and schools, houses and skyscrapers grew this way because they'd been germinating in the fertile soil of his mind while he sat staring out to sea.

I was sharing one of the tubular steel and canvas lounges with Corbu, the gray tabby with white markings who'd come to us as a kitten the summer after Mother died. The old black tank suit I was wearing had a small hole in the side which Corbu occasionally swiped at with a lazy paw. That was the scene that Tony Bain, as I said, literally fell into.

The first sign of him was a noise in the dense growth beside the deck, as if some wild animal were about to invade. Corbu pricked up his ears, and I turned just in time to see Tony come rolling out onto the stretch of clean sand. Papa didn't even turn his head at the sound. Julia's lashes fluttered, but her eyes remained closed. Only Corbu and I took notice. We both sat up. Tony struggled to his feet.

His legs caught my attention first. Beneath cutoff jeans they were strong, deeply tanned, and already bleeding. The brambles had torn his shirt, and his chest looked as hard and smooth as highly polished mahogany. His face, when my eyes reached it, made me wish I'd changed my bathing suit. Under thick dark hair that fell over his forehead, the jaw was square, the nose straight as a Roman general's, and the wide mouth at once arrogant and embarrassed. I wasn't sure if he was going to threaten to sue or apologize.

"Are you all right?" I asked.

His sunglasses had been knocked out of shape, and when he took them off, I saw his eyes for the first time. They were closer to black than brown, and flecks of gold light promised something of value. It was only later that I discovered that the soft glaze of those eyes was myopia. At that moment all I knew was that they were the most beautiful eyes I'd ever seen—and that they were focused beyond my shoulder on my sister Julia.

I turned. She'd sat and was holding her bathing suit top in front of her. I glanced back at Tony. He looked as if he might fall again.

"I asked if you were all right."

Tony must have heard the impatience in my voice because he tore his eyes from Julia and brought them back to me. "I'm okay. I was trying to get a better look at the house."

Now, I was well aware of Papa's rules. They'd been drilled into me since infancy. He did not suffer trespassers. In fact, once or twice over the years when he'd opened a second bottle of wine with lunch, he'd been known to get out his shotgun and fire a few blasts over the uninvited visitors' heads. Two summers earlier he'd come close to wounding one of Julia's boy-friends whom he'd mistaken for an architectural historian. I knew Papa's rules, but standing there looking down at Tony I managed to forget them. "You might as well come up here," I said. "You can get a better look at the house and do something about your wounds." I'd tried to sound rueful but wasn't especially successful.

Tony did not have to be asked twice, but I suspect that had as much to do with Julia who was standing beside me by then as with the famous house. His long legs took the steps to the deck two at a time.

"I'm Julia Kirkland." She held her right hand out to Tony. Her left was still holding the top of her bathing suit to her. "And this is my sister Cordelia." The dark eyes fluttered over me, light as a butterfly, then returned to Julia. She'd finally decided to tie her top. Papa was still staring out to sea, impervious to us all.

"There's a faucet over there." Tony managed to tear his eyes from Julia long enough to glance at it. "I'll get some iodine." Iodine, I thought, would hurt more than Merthiolate.

When I came back out on the deck, I handed the bottle to Julia. She made a better angel of mercy.

"I can do it," Tony said as he reached for the bottle, but she pushed his hand away. As she bent to her work, her long gold hair fell like a curtain over his legs. If his wounds took him now, I thought, he'd die a happy man.

Papa had finally deigned to notice the little drama being played out on his deck. He stood and turned to us. In his flamboyant costumes—white linen suits in summer, midnight blue velvet in winter, rainbow-colored silk shirts, and floppy artists' cravats—Papa was an imposing figure; half naked in the French swim trunks that left his deep chest and massive thighs bare to the sun, he was like a pagan god. His six-foot-three frame crossed the deck. Tony stood. My first view of him had been from above, and now I was surprised to see that he was as tall as Papa. From beneath bushy white brows Papa's hard agate eyes measured Tony. Tony held them with his own. He didn't apologize for intruding or try to ingratiate himself with praise or even explain himself. He just stood there, his own sharp profile facing Papa's leonine one.

"I could have you arrested for trespassing," Papa said finally.

"You could, sir, but your daughters invited me in, or at least up."

This seemed to set Papa back for a moment. "So you came to see Adam's Bunker." He always used the natives' name for the house. It amused him, and I think he liked the sound of his own name better than the element's. "I suppose you're an architecture student. You're too young to be a critic. Are you any good?"

"The best," Tony shot back without hesitation.

Papa's eyes didn't soften, but they did flicker with interest. "At least you've got the ego. If you don't think you're the best, it's for damn sure no one else ever will. What's your name?"

"Anthony Bain."

"Bain. Anthony Bain," Papa repeated wickedly. "I don't think I've heard of you."

"You will."

Papa's laugh came rolling out from the depths of

his enormous chest. "Do you want a drink, Anthony Bain?" Tony said he'd like one very much.

"Ellen!" Papa bellowed, and I had to remind him it was the housekeeper's day off. As I went into the kitchen to get the ice and limes, I tried to decide which would be more obvious—the hole in my bathing suit or the fact that I'd changed into another. Not that I had to worry. With Julia and Papa on hand, I held about as much interest as Corbu the cat.

By the time I came back out on the deck, Papa was presiding over the wagon with the bicycle wheels he'd designed as a bar. I watched him pour gin halfway up a tumbler and hoped Tony Bain had a strong constitution.

Papa passed two weaker drinks to Julia and me, then handed Tony the lethal one. The only thing I can say in Papa's defense is that his was just as strong. "So you're a masochist as well as a fool," he said, taking the chair across from Tony's. I went back to my chaise and arranged a limp Corbu over the hole in my bathing suit. "You want to spend the rest of your life pouring out your heart and soul and guts—assuming you have them—for a world that doesn't understand and wouldn't give a damn if it did. You want to starve to death."

Tony took a long swallow of his drink. I waited for the grimace, but it didn't come. "Like you, sir?"

Papa took a swallow of his own drink and crunched an ice cube savagely between his teeth. "You think you're another Adam Kirkland?"

"I've already told you I thought I was the best."

"You can't beat him down, Papa," Julia said, "so you might as well give up." She smiled at Tony, and he smiled back.

"Well, if you came this far to see Adam's Bunker—how far did you come?" Papa's bushy eyebrows knitted together for a moment.

"New York."

He seemed satisfied. "Then you might as well have a look at it. Why don't you show him the house, Julia?"

Unlike me, Julia knows how to play hard to get. Now that she'd hooked Tony, she was going to take her time reeling him in. "Let Cordelia show him around. She inherited the architectural genius."

I heard the irony in her voice, but Papa missed it. It never occurred to him that anyone might joke about a topic as serious as his genius. "You have a point there." He turned to Tony. "Now she"—he spoke of me as if I weren't there—"is the best. Or will be. Even as a baby she thought three-dimensionally. You should have seen her with blocks. They tell stories about Frank Wright as a child and his famous building blocks. I'll be damned if he had anything on my daughter. You should have seen the massing."

Tony turned to me, but he'd put on his dark glasses again, and I couldn't tell whether he was impressed or amused. I couldn't see anything but my own reflection, dark and grossly distorted, in the lenses of his glasses.

"Those are the words of a father, not a critic," I said. "I piled blocks on top of each other, like every other kid." I stood and started for the house. If I kept my hand at my side, he wouldn't notice the tear in my suit.

I slid open one of the massive glass doors between deck and living room and the cat scampered in between our feet. "That's Corbu. After Corbusier, of course."

"Of course," Tony repeated. "Doesn't every family have a cat named after the patron saint of modern architecture?" He was still wearing his dark glasses, but I knew now that neither interest nor amusement had been in his eyes before, only resentment. Tony was starving for success, while I, as Adam Kirkland's daughter, had already been promised a seat at the banquet.

I turned away from the anger in his voice and started my tour. I'd been showing the house to guests since I was ten, and my patter was as proficient and rote as any museum guide's. I pointed out the concrete overhang above the glass walls that blocked the sun in summer and let in the lower slanting rays in winter, an early solar solution to the not-yet-articulated energy problem. I called his attention to the morality of the materials and the purity of line. I commented on the flow of space between the vast, high-ceilinged areas.

"Your father has Wren's and Wright's weakness in reverse," Tony said.

I stopped in front of an expanse of glass overlooking miles of wild dunes and untamed ocean and turned to face him. I was not accustomed to hearing anyone, least of all an architecture student, suggest that Papa had a weakness. "What do you mean?"

He started to laugh. "Don't panic. I wasn't criticizing the great man, only making an observation. Christopher Wren and Frank Lloyd Wright were both small men. They built to their own scale. Their passageways tended to be a little narrow, their lintels an inch or two lower, that sort of thing. Your father's a big man, and the scale of this house shows it." He moved to the window and stood beside me. "I'm surprised you never noticed it yourself—with all that congenital talent."

I turned from Tony to the view. "I might be good even if I am Adam Kirkland's daughter."

He took off his sunglasses and fixed those dark velvet eyes on me until I was forced to turn and meet them. I am not the weak-kneed type, but I felt a definite unsteadiness then. "You'd better be," he said, "because from the little I've seen, you'll never forgive yourself for having a first-rate career—which you're bound to—and being a second-rate architect."

"The little you've seen is pretty little," I lied because he'd gone right to the core of my fears.

He laughed and put his glasses back on the bridge of that nice straight nose. "Oh, I don't know. That bathing suit gives away a lot. In fact, there are those who might think a torn tank suit more revealing—and sexier—than a string bikini."

I didn't ask if he were one of them, but from the way he looked at Julia when we came back out on the deck, I was willing to bet he wasn't.

"Well, Anthony Bain," Papa's big voice boomed, "what do you think of Adam's Bunker? Every fledgling architect and fourth-rate critic feels he has a right to an opinion. What's yours?"

Tony took a sip of the drink he'd left on the table. "I think it's monumental." He flashed me a conspiratorial smile. My knees turned to rubber again, and I sat down quickly.

Papa looked disappointed. "I expected something more trenchant from one of the best architects of the twentieth century."

"It's a magnificent architectural statement. Philosophically pure. Absolutely moral." Tony dropped the catchwords of the sermon that had been preached at the Bauhaus and disseminated around the world. But

47

Papa, one of the creed's chief apostles, was no fool.

"In other words you don't approve."

"I admire it."

Papa's laugh was a bark. "You disappoint me, Bain. You're one of those young men who want architecture to be easy, accessible, comfortable."

"Merely functional."

Papa looked startled, as if Tony had stolen his thunder. Though the assertion that form follows function was first made by Louis Sullivan, it has been ascribed to many architects, and none more often than Papa. "You think this house isn't pure function!"

"There are many kinds of function. There's the function of a building's structure, which your house expresses admirably."

Beneath his wild Indian color, Papa turned a darker red at the word "admirably." For him it was faint praise.

"Then there's the function of architecture itself. Architecture is shaping space for people and their needs. Churches ought to inspire, office buildings impress, and summer houses . . . well, welcome, relax, maybe even seduce."

Tony was talking to Papa, but there was no doubt that all of us were listening. Though the breeze was still light, I saw Julia shiver, and I felt the goose bumps on my own arms and legs.

Julia sat up. "I've been waiting for someone to say that for years!"

Now there was genuine amusement in Papa's laughter. He had a whole litany of fixed beliefs about my sister and me, and one of them was that despite Julia's many attributes, she was, like the general public, visually illiterate. "I don't know if you're any good, Bain, but I'm willing to bet you'll be a success. You'll design buildings the public will be able to understand." Now it was Tony's turn to flush under his deep tan.

Satisfied that he'd scored his point, Papa swallowed the last of his drink. "And what about Inter-American House? What do you think of that?"

"Now that's a magnificent building," Tony said. "Pure, honest, as moral as they come." This time there was no irony behind his words. Then he went on. "A monument to your greatness."

Papa was quiet for a moment, studying Tony the way I'd seen him study blueprints. "I suppose you know what an impudent young bastard you are."

"I can only quote Frank Lloyd Wright, sir, 'I had to choose between hypocritical humility and honest arrogance. I chose honest arrogance and I have never had cause for regrets.' I imagine you're familiar with the words"—Tony hesitated—"and the sentiment."

Papa crunched another ice cube between his teeth. "Why shouldn't I erect monuments to myself? Bernini built them to God, Le Vau and Mansart to Louis XIV. And maybe if Anthony Bain is half as good as he thinks he is, *he*'ll build them to *himself* someday."

"There's no maybe about it . . . sir."

Over the years I thought about that first afternoon frequently, and once I even asked Tony about it. "Did you mean what you said that day, or were you just trying to antagonize Papa?"

"I was a kid in graduate school. Why would I want to antagonize America's greatest living architect?"

"To get his attention. To make him see that you weren't just another kid in graduate school."

Tony laughed. "Well, it worked. But I meant everything I said that day. Including the part about your bathing suit. I couldn't take my eyes off you."

It had been Julia he hadn't been able to take his eyes off that day, but at the time of the conversation we'd been married less than a year, and I didn't want to quibble.

As I watched Tony and Julia go off in the jeep that afternoon—she'd offered to drive him back to town—his broad shoulders jostling her slender naked ones as they bounced over the ragged dirt road, I thought it was fortunate that I was more interested in work than romance, too busy competing with men, especially men who were architects, to fall in love with them.

But the knowledge that I had neither time nor a chance with Tony, at least when Julia was around, did nothing to defuse the excitement I felt when I saw him climb out of the plane that Friday afternoon of Labor Day weekend. I'd driven to the tiny airstrip to pick up Papa, who flew in and out every week or two, and Julia, who'd fled the island in boredom halfway through the summer. The plane was small, and Tony had to stoop to get his long body through the door, but I knew who he was even before he straightened and looked up. When he did, he smiled at me and waved, and a casual observer might have thought he'd come to see me rather than Julia whose duffel he was carrying in addition to his own.

Papa kissed me hello, Julia did the same, and Tony smiled down at me. For a moment he seemed almost shy, but I couldn't be sure because his eyes were hidden behind those dark glasses again. Then we all piled into the jeep and drove back to the house.

After we'd showed Tony to one of the guest rooms,

I followed Julia to hers and closed the door behind us. "Anything happen since I left?" she asked as she began to strip off her shirt and jeans. Unlike me she could have used a bra, and unlike me she rarely wore one.

"Absolutely nothing, but what's been going on in town?"

"I was turned down for three parts. One even had a speaking line."

I always admired Julia's ability to joke about her setbacks. Papa said it came from being a theater brat, at least on one side of the family, but I thought it had more to do with her supreme self-confidence. Julia knew she was good, so good that someday the world would have to sit up and take notice.

"Obviously faulty judgment on the part of the casting boards. What about him?"

"Who?"

"Him." I nodded toward the door. "Tony Bain. When did he turn up? What's he doing here?"

She pulled on her bikini and shrugged her shoulders as if the questions were silly and the answers self-evident.

"Come on, Julia. Tell."

"He called me a few days after I got back to town." I thought of asking how he'd known she was back in town, but didn't bother. That sort of thing was always happening to Julia. The minute she arrived anywhere the phone began ringing as if she gave off sensory signals. "I've seen him a couple of times. Dinner. Movies."

"It must be more than that. You brought him up for the weekend."

"It was either Tony or that method actor from Stella

51

Adler's classes, and Papa can't stand him. I figured Tony would be easier on everyone."

"You're heartless."

"Heartless? I'm giving the poor boy a perfectly nice weekend on Nantucket. Kind of a private Fresh Air Fund."

"You really are heartless. It's obvious he's crazy about you."

"According to you, Cordelia, everyone's crazy about me."

"Everyone is."

"I can name at least a dozen directors right off the top of my head who are exceptions to your rule."

"Tony Bain isn't a director."

"More's the pity. If he were, I wouldn't be unemployed at the moment."

"You see, you admit he's crazy about you."

"I admit he's taken me out a couple of times and that he'd like to sleep with me."

In the past few years, since Julia had worked her way from the boy she'd played opposite in the senior class play, through one of her instructors during a brief semester at the Yale Drama School, and an off-Broadway director, a certain gulf had yawned between us. She was a woman, I was a girl; she was experienced, I was naive. The difference between us was a cliché, but like most clichés, it hid an ounce of truth. Although Julia talked about her affairs candidly, I never questioned her about them. At least, I never had till now. "I take it, he hasn't, yet. Or you haven't, yet."

She was standing in front of the mirror tying the top of her bathing suit, and the reflection of her eyes caught mine. "Contrary to what you think, Cordelia, I am not the whore of Babylon."

"I never thought that!"

"Didn't you? Sometimes your wit cuts a little close to the bone."

"That's envy, not condemnation." When I saw the skepticism in her face, I went on. "You can get away with anything. Because of the way you look and act, and the fact that you don't give a damn about anything."

"I give a damn about lots of things."

I was about to ask her if Tony Bain was one of them, but she'd already opened the door, and Tony was walking down the hall toward us, and, anyway, I was pretty sure the answer was yes.

At least I was until the following afternoon. The morning fog had burned off, and the day was clear with a light steady breeze. Papa announced that we were going for a sail on Thomas Shaw's yawl.

Thomas Shaw was the head of a conglomerate that owned, in addition to mills and mines and electronics companies, a major television network. Whenever he wanted a new building for one of his enterprises or philanthropies, he turned to Papa. Right now he wanted one in Chicago and had sailed up on his seventy-eight-foot yawl to discuss it. Among his guests was Webster Warren.

The name "Webster Warren" is, of course, a household word in America. The face is as familiar as Goerge Washington's and smacks of as much rectitude. It's one of those faces that, by virtue of its serious but imperfect handsomeness, lends credibility to whatever issues from it. In Warren's case, it lends credibility to the television news every night at six. Webster

Warren is what is known as a television journalist. One look at him told me he was an actor. And Julia gravitated to him as if he were a magnet.

The attraction was mutual. The only guests on Mr. Shaw's yacht were assorted members of the Shaw family and a sunburned, parched-looking banker. When we arrived at Swain's Wharf, Webster Warren, a man frequently pictured with some of the most beautiful women in the world, appeared to be suffering from withdrawal symptoms. The sight of my sister Julia revived him with all the speed and kick of a bracing gin and tonic. After less than an hour, Tony looked as if he were suffering from a hangover.

Julia was cool to Tony that afternoon. He might have been a kid brother she'd been forced to bring along against her better judgment. Papa, on the other hand, could not have been warmer. He treated Tony like a protégé, and even let him administer the coup de grace in the sales pitch. Perhaps Papa felt sorry for him. Perhaps he'd already cast him in the role of son and heir that I filled so imperfectly. Or perhaps Papa was simply tired of the dramatic tricks he occasionally had to use to turn his ideas into stone and steel and glass.

Papa dashed off one of his dazzling napkin sketches with record speed—this time on the pad Julia and Webster Warren were using to keep their backgammon score—but Mr. Shaw's response was tepid. Papa went into his act.

"We've got two main problems on this site, Tom. Bracing—mainly against wind—and cost. Or, rather, one problem. How to stiffen the building without stiffening the cost to you."

Papa hated money. He hated it so much that he

made a fetish of getting rid of it as quickly as possible. He hated thinking about money, and he especially hated talking about money, but Papa was no fool. He knew that the Thomas Shaws of this world, the men who were in a position to enable him to turn his visions into reality, did not share his prejudices. And so he would force himself to bring money into the discussion.

He asked Mrs. Shaw who was playing a desultory game of solitaire if he might borrow a card and handed it to Tony. "You show Mr. Shaw what I mean, Tony."

For Tony and me, for any student of architecture, the lesson was pure kindergarten, but, as Papa knew, Mr. Shaw was no student of architecture. He relied on Papa for the most practical reasons. He valued fame more than beauty, understood rents and revenues more than renderings.

"It's really very simple, sir," Tony said to Shaw. "Do you think I can make this card stand on its edge?"

"Of course not." Shaw seemed annoyed. "Especially not underway, even in a light breeze."

"You're right, of course." Tony stood the card on its edge, and it toppled immediately. "But what if I do this?" He bent the card two thirds of the way down so it made an L and stood it on its side on the deck. Despite the light breeze, it remained that way for a few seconds.

"And that's why I want to build it this way, Tom. Wind charts for this area indicate some pretty good gusts off the lake, but if we build in this shape, you get twice the stiffness for half the price—or at least the same construction costs."

What Papa said was true. It was also true that this particular shape took advantage of the site, allowing the building to relate to the lake without turning its back on the city, an argument which had not impressed Mr. Shaw during lunch. There was a third reason for the design, one Papa hadn't even bothered to bring up. It would enable him to explore further his current obsession with angles.

Thomas Shaw was sold. Papa had pulled it off, with Tony's help, but rather than stay there to enjoy his part in the victory, Tony took advantage of a change in the conversation to drift toward the bow of the boat, and I followed. As we passed Julia and Warren, who'd given up their backgammon game and were sunning themselves on the cabin top amidships, they neither opened their eyes nor interrupted their murmured conversation to notice us.

Tony sat and let his long legs hang over the side. I did the same. At the beginning of July we'd been the same color, but he'd spent the last two months slaving over a drafting table in a low-paying, highly demanding job while I'd spent them on bikes and tennis courts, beaches and boats. I was at least three shades darker, but I wasn't proud of the achievement.

Tony rested his arms on the lifelines and his chin on his arms and stared out to sea. He didn't look happy, but I couldn't tell if he was brooding about Julia or the vagaries of practicing architecture.

"You ought to ask for a commission on that one. Or at least a job." He almost winced at the last words but said nothing.

"You think the card trick was vulgar, don't you, and that Papa's a sham?" He was still silent. "You think a prospective client ought to be able to look at a sketch or a blueprint and understand what it means. And you think your designs will be so good that even a philistine like Thomas Shaw will recognize truth and beauty when they look him in the eye." He still didn't answer me, and I laughed. I don't know where I got the courage to laugh at him, because I still thought he was light years beyond any other mortal I'd ever known, except perhaps Papa. "You're sure of all that now, but you'll change your mind."

He leaned back on his elbows and peered at me over his dark glasses. I couldn't tell whether he was angry or amused. "I suppose you're speaking from experience."

"I am. My experience with Papa. I recognize the obsession—the obsession to build. Not to draw or design but to take materials as if they were flesh and blood and forge them into something real and lasting. Without that obsession you're a draftsman or designer; with it you're an architect. And you are an architect, Tony. It's written all over you."

He took off his glasses and fixed me with a hard, inquiring gaze. "And what about you? Are you an architect too or just another draftsman or designer?"

I smiled—with some of Julia's amused detachment, I hoped—and put on my own sunglasses. "I'm Adam Kirkland's daughter. Doesn't that say it all?"

Papa never did anything in half measures. When he was working—really working, that is, not merely selling—he withdrew from the world. When he wasn't, he luxuriated in all its pleasures. During the creative stints, we kept silence around the house, visitors at bay, and sandwiches and coffee at his elbow, though none of it mattered. We couldn't have disturbed him if we'd wanted to. He lived in an isolated realm of frenzied creativity, a disembodied state where he knew no human needs. But when he returned from that world, when he came off a stint of work, he returned with a vengeance. In his studio Papa could live on crusts of bread and cheese, a childish peanut butter sandwich or cold black tea. Back in the house he relished imported caviar and truffles and lusty peasant stews, aged whiskey and vintage wines. In his studio he neither heard nor spoke; in company he gave and demanded good conversation. In the heat of creativity he could go for two or three days in the same clothes. In the aftermath he bathed like a sybarite and luxuriated in rich fabrics and his own striking appearance. The only opinion beside his own he'd ever cared for was Mother's, and his spirit was true to her memory, but his body led a more wayward existence. He might complain about the advances of strange women interested more in his celebrity than him, but he rarely discouraged them. Papa's appetites were as enormous as his abilities, and so each year on the last Saturday night of the summer he gave a blazing outdoor feast worthy of the Romans on the eve of their decline. The party was at once huge and exclusive. All summer long people jockeyed for invitations. When the night arrived, private planes swamped the airport and expensive yachts made the hop over from the Cape, the Vineyard, and points west. For someone who professed disdain for his fellowman, Papa was an excellent host.

A few hundred lobsters and as many sirloins waited on dry ice on the beach below the deck where the caterer had set up the enormous grills. There were two bars in the house and a third on the deck. The preparations had been prodigious, but Papa, striding the deck in his white linen trousers and Basque shirt that came not from some fashionable boutique on

Madison Avenue or Rodeo Drive but from a shop in San Sebastián where he and Mother had honeymooned, insisted he was merely giving an old-fashioned American clambake-cum-barbecue. In other words, though we didn't dress up, we dressed. I'd just finished when Julia came into my room. She was wearing a lacy Victorian camisole and a soft flouncy skirt that emphasized her tiny waist.

"You look marvelous," I said. "Like a cross between Alice in Wonderland and Frank Harris's *Life and Loves*."

"Don't be bitchy, Delia. Not all of us can throw on a pair of white trousers and a man's shirt and come out looking like Kate Hepburn. She should have been your godmother rather than mine. You're so damn understated, you're a knockout."

But most of the guests that evening, at least most of the male guests, agreed with my judgment rather than Julia's. From old Senator Tilden who'd come in his wheelchair to the young male model brought by Mrs. Tilden, they flocked to Julia as instinctively as the moths batting wildly and disastrously against the deck lights. There were only two exceptions: Webster Warren, whose own glow was bright enough to keep him from being burned by Julia's, and Tony. His wings had already been singed, and he kept his distance.

By three o'clock the last guest had departed, as had the host. Papa had offered to drive one of the guests back to her yacht. The last I'd seen of Julia had been her back, nestled into the crook of Webster Warren's arm, as they disappeared down the beach. Special help would return tomorrow for the massive cleanup, and Tony and I sat on the deck among the depressing aftermath of a successful party. He looked across the space between our chaises as if he weren't sure how to play the scene. "Want to go for a swim?" he asked finally.

"Are you out of your mind? This is September on Nantucket. It's three in the morning. We'd freeze to death."

I think he'd made the suggestion for the lack of something else to say, but my unwillingness seemed to strengthen his resolve. Perhaps he'd confused me with Julia.

"Come on. It will sober you up."

"I'm not drunk," I pointed out.

"Well, I am." Either he handled his liquor well or he was lying.

"You're not drunk. You're angry at Julia."

"Why should I be angry at Julia?" He finished off his drink in a single swallow. If he wasn't drunk now, he was trying to get there.

"Because of Warren."

"Listen, my child"—he stood and crossed to the bar—"I don't give a damn whether your sister goes off with Warren Webster. . . ."

"Webster Warren," I corrected.

He sat on the end of my chaise and took a sip of his fresh drink. "Don't quibble. Warren Webster. Webster Warren. No matter which way you slice it, he's a big man. With big connections. He can do our little Julia a lot of good. After all, a girl, even a girl who looks like Julia, doesn't get to be a star without a little help from her friends."

His voice was as damp and insinuating as the fog that was beginning to roll in. "Julia's not like that."

"The hell she isn't. The only difference is that in this case it's a beach instead of a casting couch."

"I knew you were arrogant, but I didn't think you

were a prig. You wouldn't be so damn holier-than-thou if she were down there on the beach with you."

I saw from his face that I'd hit home. "That's right, I wouldn't, but then Julia wouldn't be down there with me. I don't have anything she wants."

"Julia's down there because of Webster Warren, not because of what he can do for her. She's selfish and fickle, but she isn't calculating."

He started to answer, then stopped and took a long swallow of his drink. "Whatever you say. You're her sister." He finished the drink and put the glass down on the deck. I couldn't help noticing how, as he did, his shoulders pulled against the soft oxford cloth. He had wonderful shoulders. "The keeper of the flame. Julia's and your father's. Three o'clock in the morning, alone with a man, and you're busy defending your sister and worrying about what time *Papa's* going to come home."

"I don't give a damn when Pa . . . my father gets in. He can stay out all night if he wants. He probably will."

Tony laughed. "I touched something. That's reassuring. I was beginning to think you were untouchable." He put his hands on my shoulders. I could feel their warmth through the thin material of my blouse.

"You're drunk," I said weakly.

"Sober as a judge." He leaned toward me.

"I'm not Julia."

"I never thought you were." His face was coming closer, the eyes so deep and dark I thought I'd drown in them.

"And I don't pick up the pieces she's left behind."

He dropped his hands from my shoulders and drew away. "I was right about you, Cordelia. And it's lucky you have their flames to keep. Because you sure as hell don't have any warmth of your own."

They were terrible words to say to someone, especially someone who was, no matter how unwillingly, in love with you.

Papa returned around breakfast time, as I'd predicted. Julia was gone by then. She'd been invited to sail back to New York as a guest on Thomas Shaw's yawl. The fact that she had her own guest that weekend didn't deter her for a moment. Tony was left with Papa and me for consolation, but since the previous night I'd proved myself unwilling to console, he spent most of the day with Papa. I gave them both a wide berth. I was angry at Tony for his opportunistic advances, impatient with Papa for what suddenly seemed like his hypocrisy about women in general and Mother in specific, and fed up with myself. Neither of them noticed. They were too busy debating. Now and then I overheard snatches of their conversation. As I brought out a pitcher of Bloody Marys around noon, during lunch on the deck, when I lay alone on the beach in the afternoon and they walked by, their long legs and big feet keeping pace with each other in the wet sand, I heard them debating. Even when they agreed about a building, an architect, or a principle, they agreed for different reasons. By the end of the afternoon, I knew that Papa had decided to hire Tony. He wouldn't tell him yet. Tony would have to finish his last year of graduate school, go through the humbling process of an interview in the intimidating offices of Adam Kirkland Associates where he would spread his portfolio for Papa's critical eye and sharp tongue, but Papa had already made up his mind. Of course, Tony didn't know that, and I had no desire to tell him that afternoon.

I was sitting on the floor of my room, my own sketches strewn about me, trying to decide which ones to take back to school. Maybe it was the conversation between Papa and Tony that still buzzed in my head like a persistent mosquito, maybe it was only the harsh slant of the sun that had already begun its slide into the sea, but suddenly everything I'd done all summer looked tenth rate. I'd decided to chuck it all when I heard Tony's voice behind me. His bare feet had made no sound as he'd come down the hall and into my room.

"You are good, aren't you?"

I turned and looked up at him. The sun was in my eyes and I couldn't see his face, but his voice was sincere. "Don't sound so surprised," I said, though a moment ago I'd been ready to throw out the lot.

His eyes moved from my sketches to me. "I'm willing to declare a truce if you are." He held out his hand and, when I took it, pulled me to my feet. He'd just come back from the beach, and a small patch of sand clung to his chest right over his heart. It was hard to keep from brushing it away. It was hard to keep from touching him. I took a step backward.

"Would you like to go out to dinner tonight?" he asked. "We're on our own. Your father has other plans."

I couldn't tell whether the last statement was intended to tease me. "We don't have to go out. There's enough steak and lobster in the fridge to feed the teeming masses of Calcutta."

"I know we don't have to go out, but I'd like to take you out." From the edge in his voice I would have known he was poor even if Julia hadn't told me.

"I'd love to," I said. "There's a little bar in town...."

He started to laugh then, as if my insecurities were more amusing than his. "Listen, Cordelia," he said, "you're worth more than a little bar. I can even afford more than a little bar." He mentioned the name of the restaurant where he'd made a reservation. It was the most expensive on the island. I started to say something, but he cut me off. "I wasn't assuming anything. I figured I could cancel the reservation if you said no."

It was too cold to eat on the terrace that night, but Tony managed to get a corner table in front of the windows. Beyond his shoulders the sea shimmered with the reflected brilliance of the island lights and the softer glow of moonlight. Between us on the table the candle cast flickering shadows.

Papa's daughter to the core, I noticed that the wine Tony ordered with dinner was not the most expensive, but it was the best. When we'd finished the bottle but not the conversation, he ordered another.

I learned a lot about Tony that night, more, I suspect, than Julia had all summer. He'd grown up in Chicago, the city of Louis Sullivan and Frank Lloyd Wright and Ludwig Mies Van Der Rohe, he said. They were his spiritual fathers. Each had been a great architect, untamed by the world, true to his own tenets.

"And what about your real father?" I asked. "Where does he fit into things?"

Tony dropped his eyes and turned the wineglass in his long fingers. "In other words, you want the pedigree."

"Anyone who's six foot three shouldn't walk around with a chip on his shoulder."

"How do you know how tall I am?"

"You're the same size as Papa—and planning to be bigger some day."

64

"You have a sarcastic streak, Cordelia."

"And you have a reticent one. Why don't you wan to tell me about your childhood?"

He was quiet for a moment, turning the wineglass in his long slim fingers. "My father was a mason. He taught me two things. A respect for materials and the way they're handled and a hatred of meanness. He was mean with words and mean with money and mean with his hands. He was a mean son of a bitch. Does that answer your question?"

After dinner we walked on the beach. There was a cool breeze, but Tony took off his jacket and put it around my shoulders. Part of me liked the gesture, but another part of me wondered why he hadn't kept his jacket and done the job himself.

"Well, I've given you the whole story of Anthony Bain—everything except the denouement and that hasn't been written yet—but what about Cordelia Kirkland?"

"In the Kirkland household I am and always have been supporting cast. Mother was a great actress. She had enormous range—everything from Shakespeare to drawing room comedy. If she'd lived, she would have been the first lady of the American theater. As it was, she had an amazing career, considering she was only thirty-six when she died."

"How old were you?"

"I was nine and Julia was eleven. God, that was an awful time. The newspaper stories went on for days. It took them a while to find the wreckage—the plane went down in the Rockies—and we weren't sure if there might be survivors. Then when we found out there weren't, it was like losing Papa as well as Mother. He locked himself in his studio for more than a week.

Even after he came out, he wouldn't talk to anyone. He just walked around in a trance looking grief-stricken and guilty."

"Why guilty?"

The question made me realize that I'd never mentioned Papa's guilt to anyone before, not even Julia. "Mother was on her way to Hollywood. Papa didn't want her to go. He insisted she was prostituting herself. She was an actress, he said, not a movie star. They fought rarely, but when they did, it was cataclysmic. Their tempers were as big as their talents. And of course they were terribly in love. I don't suppose they would have fought that way if they weren't."

Tony gave me a sideward glance. "You know, for a cynic, you've got one hell of a romantic streak."

"Who said I was a cynic?"

"It's the role you play. And every time you open your mouth, you take a shot at me."

I didn't tell him that was self-protection rather than cynicism. "Well, they *were* wildly in love. That's fact rather than romantic illusion. They met during the war. Papa was in the army, and Mother was entertaining the troops. He likes to tell how he beat a couple of hundred thousand other men's time."

"I'll bet he does. And what happened after your mother's death?" he went on quickly.

"Papa came out of it eventually. He had his work. And us. Julia was a big help. She's so much like Mother. Not only her looks, though God knows she's got those. . . ."

"You're not exactly an ugly duckling yourself."

"You don't have to flatter me."

"I wasn't flattering you."

"Anyway, we were talking about Julia. . . ."

"You were talking about Julia. I asked you about yourself, and so far you've talked about your mother and your father and your sister."

"Maybe," I said without looking up at him, "that's because I know they're the ones you're really interested in."

He caught my arm and forced me to turn to him. His eyes were as black and fathomless as the sea. "Or at least in Papa and Julia," I added.

The wind was blowing my hair in front of my face, and I was glad because I didn't want him to see my expression, but he caught a strand and ran it between his fingers as if he liked the way if felt. "I had a nice time tonight, Cordelia."

"So did I," I answered.

We stood that way for a moment, our faces separated by a mere sliver of night. I waited for his face to come closer. I prayed for his face to come closer. Tonight I would not put him off with smart comebacks. Tonight I would not put him off at all. Then he laughed and started walking again. "Don't worry, Cordelia. No passes. I learned my lesson last night."

The following day we returned to New York, and shortly after that I went back to Cambridge. I assume Tony headed back to New Haven. I heard neither from nor about him for months. So I was surprised that February when I walked in on him and Julia in the shabby dressing room of an off-Broadway theater. Julia had just given a superb performance in a perfectly awful play. I hadn't known Tony was in the audience, and he obviously hadn't known I'd be coming backstage after the show. If he had, I can't believe he would have been kissing Julia as if he had more than kissing her in mind. Still, in all fairness to Tony, I have to admit he had the decency to look embarrassed when I walked in.

3

The following autumn, the second after I met Tony, he went to work for Adam Kirkland Associates. The name of the firm was a lie. It was not an association of equals, as anyone who worked there soon learned. Years later Tony compared Papa to one of his own buildings. He was not only the original inspiration behind it, but also the structure that supported it, the mechanical systems that brought hot air and cool, light and water to its parts, and, not least, the smooth, handsome curtain wall that presented a facade to the public. It was Papa's firm, and there wasn't a soul—from the handful of nominal partners who carried out Papa's ideas to the lowliest boys in the mail room who carried his mail, from the elderly checker who'd spent a lifetime looking for discrepancies among the hundreds of drawings necessary to a building to the greenest student slaving long hours at a summer job for the sheer experience of it—who didn't know it. To those who worked for him, Papa could be an implacable tyrant or a patient teacher, generous to a fault with praise and money or mean with both. Working for Papa was occasionally heaven, frequently hell, and always as uncertain as purgatory, but young architects fought for the opportunity like a bunch of modern day Fausts eager to sell their souls. Tony spent ten to twelve hours a day bent over a drafting board, drawing curtain wall details for a fraction of what Papa paid Ellen the housekeeper, and Tony's colleagues envied him the opportunity. I have to admit I did too. I'd be in that drafting room soon, but unlike Tony, I'd never know if I would have gotten there on my own.

But if Tony was low in the hierarchy of Adam Kirkland Associates, he'd managed to become an officer in the army of Julia Kirkland's beaux. It's an old-fashioned word, but I don't know what else to call them. "Lover" is too strong. At least it was in Tony's case. Julia still hadn't slept with him. I knew because she told me, but I would have known by looking at Tony. He had a lean, rattled look. I'll never forget the first time he came to the apartment. I could read the hunger in those dark eyes, for Julia—and for Papa's success.

It was a Friday night in November, and I'd flown down from Cambridge for the weekend and gone straight to Papa's office. He sent me down to the drafting room to collect Tony. Julia had invited him to dinner. I told myself the contraction in my stomach was merely the aftermath of flight.

Tony was bent over his board and didn't look up till I was standing beside him. His face was thinner than when I'd last seen him, which only accentuated the square jaw.

"You look tired," I said. "Julia or Papa?"

He pushed his hair out of his eyes and answered in kind. "You look a little tired yourself. Architecture or men?"

70

I turned and started away from his drafting board. "Come on. I'm hungry, and Papa wants his martini."

Tony slipped off his stool, took his jacket from a hook, and caught up with me. "If you're going to dish it out, Cordelia, you've got to be willing to take it." He threw his arm around my shoulders and pulled me to him in an infuriatingly fraternal hug.

"You still haven't answered me," he said in the elevator. "Work or play?"

"Work. I have a design studio this semester with Gaspar. One of Papa's arch enemies. He can't forgive Papa for calling his latest building a mess of circus tents left behind when P. T. Barnum packed up and moved on. And he can't forgive me for being Papa's daughter. No matter what I do, it isn't good enough."

If I was after sympathy, I'd gone looking in the wrong quarter. "Poor little rich girl," he said. "At least rich in advantages."

I didn't like his tone. "If you're talking about advantages, you've got the only one that matters. Talent."

"You've got talent too," he said as the elevator doors opened. "Only, because of your father no one believes it. Least of all you."

Papa's Rolls and driver were waiting in front of Inter-American House, and Tony tried to look blasé as he climbed in after us. He was still trying when we pulled up in front of our apartment house on Fifth Avenue, but he gave up all pretense of casualness when Papa stopped in the lobby of the building for a word with a man whose face graced the front page of newspapers around the world with impressive regularity. While Papa and the diplomat discussed a government building in Jidda and a bank in Guatemala City, his body guards regarded Tony suspiciously. Tony's face was too honest for them not to distrust him.

He'd just about recovered when the doors of the elevator opened into the foyer of our apartment. I'm not sure what threw him then—the two huge Picassos on either side of the elevator, the Rodin in the entrance to the living room, or Julia. Tony had a good eye. He knew a masterpiece when he saw one.

Papa decided to give Tony the grand tour instead of leaving it to Julia or me. The apartment had been one of those rambling mazes covering the top two floors of a prewar Fifth Avenue building, but Papa had torn down walls, stripped moldings, and gutted whole areas to make a space grand enough for his spirit. The living room, fashioned from three parlors and as many bedrooms soared two stories to a vast skylight and had three walls of windows overlooking Central Park and half of Manhattan. The library and dining room faced east toward the river. Space flowed, lines were spare, and decoration kept to a minimum, the better to set off Papa's priceless art collection.

He took Tony past the paintings and sculpture rapidly, but lingered at the personal mementos: the framed letter from Corbusier, the photograph of Papa and Gropius, the Barcelona chair that wasn't simply another of Mies's classics but one of the prototypes. Papa gave Tony a masterful lesson in worldly success and had the time of his life doing it. I don't mean to imply Papa didn't like Tony—he did—but he liked his own renown more.

Only when the four of us had settled in the living room with a pitcher of Papa's martinis and begun to talk did Tony get his bearings. He might be impressed by success and muddled by sex, but when it came to architecture, he knew his mind and kept his balance. He and Papa were debating one of their colleague's buildings when Papa dropped the bombshell.

"What title have we given you down at the studio?" he asked Tony. Papa could no more call the three floors Adam Kirkland Associates occupied an office than he could go to them in a regulation gray flannel suit.

"Junior designer," Tony answered warily. He knew when he was being baited.

"Then don't you think it's about time you started earning your keep? Don't you think it's about time you designed something?" Papa's voice held a challenge. He knew the value of what he was about to offer Tony. "I suppose you've heard through the studio grapevine about the commission for that senior citizens' home," Papa went on. "It won't make us any money, but it will bring in a lot of publicity—if it's done right."

Churches and schools, private residences and minor additions and renovations didn't make Papa as much money as skyscrapers and major government buildings, but when the client gave free rein, or at least an enlightened latitude, they paid off in the less tangible forms of professional notice and public acclaim. With these buildings, as with the more profitable ones, Papa conceived the idea and left others to realize the detailed drawings and plans. He'd never turned a commission, even a small commission, over to a junior designer from the start, but I knew he was going to now.

"How would you like to take it on?" he asked Tony.

"What do you mean by take it on?" Tony's face gave away nothing, but the gold flecks in his eyes glittered with a desperate hunger.

"What in hell do you think I mean by take it on? Design the building—if you've got the ideas, that is. See it through—if you've got the sense and stamina. In other words, be both the chief designer and project architect on this senior citizens' home." Papa pronounced the last words with a faint air of mockery. The fact that he was offering Tony this opportunity said a great deal about Tony's future. It also said a lot about Papa's fears. I don't think he wanted to have anything to do with a home for people of advancing years and declining powers.

Not only did Tony have the ideas, sense, and stamina, he was eager to put them all to work immediately. He began firing questions about site, costs, requirements, and options, but Papa had other plans. He stood and announced he was going out to dinner. The wife of a certain South American millionaire wanted his presence at her dinner table as well as his ideas for her new house in Rio.

"I saw her at that gallery opening last week," Julia said from her corner of the sofa. "Reeking of Bal à Versailles and boredom. She doesn't want your ideas, Papa, she wants you."

"Perhaps she wants both," he said and ruffled Julia's hair, "which only demonstrates her good taste." He laughed and started up the stairs without a thought for my position as a third wheel.

The three of us went in to dinner. I felt, to say the least, superfluous, but Tony took pity on me. He began to talk about his new project immediately. We discussed the needs of senior citizens, the advantages of the site, the limitations of budget.

"I don't want it to be institutional," he said. "There ought to be room for individuality."

74

"You'll be limited with materials though," I warned him. "There'll be a tight budget."

"Of course, a lot depends on the site. I understand it's overlooking Long Island Sound. I can't wait to go out and take a look."

"Maybe we ought to go right now," Julia suggested. "I'll tell Ellen to forget dinner."

Tony lifted his dark eyes to hers, and the gold flecks glinted with excitement. Then he put her expression together with her tone. "You're safe for the night, Julia. We couldn't see anything in the dark anyway." He asked her about the cattle call she'd gone to that afternoon. She said that had been several days ago, and she'd already told him she hadn't gotten a callback.

"You know," Tony said suddenly, "if the site isn't too steep, I can use ramps rather than stairs and still get a lot of mileage out of the different levels. Maybe something like this." He took a pen from his pocket and the napkin from his lap and began sketching. After a few bold strokes, he tossed the napkin across the table to me.

I took my time examining it, partly because I didn't want him to think I was willing to approve everything he did, partly because the sketch demanded contemplation. The few lines were simple, but the concept behind them was complex and intriguing.

We started to discuss it, passing the napkin back and forth across the table. I was firing questions, and Tony was answering them with words and additional sketches on the napkin. Only when Ellen entered from the pantry carrying a large silver platter did he look up and realize what he'd done.

"I'm sorry," he said to Julia, and the lights went out of his eyes. "I guess I got carried away."

Julia smiled, her small even teeth as unforgiving as a fox's. "Forget it. That's de rigueur around here. Years ago Mother replaced tablecloths with linen place mats and left a standing order with Porthault for a new supply of napkins every six months. We wouldn't think of laundering your masterpiece. It might be worth millions someday." She took the napkin that lay on the table between Tony and me and tucked it into the breast pocket of his jacket as if it were a flamboyant handkerchief. And there it sat for the rest of dinner.

Afterward we went back to the living room. Tony stood for a moment in front of the hearth that had been stripped of its mantelpiece and molding. The only decoration was a larger-than-life-size portrait of Mother above it. Though the painting dominated the room, Papa had neglected to include it in Tony's tour. Now he stood with his hands in his pockets and his face lifted to Mother's image.

"She certainly was beautiful," he said finally. "You only have to look at her face to understand your father's reaction after her death."

Julia turned from the portrait to Tony. "I never told you about Papa after Mother's death."

"Cordelia did."

Julia's eyes moved to me. They were slate blue now and tinged with disapproval, but she said nothing.

I left them then, as they'd been hoping I would. Even if I hadn't been in the way, I had my own plans for the evening. Peter Fowler was a Harvard law student who was deadly serious about his future as well as the part I might play in it. I wasn't in love with Peter, but I recognized his attractions. Foremost among them was the fact that he wasn't an architect. I'd learned early in life to avoid romantic entanglements with

76

future architects. They were either too impressed by the fact that I was Adam Kirkland's daughter or too resentful of it. Peter's legal mind managed to penetrate the aura of Papa's persona. He admired his success without being in thrall to it. More important, he regarded Papa as my father rather than me as his daughter. I found the view refreshing.

Peter had other attributes as well. He was mildly witty. He was handsome with the blandness of big blond men who have grown up with all the advantages. And sexually he was polite but persistent. I'd decided to sleep with Peter Fowler, and I'd decided to do it tonight. Time was running out. I was almost twenty-one. I was the only virgin left on my floor at school. I was beginning to think I was the oldest living virgin in captivity. And so I'd decided to make Peter happy and let him relieve me of my unhappy burden. But I hadn't expected to see Tony tonight. Two hours with him had undone two months of resolution. So when later that night I stood in the foyer with Peter, I knew there was no hope for him or for me. Even without Tony's voice floating out from the library where he and Julia were closeted and Tony's face looming between Peter's and mine, there would have been no hope.

After Peter left, I started up the stairs to my room, but Tony's voice still followed me. I stood in the darkness listening. The words, at least those I could make out, were familiar—I'd just heard many of them from Peter—but the tone was different. It was fervent and tinged with anger.

I stood there listening to my sister and Tony Bain, picturing his long, beautiful hands on her equally beautiful flesh, ashamed of myself, furious with them, and hopelessly envious. There was a long silence, and I started up the stairs, again, but now it was Julia's voice that stopped me. Unlike Tony's, it was neither urgent nor angry, only firm. "No," she said and left no room for argument.

The sound of the elevator doors opening and closing drowned out Tony's answer and Papa came in singing an aria from *Aïda* in his big baritone. Unlike me, he was not given to surreptitious night prowling. He asked about my evening and without waiting for an answer regaled me with anecdotes of his. As he bent to kiss me goodnight, I caught the aroma of Bal à Versailles but not the slightest whiff of guilt.

I sat in the window seat of my room for a long time that night. The buildings of the city are never entirely dark, and I wondered at the dramas being played out behind those neat squares of light. As architects, we're taught to think about fenestration rather than what goes on behind the arrangement of windows, but I wasn't thinking as an architect that night. I heard Julia's footsteps pass my door on the way to her room, and stood. I didn't care about the unknown dramas being played out behind unfamiliar windows, only about the one in my own home.

Julia was still in her nightgown when I went into her room the following morning. She had a penchant for opulent satins and delicate lace and had unearthed several trunks of Mother's vintage lingerie. I slept in Papa's old shirts, when I slept in anything at all.

She was on the phone and motioned for me to hand her a cigarette. I tossed her a package and picked up the fragment of her conversation. I could tell by her voice that she was talking to a man. "Tony?" I asked when she hung up.

"Webster Warren."

I was surprised. "When did that start up again?"

"It never really ended. It just isn't particularly intense. For one thing, he's been running all over the world on those specials. For another, there are too many other women competing for him. Every time I open the papers there's a picture of Web escorting a princess or a movie star or a Kennedy. I can't compete."

"Apparently you can. He's still around."

"Now and then."

"Would you like it to be more often?"

"Silly question."

"Where does Tony fit into all this?"

Julia sat up in bed, her legs crossed, her back straight, and began bobbing her head forward. "You're so eager to put us all in order, Cordelia, as if you were drawing a floor plan. Well, there's no grand scheme. I'm just trying to have as good a time as possible while waiting to have my incomparable talents discovered."

"I think Tony takes things a bit more seriously."

She stopped bobbing her head and looked me in the eye. "The one thing Tony does not do is take me seriously. He takes you seriously. He takes Papa seriously. He takes himself so damn seriously it makes me sick. But I'm nothing more than a face and body."

"You have to admit they're distracting."

She went back to her exercises. "Now you sound like him. Tony may want me, but he doesn't care about me. Remember that off-Broadway play I was in last winter?"

I remembered the show. I also remembered walking

in on her and Tony after a performance of it. As far as I was concerned, they'd played quite a love scene.

"He used to pick me up after the show. He must have seen the last scene a dozen times—and the last scene was my whole part. Every time he came backstage, he told me I was terrific. Even on the nights my timing was off or I blew a line, he said I was terrific."

"That's just the way people are. No one goes backstage and says you're terrible."

"That's the way people in the theater are, Delia, but Tony isn't in the theater. And he's a terrible liar. He simply didn't know whether I was terrific or godawful. And he didn't care. He was probably too busy thinking of the age-old corner problem or one of his endless curtain wall details." She straightened and tossed her hair back over her head. "Just like Papa."

"And you're just like Mother."

"Not exactly," she said and moved to the floor where she began doing sit-ups. "I'm not as brilliant on the stage. But I plan to be smarter in real life. At least about men."

I didn't ask Julia what she meant by that extraordinary statement, perhaps because I didn't want to know, though I told myself the real reason was because it was getting late and I had work to do.

I went into Papa's studio and sat at the drafting board he'd set up for me when I was still so small he had to lift me onto the stool. That was 1956, the same year Julia had made her theatrical debut playing Mother's daughter in a nonspeaking walk-on part in summer stock. I sat at the drafting board but didn't go to work immediately. The sunshine flooding through the windows danced off the humicant holding an array of technical pens and the forbidding white paper. Beyond the wall of windows facing south, Inter-American House and another skyscraper designed by Papa dared me to sketch a line. I picked up the pencil and took the dare.

I must have been working for an hour or two—I always lose track of time when I'm concentrating—when Ellen came in and said Tony Bain was on the phone. I suggested he wanted Julia, but Ellen said he'd asked for me.

His voice was as brisk as the wind bending the trees in the park below. "If you want to see that site, now's your chance. I'm driving out to take a look this afternoon."

"Wouldn't you rather wait and take Julia?"

There was a moment of silence, and when he spoke again, his voice held an edge of exasperation: "If I wanted to wait and take Julia, I wouldn't be asking you now. For once in your life, Cordelia, stop second-guessing everyone. Do you want to go or not?"

Of course I said I did.

On the drive out Tony lost the way and his temper. He'd given me the road map, and now he told me I was a rotten navigator. I told him not to blame me for his mistakes. "You're an architect," I added. "You're supposed to be willing to take responsibility for your decisions."

"Like the master builders in the middle ages, you mean? You want me to stand under the stone roof when they knock away the last of the wooden scaffolding?"

"You know, Papa actually did that once. It was a convention hall that spanned more than seven hundred feet, almost two city blocks, without interior columns.

Can't you just picture him standing alone in the center of that huge space, daring the physical forces to contradict him? Still, you have to admit he had courage."

"I have to admit he had a good eye for a publicity stunt. But," Tony went on before I could answer, "you're right about taking responsibility. I'll never accuse you of being a rotten navigator again. At least not as long as I'm in the driver's seat." And, of course, when it came to our relationship, he was.

The site was a low hill that sloped down to Long Island Sound. In town the air had seemed hard and bright, but out here the wind off the water was brutal. Tony didn't seem to notice it, anymore than he did the muddy flats and slippery rocks. We walked and climbed and walked some more. I was glad I'd worn boots. We went down to the water's edge and looked up at the low crest of the hill. We climbed the hill and stared down at the water. We'd arrived a little after two. By the time we left, the sun was sinking behind the barely visible skyline of Manhattan. We'd covered every inch of the site, but I don't think we'd spoken more than ten words all afternoon. I'm not even sure Tony knew I was there, though once or twice he'd held out his hand to help me over rough terrain.

We'd started back along the uneven path to the road where we'd left the car when it happened. Tony was walking ahead of me, holding back a branch here, warning me to watch a rock there. Once he stumbled in the gathering dusk and said we shouldn't have stayed so late. A minute later he asked if I was cold. I lied and said I wasn't.

Near the road the land dropped away abruptly by three or four feet. Tony made the leap easily and turned to give me his hand. I didn't slip intentionally—I swear it—but I did slip, and of course he caught me. We stood that way for a moment holding each other in the chill November twilight. His skin was burnished from the cold, his eyes glinted with excitement, and his wide mouth was half open in a smile. He touched my cheek with the back of his hand. He wore no gloves.

"You're freezing," he said.

"It'll be warm in the car," I answered, but neither of us moved.

"You're a good sport, Cordelia."

"That's me, Cordelia, the good sport," I answered a little too brightly because I didn't want him to see how the words had stung.

"I didn't mean that the way it sounded."

I wanted to ask him how he had meant it, but there was no time because his face was coming closer and his mouth on mine was suddenly warm and miraculously soft. When we stopped kissing, he looked down at me with an amused, conspiratorial smile. Then he took off his glasses and kissed me again. It was even better the second time.

When we finally got back to the car, I wasn't sure how to behave, but Tony acted as if nothing had happened. All the way back to town we talked about the site and the building he'd erect on it. He was full of his own ideas and excitement, but not so full of them that he wouldn't listen. Our minds worked well together, not so much meshing as building on each other. Each of us pushed the other a little farther than we would have gone alone.

Papa, Julia, and Peter Fowler were waiting for us in the living room. After what had happened that afternoon, I couldn't help thinking they made an unholy welcoming committee.

Julia jumped up as soon as we came into the room. "It's about time you two got back." I felt the flush of guilt on my face, but Julia was too caught up in her own role to notice. "We're celebrating tonight. I just got the most delicious, the juiciest, the absolutely bitchiest part in a made-for-telly movie that is going to be the broadcasting event of the season. To put it as modestly as possible." She put her arms around Tony's neck as if he were an Emmy award and kissed him squarely on the mouth. I remembered how that felt. Tony carried it off with considerable aplomb, but when they let go of each other, he straightened his glasses and was careful not to look at me.

"Papa's taking us all out to celebrate my triumph," Julia said.

Papa was, in fact, beaming, and I was surprised. If he'd opposed Mother's going to Hollywood to make movies, how could he be so pleased about Julia's following her to go into television? The first was a mere flirtation with compromise, the second an outright surrender to it. But apparently he'd learned his lesson. He wasn't going to quarrel with Julia before parting.

Ellen entered with a five-kilo tin of caviar, which Papa had brought back from his last trip to Russia, and a bottle of Dom Perignon. She too was beaming. "Isn't it wonderful?" she murmured to me as she put the tray on the chrome and glass coffee table. "Soon it will be just like the old days with a star in the house."

Julia was relating the details of her triumph. She'd auditioned ages ago and been called back twice, but that was so long ago she'd given up hope. Then her agent had called this afternoon. She'd got the part and third billing. She told us about the script, which

was based on a recent best-seller—"potboiler," Papa
interjected, but he seemed only amused by the fact—
and the other actors and the grueling shooting schedule. The movie would be shown this spring, she said,
and mentioned the network.

"It's Tom Shaw's network," Papa said, "but I had
nothing to do with it." I knew that was true. Papa
would not have interceded on Julia's behalf anymore
than he would have on mine if I'd had trouble getting
into architecture school. He had too much respect for
himself and for us. But it was also Webster Warren's
network. He had an intimate connection with it and
with Julia.

Papa announced that we'd celebrate at the Persian
Room of the Plaza. I knew that he used to take Mother
dancing there in the old days.

Julia was radiant. There was no other word for it.
Papa's stories flowed as freely as the vintage champagne he kept ordering. Tony was dazzled. Even Peter
was disarmed. Papa and Julia put on quite a show.

Halfway through the evening Papa decided he wanted
to waltz with me. "So you drove out to look at the
site this afternoon," he said as we began dancing. "Is
our boy genius going to design me something splendid?"

I looked up into his big florid face. His eyes were
bright, but the folds over them gave him a worn air,
and his jaw sagged a little. I wondered if the wine and
dancing and late hours were taking their toll. Or perhaps Tony was, Tony and all the time and success and
buildings—the buildings were the crux of it—he had
ahead of him.

"He has some good ideas," I said.

Papa took my chin in his big hand and raised my

face to his. "Poor Cordelia. Always so cautious. About your own ideas. About Tony's. About Tony himself." I didn't answer him, and we went on dancing. "Why don't you admit it? You think the only thing more wonderful than Tony Bain the architect is Tony Bain the man. You're in love with him, Cordelia. More in love with him than Julia could ever be, despite her flamboyance and her generosity. You're like a volcano threatening to erupt."

"You know what volcanoes leave behind, Papa? Ashes."

He drew me close to him and bent to whisper in my ear. "But while they burn, Cordelia, while they burn, there's fire and heat and glory."

I didn't see Tony again till I came home for the Christmas holidays. It was all very well for Papa to talk about volcanic eruptions, but I could taste the ashes every morning when I checked my mailbox and each time the phone in my room rang and a voice other than Tony's pronounced my name. That afternoon on Long Island Tony's passion for Julia had boiled over, and I'd been scalded. That was all there'd been to it.

He was still simmering when I came home for Christmas, simmering for Julia rather than me, but she, in the throes of several weeks of shooting, was too busy jetting back and forth between California and New York, too busy with this new turn in her career, too busy—I suppose, though she hadn't told me—with Webster Warren, to notice. I was the one who noticed. When Tony stopped by on Christmas Eve with one of his own drawings for Julia, a sketch that she barely glanced at and I would have sold my soul for, when I ran into him at the studio one afternoon, the skin beneath his eyes like two dark smudges disfiguring the clean lines of his face, when he arrived on New Year's Eve, I noticed. On New Year's Eve I would have had to be blind not to notice.

If Papa's Labor Day parties were newsworthy, his New Year's Eve celebrations were legendary. The tradition went back to the days when he and Mother, a couple so gifted and golden they took your breath away, were newly married and wildly in love. Because they needed only each other and their work, they were sought after by everyone. Within months they'd become the darlings of New York. They were poorer then, but Papa always spent like a millionaire and Mother liked to live like one. The parties were extravagant, exclusive, original. They mixed friends from their two worlds as flamboyantly as Papa mixed cocktails. Everyone knows how Cole Porter composed a song about Papa called "People Who Live in Glass Houses," and how Mies built a house of cards for Tallulah, and how one year an actress friend of Mother's brought a man responsible for a string of Miami Beach hotels. He'd dared to try to talk architecture with Papa, who'd accused him of creating the worst urban blight in modern history. Upstairs, whispering and giggling together, Julia and I heard shouts and the noise of furniture and glass breaking, and the next morning the gossip columns carried tales of Adam Kirkland's prodigious temper. There'd been a two-year hiatus in the parties after Mother had died, but gradually Papa had begun to ask friends over again, and soon Julia and I were allowed to come in our velvet dresses and try out our burgeoning womanhood. Ever since our teens, Julia had shone at Papa's New Year's Eve parties, so

I was surprised when the guests began arriving for this one and she was nowhere in sight.

Tony was one of the first to arrive. I'd never seen him in evening clothes. He looked as if he were born to wear them. I asked if he knew where Julia was.

"Isn't she here?"

"Not yet."

Guests were arriving steadily, but they hadn't yet overflowed into the library. I took Tony there.

"Do you want champagne?" I asked. "On second thought you look as if you could use something more potent." I poured him a scotch that would have done Papa proud. He downed half of it in a single swallow.

"I spoke to her this morning," he said. "She told me she was flying in sometime this afternoon."

"The flight was probably delayed. Bad weather." We both glanced out the tall windows. Stars glittered cold and bright in the winter sky. "Holiday traffic," I added lamely. "Poor Julia's probably been circling JFK for hours."

But poor Julia wasn't the one going in circles. I watched Tony pace the length of the library a couple of times, his chin jutting forward aggressively, his body taut as a coiled spring. When I put my hand on his arm and told him to relax because Julia was bound to turn up at any moment, I sensed the pent-up tension. Even a less avid observer of Tony Bain would have picked up the clues. He'd come here tonight with a purpose, a New Year's resolution of sorts. He was going to force Julia to make a commitment. If she refused, he was finished with her, or so I imagine he'd sworn to himself.

What a waste! There was enough misplaced desire in the library at that moment to fuel half a dozen affairs. It was rather like the wasted energy of the sun, I thought, except that as architects we were learning to harness that.

I made Tony another drink and had one myself. We talked about his work and my own, but for once his heart wasn't in it. He'd arrived a little after ten-thirty. It was almost midnight when we heard the commotion in the living room. Instinctively we both looked at our watches, but the old year still had ten minutes of life. I recognized Julia's voice and knew from Tony's face that he had too. Then we heard another voice, sonorous, controlled, familiar to every television viewer.

I followed Tony into the living room. Like the good actors they were, Julia and Webster Warren had taken center stage. The guests pressed toward them, glasses raised in a toast, hands stretched toward them as if toward a talisman, and in truth, Julia and Webster were magical that night. She was radiant, breathless, her cheeks flushed from admiration, her violet eyes wide with promise. Webster stood sleek and tan, feigning, I was sure, the requisite embarrassment.

"This afternoon," I heard Julia announce.

"We were married by a judge, then flew straight to New York," Webster added, ever the anchorman determined to get the facts straight.

Julia saw me at the edge of the crowd and began calling my name. I felt dozens of hands pushing me toward her, handing me over as if I were a wedding gift. I kissed her and told her how happy I was for her. "Isn't it absolutely amazing, darling!" She'd never called me darling before.

I held out my hand to Webster, but he bent toward me and placed his smooth tan cheek against mine. He smelled overwhelmingly of Oscar pour Hommes. Over his shoulder I saw Tony's back, ramrod straight, moving toward the foyer. I caught up with him as he reached the door.

"Where are you going?"

He shrugged.

"Wait, I'll go with you."

"Look, Cordelia"—the dark eyes grew darker—"don't worry about me. I'm not going to do anything drastic. I'm not going to throw myself out of a window of Inter-American House, if that's what you're worried about."

"They don't open." The attempt at humor was lame, his smile as weak.

"Or off the Brooklyn Bridge."

"Then what are you going to do?"

He shrugged again.

"Well, I'd like to do that too."

This time the smile was a little more convincing.

I grabbed a coat—Julia's as it turned out—from the front closet. As the elevator descended the nineteen floors to the street, neither of us spoke, but I was intensely aware of Tony's nearness. When he helped me on with my coat, or rather hers, this hand brushed my back where the neckline of my dress dipped low. His fingers against my skin were electric. They were also accidental.

As we came out on the street, sirens and whistles and horns were going off all around us. Tony stopped on the sidewalk in front of the building and turned to me. His smile was as thin as the cold night air. "Happy New Year, Cordelia."

"Happy New Year," I answered. And then because there was nothing else he could do under the circumstances, he bent and kissed me. It was a proper, public

New Year's kiss, a poor relation of those others in the Long Island woods.

We started walking south. When we reached the Stanhope, he said I must be cold and want a drink, but I said I'd rather keep walking. He started to say something else, but I cut him off. "Just don't tell me I'm a good sport."

He took my hand then and put it in his coat pocket. "All right, you're not a good sport. You're mean and selfish and rotten to the core. Also sarcastic and, whether you know it or not"—he rubbed the bump on my second finger—"extremely competitive."

"Me, competitive!"

He laughed. Not the small smile that was almost a wince, but a real laugh. "Yes, you, Cordelia. God knows you try to hide it, but you're in there fighting all the time. That's one of the things I love about you." I wasn't foolish enough to be misled by the word. He'd used it casually, the way he might say he loved a book or a song or a building.

We kept walking down Fifth Avenue, our hands still nested together in the warmth of his coat pocket, my heart leaping along, keeping pace with our steps. Every few blocks groups of men and women in evening clothes crossed our path, dashing from lobby to limousine or limousine to lobby. "This isn't much of a New Year's Eve for you," Tony said.

If only he knew. "I hate parties." He looked at me skeptically. "It's true. I'm the recluse of the family. Nothing like Papa and Julia."

We walked on in silence, and soon the Pulitzer Fountain, wrapped in its holiday lights, loomed before us like a galaxy of stars in the icy night. Beyond it the white marble and glazed brick of the Plaza Hotel ris-

91

ing to a richly ornamented mansard commanded the urban landscape as completely as any French château did its countryside. The facade was bathed in light and every window glowed, as if it were a huge birthday cake ablaze with candles.

"Hardenbergh knew what he was doing when he designed that baby," Tony said. "It's still one of the best buildings in New York." He squeezed my hand. "But don't tell Adam I said so. He'd have me burned at the stake for heresy."

"Your secret's safe with me. Besides, I like it too. I have ever since I was small and Mother used to take Julia and me for tea after matinees. The decor was almost as fattening as the cakes."

"Sometimes I think that we're starving man to death aesthetically. Think of it, Cordelia. Architecture is the most insistent art. You can't get away from it if you try. Now it's no secret what the layman likes. A little decoration to interest the eye and delight the senses, a bit of historic reference to give him his bearings. But we, the high priests of modern architecture, tell him he's wrong. What you really want, we assure him, is a nice clean box of glass and steel. It's morally bracing, aesthetically salutary—like medicine. As if some special sixth sense belonging only to architects lets us know what's good and bad, right and wrong."

"Then you think we ought to design for the lowest common denominator?"

Tony looked down at me. "If you could only hear the horror in your voice. You're an elitist. Like Adam."

"And you think you're not?"

"I know I am. The only trouble is I'm no longer sure that what I'm ramming down the layman's throat is right. Why can't he have a little color or decoration if he wants them? Why do we have to make everything flat and paint everything white? After all, Western civilization lumbered along for twenty-five hundred years before modern architecture came along and said everything you've been doing till now is wrong, but we'll show you what's right."

"You can always design fake Georgian houses and imitation Gothic libraries. I understand they're very lucrative." I'd meant it as a joke, but he must have heard the disdain in my voice because he took his hand from mine and put his arm around my shoulders. The gesture was half affectionate, half playful, and entirely innocent.

"Don't be bitchy, Cordelia. I have no intention of designing imitation anything. I want to go forward, not back. I want to reconcile those first twenty-five hundred years with the last twenty-five. I want to go beyond the glass box, beyond—God forgive me the blasphemy—Adam Kirkland."

His words hung opaque and misty in the crystal clear night. I wasn't entirely sure what they meant, but I sensed they were a breath of fresh air blowing through the solid glass and steel of Papa's world. What I didn't know was that breath of fresh air would turn into a wind howling through Papa's world and my own, destroying everything in its course.

"And now," he went on, his arm still around my shoulders, "the lecture is over. It's cold, and we need a drink." He gestured toward the hotel that had started the discussion. Warm invitation glowed from every window, but I had an invitation of my own in mind.

"I have a better idea. Why don't you show me the plans for your retirement home. We can get a drink there too. Papa has a bar in his office." Not to mention—and I didn't—a kitchen, shower, sauna, and sofa where he occasionally spent the night.

The watchman knew me from childhood and Tony from his long hours. If he thought there was anything peculiar about our turning up here together at one in the morning, he didn't say as much. He'd come to accept eccentricity, if not downright peculiarity, from Adam Kirkland and anyone connected with him.

There was a strange intimacy to being alone in the cold impersonal elevator at this hour, shooting skyward through floor after floor of deserted building. I suspect Tony felt it too because he didn't look at me. "I feel as if I'm luring you up to see my etchings," he joked, his eyes riveted to the lighted numbers above the door.

After the brightness of the elevator, my eyes took time adjusting to the dark office. When I bumped into one of the models in the reception area, almost toppling a thirty-three-story tower, Tony took my hand. Our steps echoed down silent corridors past empty offices and abandoned drafting boards. I felt as if we were the last two people on earth. Beyond the windows of Papa's office the lights of the uncaring city reminded me just how alone we were. I switched on the desk lamp.

"If you make the drinks," Tony said, "I'll get the plans. I'm not sure I want you entirely clearheaded when you look at them."

His footsteps reverberated down the corridors toward the drafting room. As I took the ice from the bar in the corner of the office, I noticed that my hands were trembling. I went into the bathroom, switched on the brighter light, and squared off with myself in the mirror. My face was a white mask against the black marble walls. I remembered the glow Julia had worn earlier in the evening and wondered if Tony would settle for a pale second best. I brushed my hair, but didn't put on any lipstick, and went back into Papa's office. I'd left the drinks on his desk, and now I sat behind it. Tony stopped in the doorway when he saw me there.

"What's the matter?"

"Nothing." He started toward the desk, the long rolls of blueprints tucked under his arm.

"You looked so strange, as if I'd surprised you."

"You did. I'm accustomed to seeing Adam sitting there." He was spreading open the plans and didn't look at me as he spoke. "It was a shock to see you in his place."

I stood and moved out from behind the desk. I had enough competition from Julia. There was no need to bring Papa into it.

And then I forgot both Papa and Julia. Tony's building was that exciting. It neither sat on the crest of the hill nor nestled into it as Windswept did, but moved with the low rolling terrain. The feeling of motion was at once sensual and restful. I turned from the elevation to the plans. Tony had achieved the variety and individuality he was after with a daring use of opposition, dark versus light, rough versus smooth, closed versus open. My eye traveled over the drawings again and again, always coming to rest on one thing. Where the land climbed to its highest point over the water, Tony had placed an indoor garden beneath an elegant hypar butterfly roof that soared boldly toward the sky. The roof was more than brave; it was optimistic. Tony had designed a home for the elderly where they could go on living rather than merely wait to die.

I continued poring over the plans, examining, admiring, envying. I prayed someday I'd do something as good. Finally Tony spoke: "You can admit you don't like it. I know it's not what you expected."

"It's inspired."

In the half darkness above the luminous arc of the desk lamp, I could see the gold lights exploding in his eyes like fireworks. "It is, isn't it?"

We both started to talk quickly then, pointing out strengths, considering possible weaknesses, arguing minor points, but in reality celebrating the whole astonishing achievement.

"The roof is breathtaking."

"I'm going to have to fight Adam tooth and nail for that roof."

I bent to the plans again, and he followed, his face almost grazing mine. I was drunk with his genius and with him, though I hadn't taken a single sip of my drink. Finally he rolled up the blueprints, and I raised my glass to him. "You were right that first day on Nantucket. You are the best."

We drank a giddy toast, then he put down his glass and took off his glasses. Beneath the thick lashes his eyes still glittered with excitement, but his smile was soft. I was certain he wasn't thinking of Julia.

"I was afraid you wouldn't like it," he said.

"My opinion isn't the important one."

He raised his hand to my face and rubbed his thumb gently over my cheek as if he were shading a sketch. "I trust your opinion, Cordelia. And you."

I heard the last words and wondered if he were thinking of Julia again after all, but his hand was still caressing my cheek, and his face was moving toward

96

mine through the shadowy light. I wanted him so desperately I didn't care if I was Julia's understudy.

He'd kissed me lightheartedly in the woods and formally on the street, but now his mouth was solemn on mine as if he realized the seriousness of what we were up to and wanted to make sure I did too.

His fingers against my skin where my dress dipped low in back were not accidental now, but strong and warm as they molded me to him. He tasted the way he smelled, clean and masculine and bracing.

We clung together for a long time, tasting each other, exploring each other, discovering each other. I'd forgotten my fears. I'd forgotten everything but Tony, the sensation of his beard against my skin, the desire that flickered in his eyes like flames, the thrill of his body pressed against mine. He repeated my name. Not Julia's but mine. I tasted it on his mouth. I answered with his. He kissed it away. "Come home with me," he murmured. His hands, fervent against my skin, turned the words into a prayer.

I was afraid of the distance, not in miles or minutes, but in emotions, between here and Tony's apartment. I was afraid of losing the moment—to my own fears, to his second thoughts, to Julia. I moved out of the circle of his arms, my hands still holding his. His mouth looked soft and vulnerable and almost bruised. I ran my fingers along it. His jaw tensed with desire. "There's no need to." I started to take a step backward toward the sofa behind me, but he pulled me to him again.

His body was hard against mine, his breath hot in my ear. "Not here, Cordelia. Not in Adam's office." I looked up at him. The lights in his eyes were fierce now, but his fingers running through my hair were gentle. They reminded me of sand streaming through an hourglass. I'd been afraid of losing the moment, but he'd thrown it away.

I stepped back from his arms again. This time I did not keep hold of his hands. And this time he did not pull me back to him. Perhaps something in my face warned him not to. Perhaps he'd felt my body stiffen at his recalcitrance. "You don't want me. You only want to prove something."

The lights went out of his eyes completely, and I knew that I'd been an accomplice in the murder of that fragile moment. "If all I wanted was to prove something, Cordelia, there's be no better place to do it than on that couch." He turned away from me and downed the rest of his drink in a single swallow.

"Then why?" I asked.

"If you don't understand, I can't explain it to you." The implication was clear. Girls like Julia understand matters like this intuitively. Girls like me simply blunder along, asking too many questions, wanting too much spelled out, analyzing desire to death.

"Do you want another drink?" I could hear the impatience in his voice. He couldn't wait to be out of here, away from me.

I led the way down the hall. This time he didn't take my hand. "If it had been Julia," I said in the elevator, my eyes on the lighted numbers above the door as we came down out of the sky, "you wouldn't have worried about the setting."

The doors opened, but Tony stepped in front of them, blocking my way and forcing me to meet his eyes. They were opaque. "You're right, but not for the reasons you think. With Julia there would have been only two of us in the room."

I clenched my fists. "If Julia was in the room with us, I'm not the one who brought her there."

"I wasn't talking about Julia. I meant—" He stopped abruptly, turned away, and started for the street. "Forget it," he tossed over his shoulder. But, of course, the one thing I couldn't do was forget it—or him.

4

When I awakened the next morning, I was surprised to hear the sound of Julia singing along with Mother's voice on an old recording of a Rodgers and Hammerstein show. I threw on a robe and rushed down the hall to her room. A suitcase stood open on her bed, but from the tangle of clothes I couldn't tell whether she was taking things out or putting them in.

"Even you couldn't have gotten tired of him this quickly," I said between yawns.

"No one loves a smart aleck, Cordelia. I came home to get some of my things."

"Only some? Then you're hedging your bets."

She turned from the suitcase to face me. "Damn it, Delia . . ."

"I'm only kidding." On my way across the room I gave her a quick hug. "I came in to offer my felicitations and all that. I mean it," I added in a more serious tone. "I really am happy for you."

She was still looking at me, and her dark brows, a devastating contrast to her gold hair, lifted in inquisitive arches. "You don't like Web, do you?"

I sat on the other bed and pulled Corbu onto my lap as if he might be an ally. "I don't know Webster."

"He's absolutely wonderful. And brilliant." I doubted both but wasn't going to say so. "He knows everyone, and everyone knows him." That was more like it.

"Just like Papa."

She turned from her packing. "He's nothing like Papa."

"What is he like, then?"

"I told you. Wonderful. Intelligent. Terribly imaginative. Guess how he proposed." She held out her left hand. On it a diamond, large as an ice cube and twice as clear with a veneer as hard as Webster Warren's, winked smugly. "He put this in my Perrier. We were having drinks at the Polo Lounge."

"Lucky you're not an ice chewer like Papa."

"Delia!"

"Sorry. Again. But I didn't think people really did things like that."

"*People* don't. That's one of the reasons I love Web." She'd finally said it, and I was glad.

"In that case, I'm prepared to love him too. Where is he now?"

"At the studio—the network studio, not Papa's—taking care of some last-minute business. He's flying to Camp David this afternoon for an interview, and I'm going with him, then we're going on to Sardinia. The Emerald Coast. We're staying with the Aga Khan's little brother." I started to laugh, and she did too. "Stop it! My head is spinning."

"I know. Isn't it absolutely too much?"

"Poor Tony never stood a chance. Not against diamonds as big as the Polo Lounge and Camp David and the Aga Khan's baby brother."

Julia stopped laughing. "That's not why I married

101

him, Delia. Tony will think that and a lot of other people, but you don't, do you?"

I thought of the conversation I'd had with Tony the night Julia met Webster Warren. "I know you better than that."

"Because I really do love him." That was the second time she'd said it, and I was doubly pleased.

Julia departed taking half a dozen suitcases and her happiness. She'd left me anything in her room I wanted, Tony, and the shambles I'd made of the previous night. She'd bequeathed Papa, I realized when I found him in the living room a little while later, less than that. He was sitting on the sofa staring up at the portrait of Mother, his big, valuable hands hanging limp as hanks of rope between his knees.

"I thought you were going to somebody's brunch," I said.

"A wise man knows when to leave the party, Cordelia."

I assumed he meant the holiday festivities, though he might have had a larger party in mind. His voice bristled with its usual vitality, but there was a faint shadow of stubble around his jaw. Suddenly he looked like an old man too tired to shave rather than a genius too obsessed to.

"It won't be the same around here without Julia," I said inanely.

His eyes moved from Mother's portrait to me, and I could see the disappointment in them. "Don't talk like an imbecile, Cordelia. Of course, it won't be the same. It's not the same with you away at school either. Nothing is ever the same."

"You mean Mother?"

"I mean life. Life is change. If you're any good, it's growth. Sometimes it's decline."

There was nothing I could say to that, and we sat in silence for a while, Papa staring at Mother's portrait and me, surreptitiously, at Papa. "At any rate, I don't imagine she'll be gone for long this time. The marriage won't last."

"But you seemed so pleased last night."

"How did you expect me to act in front of a roomful of guests? Besides, I'm not displeased. Julia's first marriage, perhaps her first few marriages, are bound to be experiments. Judith was married when she met me."

He spoke casually, as if he were telling me Ellen had worked for another family before us, but I felt as if someone had just taken my childhood and turned it upside down. And I could tell from the way Papa was watching me out of the corner of his eye that he realized he was not imparting casual information.

"Why didn't you ever tell me?"

"Why should I have? It wasn't important."

"It is to me."

He was smiling now. "I can't imagine why. It wasn't to me. I don't believe it was even very important to Judith, though I'm sure she thought it was when she married him. He was an actor. Not a very good one, though that wasn't the problem."

"What was?"

"Me." He no longer looked tired or old. "But Judith was not the kind of woman who could sit around waiting for the right man to come along. Julia is like her. She's not as sure of what she wants as you are, Cordelia. She's not as sure of herself." I started to say something, but he went on quickly. "You're just as

blind about your sister as everyone else. Blinded by
her beauty and the facade she presents to the public.
Julia's a first-rate actress. But beauty like Julia's is a
double-edged sword. It brings everything but trust—
trust of other people, especially men who seem to want
only your beauty, trust of your own good fortune which
seems undeserved, trust of yourself, which is simply
another word for confidence. I know. I lived with Judith for fifteen years."

"Are you saying Mother doubted herself?"

"Everything but the beauty. And she worried about
losing that. She was certain it was the only thing of
value she possessed—and she knew it would fade with
time."

"You make it sound almost like a blessing that she
died young."

He'd been staring at her portrait, but now he turned
to me sharply as if he'd been slapped. "Don't ever say
that! Or even think it! Judith's death was a curse. My
curse. I never should have let her go."

"It wasn't your fault," I said quietly. "If anything,
you tried to stop her."

"How do you know that?" His voice was peculiar,
almost wary.

I thought for a moment. "It's just something I've
always known. I remember hearing you quarrel before
she left."

The agate eyes were cautious. "You remember the
quarrel?"

"Not in detail. Just the fact that you did. You and
Mother were pretty explosive."

He slumped back on the sofa, a tired old man again,
and I knew the discussion was closed. Papa talked
about Mother often, but about her death almost never.

It was too painful for him. This morning he'd reopened the wounds for a moment, and now he needed time for them to heal. On my way out of the room I stopped and put my hand on his shoulder. He covered it with his own. We remained that way for a moment, then he sat up straighter, the familiar Papa, vital, forceful, irresistible. "Let me take you out to dinner tonight, Cordelia. Just the two of us. We'll go someplace quiet where we won't meet anyone we know and can talk, really talk." He chuckled, and I felt the strength of the laughter in his shoulder. "And everyone will stare and wonder what a lovely young thing like you is doing out with an old lecher like me." He laughed again, lustily, as if the mistaken assumption pleased him enormously. I told him I'd like nothing better and went off to try to lose myself and Tony and the mess I'd made of everything in my work.

I was just about to close the door to the studio when I heard the phone ring. There was no reason to assume it was Tony, but neither was there any reason not to. I hurried back down the hall.

"Cordelia?" Tony asked when he heard my voice. On the phone Julia and I sound somewhat alike, though my voice isn't the finely trained instrument hers is. In fact, years ago, when I'd lost courage while asking a boy to a party, she'd snatched the receiver from my hand and, pretending to be me, taken over.

"Julia's gone."

"I assumed as much. I was calling you." He sounded annoyed, as if he'd planned to take one tack, and I'd forced him into another. "How are you this morning?" he added in a more conciliatory tone.

I thought of the possible answers, then lied: "Fine."

"That's a shame. I was hoping you'd be miserable.

I am. And not because of Julia," he went on quickly. "I figured I'd beat you to the punch. I'm sorry about last night." His voice was softer now. It reminded me of his hands on my skin.

"We both are."

"Give me another chance."

I mumbled something that was supposed to be yes. It's difficult to talk with your heart in your mouth.

"Have dinner with me tonight."

I've always doubted that old chestnut about a drowning man's life flashing before his eyes, but at that moment my immediate future passed before mine. I imagined myself across a table from Papa as he talked and laughed and grew younger with each word and every glass of wine. I pictured myself across a table from Tony. He was talking and laughing too, but more softly. My imagination raced ahead at the same rate as my pulse. I saw us leaving the restaurant, my hand nested in his again, walking the cold streets, slowly, as if we had all the time in the world, because we'd waited too long to rush now. I saw myself in Tony's bed, felt myself in his arms, made out my reflection in his soft dark eyes. And I saw Papa sitting alone in the huge empty apartment, staring up at the portrait of my dead mother. I told Tony I'd have dinner with him any time he liked—except tonight.

"I see."

"I promised to spend the evening with Papa."

"Of course. *Papa*."

I lowered my voice, as if I were betraying a secret. "He's more depressed about losing Julia than he'll admit. I think it makes him feel old. He needs consolation."

"And you're the girl to give it, Cordelia."

"Another time," I prayed.

"Sure." He managed to make the word sound like good-bye.

Though I stayed in the studio all afternoon, I accomplished little. It was fortunate, I thought, that I was not given to New Year's resolutions. The year was fewer than twenty-four hours old, but my work was already at a standstill and my life a shambles. I wondered how Julia was getting along at Camp David.

On my way up the stairs, I met Papa coming down. He was wearing a scarlet velvet dinner jacket, one of his most flamboyant. "I thought we were going to a quiet little bistro," I said.

"Change of plans. The Señora Bal à Versailles, as you and Julia so uncharitably call her, telephoned." There were no lines in his face now, and his recently shaved cheeks looked fresh as a boy's. "Her impromptu dinner party won't be complete without us. Both of us." He was trying to be solicitous, but he was no good at it. I thanked him, told him to thank the señora, and said I'd rather work.

"I understand," he said, though he didn't. "When you're in the white heat of work, nothing else matters."

My particular heat had nothing to do with work, but I didn't want to tell Papa that, so I went back to the studio and waited until I heard the front door close behind him. Then I came out and dialed Tony's number. I counted ten rings before hanging up.

As I wandered through the apartment, Corbu dogged my steps, his paws as silent as the empty rooms. The only sound was a radio playing faintly in the kitchen.

Ellen was sitting at the long parsons table, humming along with a song from the thirties, a song from her youth, and poring over the day's papers. Two of them were opened to pictures of Julia and Webster, a third tabloid carried the happy couple on the front page.

"Just like the old days," she said. "Your mother made all the papers when she married your father." Ellen had started as Mother's dresser in the theater.

I cut a piece of the Sacher torte standing on the kitchen table. "You'll ruin your dinner," Ellen said without looking up from the papers, as if I were still a child, but a docile one.

I wanted to ask her about the old days, as she called them, about Mother's first marriage as well as her second to Papa, but as a source Ellen was more enthusiastic than accurate. Her memory was colored by loyalty, her judgment by admiration. I felt a sudden longing for Mother, an aching loneliness I thought I'd banished long ago.

"Men are an unreliable breed, aren't they?" I said finally.

Ellen didn't even hear me. She was lost in the pictures of Julia and Webster Warren, who'd convinced half of America as well as my sister that he, at least, was reliable.

I was to fly back to school the following afternoon. All morning I argued with myself. Finally instinct won out over reason, heart over head. Call it what you want, I went to the phone and dialed Tony's number. I was about to hang up when he answered. His voice was thick, as if I'd awakened him though it was almost noon.

Our conversation was halting and awkward. I told him I'd called to say good-bye. He sounded as if he wished I hadn't. That's when I heard the voice in the background and understood. It was a girl's voice, thick and sleepy as Tony's, but more demanding as she called his name. Obviously Tony knew more about consolation than I ever would.

As I opened the door to my room at school that evening, the phone was ringing. I didn't run for it—there was no one in Cambridge I particularly wanted to speak to—but it went on ringing while I dropped my suitcases and crossed the room.

"Where in hell have you been?" Tony's voice wasn't harsh, despite the words.

"Circling Logan Airport. For an hour and a half."

"I was worried."

"I'll bet."

"Look, Cordelia, I'm sorry about this morning. I couldn't talk."

"So I gathered."

He was silent for a moment. "I'm not a monk," he said finally.

"Apparently." I'd aimed for withering sarcasm, but hit petulance.

"You mind!" he said as if he were surprised.

"I don't give a damn."

"It didn't mean anything. I don't even remember her name."

"Is that supposed to make me feel better?" I was trying not to cry.

"Doesn't it?" He laughed, and finally I started to.

"Yes."

"When can you come home again?"

"I'm not sure. Can't you come up here?"

"I'll try."

He did, just as I tried to get home, but we were both too conscientious and too ambitious. The third weekend in January, after two abortive attempts, he swore he'd come up, but Papa sent him to Chicago. The second weekend in February, I made plans to go to New York, but a blizzard grounded the planes, slowed the trains, and put an insurmountable obstacle between us.

So we made love by phone. In the early hours of the morning, when we'd both put work aside and the rest of the world was asleep, we lay in our individual beds, separated by miles, connected by the tenuous line of a telephone, and told each other the kinds of things people tell each other after they've made love. I found out what he'd meant when he'd said that his father was mean and that he'd learned to take care of himself both physically and emotionally early in life. The physical scars had healed but the emotional ones were still raw. For the last decade, on academic scholarships and professional trial, he'd lived as a poor man in a rich man's world. He was proud and thin-skinned, arrogant about his work and more than a little sensitive about himself, often self-centered, frequently generous, and infinitely tender.

And he learned about me. He learned that for as long as I could remember Papa had cataloged Julia and me: Julia was the emotional one, I the rational; Julia was romantic, I skeptical; Julia appealed to the senses, I to the intellect. He learned that when I'd been brought home from the hospital, Julia had thrown a temper tantrum and demanded they return me, that after Mother's death and Papa's withdrawal she had protested even louder a family plan to send her to boarding school and leave me home alone, and that I

110

missed him terribly. Then at the end of March I came home for the weekend.

I hadn't told him which plane I was taking, but he'd managed to find out and was waiting at the airport. And there amid all those tired businessmen, students on standby, and crying children, he took me in his arms and kissed me, hungrily and extravagantly, as if we were seasoned lovers, and then smiled down at me shyly, because we weren't.

As we waited for my bag, I asked how he'd managed to get away in the middle of the afternoon. Papa made no allowances for personal life, not even his daughters', especially not his daughters'. Tony said he hadn't gotten away. We were driving out to a building site. He'd had a busy winter. His design for the senior citizens' home had been accepted, drawings and specifications completed, bids received, a contractor and subcontractors chosen, and—finally, miraculously—ground broken. He said he knew I'd want to see it, and he was right.

"Not that there's much to see," he added when we'd tramped up from the road to the site.

"It's all in the eye of the beholder. To some people that's a hole in the ground. To me it's a future landmark." He put his arm around me and kissed me gently, then went back to looking at what would eventually be his building. A light snow had begun to fall, and when he took off his glasses to clean them, a flake settled on his long lashes. I thought it was the most beautiful sight I'd ever seen.

By the time we left, the snow was coming down heavily, and we were both wet and chilled. "I'll build you a fire," he promised. I knew he meant in his apartment rather than Papa's.

"You have a working fireplace?"

"That's about all I have."

He'd exaggerated but not by much. Like the apartments of all young architects, Tony's was long on ideas and short on furniture. There was a table that served a variety of functions, two chairs, a wall of ingenious bookshelves, and the overpowering presence of a large mattress and box spring built into one corner of the room. At least it struck me as overpowering that evening. The room was spare and silent and isolated from the city beyond the windows.

"What you need is a hot shower." He pushed me gently toward the bathroom. "There's a robe on the back of the door."

"You're not exactly subtle." Suddenly shy, I stood my ground.

"I'm not trying to be subtle. I'm trying to be practical. Your lips are blue." He bent and touched them with his own. "Nice but blue."

I went into the bathroom, took off my clothes, and, inevitably, looked at myself in the mirror. All hard lines and sharp angles, like a cubist painting. I thought of Julia's lush body, got into the shower, and turned it on full force as if I could drown the image. When I got out of the shower, the mirror was steamed over, and I was glad.

A robe hung on the back of the door as promised. In place of the terry cloth I'd expected was a luxuriant thick silk foulard. The shoulders, wide enough to accommodate his, came almost to my elbows, the hem to my ankles. It carried a faint aroma of Tony.

He was sitting on the floor in front of the fire when I came out of the bathroom. "What on earth are you doing with a dressing gown like this?"

"I bought it the day the client approved my design. Blew two weeks salary." I started to say he was exactly like Papa but caught myself in time.

He crossed the room and put his arms around me. "Actually I bought it for both of us." His hands beneath the robe were more luxurious than the silk.

How can I describe loving Tony? It was a kaleidoscope of every heady experience I'd ever known, a fragmentation and proliferation of every moment of joy and excitement, a heightening of everything I'd felt most intensely in life. It was the fear of facing a blank piece of paper and the exhilaration of creation when something begins to take shape on that paper. It was the thrill of a work of art seen for the first time, the heat of a hearth after a long walk in the cold, the dizzying plunge from the highest diving board of consciousness into a mindless sea of ecstasy. It was wild and tender, urgent and timeless, abandoned and, finally, sweetly binding. It was like everything good I'd ever known in life—and like nothing I'd known before.

The flames in the fireplace had died to a glow, and Tony got up and padded across the floor in his bare feet to put on another log. As he bent to the hearth, I saw the movement of tendon and muscle beneath smooth bronze skin. It reminded me of a life drawing class I'd taken once, but in his individuality and our intimacy Tony was more beautiful than any model. He came back to bed and molded his body to mine beneath the quilt. We lay there in silence, his arm holding me to him, my head resting on his chest. I felt euphoric, complete, at peace, but gradually the emotions began to ebb. I was no longer sure of myself. The seconds of silence stretched into minutes. Against my ear Tony's heartbeat sounded like the ominious tattoo of a drum. "What are you thinking?" I finally asked the question women have been asking since the beginning of time.

"Nothing," Tony answered. Had I been more experienced I would have known he'd simply given the answer men have been giving for ages, but I was a novice at the game. I was certain he'd been thinking of her.

"Julia?"

He sat up abruptly. "Goddammit, Cordelia! I didn't think you could ruin this too."

I sat up holding the quilt to my shoulders. "Was it my question that ruined things or the fact that you were thinking of Julia?"

He got out of bed, wound the sheet around his waist—oh, we were both so modest now—and crossed the room to the mantel where he'd left a pack of cigarettes. "Okay. I admit it. Not that I was thinking of her now. But that I wanted her once. Julia was like a trophy. Something I had to strive for. Something I wanted to win."

"But you didn't, so you settled for me."

He stubbed out the cigarette he'd just lighted and looked at me for a long time before he answered. When he did, his voice was as tense as his face. "In the very beginning that might have been true. I didn't think it was true, but I worried that it might be." He crossed the room and sat stiffly on the side of the bed. "Only it's not. I know that now." Slowly, as if the gesture cost him a great deal, he reached across the no-man's-land of misunderstanding that separated us and put his hand against my cheek. "I want you, Cordelia." He pulled me to him, and the warmth of his body against mine was as intense as the heat of his words.

"I love you." And in the dim firelit room his body came to mine to prove the truth of his words.

Whenever I think of the next two years of my life, I think of them as a mountain range. There were peaks and valleys but no plateaus. I loved Tony and I loved my work—for Adam Kirkland Associates now that I'd finished school—but I agonized over both.

I'd started in the drafting room, like all the other juniors, only I wasn't like all the others because I was Adam Kirkland's daughter. I slaved twice as hard on the endless drawings of lintel and mullion and drywall details, and the various design partners, eager to show their impartiality, judged them twice as rigorously. There were afternoons I locked myself in the women's room for the luxury of five minutes of unobserved tears. There were nights I staggered home, my neck muscles aching, my eyes bleary from detail work. There were moments I gave up hope because other draftsmen resented my imagined influence and clients distrusted my sex and I'd come to doubt myself.

One of the worst moments occurred the first time I worked with Tony on a job. It was a condominium in the Sunbelt, a small project, at least by Adam Kirkland Associates' standards. But small as it was, I was still worried, and the fact that Tony was the designer did nothing to bolster my confidence. He was by no means my harshest critic, but his opinion was the one I valued most and therefore feared most. His and Papa's.

By rights I shouldn't have had any contact with the client—I was still too junior—but one day he turned up in Tony's office with some new ideas about the pool cabanas, which were my purview, and Tony called me in. The three of us worked all morning, tossing ideas back and forth, trying out preliminary sketches. Tony and I played off each other well, but by the time he and the client went off to their expense-account lunch and I to a sandwich at my drafting board, I knew something was wrong.

"He didn't like any of my ideas," I said to Tony that night. We were in bed in Tony's apartment, and I felt the laughter run through his body.

"He liked the ideas all right. He just didn't trust the source."

"What do you mean?"

"At first I couldn't figure out his objections either. I kept trying to talk about the plans, but he kept asking questions about you: How long had you been out of school? Were you really an accredited architect or just Adam Kirkland's daughter dabbling at being one? 'These condominiums are serious business,' he told me with a mouthful of steak." I had to admit Tony did a good imitation of the client. " 'There's a lot of money to be made—or lost.' I agreed with him. 'I can't have things coming in way over estimate. Or things breaking down and falling apart.' I told him we were in the habit of sticking to budgets and standing behind our buildings. I was so slow on the uptake that finally he came out with it. He even put down his knife and fork to make the point. 'But, my God, Bain, she's a woman!' "

I tried not to stiffen beside him. "And what did you say?"

His hand traced the line of my body, stopping along the way to pay wordless homage. "I told him I'd never noticed." He waited to make sure I laughed along with him. "You can't let them get to you, Cordelia."

"Easy for you to say. People don't doubt you on sight—and name."

Tony said nothing to that. I wasn't surprised. We had no quarrels, only silences. Some of them revolved around my advantages and his lack of them. Others around Papa. I admit that I admired Papa, but then so did most architects working today. Tony insisted, on one of the rare occasions when we actually talked about it, that admiration was one thing, blind adoration another.

And to be fair to Tony, he admired Papa too, if somewhat begrudgingly. Their relationship was intense and volatile. They argued constantly and passionately, but each respected the other's mind and talent, if not necessarily his opinions. And then there was something stronger. Each saw himself in the other. Papa remembered the young man he'd been, the future he'd once had. He'd realized that future, but reality is never quite so heady as expectation. Tony saw the giant he'd become.

I remember the day Papa made Tony a senior partner. His rise in the studio had been meteoric. No one had ever come so far so fast under Papa. I might in the future, but then I'd be second—and Papa's daughter.

Papa took Tony to lunch at the Six Continents on the ground floor of Inter-American House to break the news, and Tony replayed the scene for me that night. I would have been able to imagine it even if he hadn't. Over the years I'd heard a great deal about Papa's lunches at the Six Continents and even witnessed a few. Papa never ate there alone—he said the food was too light and the pretensions too heavy—but he frequently took prospective clients there to show off his work, and occasionally Julia or me to show off his daughters.

The Six Continents, so named because of the food that was jetted in daily from every corner of the earth, was breathtakingly handsome, rigorously exclusive, and wildly overpriced. The space, carved by Papa as an oasis of pleasure in his monument to power, was vast and soaring. The decor, designed by Papa down to the furniture and flatware, was the epitome of expensive functional elegance. And the clientele, attracted by expense, exclusivity, and Papa's reputation, was international and rich, people who had nothing to do but lunch or so much to do they continued doing it all through lunch. The joke was that those who couldn't get a reservation at the Six Continents had to settle for the Four Seasons in the Seagram Building—and it wasn't entirely a joke.

Papa didn't so much lunch at the restaurant as occupy it, the way a victorious general occupies his conquered territory. His appearance inspired awe in the other customers and deference in the employees. He was welcomed with quiet enthusiasm. He accepted the homage with booming ebullience. While all around him the fashionable and ambitious lunched on a lean diet of nouvelle cuisine and restrained whispers, Papa had the chef whip him up sinfully rich sauces or hearty bourgeois stews and told tales out of school but not out of hearing. "You see that man over there," he would say to his guest while he savored his cassoulet and the object of his conversation squirmed under his gaze. "He spent three million on his country house, and the front door is so damn heavy that his wife can't open it. She has to call the butler or sneak out the servant's entrance." "My esteemed colleague," he'd

announce over a thick steak almost raw beneath its
sauce béarnaise, as he introduced a prospective client
to another architect. "He worked for me at one time,
and I can attest to his imagination. An extraordinary
imagination. He imagined he could put air-conditioning ducts and structural beams in the same space."
Papa laughed as if it were an old and delightful joke
among the three of them.

Once Papa even took on an entire society of architectural historians in the Six Continents. They'd asked
him to speak at their annual luncheon. He'd declined.
They'd pleaded, cajoled, finally tried bribery with a
fat honorarium. Papa had agreed to speak, if they turned
the honorarium into a scholarship for a gifted architecture student, and if, in the interest of his convenience, they met at the Six Continents. There they had
assembled to have their noses tweaked and egos punc-
tured by Papa. They'd come from cities all over the
country. What was Papa's opinion of Washington, D.C.?
"It reminds me of an abandoned granite quarry." Did
Papa have any advice for the city fathers of Philadel-
phia, who were launching a program of urban renewal? "Abandon the city." And what did he think of
Los Angeles? "I try never to think of Los Angeles."

The afternoon he took Tony to the Six Continents
to celebrate his promotion, Papa was in vintage form,
and Tony loved every minute of it. They shared irrev-
erence for the pretensions of the restaurant, jokes at
their colleagues' expense, and two bottles of Château
La Mission-Haut-Brion, 1959, from Papa's private cache
in the restaurant's wine cellar. 'Fifty-nine was an excellent year, and Papa saved it for special occasions.
For a few hours all their personal rivalries and professional differences of opinion were forgotten, and they

were as close in fact as they were in spirit. But it was precisely that similarity of spirit that inspired the subtle duel between them and the tense silence between Tony and me that sprang from it.

The loudest silence of all, however, the deafening silence, was the one that surrounded Julia. I'd stopped torturing Tony about his passion for her but not myself. I occasionally believed that Tony loved me. I never forgot that he had loved Julia—and perhaps still did.

And finally there was one more issue about which we never spoke. Marriage.

For a man and woman who were supposedly in love, who spent most of their waking hours and a good many of their sleeping together, who could talk endlessly, we had entirely too many silences. And all of them exploded the night we had dinner with Julia and Webster.

When Julia called one afternoon early in March and suggested we meet her and Web for dinner, I was surprised. We saw them occasionally but never alone. Webster was much too sought after to waste an evening on Tony and me, and Julia was well on her way to being in the same position. She had a lot of television work these days, so much, in fact, that she was beginning to fear she'd never be anything but a television actress. "And that," the daughter of Judith St. John moaned, "isn't an actress at all, only a product."

So I was surprised when Julia called, and apprehensive, too, because I was fairly sure Tony's reticence about Julia was a result of his concern for me rather than his lack of concern for her. I told Julia we'd have dinner with them nonetheless. What else could I do? She was my sister, and the fact that Tony might still be in love with her didn't stop me from loving her too.

At least it didn't so long as she was happily married to someone else.

We agreed to meet at the Russian Tea Room. It was a restaurant for television, movie, and theater people, rather than architects. The ambience was grand but musty, the year-round Christmas decorations out of taste as well as season. Though Tony and I were a few minutes late, Julia and Webster arrived sometime after we did and took several minutes to make their way across the room. They knew a lot of people, and, more important, a lot of people knew them. Women reached out to stop Webster. Men stood to embrace Julia. The two of them wound their way through the maze of tables bestowing smiles, granting hands, presenting cheeks to be kissed. Had Nicholas and Alexandra returned to the Russian Tea Room, they could not have been more imperially welcomed.

When they reached our table, Julia put her hands on Tony's shoulders and touched her cheek to his. She'd done exactly the same thing to half a dozen other men in the room in the past five minutes, but Tony didn't behave as those other men had. He was stiff, distant, careful to keep a few inches of space between their bodies. Too careful, I thought. We all told each other how wonderful it was too see each other again. We ordered drinks. I tried not to worry.

I was not successful. Webster and I talked, or rather he talked and I listened; Julia and Tony talked. I picked up fragments of their conversation as greedily as if they were the caviar in my blini.

Tony said he had just finished the design for a medical office building in San Francisco. They'd be breaking ground soon. Julia said it was a shame it was San Francisco rather than L.A. She was going to the Coast the following week to begin work in a miniseries. Webster repeated a joke the Secretary of State had told him the previous week. I laughed, though I'd been too busy eavesdropping to hear the punch line.

Tony told Julia he'd caught her most recent television appearance and had thought the movie terrible but her performance moving. He didn't add that he'd caught that particular performance sitting up in bed with me. She said she'd seen his name in a recent *Newsweek* article on the young Turks of modern architecture. She didn't add that I'd pointed out the article to her. Webster asked if I'd seen the special he'd broadcast from China. I lied and said I had. I added that I'd found it marvelously enlightening. He agreed with me.

Dinner went on that way. The laughter between Tony and Julia seemed to be growing softer and the space between them, as they turned to each other, narrower, but perhaps that was only my imagination. At least Webster didn't seem to notice. I tried to concentrate on him and what he was saying. After all, a 40 percent share of the viewing public hung on every word. Why should I be contrary? He was asking me a question: "Don't you think she's being stubborn?" He plunged into his fourth or fifth drink. I'd lost count. "Damn stubborn." I made a noncommittal noise. It was all the encouragement he needed.

"All I'm asking her to do is put in a word with the old man." I realized with a shock that the old man he was referring to was Papa. No one had ever called him the old man, and I didn't like it. I was sure Julia didn't either. "After all, it isn't as if she didn't have a vested interest in this thing. My contract is her meal ticket."

I wished now I'd been listening more closely. "Meal

ticket?" I repeated inanely. The phrase had an un-
pleasant ring.

"But it's more than the money. It's a matter of saving face." He finished off the drink, and when he started
to speak again, I noticed the precision of his words.
The more he drank, the more clipped they became. I
wondered if there was a real man beneath the public
persona. "In this business you don't stand still, Cordelia. You go either up or down. And if they bring in
a co-anchor, I'll be going down." He motioned to the
waiter for another drink. For the first time I noticed
the deathly pallor beneath the smooth artificial-look-
ing tan.

"Okay," he went on, "so those on-the-spot specials
didn't do so well in the ratings. I'm still on top with
the straight news. I don't need some goddamn co-
anchor to shore me up."

I told him I was sure he didn't.

"Then you have more confidence in me than your
sister does." He was speaking quietly, but his tone
must have caught Julia's ear.

"I have confidence in you," she said. "That's why I
know I don't have to speak to Papa. Besides, it wouldn't
do any good."

"I don't understand what Papa has to do with it,"
I said.

"Don't you?" Webster grimaced. "Ask Tony." Tony
said nothing, but his silence didn't silence Webster.
"Thomas Shaw owns the goddamn network, right?
And your old man just happens to be like this with
Shaw." He held up two fingers intertwined. "The old
boys' network. Right?" he asked Tony again, and again
Tony didn't answer. I could see that his silence was
beginning to anger Webster. If he couldn't count on

123

family feeling, he'd been hoping for sexual solidarity.

"Now I, unfortunately, am not part of the old boys' network. Tony knows what I mean." This time the grimace was malicious. "But fortunately I had the sense to marry into it. So my wife says a few words to her father, her father says a few words to Shaw, Shaw lays down the law to the vice-president in charge of news, and Webster Warren is once again the sole anchorman on 'Today's News Tonight.' With perhaps another hundred thou a year thrown in for good measure."

"It's influence peddling." Julia's lovely mouth formed the words with distaste.

"Lady Julia," Webster said in a fake English accent. "You'd do a lot more than that for your own career." He made an ugly sound that I imagined was meant to be laughter. "You *have* done a lot more than that for your own career."

Julia kept her eyes, beneath the thick fringe of lashes, focused on the table. "Besides, it wouldn't do any good."

"How do you know, if you won't try?" Webster was almost whining now, but his voice was still quiet. He hadn't forgotten his public, watching and waiting at tables all around us.

"Because I know Papa. He wouldn't lift a finger to get me a part. He went out of his way not to help Cordelia get into architectural school. Wouldn't help her with her work or give her advice or even let his colleagues write her letters of recommendation."

"Don't make me laugh. He didn't have to do any of those things. All he had to do was give her his name. Just the way he gave her a job." Webster took a long swallow of his fresh drink. "Her and Tony." Webster turned his malicious grimace on Tony. "No offense, old buddy, but let's be realistic. After all, we aren't babes in the woods."

Tony didn't look like a babe in the woods. He looked like a man in a rage, but still he said nothing.

"Papa hired Tony before I—"

"I can take care of myself, Cordelia." Tony cut me off, but he couldn't silence Webster as easily.

"Before you, maybe, but not before my lovely wife. When our boy Tony here went to work for the old man, he and Julia were, shall we say, an item. I don't suppose that hurt him too much down at 'the studio.' Unfortunately for Tony, I came along and screwed up his employment insurance. But then you're resourceful, old buddy. I'll give you that." He turned his corrupt smile on me. "Now I'm not suggesting Tony isn't crazy about you, Cordelia, only that—"

Tony's tall frame looming over the table finally stopped Webster, though I'm not sure whether he was more afraid of Tony or a scene in the Russian Tea Room.

Tony reached into his pocket, threw a wad of bills on the table, and grabbed my hand. "Come on, Cordelia." His voice was as rough as his grip.

"Sit down," Julia said, aware of the dangers of a scene herself. "Web didn't mean anything."

"That's right, old buddy," Webster began, but Tony was already on his way through the room, pushing me ahead of him as if I were the prow of a ship and he the rudder.

Webster and Julia caught up with us on the street in front of the restaurant. "Listen, old buddy," he began again, the phrase becoming more offensive with each repetition. "I didn't mean that about you and Cordelia. But you have to admit the old man can be pretty helpful when he wants to. Now all I'm saying is that if he's willing to help you, I can't see why—"

Tony was bigger than Webster, and at the moment more sober, and he never should have hit him, but I couldn't help feeling pleased when he did. He hit him hard, but not, I suspected, as hard as he could have, because Webster didn't fall to the pavement, but merely staggered backward over the hood of a parked car.

I had expected Julia to race to Webster's side, but she simply stood there staring at him. Then she uttered the line that should have been Tony's: "I'm sorry, Web, but you asked for it." It was my first inkling that the marriage that looked so perfect to the public might not be perfect after all. My second came only moments later.

"Don't worry," she said after Tony had hailed a cab and pushed Webster into it. "And don't pay attention to anything he said. He's just jealous." Then she lifted her face to Tony, kissed him lightly on the mouth, and followed her husband into the cab.

Tony stood watching the taxi for a moment before he hailed another for us. He gave the driver his address, but said nothing else until we were in his apartment, and then he only asked if I wanted a drink as he poured one for himself. When he handed me the glass, his fingers did not touch mine, nor did his eyes come anywhere near me.

"Maybe I'd better go home," I said.

"Do you want to?" He sat on the end of the bed, his eyes, still refusing to meet mine, focused on the floor.

"Do you want me to?"

"Goddammit, Cordelia, if I'd wanted you to, I would have taken you home first."

126

I crossed the room and sat beside him on the bed. "Webster's an ass."

He said nothing.

"And he was drunk."

Tony remained silent.

"You know perfectly well Papa would never be influenced by personal considerations."

"Unlike you, Cordelia, I believe Adam's human."

"Maybe I'd better go home after all," I said, but he put his hand on mine.

"Don't. Please."

I didn't go home that night. I told myself I stayed because Tony needed me, but in fact it was I who needed him. All he wanted was solace. All he sought was forgetfulness. I heard it in his silence, saw it in his eyes, felt it in his touch. Any woman would have served. My sister Julia would have done splendidly.

Afterward he fell asleep, or at least pretended to. When I disengaged my body from his and got out of bed, his lashes fluttered, thick as palm leaves in a breeze, over his smooth hard cheeks. I wanted to touch his face but didn't.

I put on the silk robe, the one he'd pretended he'd bought for us, though I knew that was a lie, and curled up in one of the two Barcelona chairs. The chairs, a statement of principle as well as a sign of accreditation for every young architect, were like old friends. I needed all the friends I could find that night. Tony had lighted no fire. The ashes in the grate were cold. The view of the city, isolated and asleep behind unlighted windows, gave no comfort. I hugged my knees to me and looked at Tony. Even in sleep his lean powerful frame was coiled as if he were about to spring.

I was still sitting that way when a sliver of thin light

crossed the East River and glanced off the top floor windows of the apartment house across the street. Tony turned, his legs winding and unwinding as if he were a lazy bicyclist. The long lashes fluttered again, and he moaned quietly. I'd hoped for a name, but it was only a sound. When he opened his eyes, they were soft with sleep. He didn't reach for his glasses, and, knowing Tony, I waited for him to reach for me, but he merely squinted and rubbed his eyes, and squinted again as if he were trying to bring me into focus. Then he reached for his glasses. I hugged my cold knees close.

He went on looking at me from behind his horn-rimmed glasses. I found myself remembering how Julia looked in the morning. I wondered if he were thinking of the same thing.

"Have you been up all night?" He sounded more annoyed than sympathetic.

I shrugged. Tony turned on his back and stared at the ceiling. We remained that way for some time, the silence hanging between us as sheer and impenetrable as one of Papa's elegant glass curtain walls. Finally the radio alarm exploded with a shocking noise, and a voice sounding like an inferior imitation of Webster Warren told us the time was seven-twenty-nine and the day ahead would be grim.

"I'd better get going," I said.

Tony went on staring at the ceiling in silence.

I carried my clothes into the bathroom. When I came out, haphazardly dressed in last night's things, he was still lying in bed, his beautiful chest bronze against the white sheets, his beautiful eyes hard in the morning light. I may have said something innocuous about seeing him at the office. I'm not sure. I wanted to get out before I began to cry.

Between the hours of seven and nine in the morning the streets are filled with men and women rushing home to shower and change before going to the office, rushing between lingering pleasure and imminent work. The sight usually amuses me. Today it only depressed me.

Papa and I passed in the front hall. He was, as I trust I've made clear, casual about sex, his daughters' as well as his own—at least he had been about his own since Mother had died. Years ago he'd given Julia and me his version of the parental lecture. "I'm not going to talk to you about the mechanics of the thing," he'd begun in a voice that boomed with conviction rather than embarrassment. "I trust those damn progressive schools I've sent you to have taken care of that. But I want to tell you the important part. Do what you want—out of desire or passion or love—but do it honestly, with respect for yourself and for others. That's all that matters." Honesty was about all there'd been last night. Tony had made no pretense of love or even affection.

"You're running late," Papa said. He didn't tolerate tardiness at the studio. It was his only conventional trait.

I reached my drafting board on time that morning, but I was still later than Papa and Tony. They were both waiting for me in Papa's office. Years later I still remembered how I'd been summoned to that momentous meeting by a mundane office memo. "Mr. Kirkland wants to see you" was scrawled on the pink slip left on my drafting board. In the studio no one dared call Papa anything but Mr. Kirkland.

He was sitting behind his desk, which was bare except for a humicant, a telephone, and a photograph of Mother. Behind him the windows were gray and rain-streaked. The weather, as predicted, matched my mood. Tony sat on the black leather sofa. Above his head hung a neat line of photographs of Papa's buildings. Tony's face was as stark as their clean facades. I took a chair halfway between the sofa and Papa's desk.

"I won't have you cluttering my office and wasting my time with personal problems," Papa said. "I'm an architect not a psychiatrist."

"There's nothing personal—" Tony began, but Papa cut him off.

"For God's sake, Tony, don't make a bigger horse's ass of yourself than you already have." He turned to me. "This idiot savant just resigned from Adam Kirkland Associates."

I was stunned. I knew Webster had gotten to him, but I'd expected him to leave me rather than the firm.

"I suppose you know why," Papa continued.

I kept my eyes on him rather than Tony. "I can guess."

"If you don't mind—" Tony began, but Papa cut him off again.

"I do mind! It's my firm. She's my daughter."

"You can leave me out of this." I loathed the empty pride in my voice. I hated the idea that I couldn't hold Tony and that Papa would try to do it for me. I writhed under Tony's gaze.

"Leave you out! For God's sake, you're the problem. He has some damn fool idea that he had to stop working for me in order to marry you." Papa's voice boomed, but Tony shouted louder.

"This is between Cordelia and me!"

"Stop talking like a Victorian novel. Of course it's between Cordelia and you, and if you had any sense you wouldn't have come storming in here this morning and dragged me into it. When I married Judith, I didn't ask permission from her father or her first husband or those three hundred thousand other G.I.s."

"I'm not asking permission!" Tony was still shouting, and by now he was on his feet. The lights were going off in his eyes like explosives. "I'm quitting the firm!"

"Most men get a job rather than quit one before they marry." I could tell that Papa was having a good time now.

"I'll get a job," Tony said. "I'd planned to before I said anything to Cordelia."

"Before I stole your thunder, you mean." Papa's laughter rumbled through the office. If he couldn't be at the center of the drama, he could at least play one of the parts. "I gave you more credit, Tony. I thought you were a bigger man. I thought you were more like me." Papa was still needling Tony, but there was a faint sadness to his voice as well. "I didn't think you were so practical, bourgeois, conventional." He ticked off his catalog of condemnations.

"It's a question of pride."

"Pride! You talk to me about pride! Half an hour ago you came sniveling in here telling me you were going to resign from the best damn architecture firm in the country, in the world, because of what people might say. You were going to give up learning under the best damn architect working today because of what Cordelia might think. If you knew anything about pride, if you had an ounce of spirit, you'd trust your own

131

talent—and Cordelia—and tell the rest of the world to go to hell. So don't talk to me about pride. I wrote the book on it. And you haven't even read the first page."

Papa stood and looked at his watch. His performance was over. Now he'd lost interest. "I have a meeting. If you want to go on working here, you can—providing your work is up to the mark—but don't expect special treatment because you're married to my daughter. If you still want to leave, I'll write you a letter of recommendation, but I'll tell you now what it will say. 'Anthony Bain is a great architect—and an even greater coward.' " Papa turned his granite face to me. "As for you, Cordelia, don't go getting any misconceptions about vine-covered cottages and mewling brats. I raised you to be more than that."

"I was a mewling brat once."

"I remember—with distinct distaste. Judith felt the same way. She went into rehearsal for a revival of *Private Lives* a week after you were born. I'll be back in half an hour. I expect to find my office empty. I pay you two to make buildings not love."

When Papa closed the door behind him, the silence was as thunderous as his voice. "Are you going to leave the firm?" I asked finally.

"Are you going to marry me?"

"This is the first I've heard of it."

Tony laughed, but there was no amusement in the sound. "Typical. The first you hear of it is from Adam. He wants to design every building, conquer every man, make love to every woman. He even managed to propose to his own daughter."

"Why are we talking about Papa?"

The look on Tony's face said I'd surprised him.

132

"You're right. Let's forget him." He crossed the big office and put his arms around me. "Are you going to marry me?"

"Are you going to ask me to?"

"I just did."

"That wasn't exactly a romantic proposal."

He brought his mouth close to mine. "I offer her love, and she talks about romance." He brushed his lips against mine. "Marry me, Cordelia."

Of course, I said I would.

Tony didn't resign from Adam Kirkland Associates. Papa's argument appealed to him. It would take more courage to stay than go, to flout public opinion rather than bow to it. We both went back to work, while around us in the inbred, incestuous world of architecture our colleagues exchanged knowing smiles and sniggering comments. Anthony Bain was marrying the boss's daughter. Clever Anthony. Poor Cordelia. Canny old Adam. Papa didn't care, and I was too happy to, but Tony was another story. I noticed that he dropped a friend from architecture school when one night after a few drinks the friend said that he'd always known how talented Tony was but not how smart. The words were supposed to be a joke, but there was an ugly undercurrent in his voice.

We decided on a June wedding. Papa pretended to be horrified at my conventionality, but it was he who insisted that it be as big and splashy as possible. "If they want to talk about us, we'll give them something to talk about. The biggest damn wedding in history. I think I'll take over Madison Square Garden." I told him St. Bartholomew's and the River Club would be sufficient. Tony said he didn't know if they'd let him in. After all, he wasn't a member of the River Club. Julia told him he was marrying into aristocracy and might as well get used to it. I didn't have the nerve to tease him about it, but when she did, he merely laughed and said he guessed he could have done worse.

Julia was marvelous that spring, despite the fact that she and Webster had separated. The fight we'd witnessed that night at the Russian Tea Room had been a minor skirmish in a long war of attrition that had begun, according to Julia, only a few months after they'd married. She said she was relieved to be free of him. "I don't think Web's made for marriage," she confided to me one morning after she'd moved back into the apartment. "For that matter, I'm not sure I am. I always want what I can't have."

"Except there isn't a man you can't have."

"You're my best audience, Delia."

Nonetheless, despite the failure of her own marriage, Julia couldn't have been more optimistic or excited about mine. In fact, it was Julia—impractical, disorganized, self-involved Julia—who made all the arrangements. While I worked long hours in the studio, she talked to ministers and caterers, musicians and florists. She registered me at Tiffany's—over my objections. "You may not want all that fine silver and crystal, Delia, but most people don't want to give plain white crockery and stainless steel flatware." She saw that I got to Bendel's for the fittings of my gown. She even—I suspected though refused to ask—took Tony to buy a ring. One morning she turned up at my drafting table at the studio. "Come on, Delia. We've got shopping to do."

I looked up in horror. In this room she might still

be Papa's daughter, but I was only another draftsman. "I can't leave work."

She ran an impatient hand through her thick golden hair. "For God's sake, Papa isn't going to fire you." Her voice, trained to carry to the last rows of a theater, filled the drafting room, but it wouldn't have made any difference if she'd whispered. Every ear in the room was attuned to us. "And don't be a hypocrite about setting a bad example. Everyone knows you're Papa's daughter, so there's no point in trying to act as if you're just another draftsman. Draftswoman." She turned her most winning smile on the architect at the next drafting table. "Right?" she asked him.

"Right," he agreed and laughed. We'd worked side by side for four months, and I'd never gotten such an unguarded response from him. Julia was right. I was Papa's daughter, and there was no use pretending otherwise.

I slipped off the high stool. "I suppose I can always retire to that vine-covered cottage and raise babies."

"Fat chance," Julia said as she started out of the room. "The kid would be born with a building block in each hand, and you'd be teaching him theory and structure before he could walk—just the way Papa did you."

Julia led the way through the stores as she had through life. I'm a terrible shopper. Saleswomen intimidate me, crowds daunt me, my own image in the mirror never quite measures up to the one in my mind. Julia, on the other hand, was born to buy. She walks into a store, and the crowds separate for her as if they were the Red Sea. Saleswomen, sensing her decisiveness, fight to serve her. And her eye is as unfailing for me as it is for her. She accomplished in half a day what would have taken me a week. She also spent several thousand dollars.

"I hope you realize I can't afford any of this," I said after she'd talked me into a three-hundred-dollar silk nightgown. Not to sleep in, she'd insisted, only to laze in seductively.

"I refuse to discuss money. As Papa's daughters, and Mother's, it's positively beneath us."

"I happen to be an underpaid junior architect marrying a recently promoted senior architect."

"All the more reason to spend Papa's money while you still can. Come on, I'll treat you to tea at the Plaza. It'll be just like old times." She'd meant the old times when Mother used to take us there, but I was remembering another old time, the night she married Webster Warren and I'd managed to catch Tony on the rebound.

Several sets of eyes followed us as we crossed the Victorian fantasy that is the Palm Court, and when we were seated, one teenage girl, weak-kneed and pale with fright, approached and asked Julia for her autograph. "This really is like old times," I said after she'd given it.

"Except that Mother used to autograph the *Playbill* of her current show. Maybe I could sign a bottle of shampoo. In case you don't get the connection, that was the sponsor of my latest television debacle."

"It wasn't a debacle. At least you weren't. You gave a terrific performance."

"You are, as I've always said, my best audience."

"Now that you're back in New York full-time, you're bound to get some legitimate work."

"Spoken like Mother's daughter, Delia. No one talks about 'the legitimate theater' these days. If they admit it exists—and on the Coast they rarely do—it's 'Broadway' or 'off Broadway' or 'off-off.' "

"Places Mother never deigned to play."

"For her it was summer stock and road companies. But she hated to leave New York."

"She hated to leave Papa," I corrected.

When Julia said nothing, we both turned to the menus, but I was still thinking of Mother and Papa and the story he'd told me the morning after Julia's wedding. "Did you know Mother was married before she met Papa, or rather when she met him?" The question was rhetorical. I was sure that if I hadn't known, Julia hadn't either.

"Mother mentioned it once when I was going through some of her scrapbooks."

"And you never told me!" Suddenly I saw the years of postbedtime whispering, the girlish jokes, the heartfelt confidences in a new light. My sister had kept a secret from me, an important secret. I felt betrayed, and Julia must have sensed it, because when she spoke, she was unable to meet my eyes. Her own, deep violet and embarrassed, roamed the room.

"I didn't think it was that important. I mean, Mother and Papa never talked about it."

"All the more reason to tell me." My sense of betrayal was turning to indignation.

Suddenly her gaze met mine. "I never told you because I didn't think you'd be able to forgive Mother."

"Don't be ridiculous," I snapped, then thought for a moment. "Still, she was so crazy in love with Papa, it does seem hard to imagine her married to someone else. And Papa was so crazy in love with her. I can't imagine anyone else loving her the way he did."

"Papa's love is overwhelming, I'll give you that."

"He would have done anything for her. Remember the time she had appendicitis at that summer theater in Maine and was stuck in that tiny hospital. He chartered a plane and flew up a few dozen of her friends for the weekend. And that Christmas she couldn't make up her mind between mink and sable, so Papa bought both. And her dressing rooms. I think Papa probably did over half the dressing rooms in half the theaters in this city. Every time Mother starred in a long run, which was practically every time she opened, he moved in with his plans and his carpenters and his painters. He couldn't stand the thought of her spending so much time in those dreary little rooms."

Julia leaned across the table and put her hand on mine. Her eyes were a softer blue now. "Delia, don't romanticize their marriage too much."

I had to think for a moment before I understood her meaning. "Or my own won't measure up?"

She took her hand from mine and leaned back in her chair. "Your own will measure up just fine. You and Tony were made for each other."

"Thanks to you."

She leaned forward again but didn't touch me. "There was nothing between Tony and me. Nothing that mattered."

Everyone said, dutifully, that I was a beautiful bride. Then they added that Julia was simply beautiful. She was my only attendant. She was, I joked, one more than I needed.

We were standing before the mirror while Julia fixed my veil, and she whirled to face me rather than my reflection. "Stop it! For one day in your life just stop it!"

"Stop what?"

"The false humility. The envy. Tony's marrying you. What more do you want?" Her husky voice had turned shrill with anger, and the flush on her cheeks had nothing to do with blusher. For the first time in my life I felt sorry for my sister and cursed the quirky fate that had made the end of her marriage coincide with the beginning of mine.

But if Julia harbored any feelings of failure, she hid them for the rest of the day. Preceding me down the aisle, she was pale, lovely, and beatific as an angel. As she held my bouquet and helped lift my veil, she was as gentle and self-effacing as a handmaiden. When we arrived at the River Club for the reception, she was as gracious, efficient, and coolly beautiful as Mother would have been in her place. And everyone agreed afterward that Julia couldn't be blamed for the disruption. It wasn't her fault that as she stood on the sundappled terrace talking to half a dozen men, her voice was as seductive as the ships' whistles calling from the river below, beckoning to the romantic in every man. Nor could she be held responsible for the fact that her smile, as she moved from one dancing partner to the next, was more heady than the vintage champagne being passed by the waiters circling the room. And of course it never would have happened if one of Tony's ushers hadn't had entirely too much to drink and an architect friend entirely too much to smoke. But since each was high and both were suddenly in love, it was only logical that when Tony and I went upstairs to change, they should come to blows. And certainly it wasn't Julia's fault that when I tossed my bouquet from the top of the stairs, as one of Mother's actress friends insisted I must, it fell into a sparse circle of elderly guests. The rest of the party was on the terrace watching the battle—fervent but fortunately not bloody—for my sister.

On the way to the airport Tony and I joked about the incident. Alone at last, we'd shed the other people as easily as our formal wedding clothes, and the summer stretched before us as fresh and full of promise as the white runner I'd walked down that morning to meet Tony at the church altar. The image struck me as apt—until I remembered that Julia had preceded me down the aisle.

We were to spend the summer in Europe. When Tony had suggested it, I'd pointed out that we couldn't afford two months abroad. Tony told me I was sounding like a wife. I told him he was behaving like Papa. "Even in the beginning, if he made ten thousand dollars in the morning, he'd go out and spend twenty in the afternoon."

Tony smiled. "In that case, I'll have to spend thirty in the afternoon."

He made a good stab at it that summer. In Córdoba we stayed in a castle, sketched the Great Mosque, and made love in a canopied bed where kings had been sired. In Venice we stayed in a palace, sketched the San Giorgio Maggiore, and made love on a balcony overlooking the Grand Canal. In Chartres we stayed in a château, sketched the cathedral, and made love on the banks of the Eure under the stars. By the time we reached Athens at the end of August our money was running out but not our passion for Old World architecture or each other. We stayed in an inn that glistened all whitewash and orange tile in the morning sun, sketched the Parthenon, and made love in a sturdy old four-poster that claimed no pedigree but had given, I like to think, much pleasure.

I still have the sketches we made that summer, ordinary rough drawings that architects make as notes for the future the way writers will jot down an idea for a book. The paper has begun to yellow and some of the lines are blurred, like my memories of certain moments, but like those moments, the sketches belong neither to Tony nor me but to us. I know Tony's style of drawing and recognize my own, but the sketches we made that summer fit into neither. In one of Tony's renderings of the Cathedral of St. Pierre at Beauvais I see my hand in the delicate tracery of the chevet. My sketch of the Santa Maria del Fiore in Florence is done in Tony's style, not as if I were imitating him, but as if my vision had mixed with his and his hand were holding mine. In the open fields and ancient buildings and big old beds of Europe we hadn't become close, we'd become part of each other.

In September we returned to New York, Adam Kirkland Associates, and a small apartment that we were determined to make a testament to our ingenuity. We spent our weeks in a torrent of work at the studio and our weekends planning and planing and hammering in the small apartment. I've always thought that people who look back at the early days of struggle from the pinnacle of success with wistfulness are either rank sentimentalists or fools. I still think they are, but now I count myself among them. I had everything—except the sense to know it couldn't last.

5

Ironically, the first threat to my fool's paradise came in a real-life Eden. Adam Kirkland Associates had just finished a swank new resort at the remote tip of Mexico's Baja peninsula. The hotel was an architect's dream, as well as a sybarite's. Papa had respected the terrain without neglecting the well-heeled guests who would come there to be cared for and coddled. Instead of constructing rooms, he'd carved them from the cliffs and sand dunes. Rather than landscape with palms and rubber trees, he'd highlighted the natural wonder of more than two hundred varieties of indigenous cacti. The resort was a tribute to nature, a testimony to simplicity, and a lesson in luxury. The rooms concealed mammoth bathrooms with sunken baths, shaded terraces overlooking craggy shores and shimmering seascapes, and an aura of privacy as alien to the modern world as this remote and breathtaking site where the Pacific meets the Gulf of California. When Papa commanded our presence at the grand opening that first Christmas after we were married, Tony and I went gladly. Julia was there too.

But Julia, smooth and honey-colored beside us on the beach, sleek and cool across the dinner table each night, was not the serpent. Papa came bearing the apple.

It was late afternoon, and the four of us were on the deserted beach recovering with a round of margaritas from a day of marlin fishing. Papa was leafing through a copy of *Progressive Architecture*, and when he handed me the magazine, open to a certain page, it smacked of neither temptation nor sin. Over a photograph of the Japanese countryside ran the word "COMPETITION." I skimmed the copy quickly. The directors invited submissions for a luxurious new private club and sporting facility. The site, a hillside on the island of Shikoku with a commanding view of the Inland Sea, called for a design of opulence, drama, and architectural excellence.

I read Papa's mind immediately. Adam Kirkland Associates was too prestigious a firm to enter an open competition. He competed only when entries were limited by invitation, costs covered by the sponsor, and his winning entry guaranteed public attention. Open competitions were for novices who still had their names to make. Open competitions were for fledgling architects like Tony and me.

Tony was stretched on his stomach, oblivious to everything but the lingering warmth of the sand, the mesmerizing sound of the surf, and—I hoped—the nearness of me and the imminence of being alone in our coolly tiled cottage. I fluttered the pages of the magazine over his smooth dark back. He flicked it away lazily, as if it were an insect. If only I'd let the matter go at that. I put the magazine on the straw mat beside his head and stroked his hair.

Tony's long lashes fluttered once, a second time, then lifted, and he began to read. When he finished, he rolled over on his back, shaded his eyes, and looked up at me. "What do you think? Should we give it a try?" The question was rhetorical. He knew I'd want to enter, as much as he did.

At the sound of his voice, Julia stretched and yawned and glanced at the magazine. "Doesn't anyone in this family ever think of anything but architecture?" No one even bothered to answer her.

Though we stayed on the beach for more than an hour, neither Tony nor I mentioned the competition again. We knew each other's methods of work. Ideas germinated in privacy. Only later did we expose them to the nurturing light of each other's opinions. Yet while we lay on that primitive beach with the most sophisticated luxuries only a casual wave of the hand away, we were working as hard as if we'd been hunched over drafting boards. When Julia asked Tony for one of his cigarettes, a six-letter word meaning matched for her crossword puzzle, and a towel after her swim, I saw the blank look in his eyes and knew he had to drag himself back from Japan to comply. And as I lay on the sand and watched the cliffs turn violet in the last rays of the sun hovering only minutes above the Pacific, I was thinking of another sea and another landscape and the building that might crown it. The competition had captured our imagination, and the only time we forgot it—at least I know I did—was when we returned to our cottage. I peeled off my bathing suit and went into the shower, and Tony followed me. The contrast between the deep tans of our public selves and the pale skin of our secret bodies was seductive. The water beaded on Tony's thick lashes and cascaded over his strong shoulders. His hands worked up an exquisite lather on my skin.

"If you're thinking of the competition now," I murmured against his chest, "I'll never forgive you."

His mouth on mine told me to shut up. His hands and body reassured me he was thinking of nothing but me.

After the hypnotic warmth of tequila and sun and shower and the dizzying heat of making love, the sheets were a cool glade, and I dozed for a while. When I awakened, Tony was sitting up in bed with an over-sized sketch pad on his lap. I picked up a few of the drawings he'd scattered about the bed while I'd slept. My mind was still half dreamy, from sleep and from him, but the sketches wrenched it awake. They were not what I'd expected. Tony hadn't designed a building, he'd created an ungainly crouching monster. Its feet reached toward the sea as if it wanted to return to the prehistoric slime from which it had emerged. On its crown sat spring eaves reminiscent of a bad set for *Teahouse of the August Moon*.

"It's different from anything you've done before," I equivocated.

"You say that every time I start something new."

He was right. Unlike Papa, Tony had no single style, no personal imprint. He insisted that was because every problem had a unique solution. I suspected it was because he was still trying to find his own individual stamp.

He studied me as I continued to study the sketches. An ironic smile played around his mouth, but there was no humor in his eyes. "I was pretty sure you'd hate it." That was what he always said, but this time he sounded sincere, and this time he was right.

"Don't you think it . . . well, fades into the landscape a little too completely? I mean, given the tone of the announcement, they're probably looking for something that dominates the hill." I knew as soon as I'd spoken that I'd taken the wrong tack and was foundering, but I'd never hated one of Tony's designs before, and I didn't know how to tell him I did now.

"As Adam says"—there was no missing the sarcasm in his voice—"a building should be *of* a hill not *on* it. And incidentally, for the sake of accuracy, Wright said it first. Besides, we're talking about Japan, and that means earthquakes. Anything tall and rigid enough to dominate the hill won't dominate it for long."

"That's not so. All we have to do is drive the pilings until we hit solid rock. Papa did that with the Public Affairs Building in Turkey, and that's weathered two major earthquakes." I took the pad, sketched the idea that had been growing in my mind all afternoon, and handed it back to Tony. He studied it for a long time before he spoke.

"It looks like the box the Turkish Public Affairs Building came in. Which, incidentally, looks like the box Inter-American House came in."

I got out of bed and put on a robe. I needed armor for this conversation. "Can we stick to criticism rather than ridicule?"

Tony looked up at me from the rumpled bed as if I were a stranger. "All right, I think your idea is just a little tired. Correction, I think it's extremely tired."

"Just because something is new or different, it doesn't follow that it's better."

"You're right, Cordelia, but look at it again." He handed me several sketches. "Without preconceptions. Without Adam's preconceptions." I looked from the sketches to him sharply. "I'm sorry," he said.

I went back to the drawings. The horizontal lines

146

that hugged the earth so closely reflected a traditional Japanese style. The spring eaves shaded the upper story, letting in only the slanting rays of the sun. "I'm sorry, but I still think it looks like a fake teahouse."

"And you'd rather construct another glass box that bears no connection to anyone or anything except Adam Kirkland and a handful of modern architects? Did it ever occur to you that those historical references you and Adam are so opposed to reflect the spirit and culture of a people?" His voice had climbed until he was almost shouting, and when he stopped abruptly, the silence hung between us in the room. It was a new kind of silence. We'd never argued about work before.

"Maybe we should forget the competition," I said quietly.

"We'd never forgive ourselves—or each other."

He was right, of course. I picked up his sketches again and tried to look at them with a fresh eye. Honestly I did. "You talk about earthquakes, but the way you've positioned the building, on the side of the hill, so close to the water, you won't be able to drive your supports deep enough to reach hard rock."

"I don't want to. Look." He took the pad and began sketching again. He was excited now rather than angry. "To begin with, we put the columns here, a short way in from the corners. It's not only the most economical position for support, but it takes away the boxiness of the building. Then if we drive the pilings not into rock, but soft mud, the building will ride the earth's movement. We'll float it—like a ship!"

I thought he was joking. "You're crazy."

"That's what they told Copernicus and Newton and Columbus, to cite a mixed bag."

"Even if you're right, and I don't think you are, no team of judges will ever buy the idea."

"Are we trying to design a great building or humor a bunch of stodgy old reactionaries?"

"Can't we do both?"

"The way Adam does, you mean? Thumb his nose at the masses while he panders to the money men."

"Let's leave Papa out of this."

"I wish to hell we could!"

We'd reached the shouting stage again, and again silence followed. We dressed for dinner without a word. By the time we joined Papa on the terraced dining patio that descended gracefully toward the sea, we still hadn't spoken. The lights of the resort glowed like colored jewels in the black sea, the night air caressed my skin, and the scents of the tropics made a heady brew. The setting throbbed with romance, but I was no longer in a mood for romance. Julia was another story. She'd wound a garland of flowers through her hair, and as she crossed the terrace toward us, the breeze swirled her pale chiffon dress around the smooth curves of her lovely body. She looked tender and soft and accommodating. She looked like everything I was not and could never be. Tony must have been thinking the same thing as he held her chair for her.

"How's the competition coming?" Papa asked when he'd dispensed with the wine list and the wine steward.

Julia sighed. The sound, meant to be deprecatory, was merely sensual. She couldn't be abrasive if she tried. It seemed I couldn't be anything else.

"Competition is right," I said. "Our ideas are, to put it mildly, dissimilar."

Tony's eyes caught mine for a moment, and I read the annoyance, but he must have known that Papa would ask about our ideas and that I'd answer.

Papa watched as the wine steward poured a fraction of an inch of chardonnay into his glass, then he sniffed it, rolled it around on his tongue, swallowed, and nodded. It was quite a show, but it was not just a show. "I've never believed in design by committee," he said slowly as if he were savoring the words as he had the wine. "A great idea is a great idea, but two great ideas combined are only a compromise." All our glasses had been filled, and Papa raised his as if he were about to propose a toast. "Why don't you enter separately?"

Above the muted sounds of the Mexican music, the other diners, and the waves breaking on the beach below, I was sure I could hear the unsteady beat of my own heart.

"Compete against each other?" Tony was incredulous.

"Why not?" Papa went on. "I'd rather have one of you win than both of you lose."

"You're just thinking of the firm." I laughed, but uneasily.

"Of course I'm thinking of the firm, but I'm also thinking of the two of you. I'm not in such dire straits that I have to go begging for another commission or award, but neither of you is so well established." Papa sipped his wine pleasantly. "And surely neither of you is afraid to lose to the other. In fact, wouldn't you prefer to see Tony win, or he you, than some stranger?"

Tony and I were silent, but Julia was not afraid to

answer. "No," she said. "But then what do I know about marriage?"

We returned home and said no more about the competition, but we were both thinking of it and planning for it. I could tell by the half-finished sketches scattered around the apartment. Perhaps they would have remained just that—unfinished designs—if it hadn't been for the Butler Building. The Butler was an office building in Dallas. It was neither large by Texas standards nor especially lucrative by Papa's, but it was a challenging commission. Tony was the senior designer on the project. I was working under him, but as Tony was the first to admit, I'd come up with the central structural idea. The Butler was to be a concrete tube, but because of location and budget limitations there was some question as to how to distribute the wind load. I suggested diagonal members, rather like huge x's, crisscrossing all four sides of the building. The idea was mine, but it was Tony who sold it that afternoon in Papa's office. Maybe that was why everyone insisted on giving him the credit.

The client admired the sketches, liked the plans, and loved the specifications, which promised to bring in a handsome building within his budget. "There's just one little problem," Mr. Butler drawled. His accent made him sound slow, but he was quick and canny. "These x's that look so pretty and work so well and save me a bundle of money cover up an awful lot of windows. Now you tell me, Adam, because you're the fella who knows about this stuff, how'm I gonna rent offices with no windows. How'm I gonna get top dollar if I don't give 'em a top view?"

All eyes turned to Tony. The idea may have been

mine, but the position of chief designer was his. "Why do you get more money for offices with windows, Mr. Butler?"

The client looked at Tony as if he were simple-minded. "I reckon people like the view."

"Of a blank wall? Of a parking lot? Of an office building across the street. Incidentally, I've seen that building, and I don't believe you could charge a penny extra for a view of it."

Butler looked at Tony as if he weren't so stupid after all. "I reckon they like the idea of a window. You might say it shows how important they are."

"In other words, your tenants don't pay more for space they want but want the space they have to pay more for. The higher the rent, the greater the prestige?"

"Something like that."

"So if word gets out that the largest and most expensive offices in the Butler Building are the ones behind the structural crosses, the ones protected from that eyesore across the street, the ones that have some sculptural interest, they'll be the most prestigious. Prospective tenants will be clamoring for them."

A canny smile crept across Butler's face. Papa was almost beaming. "Or as H. L. Mencken said," he put the cap on Tony's sales pitch, "no one ever went broke underestimating the intelligence of the American public."

"A hell of a job," Papa said after the client had signed the contracts and left. "A good building and a great pitch."

"You can thank Cordelia for the building," Tony said. "All I did was sell it."

"In that case, you two make quite a team."

Papa may have thought so, but he was the only one. Word traveled fast in the studio and almost as quickly among our colleagues. It was Tony's building, and Tony's cleverness had sold it. The more credit he gave me, the less people believed I'd had anything to do with it. I was the little woman, his right-hand man, his support, his aide, but not his equal.

"Maybe Adam's right," Tony announced one night about a week later. We'd just finished a long afternoon with the engineering consultant who had complimented Tony on the Butler Building. "About working separately."

"Papa said we made a good team."

We were standing on opposite sides of Tony's office, and he looked at me over the model of the Butler Building. "Only you do half the work, and I get all the credit. Maybe we ought to enter the competition individually. Each stand on our own work."

"I'm not that sure of myself."

"All the more reason to enter on your own."

"I'm frightened."

Tony walked around the model until he was standing close to me and put his hands on my shoulders. "Of winning or losing?"

"Both."

We each went to work with a vengeance, but for the first time since I'd known Tony, it was a separate vengeance. No longer did we pass drawings back and forth, ask for help, offer advice. And then, in case I hadn't noticed the change, Tony underscored it for me.

We'd finished our apartment, and it had been duly photographed by several prestigious journals. The crowning achievement was the studio. We'd broken through the roof of the building and constructed a large room with a skylight, fireplace, and plenty of space for both of us to work. On a Sunday morning in February with sullen rain pelting the skylight, I found Tony at work there. It wasn't unusual for him to rise early and begin working immediately, but it was unusual for him to have moved his drafting board halfway across the room.

"The light's better here." His face was naked with guilt, as if I'd caught him with another woman rather than his own ideas.

We worked all day as we frequently did on Sunday, but we'd never before worked this way. Neither of us could see the other's board, and we rarely looked up to see each other.

I pursued my original design, just as Tony did his, and I was feeling pretty good about it. From the outside it might look like a classical Adam Kirkland building—I admit I've been influenced by Papa, but so have 90 percent of the architects working today, including Tony—but inside, a Japanese garden softened the stark lines and lent an aura of repose. That evening in Mexico Tony had talked about the spirit and culture of a people, and I was sure I'd captured both in this space. Japan has four distinct seasons, and the enclosed garden, which mimed classical Japanese tradition without copying it, would bring all of them into the building. The rooms would explode with the colors of autumn foliage and pale with the snow, blossom with the cherry trees and turn cool beneath summer greenery. Tony could talk all he wanted about using nature rather than taming it, but my spare glass box did both. I was sure of it. So sure that when Julia asked me what I'd do if Tony won, I smiled and said I'd be terribly happy for him.

She and I had run into each other by accident at the hairdresser's. I manage to get to Jonathan at Monsieur Marc only about every second month for a trim, but Julia spends at least one morning a week there caring for an appearance that appears to require little care and gossiping with Jon. Her head was wrapped in a steaming turban, her fingernails were splayed over a white towel like drops of fresh blood, and her toes had been trimmed and creamed and massaged until they were things of beauty. She was in disarray, but I was the one who felt gauche.

"And what will Tony do if you win?" she asked, examining her nails critically.

"His ego isn't that fragile."

Her eyes moved from her nails to my face. "You know Papa did it intentionally, don't you?"

"Did what intentionally?"

"Set you competing against each other. He's jealous. Papa admires Tony's talent, but he resents it too. Just as he resents Tony's hold on you."

I examined my own nails, short, squared-off, and milky white except for an errant ink stain, while I weighed her interpretation. It was flattering but incorrect. Julia, not I, was Papa's darling. And his hold, or at least influence, on me was as great as Tony's, as Tony occasionally pointed out.

"Why don't you give it up, Delia?"

"Would you give up a juicy part?"

She sighed. "No, I guess not."

"You see, you're Mother's daughter as much as I'm

Papa's. The amazing thing is that they managed to stay together so blissfully."

Julia leaned her turbaned head against a cushion, closed her eyes, and murmured something. It sounded like "poor Cordelia," but I couldn't be sure.

Spring and summer slipped away almost without my noticing them. I was working hard at the studio, slaving on the competition at home. For days at a time Tony and I communicated only through secretaries in the office and hurried notes left on each other's pillows at home.

"Mr. Bain has to fly to Dallas this afternoon," his secretary would call to report.

"A crisis in the drafting room. Don't wait up," I'd scrawl hurriedly on a note on my way out the door.

He didn't wait up, but he awakened when I slipped into bed beside him. "It's like having an affair with a mystery woman," he whispered. "Each night she steals into my bedroom in darkness"—his mouth murmured against mine—"takes off all her clothes"—his hands traced the curve of my body—"and climbs into bed beside me. I can't see her face"—his fingers traced the line of my features—"I don't know her voice"—his words were warm against my skin—"I have no idea what goes on in her mind"—his body was hard against mine. "All I know is how badly I want her.

"Why don't we do something extraordinary," Tony suggested the next morning, "and spend the evening together."

I reached over and brushed the hair back from his forehead. "I suspect your intentions are strictly dishonorable."

"Not strictly. I thought we'd leave the office at an

unheard of hour, say six or seven, together, and go out for dinner, together. My intentions are strictly honorable up to that point. After that we'll play it by ear."

"What about that mystery woman who steals into your bed in the darkness each night?"

"Not tonight," he said and moved closer to me beneath the comforter. "Tonight I have a date with my wife."

We had a date, but I had a crisis—another crisis. I was working on one of Papa's projects now. They were all his projects, of course, but he kept a tighter rein on some. He'd kept a very tight rein on this one. It was a government building in Kuwait and would bring the firm millions of dollars and much attention.

It was a little after five when Papa entered the drafting room. You didn't have to look up from your board or turn around to feel Papa's presence in that room. In the old days when the head architect entered a drafting room, all the assistants automatically stood and turned to face him. We were not so archaic. Our bodies remained at our drawing boards. Only our spirits snapped to attention.

I felt him standing beside me but went on working. The government building was a glass tower with triangular black granite columns rising without a break to its full height. Papa had been playing with the facade for weeks. I felt as if I'd been drawing the details for years.

"Cordelia," he said. He called me by my first name, but then he called all his employees by their first names. Nothing in his voice indicated that I was any more than another draftsman. "You'd better get to work on this." He covered my drawings with one of his own. It was the same building but now there were shorter columns along two side galleries. They were not an improvement, but it was not my place to say so.

He started to laugh. In that drafting room the only sound more welcome than Papa's laughter was Papa's praise. "The vagaries of dealing with other cultures. Some high government official saw a sketch of the wrong building. The other one had open galleries with columns. Now he has his heart set on open galleries with columns. I'm leaving for Kuwait in the morning so you'll have to do the plans tonight." He turned and left without waiting for my answer. In the drafting room as in life, he demanded obedience and got it.

I called Tony and told him what had happened. Though I tried to make a joke of it, he didn't sound as if he thought it was funny.

It was a little after eleven when I finished the plans and took them up to Papa's office. He went over them carefully, critically, without a word. They were meticulous drawings of a design Papa had no intention of building. Finally he laughed as he had in the drafting room. "You make it crystal clear. If this doesn't convince the bastard he doesn't want open galleries with columns, nothing will." He put his arm around my shoulders. He was satisfied with the job. Working hours were over. I was his daughter again. "How about a drink?"

"I ought to get home."

"Why?" Sometimes Papa could be maddening.

"It might be nice to see my husband."

"He's either working or asleep. Whichever, he'll still be at it half an hour from now. Stay and have a drink." He'd already poured two, and now he handed me a glass and settled into the sofa. The photographs of his buildings sat on the wall above his head like a crown.

The carefully lighted models placed around the office glowed like pale jewels. I remembered the New Year's Eve Tony and I had come here with a drink in mind and perhaps more. Papa had come between us then.

"How's the competition?" he asked when I'd settled into the other end of the sofa.

"From my point of view, or Tony's?"

"Both. I expect one of you to win."

"And which of us do you think will?" Papa had seen some of my plans, and I'd told him about Tony's ideas.

"It isn't a question of which design is better, but of which design the judges believe is better. And you know what I think of most of my colleagues, Cordelia. If you rubbed all five of those judges together, you still wouldn't ignite a spark of imagination. In this particular case, that fact happens to be in your favor." I started to say something, but he went on quickly: "I'm not saying your design isn't fresh. It is. It's also sound, and that will appeal to the judges. Form and function are one, the nature of the materials will be apparent everywhere, and the structural methods are proved. Your design, in fact, is everything Tony's isn't. Of course, I haven't seen his plans, but from what you've told me I'm skeptical. For one thing, I don't trust the structure. For another, I don't like all this playing around with cultural references and local color. It's too flashy, too much of the moment. Tony is trying to be different just for the sake of being different."

"That's not fair. There's a philosophy behind his design."

Papa's eyes glinted with wicked amusement. "Are we discussing plans or your husband, Cordelia?"

"It's just that sometimes I think you're too hard on Tony."

158

"Hard on him? I've brought him along faster than anyone who ever worked for me—including you. I recognize his talent, but I also recognize his faults. Notice I said faults, Cordelia, not limitations. I agree with you. I think Tony has the makings of a great architect. I also think he has the instincts of an angry young man. Sometimes his resentment of the establishment, society—call it what you will—gets the better of him."

"You've always hated the establishment."

Something between a wince and a smile flickered across Papa's face. I never knew how he felt about having Tony compared to him. His own uniqueness was one of the cardinal tenets of his religion. "I regard the establishment with the amused disdain of one who has turned his back. Tony hates it with the sullen fervor of one who never belonged. I wouldn't mind that if it didn't color his work, but every now and then Tony feels obliged to thumb his nose at the establishment. And that's what he's doing in this competition. Tony's design is a gesture of rebellion. I'm sure there are brilliant touches to it—Tony couldn't design a building without some brilliance—but it has no central reason, only reaction. Reaction to modern architecture as we know it today and—face it, Cordelia—reaction to me. That's why I think you're going to win. Because you haven't let your own emotions and uncertainties creep into your work. Because you've stayed true to the eternal principles."

I didn't know whether to laugh or cry. I was excited about my work and terrified for my marriage. I wanted to run home to my drafting board, but I didn't have the courage to go home to my husband.

"But don't pack your bags for Japan yet, Cordelia. Keep in mind that I'm a genius, and you're dealing with mediocre minds. It's entirely possible that they'll be swept off their feet by what I regard as mere showiness in Tony's design. It's also possible that the blind bastards will revert to type and pick a third entry that's a monument to mediocrity. God knows they have in the past."

Papa was wrong. Tony was neither asleep nor at work when I got home. He was in the living room with Julia. I heard their laughter as I put my key in the door. It seemed to me that it stopped abruptly. Can you hear guilt in silence?

"We've been waiting for you," Julia said.

I doubted it but didn't contradict her.

"We've been celebrating," Tony informed me. "Julia landed a part on Broadway."

"A choice part on Broadway," she corrected him. They sounded like a damn duet.

"It's not the lead, only the ingenue, but I get third billing and a stupendous scene where I tell the leading man off. There are actresses all over New York who would kill for that scene."

I congratulated her and kissed her, and we toasted her success. When Tony and I were married, we'd been given a case of Dom Perignon, and we'd got into the habit of opening a bottle for special occasions. He'd opened one tonight with Julia.

"Tell me more about it," I said, taking a chair across from the sofa where the two of them were sitting. She did with help from Tony, who'd already heard the details but showed no sign of growing bored at their repetition. In fact, he kept interrupting her to add a point or remind her of an anecdote.

When we finished the first bottle of champagne, Tony

was all for opening another, but Julia stood and said she had to get some sleep. "Nobody wants a haggard ingenue." Her smile at Tony was dazzling as a spotlight. He looked as if he'd take that particular ingenue in any shape she came. He said he'd see her downstairs and put her in a cab.

"Are you sure you don't want to see her home?" I said to the empty room when they'd left, and was thoroughly ashamed of myself.

I swore I wasn't going to watch them from the window overlooking the street, then went into the next room and, without turning on the light, stood looking down at them. All the taxis that passed were full, but neither of them seemed to mind. Tony was looking down at Julia as they talked, and her face was turned up to him. Even at this distance, in the faint light from the street lamps, I could read the pleasure in it. She was wearing her Burberry trench coat, which I happen to know is fully lined, but she shivered and hugged her arms to herself once or twice, and finally Tony put his arm around her shoulders. A few seconds later an empty taxi pulled up, and he put her into it with a properly brotherly kiss on the cheek. At least it looked that way from where I stood.

"You worked pretty late," he said when he returned to the apartment. I'd taken the glasses and ashtrays into the kitchen and was plumping the pillows. Playing the good little wife, I thought, while my husband was playing around.

"You don't seem to have missed me."

Tony stopped on his way to the bedroom and turned to me. "What's that supposed to mean?"

"Nothing. You just seemed to be having an awfully good time with Julia when I walked in."

"If you're trying to make something of this, Cordelia, you picked the wrong night. You were the one who begged off."

"I had to work."

"I know you did. And after you finished, you had to stop for a drink with Adam. That and a little father-daughter talk."

"How did you know I had a drink with Papa?"

His smile was quick and cruel. "You couldn't have helped yourself."

"He's getting older, Tony. He's lonely. He'd never admit to either, but I can see it. Even with Julia home, he's all alone."

"Not as long as he has you." Tony turned and went into the bedroom. By the time I followed him a few minutes later, he was lying on his side of the bed, his back turned ominously to mine, feigning sleep. Or maybe he wasn't pretending. Either way, the message was clear.

The following morning we both apologized and blamed the champagne. I didn't mention Julia, and he didn't speak of Papa. We patched things up, and good marriages, I reassured myself, marriages that last, are like patchwork quilts. I felt terribly mature in my wisdom.

For the next few months I needed all the maturity and wisdom I could muster. Life had turned into a three-ring circus. Papa had been successful in Kuwait. The government official had relinquished the open galleries with columns, but he was still demanding changes, and Papa was driving himself and the rest of us at an unprecedented pace. After hours Tony and I were running our separate races to complete the sketches and plans before the competition deadline. We ate little, slept less, made love infrequently. And as if our own frenzy were not enough, every few days Julia came hurtling through the apartment like a beautiful demon. Rehearsals for *Eastward* were progressing with customary chaos. Julia was in her element. She adored the director but hated the leading man. The director didn't know stage right from stage left, and the leading lady still hadn't learned her lines, but the leading man was a dream to work with. The costumes were terrible, but the lighting was inspired. The costumes were terrific, but the lighting made her look like the oldest ingenue in captivity. The play would win the Pulitzer and run forever. They'd fold opening night. She was going to score the success of the season—the decade. She'd never work in the theater again. I would have laughed at her if I hadn't been going through the same cycles myself. One day I worried how Tony would take my triumph, the next how I'd live with my failure, the third how we'd both feel when some monument to mediocrity, as Papa put it, took the prize. Though all the materials had been mailed, I was still too close to my design, and to Tony, to be able to judge them clearly. Preston Hunter had no such problem.

Preston Hunter is, as everyone knows, America's most widely read—and widely hated—architectural critic. He has an excellent eye and a vicious tongue. He makes reputations with a single article, breaks them with one withering phrase. He cannot be fooled or charmed, bought or bargained with, as many young architects have learned. Plump and squat with a long mournful face that gives him the appearance of a balding horse, Preston Hunter is also known for his prodigious and eclectic sexual appetites. He likes women; he likes men; he likes various combinations thereof. But a night in Hunter's bed does not ensure a good word in his column the following morning. I know at least two women and one man who found that out the hard way. Just talking to the man makes my skin crawl, but there was no avoiding conversation with him at the opening of a show of Papa's early sketches.

Over the years the value of Papa's drawings has kept pace with his reputation. They've been collected in three volumes and hung in museums around the world. This particular showing of them was at a gallery so prestigious it hadn't displayed the work of a living artist for more than a decade. On the night of the opening—a week before the results of the competition were to be announced, and, coincidentally, a week before Julia's debut—Papa said he felt like a corpse celebrating his own wake.

The room was, of course, too warm, too smoky, and too noisy. The crowd was, of course, too busy looking at each other to pay much attention to the sketches. Tony and I tried to, but a crowded opening is no place for an art lover. People kept popping up between us and the drawings or pushing us up against the wall or merely demanding our attention. Finally we gave up and settled for some bad champagne and mediocre conversation—until Preston Hunter appeared. Tony and I were both on our guard.

"I have to congratulate you, sweetpea," he said to Tony. Preston called everyone—man, woman, and child, friend, foe, and stranger—sweetpea. "I just got back from San Francisco. That medical office building isn't bad. In fact, it's damn good. Almost great."

Tony was still wary. Hunter's most vicious attacks

were often sneak. "An impossible site made more so by zoning restrictions, but the seven floors of setbacks stepped down to one work. The scale is human, and all that planting on the terraces helps." Hunter took a sip of his champagne, then licked his thick lips. I had to avert my eyes. "You know, sweetpea, you're the only architect working today in what we still laughingly call the modern idiom, who doesn't think every building has to be an assertion of his own fragile and dubious masculinity. Including the great man himself." He tossed his long head in Papa's direction like a horse whinnying. "Now I know Cordelia doesn't agree with me, but you understand what I mean, don't you?" If Tony did, he gave no sign. "Adam Kirkland has erected phallic symbols in every major city in the world—and cuckolded the public at the same time. I mean, skyscrapers in the middle of the Sahara! With all that empty land. What's the point?" Hunter turned to me. "You tell us, sweetpea. You explain the Kirkland mentality to us."

"The point is," Tony began before I could, "that every Third World government wants its own skyscrapers, and Adam Kirkland has given them damn good ones."

Hunter turned to me. "Loyal as well as gifted. My, you are fortunate, sweetpea."

"You used to think those skyscrapers were pretty good yourself, Preston. 'Monuments to order, logic, and clarity,'" I quoted his evaluation of Inter-American House.

"How sweet of you to remember. I wrote that years ago. But unlike your illustrious father, I don't go around repeating myself year after year in city after city." I started to say something, but he went on quickly:

"Neither does Tony. At least he hasn't yet. Rumor has it your entry in the Japanese competition is like nothing you've done before, like nothing anyone's done before. Is it any good?"

Tony laughed. "It's not good, Preston, it's sensational."

"I hear it doesn't change the skyline at all. Simply nestles into the hill."

"You've heard too much. The entries are supposed to be secret until the results are announced."

"Pillow talk. The wife of one of the judges was quite taken with your design. And the little boy who works for him was positively captured."

Tony laughed again. "Tell me, Preston, is there anyone in this business you haven't slept with?"

Hunter threw an arm around each of us. His touch was clammy. "Yes, sweetpea. The two of you."

"What a repulsive little man," Tony said after Hunter had drifted away, but he still sounded pleased.

"Repulsive but with a good eye. And taped in. I wouldn't be surprised if he knows the winner already."

"That's exactly what he wants you to think. They haven't chosen the winner yet, Cordelia. Hunter was only gossiping."

"Then why," I said, trying to joke, trying to hide my disappointment from him, "do you look like a cat who just swallowed the biggest, fattest canary of your life?"

He did look that way, and he acted that way for the rest of the party, and afterward. I suppose there are as many ways of making love as there are of loving. Tony and I had made love playfully like children and passionately out of hunger, tenderly with the trust and intimacy of two people who share a great deal and casually because every now and then we began to take this miraculous thing for granted. But that night for the first time, Tony made love to me triumphantly.

Julia's play opened on the first Wednesday in October. It was the same day Tony and I were to hear the results of the competition, at least if one of us won. If we both lost, we would have to wait for the public announcement of the winner the following day. But of course that announcement would no longer matter to us. By noon we'd received no word, but noon, we told each other over sandwiches in Tony's office, was still early in the day. We'd used the excuse of too much work to keep from going out for lunch, but we both knew that neither of us wanted to leave the phone.

"This is the damnedest feeling," Tony said, pushing his half-eaten sandwich away. I'd done even less well with my own. "I want to win so much I can taste it, but I want you to win too."

"Maybe we should have entered together after all."

His eyes held mine. "Maybe we should have."

"Only then neither of us would have won," I said. "Compromise of first-rate ideas only produces second-rate design, as you pointed out."

"Adam said that, not me."

Tony had a meeting at two. As we left his office, he told his secretary to call him out of it if there was any word on the competition. When he returned to his office a little after three, there were no messages about the competition.

At three-thirty I had to leave for a site inspection. Fortunately, it was in town, and Tony promised he'd run all the way over if he had any news. I returned to the office at six. There was still no word.

"I guess it's the monument to mediocrity," I said in the cab on the way home.

"I guess you're right," he answered, though I could see he hadn't given up hope. Neither had I.

The mail was in a great pile in front of our door. Tony scooped it up and riffled through it in seconds. "No telegrams," he reported.

"It's better this way," he said half an hour later when I came out of the shower. He'd made a small pitcher of martinis and handed me one. "No rivalry, no jealousy." He touched his glass to mine as if the words had been a toast.

"Much better," I agreed. The liquid was smooth on my tongue. In a few minutes it would dull some of the pain.

Tony was fastening a necklace for me—Mother's emeralds; Julia had taken the sapphires because they matched her eyes—when the phone rang. We were both standing beside the night table, but since his hands were occupied with the clasp, I picked it up. I spoke with Preston Hunter rarely, but I recognized his voice immediately. The accent was impeccable, but the tone was thin and nasal.

"I understand congratulations are in order." I tightened my grip on the phone. "The judges were enthralled. Only one of them had a single reservation. He said Tony's design will be better appreciated in ten years than it is now."

"Then he won!" Tony had closed the necklace, and now his hands gripped my shoulders as if he were holding on for life.

"Do you mean you haven't heard?"

"Not a word."

Preston's laugh was shrill and vaguely cruel. "Well,

just think of it. You two children pacing the beautifully finished floors of Adam Kirkland Associates all
day, chewing those ink-stained nails, wondering which
of you would walk off with the prize—pity it can't be
both of you—then enter Preston Hunter, the bearer of
good tidings."

"Did he win?" I demanded.

"Did Tony win? she asks me."

"Preston!"

"All right, sweetpea, I'll put you out of your misery.
You and that handsome husband of yours. I am pleased
to announce on behalf of the illustrious judges—shall
I name all the judges for you in case you've forgotten?"

"Preston!" I screamed this time.

"He didn't win, sweetpea. You did."

"Preston!" I screamed again.

Tony grabbed the phone from my hand. He was just
in time to receive my congratulations. His face collapsed as suddenly and completely as a building in
an earthquake. Then he recovered. His smile was wide
and warm. It wasn't his fault it didn't extend to his
eyes. "I'll give her your congratulations, Preston." Tony
laughed. It had a hollow sound. "And I agree with
you. I preferred my design too, but I'm glad for Cordelia's sake that the judges didn't."

"I am glad for you," he said when he hung up the
phone. "You did a good job."

"But not as original as yours. Did Preston tell you
what one of the judges said about your work?"

"Sure." He laughed. Another hollow sound. "Like
all geniuses, I'm bound to be a big success—posthu-
mously."

"You are a success. And you're ten times more talented than I am. It's just as Papa predicted. They chose the monument to mediocrity."

"Don't denigrate yourself, Cordelia. And don't patronize me."

I started to say that I wasn't patronizing him, but the phone rang, and it was just as well because I had been. I felt sorry for Tony, but my pity was diluted with pure joy at my own success, and by the time I got off the phone with Papa who'd just heard the news, I'd almost forgotten Tony's disappointment. I was intoxicated by triumph, and like every drunk, my vision was clouded, my judgment faulty, and my interests entirely self-centered. The telegram confirming the news that arrived as we were leaving the apartment was like another shot of whiskey.

Only years later when I'd sobered up, when I began tracing events back to that night, did I remember one peculiar aspect of Tony's behavior. He'd done all the right things. He'd smiled and congratulated me and pretended to be happy. But he hadn't been able to bring himself to kiss me.

Papa did that at the theater. He was pacing the familiar lobby of the Sarah Siddons when we arrived. Funny now to think that none of us even noticed the theater that night. Papa had lived through dozens of opening nights with Mother, but experience had only sharpened his anxiety. He knew what could happen. Though he trusted Julia's talent, he had no such confidence in the critics' judgment.

The theater was filled with famous names and faces. Papa knew them all, and they all knew Papa. Many of them stopped to speak to him on their way to their seats. "Just like old times," said America's greatest living lyricist. "She's going to make theater history tonight," predicted a man who'd proved Shakespeare could be box office magic if you updated the action and added a little music. "If only Judith could have lived to see this," whispered an actress who had outlived her own career. No one mentioned my success, but then I reminded myself that no one knew about it. The results would be announced at a press conference the following day.

As the lights dimmed, I sensed the familiar opening night tension in the audience. On one side of me, Papa bristled with expectation, on the other, Tony sat rigid and removed. I wondered whether he was hoping for Julia's success or wishing for a failure to offset his own. It isn't easy to be generous in despair. Fortunately, I had no such problem. At that moment I prayed for Julia's triumph almost as fervently as I savored my own. My hand crept through the darkness to Tony's. He didn't return the pressure, and after the burst of applause greeting the leading lady's entrance, he didn't take my hand again. Papa did. He squeezed it hard and whispered, "Let's hope she breaks a leg."

Julia made her entrance during an argument between the two leading characters. It was a difficult entrance, and an actress without stage presence would be overlooked. The audience noticed Julia. I could feel the attention sway to her, then back to the leads as surely as heads turning at a tennis match. When she spoke her first lines, I knew she was nervous, but I doubt anyone else in the audience did. In any event, the nervousness worked to her advantage. It gave her a breathless, innocent air. She was the perfect ingenue.

By intermission I was certain of her success. As Papa, Tony, and I stood in the lobby, more celebrities drifted by to concur. "She's magnificent." "She's stealing the show." "You've got another star on your hands." But Papa wasn't taken in. He knew theater people. "It's not what they say to your face that counts," he always warned, "but what they whisper behind your back."

The warning bell sounded, and we returned to our seats. Julia was even better in the second act. She was building in the part. And the audience was warming to her. I didn't care what Papa said. I could feel it all around me. By the time she came to her final scene, the one she said half the actresses in New York would kill for, she was at fever pitch. This time she entered unobtrusively. There was no business, no intense concentration to call attention to herself. And so when she finally spoke, the audience was almost surprised to find her onstage, as surprised as the leading man was supposed to be. The lines were only moderately good, but in Julia's mouth they sounded inspired. When she tweaked the leading man's vanity, the audience roared its laughter. When she told him what she thought of him, a single shocked gasp ran through the house. When she turned and walked off stage, she brought down the house. It was some time before the applause died and the leading man could go on with his lines.

"Don't tell me this is insincere," I whsipered to Papa, but he was too busy applauding to answer. Tony was applauding too and looking genuinely pleased. More pleased, I thought with a sudden pang, than he'd been at my success. But of course Julia hadn't been competing with him. Her triumph didn't diminish his worth.

Afterward we fought our way backstage, but there was too much of a crowd for more than a few brief shouts of congratulations. Half the theater was in Julia's dressing room. The whole world lay at Julia's feet. Papa, who'd reserved a table at Sardi's, told Julia we'd wait for her there. "That gives her," he explained as the three of us headed for the restaurant, "the chance to make a grand entrance."

Grand entrance was an understatement. I don't know if she'd dawdled intentionally taking off her makeup and changing her clothes—Julia always did take forever in front of a mirror—but she managed to arrive after the leading lady. The star had gotten a respectable round of applause as Vincent led her to her table. Julia got a standing ovation as he led her to ours. Part of it was in memory of Mother, but only part.

She crossed the room to us slowly, as if she knew it was the most delicious walk of her life and wanted it to last. Her eyes were as deep and shining as the sapphires at her throat, her smile as bright as all the neon on Broadway, her pride as simple and honest as a child's. I loved her deeply. I think everyone in that room loved her at that moment, everyone, that is, except the leading lady.

By the time Julia reached our table we were all standing. When Papa folded her in his arms and held her for a moment, there wasn't a dry eye in the room. I kissed her and told her how wonderful she'd been, and she beamed and said, yes, hadn't she been after all. Then she turned to Tony and raised her face to his, and he bent until his mouth touched hers lightly and gave her the congratulations he'd been unable to give me.

All night long people kept coming over to the table to congratulate Julia. Occasionally, when they were old friends, Papa told them we were celebrating two great events, and then they'd congratulate me too. But mostly these were theater people, and Julia had scored a theatrical triumph. It was her party and one after another people joined us to celebrate it. Over and over they chanted the same litany of praise. Subtly shaded. Alive. Dynamic. Superb. Stupendous. After an hour or two and several bottles of champagne, the words floated in my head like figures lost in a mist. But through them all a single sentence that had been repeated again and again rang as insistent as a fog horn. "You're bound to win a Tony," the well-wishers told her again and again. I remembered the way Tony had kissed her. I thought of the fact that he'd neglected to kiss me. And I knew the well-wishers were right. Once again Julia had stolen my thunder. It seemed only a matter of time before she took my husband as well.

BOOK TWO

Julia's Story

6

I love my sister Cordelia. She's generous to a fault. For as long as I can remember she's shared everything—toys, clothes, books, even her allowance. She's loyal. No matter how I tortured her, and as an older sister I did my share of minor torturing, she never tattled. She's witty and intelligent and beautiful. She is, despite everything, my dearest friend in the world. As I said, I love my sister Cordelia. But if I were you, I wouldn't believe everything she says.

I don't mean to suggest that Cordelia lies. On the contrary, I think she's incapable of lying. It's simply that she doesn't always see things clearly. Like Papa, she's a great maker of myths. She accepted as gospel Papa's view of himself and Mother and their marriage. Again, don't misunderstand me. Papa is a great architect and an extraordinary man, but he is, after all, human. Mother had as much charm and talent as she did beauty, but she also had her weaknesses. And I realize now that their marriage was pretty good, all things considered. But for Cordelia there was nothing to consider beyond their perfection. And then, as if Papa's myths weren't destructive enough, she set about making her own. The first, and I suppose the most dangerous, was about me.

Cordelia always called me a golden girl. Translation: dumb blonde. I don't mean that Cordelia thought of me that way, only that she didn't understand a lot of other people did. Even Papa. Of course, he never said as much, but the implication was always lurking beneath the words. He used to say I knew nothing about architecture. And since to him architecture was the world, he meant I knew nothing about anything. All I was good for was dressing up a stage, decorating a man's arm, and filling a man's bed. I sometimes wonder if he was as condescending to Mother as he was to me—and if so, how she put up with it.

Not that I'm asking for sympathy. I have a great deal to be thankful for. I inherited Mother's looks, some of her talent, and, most important, her willingness to work hard to make the most of both. Contrary to Cordelia's opinion, not everyone in the theater recognized my gifts on sight. I've fought as long and hard and—I admit it—ruthlessly as every other successful actress. As for my looks, I admit that I was born lucky—and that I've struggled all my life to stay that way. Cordelia's the natural beauty. Her eyes are like mine, except that the intelligence radiating from them is uniquely hers; her bones are beautiful as well as visible; and her air of not thinking twice about her appearance makes her three times as attractive. I, on the other hand, am a monument to man's—or rather woman's—ingenuity, vigilance, and determination. I run five miles each morning and spend at least ten hours a week at the gym. Cordelia occasionally walks to work. It takes me twenty minutes to do my face, not for a performance but for life, though most people think I wear no makeup offstage. Cordelia owns a lipstick, some blusher, and mascara, though she rarely remembers to wear all three at once. I've been on the Scarsdale, Cambridge, and several hundred other diets, lived on oranges for a week and liquids for a month, fasted for days and eaten three mouthfuls every hour. Cordelia never thinks about food; she just enjoys it. I value my face and body as the instruments of my craft, but I also fear the day they will become my enemies. Cordelia knows no such terror.

There's one more point I'd like to get straight. Contrary to Cordelia's opinion, every man I meet does not fall head over heels in love with me. I admit that a good many of them would like to take me to bed, especially now that I'm famous, but lust is not love. And Tony, the best of the lot, wasn't in love with me, at least not the way he was with her. It may have taken the two of them some time to realize that—perhaps they still haven't—but I knew it that first afternoon on Nantucket.

I was as taken with Tony as Cordelia was. It wasn't merely that he was handsome, though heaven knows he was. Not handsome like so many of the actors I know who always seem to be giving you their best profiles or posing against some backdrop, but handsome almost as an afterthought. Still the strong-boned face and hard body, intriguing as they were, couldn't have done it alone. It was the way he stood up to Papa. Tony was impressed by Papa, I think he was even a little afraid of him, but he was determined not to show it. When he told Papa what he thought of the house, I wanted to applaud. When Papa called him an impudent young bastard, I knew he thought Tony was special too. And I knew, when Cordelia came back from showing Tony the house, that he saw something in her he'd never even bother to look for in me. The more I saw of Tony, the more certain I became of that. Ever since we were children Papa has always compared Cordelia and me as if we were separate poles and he the magnetic force. Tony did the same thing, not in words but in actions. Cordelia was mind, I was body. Cordelia was talk, I was touch. Cordelia was serious, I was frivolous. Cordelia was a person, I was an object. I sensed all that from the beginning, though I pretended not to, but after the night Tony came to the apartment for dinner for the first time, the night Papa gave him his first crack at designing a building from scratch, I couldn't pretend any longer.

I suppose I could have forgiven the way he acted at dinner. Papa had just dropped a bomb in his lap, and Tony wouldn't have been Tony if he hadn't been exploding with a hundred different ideas. I didn't even mind the fact that he insisted on trying them out on Cordelia. After all, she'd be more likely to understand them, though I am not the visual illiterate Papa believes. And I certainly didn't mind all those drawings on the napkins. God knows I'm accustomed to them. I could have forgiven Tony for turning to Cordelia in his exhilaration, but I couldn't forgive him for, that same night, turning to me for sex. Because that was all he wanted from me. And the funniest thing of all, though I didn't think it was so terribly amusing at the time, was that if it hadn't been for the way he'd behaved earlier in the evening, if it hadn't been for Papa's gift of the design job on the retirement home—I suppose it always comes back to Papa in the end—I would have slept with Tony that night. I'd wanted Tony, emotionally, sexually, completely from the very beginning, and maybe that night he came to the apartment for the first time would have ended differently, even after the way he'd treated me at dinner it might have ended differently, if I hadn't heard Cordelia come in. Tony heard her too. I could tell because he stopped what he was doing at that moment to listen. And when a man stops making love to you to listen to another woman, it's time to get up, put on your clothes if you happen to have taken any off, and we had, and call it a day. I know I sound cavalier about the incident, but remember, it all happened some time ago. Remember too, I'm a good actress.

I realized that night that there was no hope for Tony and me. And when he and Cordelia returned from their drive out to the site the following afternoon I knew I was right. Something had happened between them. For one thing, Cordelia was positively dripping guilt. She looked the way she used to when we were teenagers and she'd appropriated one of my skirts or sweaters without asking. For another, there was the tiniest smudge of lipstick near Tony's ear. Maybe it was the lipstick that did it. Whatever, that was the moment I decided to concentrate on Webster Warren.

But I'd rather not talk about Web. There's nothing wrong with my former husband, nothing that an injection of backbone wouldn't cure. I suppose I should have seen through Web from the beginning, but I seem to have a fatal weakness for choosing the wrong men—except Tony, and I let him get away. At any rate, what I saw in Web was that he was gravely handsome, wildly successful, and nothing like Papa—or Tony. By the time I returned from our wedding trip, I'd realized that those traits weren't enough—and that I'd made a serious mistake. In more ways than one. If I'd ever had a chance with Tony—and I admit that I sometimes still toy with the idea that I had—I'd lost it. Tony had discovered Cordelia. He'd seen the fire beneath the cool exterior, the passion behind the controlled demeanor, the sensuality lurking in all those clean angles. Cordelia had become mind *and* body. I knew it the first time I saw them together. And I was glad for her. Really I was.

All right, I'm exaggerating just a little. There was some envy, an occasional surge of sibling rivalry, a feeling during the time I was trying to muster the courage to leave Web that my life was falling apart while hers was coming together. But the envy didn't last. I'd been in love with Tony, but I loved my sister too. And I was occasionally, if temporarily, capable of falling in love with someone new. But most of all, I was in love with the theater. And that, rather than Tony, is the reason I can't forgive Cordelia now. Because she wants to destroy part of what I love best in the world. I don't care what her motives are—ignorance, ambition, revenge—I care only that she wants to demolish one of the best theaters in New York, the building where dramatic history was made, where Mother scored some of her greatest triumphs, where I made my debut. She wants to replace a monument to Mother's achievements, and mine, with one to her own.

7

The first few years following my Broadway debut in *Eastward* were the happiest of my life. I know that sounds strange in view of all that happened afterward, in view of the consequences, but of course I didn't know then what the consequences would be. None of us did. And I was happy. There's nothing like the early days of success when every pleasure seems newly minted and you believe nothing in life will ever tarnish.

I'd won my Tony, as everyone had predicted. I suppose I also won Tony, in a way. I don't mean to imply that I took him away from Cordelia. No one could have done that. But Cordelia was spending a great deal of time in Japan, and Tony was lonely. I admit I was attracted to Tony, and I suppose he was attracted to me. Wait, let me rephrase that because I want to be honest. I know Tony was attracted to me. But we were both on our guard against that attraction.

Perhaps in the further interest of honesty, I ought to say a few words here about the men in my life, for, of course, there were still men in my life. My marriage had soured me on one specific specimen but not on the whole breed. Papa's wrong about many things, but not about that. I am not a one-man woman, though there was a time when I thought Tony might make me one, but I'm getting ahead of myself. I don't mean to imply that I'm unfaithful. I'm not. I believe in mutual trust. I abhor betrayal. I don't like sneaking around to secret trysts in shabby hotels. In any event, these days I'm too well known to. In other words, I believe in fidelity, but not suttee. I grieve, but I refuse to grieve eternally or publicly. Besides, I've always found that the best way to get over one man is to find another. Which only complicated matters that winter because I was in the process of recovering from a romantic disaster. I'd just come off an affair with . . . well, I'd rather not say with whom. I've never thought much of men, or women for that matter, who begin writing their memoirs and end up naming names and betraying confidences. Let's just say he's one of those actors whose name appears above the title of a movie. Unfortunately, he's considerably more attractive on screen than off, and I don't mean only physically. The beginning of the affair was heady, the middle stormy, and the end merely tawdry. He was, not to put too fine a point on it, an unadulterated rat. Jack the Ripper would have looked good by comparison, so you can imagine how Tony appeared to me that winter. And I suppose during Cordelia's repeated absences, I began to look pretty good to Tony too. But as I've said, we were on our guard against that mutual attraction.

I was living at home at the time, I'd moved in temporarily when I'd left Web, and, given the size of the apartment and the strength of Papa's convictions about personal freedom, never gotten around to moving out. I stayed for my own convenience and pleasure, and for Papa. Not that he ever admitted he needed or even wanted me around. That would have been admitting to a weakness, and Papa was convinced he had no weaknesses. Still, I could see the change in him. His work continued to consume his time, but no longer yielded the same all-consuming pleasure. As for the variety of women in his life, though they filled his evenings, they'd never managed to fill his life. So Papa and I made one for ourselves, aided and abetted by Cordelia, and in her absence, Tony. Papa and Tony continued to debate, disagree, and even quarrel, but I think Papa needed Tony's presence as much as he did mine. And when he announced that Tony was coming for brunch one autumn Sunday morning, his voice was positively gleeful. "I believe he's going to resign—again."

"I think you enjoy torturing him."

Papa put down his paper. His proud face was almost tender. "I don't torture him, Julia. I keep him on his toes. And he ought to be grateful. Tony's so good that if he worked for someone who was only half as good as I am, he'd never be challenged, and he'd never grow. Besides, if I really wanted to torture him, I'd accept his resignation."

Ellen was in the kitchen whipping up one of her outrageously fattening brunches, so I met Tony at the door. He touched his cheek to mine. His skin was cold, and he smelled of soap and the outdoors. Tony is the only man I know besides Papa who doesn't use some cloying aftershave. I suspect he knows his own scent is sufficiently heady. I lingered beside his cheek a moment longer than I should have.

"Papa says you're going to resign—again," I warned him. "Fool him. Don't."

"He hasn't left me any alternative." Tony's voice

was deadly serious. Architecture was not something he joked about.

Papa, on the other hand, could be terribly amusing on the subject—providing it was at someone else's expense.

"How are the plans for the Museo Nacional coming?" he asked Tony as he handed him a Bloody Mary.

"You ought to know. You've rejected everything that's come across your desk this week."

"Give me something true to the concept, and I won't reject it. I sold the Mexican government a building true to its structure and use. You give me fake Aztec temples."

"I give you plans that reveal where the museum is and whom it serves as well as what it does."

"If a building is right, moral, pure, it doesn't matter where it stands."

"Right! Moral! Pure! What are you, God or an architect?"

Papa smiled wickedly. "A little of both." The smile slipped from his face, and he turned suddenly serious. "In the last fifty years we've made great strides, Tony, and I don't mean only technologically, though that's a big part of it. Architecture is technology. Hell, we couldn't even begin to think about skyscrapers until we had elevators. But it's more than a question of technology. In the last century, if not longer, all architects did was borrow. No, why not call a spade a spade. All they did was steal. Mr. Richard Morris Hunt and Mr. Stanford White and all the rest were worse than the robber barons who gave them commissions. Want a mansion? How about the Petit Trianon, American style? Need a railroad station? Let's copy the Baths of Caracalla. Then along came Louis Sullivan and Frank Wright here and a little later the Bauhaus in Europe, and architecture was reborn. No more copying the Greeks and Romans and Renaissance master builders. They began looking at each problem and solving it—brilliantly, beautifully, originally. They began thinking about function and structure, and designing accordingly. And now what do you want to do? Go back a hundred years to the imitators, the thieves. Go back a couple of thousand to borrow a gratuitous roof from some ancient sun worshipers. You want to throw out all the beautiful, logical, moral rules for your own whimsical exceptions."

Tony had listened to Papa's diatribe calmly, but I could see the muscles in his jaw tightening. "My whimsical exception, as you call it, is the courage to say that I don't think a steel and glass box solves every problem or meets every need."

"I never said it did." I heard the tinge of anger in Papa's voice and was relieved to see Ellen beckoning us to brunch.

"Look, if you don't like my work . . ." Tony continued when we were at the table.

"I admire your work." Papa had calmed himself. His voice was as smooth as the maple syrup he poured over a stack of sour cream pancakes. "What I don't admire is your self-indulgent rebellion. You take a brilliant plan—and your arrangement of the first floor galleries is brilliant, I give you that—and ruin it with fake Aztec carving. A grandstand gesture. You're thumbing your nose at the establishment, nothing more."

"If I wanted analysis, Adam, I'd go to a psychiatrist. I'm trying to design a building that will draw people in, not put them off."

187

"In other words, you're pandering to the masses."

Tony stirred his coffee and took his time answering. "Not pandering to them, but taking into consideration their tastes and needs, the limitations of their lives, and their hunger to transcend those limitations. Because you know as well as I do what happens when you don't take all that into consideration, Adam. The Pruitt-Igoe housing project in St. Louis." Tony pronounced the name solemnly. He knew its significance, to the world and to Papa. "The Pruitt-Igoe met all your requirements, right? Well, the architects may have raved, but the people, the poor blind, misguided masses, didn't see all that morality, all that purity, all that functionalism. All they saw was a grim, sterile housing project, as grim and sterile as their lives, and they rebelled. They refused to live in it. So the city had to dynamite it. That explosion was heard around the world, Adam, because the dynamiting of that building sounded the death knell for modern architecture as we know it." Tony must have seen the rage in Papa's face because he hesitated, then went on solemnly. "Now it's time for a rebirth."

"I suppose you plan to be the midwife."

Tony met Papa's hard gaze. "Can you think of anyone better suited to the task?"

Papa pushed his plate away, leaned back in his chair, and lighted a cigarette. He studied Tony across the table as he might a blueprint. "All right. I'll approve your plans. I'll even leave in the goddamn Indian bric-a-brac." Tony looked pleased but wary. "On one condition. You go back and do your homework on the foundation."

Tony no longer looked pleased. "What do you mean?"

"I mean Mexico City is built on a mixture of sand

188

and water. Don't you know what happened to the National Theater? If you weren't so busy being a boy genius, if you weren't so sure you had nothing to learn from anyone, you'd know what happened to it. The theater was built at grade level with a cladding of stone. Needless to say, the weight of the building squeezed out a good deal of water. In a few years it sank more than ten feet. They had to build stairs down to its entrance. Then a few years later it started to rise again. Mexico City was enjoying a building boom. All the skyscrapers going up in the area had pushed water out from under them and back under the theater. So they built another stairway, this one going up. It was a great joke in architectural circles." Papa's eyes cut through the cloud of smoke he'd created around himself like twin searchlights. "But I'm not about to become the butt of a joke. You know what name will be etched on the cornerstone of the Museo Nacional? Not Anthony Bain. Adam Kirkland Associates will be written there. Keep that in mind. About this and every other building. Keep it in mind next time you offer your resignation. Because the minute your buildings don't meet my standards, the day I'm unwilling to put my name on them, you're of no use to me."

Tony's profile, more chiseled but no less proud, faced Papa's across the table. They reminded me of duelists. "And when that day comes, Adam Kirkland Associates is no longer of use to me."

Lesser men might have broken after that—Tony could have stormed out of the apartment, Papa could have ordered him out—but they were not small men. Each swore by his own probity and thrived on the other's opposition. A few minutes later, every trace of animosity had vanished, and we were back in the living room talking about Cordelia as if we were any family discussing an absent member. Tony missed her desperately, but wouldn't admit it for fear of looking like a bad loser. Papa missed her too, but wouldn't say as much for fear of giving away how much he'd come to depend on her. I missed her and wasn't afraid to confess it. An hour later Papa went off—to work, he said; to nap, I suspected—leaving me alone with Tony.

He asked about the show, but I knew he didn't want to hear about the show. People say actors are egomaniacs. Maybe we are more self-involved than ordinary mortals—or maybe we're only less hypocritical.

"Since this is my day off—no Sunday matinee fortunately—and since I did two shows back to back yesterday, I don't particularly want to talk about it. And you don't want to hear about it. The show is fine, thank you, and what's really going on with the Museo Nacional?"

"The same thing that goes on with everything I do for him. I never thought I'd say this about Adam, but I think he's afraid."

"Of what?"

"Originality."

"But Papa was always the one who broke the rules, came up with the innovations, made history."

"That's right, Julia. He was. But he isn't any longer. It's not only that he keeps repeating himself. He wants everyone else to keep repeating him as well."

"I can't believe it."

He came and sat beside me on the sofa. I wished he hadn't because I was worried about Papa, and Tony's nearness made it hard to concentrate on Papa. There was a fine red line, like a cleft in his chin, where he

190

must have cut himself shaving, and I fought the urge to touch it.

"It's true, Julia. And I'm not the only one who thinks so."

"But his reputation is bigger than ever."

Tony took off his glasses and rubbed his eyes. When he looked at me again, his gaze was as soft as velvet. I told myself the tenderness was for Papa rather than me. "That's just the problem. He's living on his reputation. Have you seen the spate of articles on the Kuwait government building? 'Tired. Stale. Sterile.' To quote just a few adjectives."

"Papa never cared what the critics said about him."

Tony smiled sadly. It made delicious crinkles around his eyes. "He never cared when they called him impossible or outrageous or flamboyant. But that's a far cry from tired, stale, and sterile."

"Does he realize what's happening?"

"Does anyone ever realize something like that?"

"What about Cordelia?'

He looked away from me. It didn't help. His profile was even better than his full face. Even his ears were beautiful. "What about Cordelia?" he repeated.

"Does she agree with you?"

"I don't know."

"What do you mean you don't know?"

He still refused to meet my eyes. "I can't talk about Adam with Cordelia."

My heart fluttered like a pathetic wounded bird. And I hated myself for allowing it to.

Tony was wrong about Papa, at least partially. He did know what was happening to him. I found that out one night early in December. It was a Wednesday,

I remember, because I'd done two shows back to back and come home to find him in the library with a volume of Corbusier's notebooks. "How did it go?" he asked as he used to ask Mother.

"I suppose it could have been worse but not much. Matinee audiences."

"Judith used to hate them. Especially the Wednesday one. She called it the gastrointestinal brigade. Said they spent the first act thinking about where they'd lunched and the second wondering if they'd get home in time to make dinner."

"I guess that explains it. I felt as if I were playing to an empty house. It rattled me so much I was off tonight as well. Threw away the best line in the show."

I made a drink for each of us, and he closed the book and put it on the coffee table. "I've been sitting here thinking about Corbu." At the sound of his name, the cat stirred, stretched, and went back to sleep. "How much he saw and knew and how little he built. He left an enormous legacy, but few buildings."

"Which is better, the influence or the reality?"

"Both."

I laughed. "I love you, Papa. You're outrageous. Greedy. Larger than life. You know, if Freud is to be believed, you've probably ruined me for any other man. I'll never find one who measures up to you."

The laughter rolled out of his deep chest. "Of course, you won't, but if I know you, you'll go on trying."

"You know me too well," I said and turned on the television, because I didn't want to pursue this particular conversation. If you were looking for a man like Papa, you didn't have to look any farther than Tony, and we both knew it.

But Papa was ahead of me. "Don't worry, Julia. I

wasn't about to pry into your personal life. I just hope you didn't turn that thing on to subject me to your former husband."

"Web's not on at this hour." I began switching channels and stopped at one of the so-called educational ones when Preston Hunter's face appeared on the screen.

"On second thought, I think I might prefer your former husband," Papa said, but before I could answer him I heard Hunter pronounce Papa's name.

"Now I don't suggest his more recent work is on a par with the earlier buildings, but when you talk about seminal architecture of the twentieth century, you've got to talk about Adam Kirkland."

"Well, of course," the host agreed, "but I thought we were discussing living architects."

On the large screen Preston Hunter opened his soft, thick lips and let out a macabre laugh. "Adam Kirkland is very much alive. I don't say alive and well because I've seen the model of the government building in Kuwait." The host guffawed in encouragement. Despite his pretensions to high-minded criticism, he knew that viciousness was good for the ratings.

I reached for the television controls, but Papa stopped me. "Leave it on, Julia. How many men live to hear their own eulogies?"

"Preston Hunter is an idiot, as you've often said."

"As a man, he's an idiot. As a critic, he's as good as we've got. And he happens to be right about Kuwait. I made too many compromises on that building. When I saw what was happening, I should have resigned the commission, but I've gotten old and soft. I've become a fat cat. I like building too much. And so I gave in to their demands. I never would have done that twenty years ago."

"Not every building can be great. Anymore than every performance can be. In a long career, a monumental one like yours, there are bound to be failures."

He turned from the television screen to me, and his eyes were like that electronic one, blind to everything but what went on within it. "Exactly! Failures. I respect an honest failure. I admire it. Sometimes the honest failures turn out to be the real masterpieces. But Kuwait isn't an honest failure. It's only a compromise. And I despise compromise."

There was nothing I could say to that. He'd spoken from his heart, and it had touched a chord in my own. He and Mother hated compromise and had brought us up to do the same. I suppose that was why I'd been drawn to Tony—and why I'd relinquished him to Cordelia, though I was beginning to wish I hadn't.

I'd relinquished Tony to Cordelia, but in the wake of her triumph in the competition, she'd gone to Japan and left him, or at least left him for the time being, so it was only natural that I should be the first one he told when he won the award for that addition to the university library in Boston. He was positively crowing.

"Have you called Cordelia?" I asked after I'd congratulated him.

"I didn't want to wake her. It's four in the morning there. I'll call her in a few hours. Let me take you to dinner to celebrate."

"This may come as a shock to you, Tony, but theater people don't work from nine to five. I have a performance tonight."

"Then supper. After the show."

"Do you think you can wait that long to start celebrating?"

"No!" His laughter was soft and woolly, like a blanket, and I wanted to wrap myself in it.

Tony sat through the play again that night. "You were marvelous," he said when he came backstage afterward.

"Tonight you happen to be right, but you wouldn't have known if I'd been dreadful. Where are you going to take me? I'm famished."

"Anywhere you want to go. So long as it's very exclusive and terribly expensive. I'm an important man, and we have to go someplace befitting my position."

I told him I thought he'd been drinking, and he said he didn't have to tonight. "But if you don't believe me, see for yourself. No telltale aroma of the evil demon rum." He brought his mouth close to mine which was a dangerous thing to do. I stepped back. The current between us was electric, and I was wary of shocks.

"I'll take your word for it. Now get out of here and give me a chance to shower and change.

"Have you decided where we're going?" I asked when I came out of my dressing room a little while later.

"To Sardi's. I went there in defeat, and I'll be damned if I won't go there in victory."

"And I thought you'd chosen it out of deference to me."

"The thought crossed my mind."

I don't remember what we talked about over supper, though I recall that when Vincent showed us to what had already become my table, Tony glanced at the caricature of me hanging above my head and said that he liked coming there with me. "I get double value." I certainly don't remember what we ate, or if we ate.

I recall that we sat across from each other and occasionally, to make a point, Tony touched my hand, and once, when he joked about something or other, I touched his. When he helped me on with my coat, he lifted my hair out from under the collar and let it fall on my shoulders. It's not the sort of thing most men, do, but Tony did it naturally and gently and, well, lovingly.

It was strange being alone with Tony in the back seat of a cab again. We'd grown close during dinner, but being close in a crowded restaurant is one thing, and being close in the dark privacy of a taxi is an entirely different affair. A thick silence hung between us. Then the cab turned onto Park Avenue and Inter-American House loomed into view like a mutual acquaintance shattering the intensity of our privacy. As we sped past, Tony and I both turned for a last glimpse of it through the rear window. Illuminated by a specially designed lighting system, it blazed against the black sky like an ice palace.

"Whatever else, you have to give him that." Tony's voice was hoarse with emotion but it wasn't direct at me.

"Sometimes it's uncanny how alike you and Papa are."

Tony frowned slightly. Like Papa, he believed he was unique. "I'm not pigheaded."

I couldn't help laughing. "Any man who insists he's not pigheaded is, by definition. You can be as intransigent as Papa and as generous. You're certainly as proud and"—I hesitated because I wasn't sure I should say the rest—"as greedy for life. What was it you said about him once? He wants to design every building, conquer every man, make love to every woman." He'd said that to Cordelia, but she'd repeated it to me, and

196

now the thought of her as well as the last part of the sentence hung between us as portentously as the silence.

"The only real difference between you and Papa is in your work," I went on. "You're both wildly gifted, yet your styles are so different. Papa's buildings are cool, sleek, philosophical; yours are warm, sensual, human."

Tony looked at me as he never had before. There was surprise on his face but also admiration, a new kind of admiration. "Don't ever let anyone call you a visual illiterate again, Julia. You've got a keener eye than Preston Hunter."

"I see the difference, but I'm not sure I understand where it comes from. Papa's not a cold man. Or rather he can be, but then so can you."

"Part of the explanation is so simple you won't believe it. How did Adam become an architect?"

I didn't understand what he was getting at. "Harvard. Undergraduate as well as graduate. But it goes back farther than that. As he tells it, he knew he wanted to be an architect from the moment he saw the Parthenon. I think he was six or seven at the time."

"Exactly. Adam came to architecture through art and intellect—and money. On his first trip to Greece at the age of six or seven. Adam came to architecture through his eyes. I came to it through my hands. Like Palladio and Gropius. My father was a mason. A mean son of a bitch but a good mason. I started a kind of apprenticeship at twelve. While other kids were racking up batting averages, I was piling up bricks. Learning about Flemish and English and common bond."

"I never can remember which is which."

With his index finger he traced the three patterns

197

in which bricks are set on the inside of my palm. This time, I thought, the differences were indelibly etched.

"Don't misunderstand me. I'm not complaining. Baseball bored me, and I loved hanging around half-finished buildings. The work was hard, but I loved watching them climb from the foundations, grow like a living organism. So by the time I got to Yale—on scholarship, unlike Adam—"

"Now that was bitter."

"You're right. I apologize. It seemed only logical for me to work my way through with construction jobs. Besides, you make more money laying bricks and pouring concrete in the broiling sun than you do sitting in an air-conditioned drafting room, and I needed money."

The cab swerved at that moment, and when I felt the strength of Tony's shoulder against mine, I thought that he owed more than his style to those arduous summers in the hot sun.

"And that," he said as if he suddenly realized he'd gone on more than he'd meant to, "is the secret of my style—and my success."

"And what about Cordelia?" I asked as the taxi pulled up in front of the apartment house. "What about her style?"

"You tell me. You're the one with the critic's eye."

"I'd say she doesn't have one yet."

"She will someday. A damn good one."

"When she breaks away from Papa?"

Tony didn't answer me. He was always loyal in word.

Tony followed me from the lobby to the elevator and from the elevator into the foyer. Then the elevator doors closed behind us, and we were alone again. We stood only inches apart in the half-darkened room. I suppose what happened next was inevitable. It was also wrong.

I thought I remembered what kissing Tony was like, but the memory was a pale echo of the reality, because memory is cerebral but the warmth of his mouth, the taste, the thrill of it assaulted my senses. His body pressed against mine hungrily, his hands were dizzyingly skillful beneath my coat. He'd said he'd learned about life and art and reality through those hands, and as they moved searchingly, I felt their wisdom and their pleasure.

I'm not sure how long we stood that way. A few seconds? A lifetime? When we broke away, I could hear the sound of my own breathing and Tony's. Even in the dimly lighted room I recognized the desire in his eyes. The fact that he wanted me as much as I wanted him didn't make it any easier.

"That shouldn't have happened," I said.

"It had to. And it will happen again if we go on seeing each other this way."

"That's why we're not going to."

He agreed. We walked to the elevator. Tony pressed the button. We waited in silence. When it arrived, he got into it without turning to look at me. The doors closed behind him. I heard the sound of the machinery taking him away from me. We'd done the right thing, if only after a dangerous flirtation with the wrong.

The next afternoon Sean Wellihan called. Sean is one of those people I've known forever, or at least since early acting classes and various workshops. He calls regularly, if not frequently, to ask me to a party or play or dinner. My acceptance or refusal usually depends on the state of my romantic life at the moment. That afternoon I accepted.

We went to a preview of an off-Broadway play directed by a friend of his. I knew the friend and didn't particularly like him. I didn't think much of the play either. Sean agreed with me. Afterward we went backstage and lied through our teeth, then on for drinks, inevitably at Sardi's. Of course, Sean couldn't have known, but it was not a wise choice. Though I was sitting across from an extraordinarily attractive man—Sean is frequently likened to a young Bill Holden, and the comparison is apt—the ghost of Tony lingered. Perhaps I'm attracted to dark men, I thought as Sean pushed the shock of fair hair back from his forehead. But I knew it had nothing to do with type, only with Tony.

"I think I finally got the timing right," Sean said.

I didn't understand what he meant. He'd given up acting, and though he was in the middle of his second play, he never talked about his writing. "I thought you didn't discuss work in progress."

"I don't. I was referring to you. Ever since I've known you, I've been waiting to catch you between men. Rumor has it that things are over between you and the first gentleman of the silver screen. Rumor also has it that he's no gentleman."

"Rumor is right. At least on the first count." It was right on the second as well, but I didn't believe in kissing and crying anymore than I did in kissing and telling.

"Then what's holding you back? Or as Rhett said to Scarlett, I've waited for you longer than I've waited for any woman, Julia."

"Small compliment, darling. You've never waited for a woman in your life. They just fall into your lap."

"All the more reason you should be flattered. I can't

understand why you aren't madly in love with me."

"Because you're a good friend, and I'd like to keep things that way."

Sean looked at me over the rim of his glass. He had Bill Holden's looks and Clark Gable's—or at least Rhett Butler's—charm, and I suppose I was terribly perverse.

"Thank God," he said with a slow smile, "they give you better lines on stage."

I thought the subject was closed, but Sean returned to it as we were leaving the restaurant. "Is there someone else?"

"Of course not."

"Bad reading, Julia. If there really weren't anyone else, you wouldn't be so vehement about it. And since you're so eager to deny it, I see trouble on the horizon."

Unlike Tony, Sean left me at the elevator in the lobby. Too many women wanted Sean for him to make a pest of himself with one who didn't. He took my hand in both of his. "I won't say I'll always be here, Julia. For one thing, it's a corny line. For another, it's not true. But I'm not giving up yet."

The following week one of the columns carried an item about Sean and Liza Minnelli. I was fairly sure it was a plant, but I was still disappointed.

Cordelia returned home for the holidays, bringing me a Japanese kimono for Christmas. I wore it to Papa's New Year's Eve party. Cordelia wore a similar one in another color. I looked as if I were wearing a costume. Cordelia, her straight dark hair pulled back in a smooth chignon, carried it off with an aura of quiet serenity. Tony couldn't keep his eyes off her. Neither could another of Papa's guests, a man named

Graham Fowler. He spent a good part of the evening talking to Cordelia, and not, I knew, because she'd been a friend of his nephew Peter Fowler at Harvard. In fact, when Cordelia asked if he were related to the younger man, Fowler looked a little put out, as if he resented the reference to their different generations.

On New Year's morning Cordelia flew back to Japan. We gave a special holiday matinee that afternoon. Tony was waiting in my dressing room afterward. He was wearing the cashmere muffler I'd given him for Christmas—not exactly imaginative but correct—and an air of despondency.

"Do you feel like some supper?" he asked. "Or a drink?"

I thought of our agreement. It seemed impossible that he'd forgotten it. Then it dawned on me. He'd forgotten not only the agreement but the evening. Cordelia's presence had obliterated it. I was no longer a threat to his marriage, merely an ear to listen and a shoulder to cry on in his loneliness. It was not a flattering portrait, but it was a safe one. I said supper would be fine.

I was right. We talked about his work and Cordelia, and Papa and Cordelia, and Cordelia and me. When he left me at the elevator, he thanked me for keeping him company. I felt extremely virtuous. It's a highly overrated sensation.

And so Tony began drifting by the theater again to see me, and the apartment to see Papa and me. I found him there when I came home from the theater a few weeks later.

"You're not seriously thinking of accepting it!" I heard Papa's voice boom from the library as I hung up my coat.

Papa was sitting beneath the windows. Tony was sprawled on the sofa. Some tall men look ungainly when they sprawl. Tony looked inviting. "Accepting what?" I asked and sat a safe distance away from him.

"The mayor has appointed him to some asinine council on urban design," Papa answered for him.

Tony laughed, and the crinkles gathered around his eyes. "In case you can't tell, Adam doesn't think I ought to accept."

"It's a committee, and men like you and me don't join committees, Tony. Men with imagination and integrity and guts don't sit around debating and equivocating and compromising. You'll give them six months of your life, and all you'll end up with is some harebrained report saying maybe, under certain conditions, in certain instances, a certain thing might not be advisable. Then someone with the will to action will come along and do exactly as he pleases."

"Someone like you?"

Papa laughed. "Someone like me. Or someone like you. You don't belong on committees, Tony. You sure as hell don't belong on a government committee. You'll drown in the bureaucracy."

Tony sat up and stretched, his body as supple as Corbu's. "You're probably right, but I'm going to accept the appointment anyway."

Papa looked at Tony, his eyes glinting like marbles. "Tired of thumbing your nose at the establishment, eh? Finally ready to join it?"

Tony smiled back, icy as Papa. "Isn't that what you've always predicted, that someday I'd sell out?"

"But I thought, or at least hoped, that your price would come higher than a pathetic appointment to some minor-league municipal committee."

Tony laughed. "You're terrific, Adam. You really are. Your motives are always above question. And everyone else's are always beneath contempt. I hate to disappoint you, but I'm accepting the appointment because I want to put a stop to what's happening to this city. I want to put an end to too many bad buildings on too little space."

"The only way to stop bad buildings is by designing better ones."

"You heard only half of what I said. Good design isn't enough. We need good planning too. The problem of architecture today, the province of architecture today, isn't the individual building but the entire city. We can't go on filling every inch of empty space with stone and glass and steel, jamming people together until they hate the sight and sound and touch of each other, shutting out every ray of sunshine from the streets. We can't go on turning the cities into inhuman jungles."

"And you and your committee are going to put a stop to it?"

"We're going to try."

Papa threw back his leonine head and let out a roar of laughter. "They're going to eat you alive, Tony, you and your committee. And I'm going to be there for the feast. As long as a foot of space on or above this overcrowded, inhuman island commands several hundred dollars there will be men fighting, kicking, and clawing to provide that space. And as long as they are, I'll go on designing that space, turning their filthy lucre into steel and glass and greatness. I'll go on giving your poor benighted overcrowded public more beauty than it can recognize, more than it deserves." Papa drained his glass in a single swallow. "But you

204

might as well join if you've got your heart set on it. Publicity is always good for the firm."

Cordelia flew in the following Friday and left on Monday. When Tony turned up in my dressing room after Tuesday night's performance, he looked like a starving man who'd been promised a banquet and given a sandwich. And I'm not referring only to sex, though I'm sure that was part of it. Tony was that peculiar breed of man who is a loner among men but needs a woman in his life.

"You look tired," I said. Actually he looked depressed, but I'd hit on "tired" as an innocuous euphemism. "Is the mayor's council wearing you down?"

"Can we drop the sarcasm? God knows I get enough from Adam and Cordelia." He looked surprised, as if the words had slipped out without his meaning them to.

I sat at the dressing table and began taking off my makeup. "That's not true. Cordelia is proud of your appointment."

He flopped down on the chaise and pretended to examine a wig I wore in the second scene. "Did you speak to her before or after she spoke to Adam? No, don't answer that. I don't want to talk about the council or Adam or"—he stopped abruptly—"or work." He twirled the wig on his index finger. "Do you really wear this thing?"

"You've seen the play."

"Well, it looks a lot better onstage."

"Don't we all?"

"No." He stared at me hard, so hard that I was embarrassed. Every night several hundred pairs of eyes focused on me, but only Tony's made me feel that way. "No, you don't look better on stage. You look just fine sitting here with cold cream on your face and without illusion."

I'd forgotten about the cream and began rubbing furiously. "Do me a favor, Tony. I won't talk about architecture, and don't you talk like—" I stopped abruptly because I knew what I meant, but I didn't know how to phrase it.

"Like every other man on the make?" he finished for me. He stood and put his hand on my shoulder. "I'm sorry. I didn't mean to."

"I know you didn't." We were silent for a moment. I was intensely aware of the way his hand felt on my skin. I remembered that night in the foyer when we'd agreed to stop seeing each other. I realized now that he remembered it too.

I reached for the hairbrush. His hand fell from my shoulder. "Now ..." I began in a voice that was brighter than I felt.

"I know. Get out of here and let you shower and change."

So you see, Tony and I were very much on our guard. Whatever was in our minds or our hearts or wherever in the anatomy you happen to place love and desire, Cordelia was on our consciences. She was there in my dressing room that night, and she was still there a few hours later when I asked Tony in for a drink.

I'm not sure why I asked him in that night. Perhaps I was only being polite. Perhaps, given the hour I thought he'd refuse. No, those are lies, or at least self-deceptions. I want to avoid self-deception, the hereditary affliction of the Kirklands. I asked Tony in because I was in love with him again or perhaps still. And as it turned out, there was no reason I shouldn't

206

have asked him in. Tony and I behaved ourselves—thanks to Papa.

There was a light in the foyer but the living room was dark, and when I switched on a small lamp I was surprised to see Papa sitting in a chair beside the southern wall of windows. At first I thought he'd fallen asleep, but when he turned to us, I saw his face was alert and thoughtful.

"I was just looking at Inter-American House," he said. "Come in and talk to me, Tony. I need company. Not that you aren't good for the spirit in your own way, Julia. But I want to talk about architecture, and you're no good there."

"Julia sees more than you think," Tony said.

"If you mean she sees more than the average layman who sees nothing, I should hope so. I like to think I've left some mark on her."

"You've left your mark, all right," I said.

He turned back to the view of the skyline, dominated by Inter-American House. It wasn't the tallest skyscraper, but its power and elegance made it appear to be. "On the century. I'll be damned if that isn't the best building of the twentieth century." It was only an expression, but in a sense Papa was speaking literally. His salvation lay in his architectural legacy. Without that he would consider his life wasted, himself damned for all posterity.

"I finished it in '58," he went on, though Tony and I knew the dates as well as he did. "But what have I done since then?"

"A couple of hundred buildings," I suggested.

Papa turned from the view to Tony. "What would you say, Tony? What would you say I've done since then?"

"I agree with Julia," he said, and I heard the uneasiness in his voice.

"You agree with Julia," Papa repeated in a withering tone. "Only Julia doesn't know what I mean, and you do, don't you?"

"I think so."

"You damn well know so. A couple of hundred buildings but only one masterpiece."

"One masterpiece is more than most men can claim in a lifetime."

"Most men, Tony! Most men. Do you want to be like most men?"

"No."

"Then why the hell should I? I'm going to build another one. Another monument to my own greatness." Papa's laughter crackled through the room maniacally. Mother used to say that in genius there was an element of insanity. "Isn't that what you called it that first day, Tony, a monument to my own greatness? And you were right. Well, it's time for another. Two masterpieces. They'll be like bookends, standing at either end of my life, supporting my reputation. Bookends on either side of this absurd island that crowds all the vitality and power of the world into twenty-two square miles." Papa took a long swallow of his drink. "Do you think I'm crazy?" he asked Tony.

"I know you too well for that."

"Come into the studio."

Tony followed Papa down the hall, and I tagged along, curious but superfluous. When Papa switched on the light over his drafting board, the gesture brought revelation. I can't describe the design as Cordelia would. I'm vague on terms and naive about technicalities, but I am not, as Tony pointed out, without eyes. Suspended several floors above the ground, supported by a series of graceful piers, a curved glass tower, almost like a four-leaf clover, seemed to float in space.

I looked from the sketches to Tony's face. I'd seen that expression when he looked at works of his own of which he was particularly proud. I'd even, years ago, seen it on his face when he looked at me. Tony was in love. So in love that he didn't have to articulate the words. He and Papa simply stood there staring down at the flowering of Papa's imagination and expertise and genius, the idea that would someday be art and structure and reality.

"Didn't think I still had it in me, did you?" Papa said finally, and Tony only laughed because he'd had his doubts.

"It's for the International Banking Group. They wanted something different. And I was ready for something different. I've done all I can with the box. I've exhausted angles. So I gave them fifty-five stories of curved glass. Only it isn't glass. That's the beauty of it. I'm going to use high impact plastic. Use it as it's never been used before. If I did this in glass, the skin would be too thick and we'd have a hell of a time with heat and light and condensation. But the plastic solves all that. The plastic lets me get away with anything—with everything."

Tony laughed again. He was giddy with infatuation. I supposed we all were. "Everything is right. You've pulled out all the stops. Do they know just how good it is?"

"Probably not. Clients never do. But they're impressed. They think it's 'imposing.' The president allowed as how the shape was distinctive enough to put on the letterhead." Papa roared with laughter, and

Tony joined him. The foibles of clients couldn't touch them now.

"I'd like to work on her with you, sir." Tony hadn't called Papa "sir" in years.

"Of course you would. Half the architects in the country would give their right arms to contribute a single detail to this. But you're the one who's going to get the chance. You and Cordelia when she gets back. This is going to be the best damn building since Inter-American House, maybe even better than Inter-American House, and I want the best damn designers on it."

I moved to the wall of windows and looked out at the skyline. "Where will it be?" I asked, trying to imagine it in relation to Inter-American House.

"Fifth Avenue and Forty-second Street. Bryant Park will be its backyard," Papa tossed over his shoulder as he and Tony went on poring over the plans.

"But you said bookends, opposite ends of Manhattan." ·

"I was speaking figuratively, Julia," Papa answered and went on explaining something about the plans, but I could tell Tony was surprised too.

"But that's where the library is," Tony said. "You wouldn't tear down the library!"

"The hell I wouldn't—if they'd let me. But they won't. The library has landmark status. The kind of thing you boys on the mayor's council are very serious about. But my building will stand over it. Soaring on five-story piers. It will float above the library, float a hundred and ten feet above street level."

"But you can't." Tony's voice had moved from respect to incredulity. "The library is a monument too."

"So it is. An ornate, anachronistic monument to Beaux Arts pomposity."

"You mean because it's old, it's outdated."

"If you're referring to me, Tony, I don't admit the comparison."

"I wasn't. I was talking about architecture. I suppose you think the Parthenon ought to be torn down too. Put some nice, functional, technologically up-to-the-minute skyscraper in its place."

"The Parthenon is a creation of genius. The New York Public Library is the work of a bunch of hidebound imitators. Why do you think they call it Beaux Arts eclectic? Because those boys didn't have a single original idea between them. All they could do was steal—a column from the Greeks, an arch from the Romans by way of Palladio, a line-for-line French château from Mansart."

"It's part of our architectural heritage. Adam—of the city's and the entire country's."

"Heritage! What are you, an historian or an architect?"

"An architect. And an architect creates space. The steps of that library are the best open space in the city, a place where people can go to meet friends or eat lunchs or just sit and enjoy the passing parade."

"For God's sake, Tony, the sidewalks of Fifth Avenue are twenty-two and a half feet wide. Isn't that enough public space for you?"

"No, no it isn't. The sidewalks are canyons. How many hours a day do they get the sun—one, two at the most? The library steps are one of the last places in midtown Manhattan people can still sit in the sun. You put up that building, and you'll create a permanent total eclipse."

"I'm talking about one of the greatest buildings of the twentieth century, and you're worrying about sunbathing, as if this were some Caribbean hotel. I'm talking about man's triumph over gravity, Tony, about pride and power. You know what Nietzsche called architecture, or have you forgotten? He called it 'a veritable oratory of power made by form.' "

"And I'm saying it's time we started thinking a little less about power and a little more about the quality of life in the cities. If you erect that building on that site, you'll diminish the quality of life in this city as surely as if you put up an eyesore."

"Does that mean you don't want to work on it after all? Does that mean you're turning down a chance to contribute to the greatest work of architecture of the twentieth century, because make no mistake, Tony, it will rise, and it will be great." The words were a taunt rather than a question, and Tony took a long time to answer. When he did, the reply was out of character.

"I don't know," he said finally.

8

I didn't hear any more about Papa's new building or Tony's opposition to it for a few weeks. Two days after Papa showed us the sketches, Tony left for Mexico City with his plans for the Museo Nacional. A week after that I left for the Coast. I'd taken a leave of absence from the show to do a small but meaty part in a movie. I'd expected Papa to tell me I was crazy, but his only advice was to remember that my left profile photographed better than my right and that Hollywood was a place of small minds and big egos. For a moment a fragment of memory surfaced, and I remembered his saying the same thing to Mother, though I wasn't conscious of having heard him at the time.

I'd been on the Coast for a week, and I can't actually say that I'd forgotten about Tony, only that I was thinking of him a little less, when he called. I was having breakfast with a producer in the Polo Lounge when they brought the phone to our table. The producer reached for it automatically, and I was amused when the waiter told him the call was for me.

"I thought you were supposed to be shooting a movie. Instead I find you hanging out in the Polo Lounge with some thoroughly disreputable Hollywood type—or is that redundant—at seven-thirty in the morning."

"How do you know whom I'm with?"

"I don't, but I know human nature. If you're sitting at a table, Julia, there's bound to be a man across from you, maybe more than one. I'll bet they're after you like flies."

"Gnats."

"When can this particular man sit across the table from you?"

"Are you in town?"

"Ten minutes away."

My mind raced through the day's schedule. I had a class at Bikram Choudhury's Yoga College of India on Wilshire at nine and was supposed to go over to Alex and Walter's gym this afternoon for a workout, but I decided I'd rather see Tony than hang by my heels for half an hour. I told him to drive out to Leda Harris's house for lunch.

Leda had been a friend of Mother's in the old days. Actually she'd wanted to be more than a friend, but Mother had managed to deflect Leda's advances without losing her friendship. Leda was on location in Africa—she still worked regularly and insisted she'd go on working until she finally starred in her own funeral—and I had the house to myself.

I was lazing around the pool, kidney shaped of course, when the houseboy, Japanese of course, showed Tony out. He stood at the foot of my chaise and looked from me to the rear facade of the pink stucco mansion, then back to me. "My God, when you go Hollywood, Julia, you really go Hollywood. If Adam knew you were staying in a place like this, he'd never forgive you."

"I know. It's ostentatious, vulgar, entirely without

redeeming aesthetic value. And I absolutely adore it."

He bent and kissed me on the cheek—a proper fraternal kiss that I accepted with good grace and mixed feelings—then sat on the end of my chaise. "I take back what I said. Adam's right. You're a visual illiterate."

"Nope, just someone who has to binge every once in a while. I've been on an aesthetic diet all my life. Permitted to feast my eyes on only the leanest, purest forms. Now I'm living inside a perfect ice cream sundae of a house. Mother was like that too, except she couldn't get away with it. She used to clutter her dressing rooms with all sorts of mementos and useless objects, but once the play was a hit and Papa knew she'd be there for some time, he'd move in with his workmen and strip it all down to pure, functional space. I remember once when the opening night reviews were devastating—not of her, only of the play— and I felt just awful for her, she told me to look on the bright side. 'The play will run for only a week or two, but at least I'll have my own dressing room for that long.'"

Tony smiled at the story. "You know, you're the damnedest family. Like a prism or a diamond. The facets change depending on the angle of vision."

"I imagine that's true of all families. Anyway, don't say *you* that way. You're part of the family. How's Cordelia?"

He stood, took off his linen blazer, and loosened his tie. His shirt was custom made and followed the lean lines of his back closely without straining at his wide shoulders. I tried not to think about those shoulders.

"Fine. I suggested she fly over from Japan for a few days and meet me here, but she said she couldn't get away." He sat on the edge of my chaise again, rolling up the cuffs of his shirt as he did. His arms were tanned, from Mexico, I suppose, and strong. On the inside prominent veins made a delicate web. I fought the urge to trace the pattern with my finger.

"Do you want to swim? There's a complete array of guest suits in the pool house."

He said he did and disappeared into the cabana to change. Since I do not believe in sins of the mind, only of the flesh, I watched him shamelessly in the theater of my imagination. I saw him remove the beautifully tailored clothes piece by piece to reveal the more beautifully fashioned body beneath. I pictured him standing naked in the shadowy bathhouse while he selected a pair of trunks. When he finally emerged and crossed the patio toward me in his long easy stride, his body strong and bronze in the revealing sunlight, I almost blushed. Or maybe I did blush, because he looked at me, then away, then back at me with a peculiar smile.

He swam—his long, brown body cutting through the pale blue water like a knife—and the Japanese houseboy brought us gin and tonics, and Tony stretched out in the chaise beside mine and told me about the commission that had brought him to the Coast.

"And what about Papa's new building?" I asked. "What about his monument?"

"They're going to crucify him."

"Who?"

"The preservationists, the conservationists, at least half the architectural establishment—including Preston Hunter—probably half the city."

"It sounds like the kind of odds Papa likes."

"It's no joke, Julia. They'll never let him get away with it."

"They got away with building the Pan Am over Grand Central, and Papa will get away with hiding the library with his tower. Papa always gets what he wants, and this is the first thing he's wanted, really wanted, since Mother died."

"That's why it's going to destroy him when he doesn't get it."

"What makes you so sure he won't?"

"There are too many people who care too much about the library."

"There were a lot of people who cared about Penn Station and look what happened to that."

"That was 1963. This is 1975. Times have changed. There's a new respect for the past. And a new dissatisfaction with Adam's kind of architecture."

"I suppose you told him all this."

"I tried to tell him that night in his studio. I've been trying to tell him ever since. He called me into his office the morning after he showed us the plans. He was working on an as-of-right model. That's a rough model, almost like a lump of unformed clay, that shows what kind of massing is possible under current zoning restrictions."

"For God's sake, Tony, I know what an as-of-right model is."

He smiled. Fortunately he was wearing dark glasses, and I didn't have to watch the crinkles gather around his eyes. My resistance was diminishing. "Sorry. Sometimes I forget you're Adam's daughter too. Anyway, he wanted to know what I'd decided about working on the building."

"And what did you decide?" I was as sure of the answer as Papa had been, and as wrong.

"I told him if he were going to build it anywhere

217

else, I'd do anything to work on it. But that I couldn't work on the plan as it stood now." I turned to face Tony, but the glasses hid the expression in his eyes. I could only guess at how much the decision had cost him. "And then, of course, I offered my resignation for the twelfth or thirteenth time."

"And he finally accepted it?" There was no telling what either of these madmen would do.

"No. He said I was a damn fool but a good architect. Then I told him I was going to resign from the mayor's council. I said I didn't support the building personally, but I wouldn't oppose it publicly."

"How'd he react to that?"

"Exactly the way you'd expect him to. Laughed his head off. Said he didn't give a damn whether I stayed on the council or not. Said for all he cared I could lead the opposition. According to him one more bureaucrat in the army of bureaucrats against him wasn't going to make a bit of difference. According to him, this thing has been in the works for months, and it's just about sewn up. Do you remember a man named Graham Fowler? He was at Adam's New Year's Eve party. Tall, bald, arrogant as hell."

Just for the record, though Graham Fowler's hairline is receding, he is not bald, but I wasn't going to quibble. Fowler didn't interest me, Tony and Papa did.

"The one who spent a lot of time with Cordelia?"

Tony looked at me for a moment. "Did he? Well, if he did, he didn't mention anything about this deal. Of course, he wouldn't. He's smart. At least about money. Apparently everything he touches turns to gold. Big developer in the West and Southwest. Likes to build towns in the desert, that kind of thing. Now he's decided to move East, or rather back East. Apparently, Fowler inherited his first million from an old New England family, but he made the other ninety-nine himself."

"Is he really worth a hundred million?"

Tony laughed. "You little gold digger. All I know is he's worth a lot. Anyway, I digress. Graham Fowler sits on the board of the New York Public Library. He also just happens to sit on the board of the International Banking Group, but that comes later. Now the library is in financial trouble. It's supported by a private trust and contributions rather than by the city. But Graham Fowler didn't get where he is in this world by being unable to solve financial problems. He suggested the library sell the air rights over the building. Even convinced the mayor and the City Council and the Board of Estimate, who have control over any alterations to the library building, that they ought to, and if you think getting those three to agree on anything is easy, you've never tried it. Our friend Mr. Fowler is very persuasive. Anyway, according to him, this land, or rather the air, is worth about five hundred dollars a square foot and climbing. So Fowler, as a director of IBG turned to Adam, and Adam rose to the occasion. The design really is a beauty. Only the site is a disaster."

I put my hand on his shoulder. It was warm from the sun. "What are you going to do?"

"There's nothing I can do. I can't work for Adam on this, and I won't work against him. At least not openly."

"What about Cordelia?"

Tony stood and moved toward the pool. He said he wanted another swim, but I think he wanted to escape my question. We both knew where Cordelia would stand on this issue. Squarely behind Papa.

A week later I flew back to New York. The following morning a full page ad in the *Times* announced that Julia Kirkland had returned to the cast of *Eastward*. A smaller article, but on the front page, fired the first public shot in the war over Bryant Park Tower, as Papa's new building was to be called. Under a photograph of Papa with his model ran a headline:

TOWER TO RISE
OVER LIBRARY

Not exactly inflammatory, not unless you happened to care about the face of New York, its past, and its future. By the time Ellen brought me the paper on my breakfast tray, the telephone, which I turn off in my room, had been ringing for hours. According to Tony, things were even more hectic at the office.

That evening I switched on the six o'clock news before I left for the theater. I watched it rarely, but when I did, I turned to Web's channel, more out of habit than lingering affection. There was Papa looking confident and slightly amused. "The city," he told the reporter, "is a living organism. It changes and grows. The city needs office space, the library needs revenue, and we plan to meet both needs. Regardless of the whimpers of a few reactionaries."

Web reappeared on the screen. "Adam Kirkland," he intoned, "may be surprised when the 'whimpers of a few reactionaries' turn into the roar of an enraged public." I turned off the set, wondering how I'd ever found that smug superior face attractive.

The fact that I had seemed even more absurd when

I came off stage later that night and found Tony waiting in my dressing room. His face was still tan, his hair was falling over his forehead, and it took every ounce of willpower to keep from walking straight into his arms. Every ounce of willpower and the fact that he hadn't held them open to me. He was sitting on the chaise, smoking a cigarette. From the ashtray, I gathered that he'd been there for some time, chainsmoking all the while.

As I walked past him to the makeup table, I pushed the hair back from his forehead. There was no harm, I told myself, in one small touch. He looked embarrassed, and pleased.

I took off my makeup while we talked. When I started for the shower, he didn't stand to leave. I went into the bathroom, closed the door behind me, and stood there holding my breath. I heard the creaking of the chaise as Tony stood. I couldn't do this to Cordelia. I heard his footsteps. I wouldn't do this to Cordelia. Then I heard the door to my dressing room open and close. Tony was smarter than I, and more loyal and more in love—with someone else. When I came out of my dressing room a little later, his face showed traces of impatience but no struggle.

"I saw your former husband on the news tonight," he said after Vincent had showed us to the usual table and we'd ordered drinks. "Talk about vultures. He's just circling above Adam, waiting for the others to move in for the kill so that he can feed off the carrion."

"He's never forgiven Papa for not helping him when they brought in his co-anchor. Or me for not asking him to. You remember that night."

Tony smiled and rubbed his chin as if he were the one who'd been hit. "I'm not likely to forget it."

"You know, this is a terrible thing to say, and I never would have admitted it at the time, but when you hit Web, I wanted to cheer. I felt as if someone had finally avenged me."

The smile was broader now. "Glad to be of service." Gradually the smile faded, and he toyed with his glass thoughtfully. "I never did understand why you married him," he said finally.

"That's not what you said at the time. I remember a night, a month or so before I married Web, when you said you knew exactly what I was doing with that network nitwit. I believe that was the way you described him. You would have been funny, if you hadn't been so angry."

"I was crazy about you."

He spoke so quietly that I wasn't sure I'd heard him correctly. I pretended I hadn't. "You were wrong though. I didn't marry Web because of what he could do for me. I'm ambitious but not immoral."

"I know that now."

His voice made me shiver, and I had to summon memories against it. "You said terrible things to me."

"You left some pretty good scars yourself." His eyes were darker than I'd ever seen them, and as soft as a caress. I was frightened of what might happen and what might not. Then suddenly Preston Hunter was standing beside our table, and the moment shattered as if it had been a piece of crystal.

Preston took my hand in his own soft, damp one. "Adam Kirkland's real masterpiece. How are you, sweetpea?" I told him I was fine. "Yes, you're looking fine. Do we have Anthony Bain, brilliant young architect, to thank for that?" He turned his long face with its salacious smile to Tony. "You know, I really

222

envy you, sweetpea. When you married into the Kirkland family, you certainly got your money's worth. A beautiful and talented wife. An extremely useful father-in-law. And"—he turned back to me—"a perfectly ravishing sister-in-law. It must make Cordelia's repeated absences somewhat easier to bear." I saw Tony's jaw tighten, and Preston must have too, because he went on quickly: "How is Cordelia? I hear delicious things about what she's doing in Japan."

We talked about Cordelia and her work for a moment. Neither of us asked Preston to join us, though he showed no sign of moving on. "Well," he said finally, "it's nice to know that one member of the family is doing well." Again Tony's jaw tightened, and again Hunter went on quickly: "I wasn't comparing her to you, sweetpea. I'm still your biggest fan." His eyes moved to me for a split second. "Or almost. I was referring to the great man himself. We're going to crucify Adam Kirkland."

"I thought you admired his work," Tony said.

"I admire Inter-American House. I admire what I've seen of the plans for this new building. But I don't admire where he plans to put it. Hubris, pure hubris. It's time Adam learned there's more to the world than his own vision of it."

Tony's jaw relaxed, and he leaned back in his chair and looked up at Hunter with undisguised distaste. "Tell me, Preston, do you really care so much about the library—and the city—or is this just a test of power?"

Hunter's laugh was easy, but his tongue darted nervously over his soft, full lips. "I can't imagine what you mean, sweetpea."

"You helped make Adam Kirkland's reputation and

had a good time doing it. And now you're going to have an even better time breaking him."

"What an absurd idea! Only not so absurd if you stop to think." Preston's tongue flickered over his lips again, but not in nervousness. Now he was like a man anticipating a tasty meal. "If you stop to think," he repeated, "where the idea came from. I'm not the one who's competing with Adam Kirkland. I'm not the spiritual son who has to slay the father in order to become a man. I'm not even an architect." Preston looked down at Tony with gimlet eyes. "But you are. The best damned architect to come down the pike since Adam Kirkland. Need I say more?"

He had already said more than enough.

Tony was quiet most of the way home. As the cab neared the apartment, he finally spoke: "Do you agree with Hunter?"

I started to ask about what, but there were enough masquerades between us. "I know you better than that."

He paid the driver and followed me into the lobby in silence. We stopped at the elevator as we'd trained ourselves to do.

"Cordelia's coming home tomorrow night," Tony said. The statement sounded like a non sequitur, but we both knew it was not.

The following morning the opposition fired its first round. Again the front page of the New York *Times* served as the battlefield.

"If we don't care about our past, we cannot hope for our future," said Mrs. Aristotle Onassis.

"Europe has its cathedrals, and we have the New

York Public Library," announced noted architect Philip Johnson.

"Would you construct an office building over the Parthenon?" demanded Preston Hunter.

"They've certainly wheeled out the big guns," I said to Ellen, who'd brought the paper with my breakfast tray.

Throughout childhood Cordelia and I had hungered for breakfast in bed, but nothing less than a fever would induce Mother to let Ellen climb the stairs with a tray for either of us. Mother believed in strict rules and unalterable conventions, especially in an erratic and unconventional family. Ellen had continued to adhere to Mother's instructions after her death and into our adulthood—until I'd opened in *Eastward*. The following morning she'd brought me breakfast as well as all my reviews on a tray, just as she used to for Mother.

"It's a disgrace," she pronounced as she opened the curtains. "The very idea that they should try to stop your father from putting up one of his buildings." Ellen knew nothing about architecture, but she was an expert on loyalty.

Tony didn't come to the theater that night. Cordelia had arrived home on schedule. I always have trouble coming down after a performance, but I was down that night. Strangely enough Sean Wellihan stopped by. "You get better and better," he said. "When I saw it opening night, I didn't think you could improve that performance. I was wrong. There's less business. You're quieter, deeper. And much funnier in your first scene."

"That's one of the things I love about you, Sean.

You may be a liar, but you're a convincing one. Other people just say, 'Darling, you were wonderful.' "

"Then the other people you know are fools. Incidentally, who was that particular other person you were with at Sardi's last night."

I stopped taking off my makeup and faced his reflection in the mirror. "I didn't see you."

"Neither of you saw anyone. I took one look and said to myself, 'Julia's in love again.' Well, I've waited out the others, and I can wait out this one."

I went back to creaming my face. "Sorry to disappoint you, Sean, but you're wrong. That was my sister's husband I was with last night."

Sean's eyes caught mine in the mirror. "Poor Julia," he said. "And poor, poor Cordelia."

I called Cordelia at her office the following morning. I'd tried her apartment—hers and Tony's I reminded myself—but no one had answered. "Welcome home," I said, "though I'm surprised to find you there instead of home."

Only Cordelia could have asked why.

"Jet lag," I suggested. "The fact that you haven't seen your husband in weeks. I should think you'd both take the day off."

She laughed. "Don't think we didn't toy with the idea."

I decided that if I'd awakened next to Tony, I would have done more than toy with the idea. I also decided I had to stop thinking about things like that.

"I was just going to call you," Cordelia went on. "I don't suppose a successful star of stage and screen is free for lunch."

"I'm not, but I can be."

"Don't break anything on my account," she said in a voice that made it clear she hoped I would.

"It's only a movie director."

"*Only* a movie director."

"Two years ago he wouldn't have bought me a hot dog on a street corner—unless of course I agreed to go to bed with him. Now he can wait."

"Vengeance is sweet."

"And fleeting. Two years from now he could be refusing to take my calls again, so I might as well enjoy success while I've got it. Should I leave him cooling his heels at the Russian Tea Room the way he left me in his reception room once or should I give him the courtesy of a cancellation?"

"The courtesy, by all means. Remember what Mother used to say. 'The greater man the greater courtesy.' "

"Shakespeare."

"Why does everyone in the theater always ascribe everything to Shakespeare? Or Shaw? It's Tennyson."

We agreed to meet at the Six Continents at one.

The maître d' greeted me effusively and said Mrs. Bain was waiting. Sitting alone and erect at a corner table, Cordelia was a piece of art, cool, smooth, beautifully sculpted. The severe black suit accentuated her long slender body; the soft light filtering through the tall tinted glass windows defined her like a gilt frame.

"Welcome home," I said.

"Same to you. Tony said you were in California for a few weeks. He said he stopped by to see you—at the most fantastic pink palace. All cupolas, turrets, and spires." She said it casually, as if she were more suspicious of the architecture than of me, and I thought how ironic that she should finally begin to trust me with Tony at precisely the moment I was beginning to distrust myself.

The headwaiter approached with deference. Cordelia bypassed the menu and asked him to make her the pasta with cream and truffles he'd devised for Papa. My ever vigilant conscience toted up the calories, and I settled for the poached salmon—without sauce.

"How do you think Papa is?" she asked after we'd ordered.

"Happy. Really happy for the first time in years. There's nothing he likes better than a good fight. Providing he's got something worthwhile to fight for."

"He's got something worthwhile, all right. Have you seen the plans? They're astonishing. The best he's ever done. Better than anything Wright or Corbu ever dreamed of."

"But what if he doesn't get to build it?"

"He has to." The intensity of her voice made the two men at the next table turn to stare.

"Tony doesn't think he will."

There was a long silence, and I realized it wasn't Papa she'd wanted to talk about, or at least not only Papa. She bent her head and covered her eyes with her hand for a moment, the way she used to when she didn't want to cry, and a shared lifetime of skinned knees and broken toys came flooding back. "I don't know what to do."

"About what?" I asked, playing for time. For once I wasn't sure I wanted my sister's confidences.

"About Tony. About the fact that he refuses to support Papa."

"He refuses to support Papa's building. And if Papa can accept that, why can't you?"

"He doesn't accept it. He's just too proud to admit he cares. But he feels betrayed. I'm sure of it."

"Tony has a right to his own opinion."

Her eyes, so miserable a moment ago, glinted with anger. "Tony admits the building is superb. The only thing he's opposed to is the site. Suddenly he's in love with Beaux Arts architecture. All he can talk about is that half-acre reading room. He insists it's the best public room in the city, and Papa's building will cast it into gloom."

"Maybe Tony's right."

"It doesn't matter whether he's right or wrong. He owes this to Papa."

"I hope you didn't say that to Tony—that he *owes* Papa something."

She glanced away, unable to meet my eyes. "I didn't mean to. It slipped out."

"The things we say in anger."

"More in desperation than anger. But he does owe Papa something. Papa hired Tony right out of school, let him start designing while everyone else was still doing detail drawings, made him a senior partner in record time."

"Do you know who you sound like?"

"Who?"

"Web. The night he said Papa was doing so much for Tony's career he might as well pull a few strings for him too. The night Tony hit him."

Cordelia flushed with embarrassment. "I didn't mean it that way."

"What way did you mean it?"

"Tony's brilliant," she said as if that were an answer.

229

"That's one point on which all of us, including Tony, agree."

"And he would have been successful even without Papa. The point is that he's been successful with Papa. And now he wants to turn around and betray him. It's almost as if he's jealous of Papa, as if he thinks he can't be any bigger until he makes Papa smaller."

"Now you sound like Preston Hunter."

Her mouth opened in surprise, then closed in a stubborn line. "Maybe it's true."

"Do you really trust Tony that little?"

Her answer said a great deal about Cordelia and her marriage: "I don't think he's doing it intentionally or even consciously. He just can't help himself."

"If you believe that, God help both of you."

"Do you know what will happen to Papa if he loses this?"

"Do you know what will happen to your marriage if you keep this up?"

Her mouth was set in an angry line again as if she were determined not to speak, and I could guess what she was thinking. "I know," I said, "I'm not exactly in a position to give marital advice. I made an unholy mess of mine, and my affairs haven't been much to write home about either." I hesitated for a moment. I knew the right thing to say, and since I was sitting across from Cordelia rather than Tony, it was not even difficult to say it. "Well, I may be stupid, but I'm not blind. If I had what you do—"

"You threw Tony over," she said, and the old suspicion flared in her eyes.

"I didn't mean Tony." It wasn't entirely a lie. I'd meant Tony, but I'd meant more than him. "I meant if I had what you and Tony have together. If I had that, I wouldn't let anything or anyone ruin it."

"Not even loyalty?"

"Loyalty to whom? That's what you have to decide."

I'd lunched with Cordelia on Thursday. When she and Tony arrived for brunch the following Sunday, I knew she'd taken my advice. The cool architect had given way to a soft woman. The lights in Tony's eyes glowed rather than sparkled. They looked as if they'd had difficulty dragging themselves out of bed. I felt ashamed and more than a little foolish about the thoughts I'd entertained during Cordelia's absence. I also felt more than a little lonely. And the fact that I'd run into Sean with an actress who was being touted as the new Monroe two nights earlier didn't help.

Ellen came out to welcome Cordelia home, told her she'd grown thinner in Japan, and returned to the kitchen to make eggs and bacon, waffles, and fresh whipped cream for Papa's Irish coffee. I steeled myself against the aromas. Cordelia used to call my body a lethal weapon in the war between the sexes, but she's never understood that there's such a thing as too much ammunition.

After brunch we went into the living room for Papa's Irish coffee. With a fire on the hearth and the Sunday papers strewn around the floor, we made a handsome picture of a happy family at ease with themselves and each other. But pictures, contrary to common belief, can lie.

"Have you seen the morning papers?" Papa asked.

Tony and Cordelia said they hadn't looked at them yet. I wasn't surprised.

"Things are heating up." I could tell Papa was enjoying himself. "The media, in its unrelenting struggle to bring both sides of the question to the common man—as if the common man had enough intelligence to evaluate both sides of any question—has printed two articles on what they call the pros and cons of the Great Library Debate. One was written by Preston Hunter, of course. The other is by Graham Fowler."

"I didn't know developers could write."

"Watch yourself, Tony, you're beginning to sound like an elitist. You're beginning to sound like me. Undoubtedly the article was written by someone in Fowler's office. But don't underestimate Fowler himself."

Papa handed the section of the paper to Cordelia and Tony, who read the pieces and passed them on to me. I'd already heard Preston Hunter's arguments from Tony. Fowler's article was a masterpiece of public relations. It contained just enough honesty to make the hypocrisy convincing.

> Critics tell us to build somewhere else, as if there were a dozen sites like Fifth Avenue and Forty-second Street, as if there were a dozen corners called the Crosswords of the World. I answer them with the first three rules of real estate. Location, location, location.
>
> As for the library itself, I am a voice in the wilderness crying out that I don't think it's either untouchable or irreplaceable. I don't think a Beaux Arts facade is worth twenty thousand new books, locked doors two days a week, or cuts in library staffs. I don't think an old building is more important than the people who use it. I don't think deference to the

past is more important than a living library
that looks to the future.

"I don't know who Fowler's PR man is," I said, "but
I want him."

Tony laughed. "Success is making you cynical."

"I think he has a point," Cordelia said.

Tony reached over and tousled her hair. "And it's
making you naive. He doesn't give a damn about the
library, Cordelia. You could burn every book in it, and
Fowler's only thought would be how he could harness
the heat to cut energy costs in one of his buildings."

Papa chuckled, but Cordelia was more protective of
him than he was of himself. "Whether he means it or
not, he has a point," she insisted.

The way Tony pressed his lips together was more
eloquent than any words. He was determined not to
argue with Cordelia, or perhaps not to argue with her
again.

"Well"—Papa stood—"Fowler's due any minute so
you can tell him what you think of him and his article
to his face."

Graham Fowler arrived on schedule, wearing an as-
cot and managing not to look like something out of a
Noel Coward revival. He had that much presence. He
was not a handsome man, but his thin features were
sharp and regular. Fowler was as smooth and rich as
Papa's Irish coffee, but like it, he packed an unexpected wallop. Beneath the correct appearance and
beautiful manners, Graham Fowler radiated heat. He
had a secret sensuality. Other men would not guess
at it, but women would sense it immediately. I did,
but I was not attracted by it. For one thing, he was a

little too slick for my taste. For another, he was more Papa's contemporary than mine, and I've never had a penchant for older men. Papa is more than enough father for me.

"We were just discussing your article in this morning's paper," Papa told him. "Cordelia was much impressed, though the rest of us took a somewhat more cynical view of your arguments."

Fowler's smile was quick, perhaps even sincere. As I said, he wasn't a cold man, only a reserved one. "I meant every word of it. After all, I sit on the board of the library. I'm genuinely interested in its welfare. And I like its location." He laughed. "I meant that part of the article too." He seemed to be speaking to all of us, but his words were intended for Cordelia. I've attracted enough men in my life to recognize the signs when they're drawn to someone else. Fowler had been to Cordelia ever since he'd met her, though she didn't realize it. Of course, Cordelia never did realize the effect she had on men. And I suppose the fact that she didn't was part of her attraction.

"You still think he's sincere?" Tony asked after Papa had taken Fowler into his studio to look at some new sketches.

"I never said he was sincere. I said his arguments were cogent. And I don't understand what you have against him." She really didn't, but then I don't think Tony did at the time either. He wasn't jealous of him yet. He just didn't like him.

"I'm against developers on principle. For an architect they're a necessary ally and a natural enemy."

"I'm not against a developer who can recognize the greatness of Papa's design."

"Cordelia," Tony said, "that man would put up a

fake colonial or neo-Gothic monstrosity so long as he could do it at Fifth Avenue and Forty-second Street."

"Maybe, but he's going to put up Papa's masterpiece."

"He's no fool. He knows he stands a better chance against the opposition with a building by America's leading architect than with a second-rate design by an unknown."

"Tony has a point there," I said and immediately regretted my words. I'd made up my mind to stay out of their arguments and Tony's life, but neither of them paid any attention to me.

Cordelia stood, walked to the fire, and turned to face Tony. She's Mother's daughter as well as Papa's and has a nice sense of dramatic movement. "That's right. I keep forgetting you're the opposition. No, that's not true. I never forget it for a moment—"

"So I noticed."

"—but I keep hoping you'll see reason."

Tony started to say something, then stopped. He took a sip of his Irish coffee, and when he finally spoke, his voice was controlled. "Couldn't we drop the subject? Just for a while? Just until you leave? Then we can quarrel long distance," he added in a weak attempt at humor.

"When are you leaving?" I told myself I was only trying to change the subject.

"Tomorrow." She returned to the couch and sat beside Tony. I knew she was sorry, though I wasn't sure he did.

"But you just got home."

Tony put an arm around her shoulders. "That's what I get for marrying an architect. A brilliant architect."

He said the same thing a week later when I mentioned Cordelia's absence. He was alone and lonely, and it was only normal that he should drift by on Sunday to eat one of Ellen's stupendous breakfasts and read the papers with Papa and me. "But don't you mind her going?" I asked after Papa had disappeared into his studio.

"Of course I mind her going. But I wouldn't respect her if she didn't. I knew when I married her she was an architect as well as a woman."

"God, Tony, if there were more men like you, the world would be a saner place."

I heard the irony in his laughter, but it was directed against himself. "Don't you believe it. I talk a good game, but sometimes I think it's just talk. I'm mad as hell that she's gone." He was silent for a moment, contemplating some truth in the middle distance. "And I was jealous as hell when she won the competition," he said quietly, still not looking at me.

"That's only normal," I answered because I didn't know what else to say.

"At the risk of sounding like Adam, I don't want to be normal. I was jealous, and I hated myself for the jealousy. Sometimes I think it would be easier if Cordelia were a painter or a sculptress or—" He stopped as if realizing he'd already said more than he'd meant to.

"Or an actress?" I laughed.

He picked up my tone gratefully. "Anything but that. You people are the most egomaniacal in the world."

"I resent that. Have I read you my latest raves? Have I shown you the series of pictures of me that ran in last month's *Vogue*? Have I told you of my latest movie offer?"

"My God, I had no idea I was in the same room with a celebrity."

"The trouble with you is that you knew me when."

"And the nice thing about you is that you're even better now."

"You mean success hasn't spoiled Julia Kirkland?"

"Success has improved her. If, in fact, perfection can be improved."

"Flattery will get you nowhere," I said in the same tone, then immediately regretted it. We'd both been joking, but even in fun, there was no reason to assume he was trying to get anywhere.

A week later I received a letter from Cordelia. I was surprised. She telephoned Tony and telexed Papa, but she claimed she had no time for letters. There was nothing of importance in it or at least nothing I realized as being important at the time. I think she was simply lonely.

Most of it read like a travelogue. She told me about the traditional inn where she was staying, the gentle care of the kimono-clad women who spoke no English but still managed to anticipate her every need, the spare beauty of the culture. If she was having second thoughts about the historical references in Tony's losing design, she didn't say so. Only at the end did the letter turn personal, though I doubt Cordelia realized how personal.

I had quite a surprise the other day. Graham Fowler turned up here. He'd been in Tokyo on business, and since he knew I was here, he took the high speed train down. He said he'd always wanted to see the Inland Sea and thought I ought to as well. He hired a hydrofoil for the tour, and I have to admit it was a wonderful weekend. The sky was clear, the water sparkling, and the islands simply breathtaking. When the water comes swirling in from the Pacific through the Naruto Strait, the whirlpools are absolutely terrifying. Graham is the perfect tour guide. He's exactly like Papa that way, knows everything about the place though he's never been there before, and has a wonderful eye and a quick, open mind. It was awfully kind of him to come all this way to keep a lonely American company for the weekend.

As I've said, Cordelia never did recognize the effect she had on men. She'd compared Graham Fowler to Papa, but Fowler's interest in her, I felt sure, was anything but paternal.

The battle over Bryant Park Tower dragged on through the winter and into spring. I heard about it from Tony and from Papa and from Cordelia during her brief visits home. Tony said one night, when I asked about her, that it was lucky she was home so rarely these days. They had less time to quarrel. He was half joking but only half.

The play was turning into a long run, and I was slipping into boredom. The theater's an upside-down world. We pray for a hit, then complain when our prayers are answered. I still liked going to the theater, the greeting at the stage door from the old man who'd known Mother, the nightly panic when the call "five minutes, five minutes," echoes through the corridors backstage, the sheer heart-thumping thrill of the applause, but I'd begun to tire of repeating the same lines every night, of crossing from stage left to stage right at precisely three minutes of nine every night, of having to kiss the leading man as if I meant it every night. My agent who'd been so eager to get me a run-of-the-play contract when I was unknown was now looking for ways to get out of it. In the meantime I was trying to keep my performance fresh and my feelings for Tony dormant. Both demanded constant vigilance and considerable effort, and I'd almost forgotten Bryant Park Tower when it blew up in all our faces.

The first inkling I had was a call from Tony early one morning in April. He'd managed to persuade Ellen to wake me. "Have you seen the paper?" he demanded. I steeled myself for the worst. It seemed to be the fate of our family to have our personal dramas played out on the front pages of national newspapers and the air waves of network television.

"The Consolidated Life Building." Tony breathed the words as if he were asthmatic. " 'A group of independent engineers,' " he read from the newspaper, " 'canvassed by Preston Hunter, warned of a possible defect in materials in the proposed Bryant Park Tower similar to the one that befell Adam Kirkland's Consolidated Life Building in Houston more than fifteen years ago.' "

"Is there really a similarity?"

"No. But the argument is sensational enough to win them plenty of converts."

I sat up in bed and ran my fingers through my hair. "How is he?"

"Who ever knows with Adam? He's called a press conference for eleven o'clock. I think he might like to have you there."

"Will you be?"

"I offered, but he just laughed and said he didn't want me to compromise my principles for family feeling."

I dressed quickly in a navy and white Chanel suit. Chanel is solid, respectable, safe. A defect in materials is not a subject to be met lightly.

"What are you doing here?" Papa asked when I arrived at his office a little before eleven. "Think I needed moral support?"

I sat on the edge of his desk and crossed my legs, as if I were posing for an old-fashioned cheesecake shot. "Nope. Just cashing in on the free publicity. You know how we actresses are."

He put an arm around my shoulders and hugged me roughly. "Just watch those legs. I want those damn reporters to keep their minds on my building."

Papa was glorious that morning. Charming, witty, arrogant, absolutely certain of himself and his infallibility. His only defense was offense. I knew that for the rest of my life I'd remember him the way he was that morning.

Though he received the reporters sitting behind his huge desk, he seemed taller than any of them standing and jostling for position with their cameras and microphones. His proud hawk's face and mane of white hair were silhouetted against the backdrop of the skyline he'd helped fashion. His powerful voice filled the vast office that was the symbol of his success. His air of assurance was as sturdy as the buildings pictured on the walls and re-created in the models around the room. He was—I'm not ashamed to say it—godlike.

The reporters wasted no time getting down to business. They demanded an answer to Preston Hunter's charges. They demanded to know if what had happened to the Consolidated Life Building was likely to happen to Bryant Park Tower.

Papa gave them his best smile. For a moment every man in the room wanted him as a friend, every woman as a lover. "The Consolidated Life Building is Preston Hunter's red herring. He can't find any faults in Bryant Park Tower"—another disarming smile—"he even admits to the excellence of design, so he's gone back more than fifteen years and dug up a minor problem in an entirely dissimilar building."

"A woman was killed by falling glass. Do you call that a minor problem, Mr. Kirkland?"

Papa's face was a mask of concern and regret. The expression won as many converts as the smile. "I call that a tragedy, but one that has no bearing on the building under discussion. The materials aren't the same. We didn't even have high impact plastic then. Moreover, subsequent studies of the Consolidated Building found no flaw in either the plans or the specifications, and the courts ruled accordingly. They found no negligence."

"But didn't the hotel across the street from Consolidated Life win their suit?" shouted a woman I recognized from Web's network.

This time Papa's smile was amused. "As a matter of fact, they did. That, of course, was not against Adam Kirkland Associates, but against Consolidated Life. It seems our mirrored curtain wall reflected the sun and increased the air-conditioning needs of the old Houston Arms. Consolidated was required to pay damages."

Papa had deflected the first thrust, but the reporters were pros too, and they wanted a story. "What about reports that the drilling and sinking of the structural pilings will weaken the foundations of the library and other buildings in the area?"

Papa permitted himself a small frown, as if a student had asked a stupid question. "Not a single day goes by without some sort of blasting in midtown Manhattan. The city has stringent safety codes. We plan to exceed them with safety measures of our own. Blasting will be broken up into more than ten thousand separate explosions. We will be using Tovex, a nitroglycerin derivative gel. Some of the explosions will use as little as three ounces of Tovex. Nonetheless, no matter how small the explosion, it will be covered with a steel blanket weighing three to four tons and carefully monitored by seismograph. We do not toy with the public safety or that of other buildings. Moreover, the bedrock in this part of Manhattan is mica schist. We won't have to treat the soil as they did at the site of the World Trade Center for safety purposes."

The questions continued for a few minutes, but Papa had answered the important ones, and the conference was effectively over. The reporters were hungry but realistic. They knew innuendo could go only so far, even with a man as successful, arrogant, and ripe for pillorying as Papa.

Papa had beaten back the attack, but, though the enemy didn't know it, he'd suffered casualties. Old wounds, both professional and personal, had been opened.

"You were superb," I said after the crowd had moved out trailing cameras and cables and occasional wishes of good luck to Papa.

"Was I?" His voice was hollow. He sat slumped be-

242

hind his desk, a broken relic of the man he'd been a moment ago. I'd never seen him like this, or at least I hadn't seen him like this since Mother's death.

"Can I get you a drink?"

His eyes moved to me as if from a great distance, but they didn't focus. "I'd like to be alone, Judith." He turned to the window behind his desk. I was certain he didn't realize he'd called me by Mother's name.

That night before going to the theater I turned on the news to find out how Papa's press conference had played. I was surprised to see that Web had grown a mustache. He'd been considering it for years on the assumption it would give him more character. I'd never told him it would take more than a mustache to do that.

The video tapes of the press conference came late in the broadcast, a mere few seconds of a handsome and confident Papa assuring the public that he did not take chances with their safety. Webster's mustachioed face reappeared on the screen. "There were comments from others in the city too."

Preston Hunter grinning foolishly into the camera: "A crime against our architectural heritage. A blight on the already overcrowded midtown area. And dangerous."

A balding man with a beard, identified as an engineer: "The risks are too great. Especially to the library during construction."

And then, shockingly, Tony. The camera did not, as the saying goes, love him. It caught the dark circles under his eyes and the trapped expression in them. "The right building in the wrong place at the wrong time."

"How did you get him to say that?" I demanded of the screen as my former husband's face reappeared.

"Those last words," Web said with a hint of the famous smile reputed to instill confidence in the most skeptical viewer, "came from Anthony Bain. Mr. Bain is a partner in the firm of Adam Kirkland Associates. A house divided, eh, Bill?" he said with a nod to his co-anchor and nemesis.

I debated whether to call Tony. He didn't give me the chance. "I suppose you saw it," he said.

"I won't even bother to ask how they trapped you. I've seen them work."

"They were in the lobby when I came down for lunch after Adam's press conference. One of them knew I was Adam's son-in-law as well as a partner—and that I'd resigned from the mayor's council. They started asking—no, badgering—me about high impact plastic, but they weren't interested in my answers."

"You poor dope. They probably didn't understand a word you were saying. And they didn't want you to defend Papa, they wanted you to turn against him."

"Well, they got what they wanted. I kept defending the structure and design, but they kept firing questions—you know how they do it, five at a time, all rapid-fire—about why I'd resigned from the council and where would the conflict of interest be if I was genuinely in favor of the building. After a while the 'no comments' began to sound as if I really did think there was some failing, so I blurted out that line about the right building in the wrong place at the wrong time."

"And of course that was the only line they picked up."

"While your former husband added a few of his own."

"You're not one of Web's favorite people—in case you didn't know it. Have you seen Papa?"

"He left the studio. I was hoping he'd be there." Strange what we notice in a crisis. Papa's dream was falling apart, and, for all I knew, Tony's career as well, and all I could think of was that he hadn't called to speak to me but to Papa. At that moment I heard the elevator approaching. The doors opened, and Papa stepped into the foyer. His broad shoulders sagged beneath the weight of the usually dashing cape.

"He's here now," I told Tony and handed Papa the phone. He did not have to ask who it was.

"A nice turn of phrase," I heard Papa say. "Perhaps you missed your calling. Should have been a writer rather than an architect."

Papa was silent for a moment, and when he spoke again, his voice was a pounding hammer: "You think I'm that petty! You think I'm a smaller man than you are! To hell with your resignations! I don't need your support, but the firm needs your work." Papa straightened his shoulders, and his voice became a silvery knife again. "It's a lot more valuable than your opinion. You've chosen the wrong side, Tony. I'm going to win."

I was sure Tony would be waiting in my dressing room that night, certain that in his guilt and pain and loneliness he would turn to me, but I was wrong. When I came off stage my dressing room was empty, as empty as my life. I faced myself in the mirror, skin shiny from cream, features a little weak without the delineation of makeup, eyes hollow. "He doesn't need you," I told myself. "Cordelia's life blood, Papa's oxygen—

both critical to his existence—but you're nothing but an afterthought."

The following night I found Tony waiting in my dressing room, and my heart contracted as if he'd reached in and touched it. The skin beneath his eyes looked as if it had been shaded with charcoal, and there was a grim cast to his mouth, but I could feel nothing but pleasure. I am, I suppose, a selfish woman.

"Feel like some supper?" The invitation was familiar, the tone tortured.

"You look as if you could use some, but you don't look fit for a restaurant. Come home. I'll scramble eggs or something."

"No." I looked at him in surprise. "I don't want to see Adam. I haven't got the stomach for it."

"Okay we'll go to your place. I can scramble eggs there just as well." I suppose a warning bell should have gone off then, but I didn't hear one, and if Tony did, he ignored it. We took a taxi to his apartment, his and Cordelia's. I suppose it was just as well we did. Cordelia called a few minutes after we arrived.

Tony picked up the phone in the living room. I went into the kitchen to fill the ice bucket, start the supper neither of us wanted, and pretend not to listen. But of course I was listening, as closely as I'd listened to Papa's conversation with Tony the previous evening.

"How the hell did you hear about it?" I heard him shout. "No," he went on in a quieter but no less defensive tone. "I didn't think I could keep it from you. I'm just surprised you saw it halfway around the world. You are halfway around the world, you know, Cordelia." There was a brief silence. "I'm sorry."

There was a longer silence this time, and when he spoke, his voice was strident again. "Did you expect me to lie? To cut my conscience to fit his?" Another pause. "That's right, Cordelia. Your father. Not God. And while we're talking about relationships, I'm your husband. I know that ranks considerably below father and somewhere after career in importance, but I thought I'd remind you anyway. In case you'd forgotten."

Her answer, whatever it was, was brief. "I know fighting isn't going to help, but you called to fight, didn't you? Or did you just want to tell me how much you liked my comment to the press?" He apologized again and mumbled a few more words. "I love you" were not among them.

When I heard him hang up, I went back into the living room and handed him a glass with a little ice and a great deal of scotch. "A bad connection," he said. I looked for a trace of irony but found none.

I started back to the kitchen, but he stopped me. His hand on my arm was strong, but he let go immediately. "I'm not hungry." I said I wasn't either, and we settled on opposite sides of the sofa, a no-man's-land of suede upholstery between us.

"I suppose you heard."

I could have said I hadn't, perhaps I should have, but I merely nodded. "Do you think I've betrayed Adam too?"

"I think you did what you had to do."

"Why can't Cordelia see that?"

"Because she's always had a blind spot where Papa is concerned. And she's always been terrified of disappointing him. It's not her fault. He always demanded so much of her."

Tony looked across the space between us, and I felt as if I were under a microscope. "And not of you?"

"I was less important. After all, an actress is not an architect. Acting is recreative, not creative. The theater is transitory, ephemeral. Buildings are . . ." I hesitated, trying to remember the quote, and Tony finished for me.

" ' . . . man's pride, man's triumph over gravitation, man's will to power.' Our boy Nietzsche again."

"He believes it, Tony. So do you. That's why you couldn't lie to help him. And so does Cordelia. This business with Papa works both ways. I love the man. She's in thrall to the genius as well."

He was silent for what seemed like a long time, contemplating some truth in the bottom of his glass. "I went to the public library this afternoon. To find out some things."

"Like whether it's worth the battle?"

"No, I knew that. It is. I looked up the accounts of the Consolidated Life accident and the trial."

I was surprised and, for some inexplicable reason, frightened. "So Preston and his little band are right?"

"Hell, no. Adam's too good to make the same mistake twice. There's nothing wrong with this high impact plastic. I'm sure of that. And the mistake in Houston wasn't his but the glass manufacturer's. Insufficient testing. Like the U.N. Secretariat where the pressure differential inside and outside the windows causes it to rain up into the ducts rather than down. Adam's problem was sun rather than rain. He used mirror-coated, double-glazed windows for that curtain wall. The ultraviolet buildup inside the double-glazed sandwich wreaked havoc on the sealant. No one could have guessed the glass would fall out. The tests didn't even hint at it."

"What about the tests on this plastic?"

"Much more extensive. Adam's had them checked out thoroughly and even had his engineers run some of their own. I told you, he's learned his lesson. In more ways than one, I think."

"What's that supposed to mean?"

Tony stood, took off his jacket, and loosened his tie. As he moved to drop the jacket over a chair, his shoulders strained against the fabric of his shirt, and this time my stomach rather than my heart contracted. Funny how men can spot the seductive in a woman but never in themselves. Not that I'm suggesting Tony was being intentionally seductive at that moment. But intention had nothing to do with it.

"There was a lot of personal stuff in the coverage of the Consolidated Life accident. Adam Kirkland and Judith St. John were celebrities, and the public was, as usual, hungry for dirt. The papers managed to dig up a little." He refilled our drinks and sat on the opposite side of the sofa again. "Do you want to hear?"

"Of course."

"Cordelia wouldn't." He stopped, as if guilty at the words. "What I meant was the perfect marriage, the one she's created in her imagination, the perfect marriage to the perfect man wasn't so perfect after all. Neither the marriage nor the man. According to several papers, Judith St. John was about to divorce Adam when she died."

I put my glass down with a clatter of crystal and ice, but my hand was still cold. I rubbed it absentmindedly against my skirt. "What?" I asked stupidly.

"The rumors appeared a few days before the plane crash. Then they disappeared. Maybe the press had pangs of conscience, though I doubt it. More likely someone hushed them up. Or maybe the tragedy was more poignant if the couple was still young and in love. Whatever, the rumors disappeared from the papers, along with the woman in Houston."

"What woman in Houston?"

"Just a woman. Pretty, judging from the picture in *Time*, but not nearly as beautiful as your mother. Don't forget though, that was the time of the lawsuit against Adam. He spent a lot of time in Houston that winter."

"And Mother spent it in New York. She was starring in *Separate Tables*." I stood and paced the room several times. What Tony had just told me was impossible. It was also, I knew instinctively, true. "Suddenly it fits together."

"His guilt after the accident and his excessive grief."

I sat beside Tony again. "More than that. I don't remember Mother's death very clearly. Or rather certain images are clear, but I can't remember the sequence of events coherently. I remember friends and relatives turning up at the apartment and lots of reporters and Papa locking himself in his studio and a lot of people saying a lot of things that didn't make sense to an eleven-year-old child. And I remember an argument, just before Mother left for the Coast. When Mother and Papa quarreled, you remembered it. But I couldn't understand what the argument was about. I knew vaguely that Papa had been in some kind of trouble, but he'd come home that last time saying everything was all right. I imagine by then he'd won the lawsuit and thought he was in the clear. But he wasn't counting on Mother. She had her bags packed and standing in the hall when he walked in the door. There was a lot of shouting. I didn't understand most of it, but I can still remember some of it. Papa said if she'd gone with him as he'd asked, if she'd been there hen he needed her, none of it would have happened.

"And Mother said—God, I can still hear her voice—
'm your wife, not your faithful dog.' Then she said
he'd send for us as soon as she arranged things on
he Coast and walked out the door."

"Your mother had a lot of pride."

"She needed it to live with Papa."

We were silent for a while, and when Tony finally
poke, his voice was strangely husky. "Do you blame
im?"

I thought for a moment. "For Mother's death, not
t all. For what he did, not much. I know him too well.
'apa's a powerful man, but sometimes he's not very
trong. He has a habit of giving in to his temptations
nd justifying his behavior by his greatness. He has a
abit of forgetting there are other people in the world.
Vhen he had an affair with that woman, he was only
unning true to character. Just as Mother was when
he walked out. Just as you were when you came out
gainst him."

"And what about loyalty?" He took off his glasses,
nd his eyes were like velvet.

"I'm afraid I don't know much about that, or so I've
een told."

"You're wrong. You know a great deal about it. There
re many kinds of loyalty, Julia. To many people."

"Are you going to tell Cordelia?"

"About Adam and Judith?" He'd made no move to
ut on his glasses, and his eyes were naked with sor-
ow and suffering—and desire.

I stood and took my coat from the chair where I'd
ossed it. "There's nothing else to tell her," I said firmly,
;iving the words a perfect reading.

Tony took the coat from my hands. For a moment

I thought he was going to stop me, but he merely helped me on with it. This time he did not lift my hair out from under my collar. He did not touch me in any way.

"Nothing," he agreed.

9

As spring melted into summer, the battle over Bryant Park Tower dragged through the courts. Since the library was a landmark, there were innumerable hearings and an infinite number of legal actions. Lawyers came and went. Appeals were made, public opinion molded, influence peddled. It was a long, tedious, and not particularly inspiring war, though both sides managed to mouth a good many uplifting phrases.

Tony stayed out of it as best he could. Cordelia was violently partisan. She managed to get home from Japan in June, and she and Tony went to Nantucket for two weeks. Papa flew up for the weekend, but Saturday performances kept me in town. Tony looked relieved when I told him I wouldn't be joining them. I didn't blame him. We'd become too close during Cordelia's absence. Not that Cordelia noticed. She'd become too distant. She had her own work and her own cause, or rather Papa's, and her own resentment. She couldn't forgive Tony for his defection.

Papa was more observant. "I saw Preston Hunter at the hearing today," he said one evening in July after Cordelia had returned to Japan. "He mentioned that he ran into you and Tony last week. Said you were having supper after the show. He said it with innuendo."

"Preston Hunter says hello with innuendo."

"True," Papa said in a maddeningly noncommittal tone.

"Tony stops by the theater occasionally. He's lonely without Cordelia."

"No doubt," Papa said and went on leafing through one of those opulent, overpriced, coffee table books a colleague had sent him in hope, futile, of praise.

"He needs someone to talk to."

Papa slammed the book closed. "Lies!" I looked up from the magazine I was pretending to read, startled. "Every line that man draws, every building he designs is a lie. Of course, if I understood structure as little as he does, I'd try to hide it too. What do you and Tony talk about?"

I shrugged, then realized too late it was, as we say on stage, a piece of business and a bad one at that. I don't usually shrug. "I don't know. What do people talk about over supper? His work. Mine. Cordelia. You."

Papa put the heavy volume on the coffee table, stood, and walked to the wall of windows facing south. The most famous skyline in the world glowed against the black sky. "Right there," he said. "In two years it will stand right there. Are you having an affair with Tony?" he asked without a pause between sentences, without a change of tone.

"Of course not!"

He turned from the window and his dream, and faced me, eyes searching, face serious but not unkind. "Just friends, eh? A beautiful woman, young, healthy, not exactly made of ice. A man, also young, also handsome, also passionate by nature, a man whose wife is halfway around the world, has been halfway around the world for the better part of a year, and they meet to talk architecture and art. What is this, Julia, theater of the absurd?"

"For God's sake, he's Cordelia's husband!"

"Don't shout at me. Do you think we'd be having this conversation if he weren't? I find it as distasteful as you do."

"Then why did you start it?"

"Because I don't want Cordelia hurt. Or you. Or even Tony."

"If what you're implying were true—"

"I'm not implying anything, Julia. Words don't frighten me. I'm saying that you and Tony are lovers."

"If we were—and we're not—I should think he'd be the last one to be hurt."

"I wouldn't be so sure."

We sat in silence for what seemed like a long time. "You have nothing to worry about," I said finally. "I admit I'm in love with Tony, but I won't do anything about it."

"Permit me a bit of paternal skepticism."

"Are you saying you don't believe me?"

"I know you, Julia. You're my daughter as well as Judith's."

I'd had enough. "And so you judge me by your standards, yours and that woman's in Houston."

The big, proud face collapsed into lines of pain. "I didn't think you knew about that."

"You didn't think Mother did either."

"There were . . . circumstances. I'm not excusing myself, just explaining."

"You don't have to explain anything to me."

"I tried to explain to Judith, but she refused to listen. She betrayed me."

"*She* betrayed *you!*"

"I needed her that winter. I asked her to come with me. I begged her to." His voice rasped with harshness, like a nail scraping steel.

"She couldn't leave New York. She had her own career."

Papa straightened his big shoulders, and when he spoke, I knew he'd pulled himself together. "That's right, and I forgave her that."

"You forgave her her career!"

"I forgave her for putting it before me. Why couldn't she forgive me? It didn't mean anything. It was only a way of getting through those nights without her, through that long awful winter without her."

There was nothing I could say to that, and again we were silent. "Do you blame me?" he asked finally, as Tony had.

"No, but you blame yourself." I started from the room then, not because I didn't sympathize with his guilt but because I didn't want him to sympathize with mine.

But Papa wasn't quite finished. "Does Cordelia know?" he asked.

"No. She still thinks you're perfect."

His voice stopped me at the bottom of the stairs. "And you hate me."

"No," I repeated without turning. "I love you. I love you very much. But unlike Cordelia, I realize you're human."

Though the war was beginning to turn against Papa, he remained optimistic and undaunted. Unrealistic,

Tony said. Judges would decide, but judges do not make decisions in a vacuum. They're political animals. They listen to the people, and the people listen to the media. The media had spoken again and again of the Consolidated Life Building. The Supreme Court handed down its decision in October. The library was a landmark. Papa's building would deface that landmark. Papa had lost. His monument would stand only on paper.

The following day the American Institute of Architects awarded its gold medal, architecture's most prestigious award, to Adam Kirkland. Papa announced he would not accept it. "A gold medal," he told the press, "awarded by men with minds of dross." Even beaten and broken, he had twice the courage and three times the pride of most men.

"Unless you want to accept it on my behalf, Tony, on behalf of all the right-thinking, backward-looking architects who are making a profession of *not* building. Because that's what the award is for—for not erecting one of the greatest buildings ever designed. For not working. As long as I was working, I was too controversial."

"You're still working," Cordelia said.

We were on the deck of the house on Nantucket, and Papa put his arm around her shoulders. "Don't patronize me, Cordelia. I may be finished, but I'm not senile."

"You're not finished," I added lamely.

Tony was silent. Papa didn't really blame him for his defeat; he just envied him his youth. But Tony blamed himself, almost as much as Cordelia did. I suppose I was the only one who didn't blame Tony. And I suppose that was one of my attractions for him.

That and Cordelia's absence. She was still spending a great deal of time in Japan, and this was the first weekend we'd all been together in months. I was not enjoying it. I don't think Tony was either, though that might have been wistful thinking on my part. At night I lay alone in my childhood room and thought of Tony and Cordelia in hers. I pictured him crossing the strip of bare wood floor between beds, the Rubicon of a tense marriage. I speculated on Tony and Cordelia and tortured myself with images of them. I saw desire flicker like a flame in his eyes, tasted the warmth of his mouth, felt the strong network of tendon and muscle beneath smooth suntanned skin. I imagined ecstasy. I lived with agony. And if you think I'm being melodramatic, you've never been in love.

The weather was magnificent. Each morning dawned cool and clear. As the sun climbed across the cloudless October sky, the air grew warm enough to sunbathe. The island had already assumed its autumn personality. Tourists no longer clattered over the cobblestones of Main Street, most of the cottages were boarded up for the winter, and the reds and violets and whites of the summer wildflowers had turned to more autumnal hues. They were brighter than our somber mood. I don't mean to imply that Papa was feeling sorry for himself. His behavior made it clear that the world rather than Adam Kirkland was the loser. He refused sympathy and avoided self-pity. Each day he arose before the rest of us and walked on the beach. Though he said he wasn't working, he spent the mornings in his studio. At lunch he ate well and seemed to enjoy the wine. On Saturday afternoon he trounced Tony on the tennis court.

"That was nice of you," I said afterward when Tony

258

joined Cordelia and me on the beach. "To let him win, I mean."

Tony mopped his forehead with a towel and laughed. "I didn't let him win, Julia. I gave it everything I had and still couldn't beat him."

Saturday night we sat up late with several bottles of Papa's splendid Château Palmer and his wonderful stories of this architect and that building and the old days with Mother. He wasn't thinking of the days just before she died now, but of earlier happier times. I was sure of it.

On Sunday Tony suggested a rematch, but Papa said he didn't feel like tennis. He said he'd rather walk on the beach. When Cordelia offered to go with him, he said he wanted to be alone. I remember thinking at the time that it was strange he'd gone back to the house instead of starting off across the dunes, then decided he wanted to get a sweater. The breeze was freshening, and October afternoons can turn cold on the island.

After he left, the three of us sat on the beach making desultory conversation. We were not a comfortable group. I was leafing through a script I'd been sent, and Tony asked me about it. I started to say that I'd told him about it a week ago, but caught myself. We didn't lie about the time we spent together when Cordelia was away; we simply didn't mention it. I told him it was a screenplay that my agent wanted me to do. He asked if I was going to. I said I couldn't decide. Neither of us dared to say what we meant. Tony wanted to know if I was going to leave. I couldn't decide whether I should stay. Cordelia lay on the sand and pretended to sleep, or maybe she wasn't pretending. I didn't know what Cordelia was thinking these days. We spoke little and then only about Papa.

We were silent again, each lost in individual thought. The sound of the surf was mesmerizing, almost reassuring. It was late in the season, and no gulls screeched overhead in warning. The wind whispered through the brush. I remember thinking that afternoon that the island was as quiet as I'd ever heard it. Then it came. I didn't recognize the sound at first, and I don't think Cordelia did either, but Tony knew it immediately. Tony had hunted as a boy.

At the sound of the rifle report, he was on his feet. Cordelia and I looked at each other. I saw the chilling fear in her eyes, and I suppose she read the same in mine. We began running after Tony.

I hadn't stopped to put on my sandals, and the rocks and shells hurt my feet, but I kept going, running as fast as I could, listening to my own shallow breathing and the terrible prayer that kept running through my mind. *He couldn't have. He couldn't have. He couldn't have.*

Tony's long legs carried him swiftly, and Cordelia and I were straining to keep up. I saw him climb a dune, then disappear down the other side of it. As we reached the bottom, he reappeared at the crest. His face, beneath the tan, looked as bleached and worn as a piece of driftwood.

"Don't!" he shouted. "Don't come any farther!" But Cordelia and I kept running over the sand, soft and sucking beneath our feet. Cordelia stumbled once, and I fell to my knees, but we kept going, crawling, clawing our way up the dune. When we reached the top, we saw Papa on the other side. His blood made a crimson stain on the sunbleached sand. He'd left his final mark on the landscape.

I heard a scream. I don't know whether it was Cordelia's or my own. I had no awareness, no will. I moved to Tony as if driven by some outside force, and he came to me the same way. I felt his arms around me, comforting me, seeking comfort for something that admitted no comfort. I knew nothing but that Papa was dead. But Cordelia, always the rational one, always the intelligent one, knew that and one thing more. She said later that at that moment, at the moment we came upon Papa's lifeless body, she knew that her sister and her husband had become lovers.

Papa had been right that night we'd argued. I'd lied to him, and Tony had lied to Cordelia, and perhaps we'd even lied to each other. But we hadn't lied to ourselves. We knew from that night in Tony's apartment, that night I'd put on my coat to leave but hadn't left, that we were not nice people.

BOOK THREE

Tony's Story

10

The first debate I ever had with Adam Kirkland was about monuments. Every successful architect, he'd argued, builds monuments to himself. I suppose he was right, and I suppose I'm no exception to that rule, but sometimes I think the clearest statement I could leave for posterity would be a single line on my tombstone. *Here lies the man who loved both Kirkland sisters.*

Because I did. I loved them both, and I lost them both. Don't misunderstand me. I'm not asking for pity. I don't have any for myself. I knew what I was doing when I married Cordelia. By then I was over Julia—for good, I thought. It never occurred to me that if things had changed once, they might change again. I was too young to know about time and the nasty tricks it plays. Adam used to worry about its ravages on the creative spirit and the body and, I knew from a comment he made once when we were alone, the sexual appetite. No, not appetite, performance. I recognized those changes, and thought, with the unbridled arrogance of youth, that I was prepared for them. I was prepared for nothing. Especially not for Adam. He cast a long shadow over both his daughters' lives, but especially over Cordelia's. When we married, I thought love and reason and intelligence would illuminate our lives so completely there would be no shadows. I was wrong.

I'm not trying to put the blame on Cordelia. Or excuse myself. There are those who say I was just greedy, and I suppose I was, but before you judge me, put yourself in my place.

I can still remember the first time I saw them. I'd gone to Nantucket for a look at Windswept. The only romance I had on my mind that day was the romance of that clean concrete and glass bunker that I'd seen in dozens of books and magazines. The powerful concept and the pure expressive structure were more exciting to me than any flesh and blood girl. Oh, I liked girls well enough. I dated them when I could and slept with them when I could, but I wasn't ready to get seriously involved with any of them. For one thing, I didn't have the money. For another, I didn't have the time. Architecture was my vocation and avocation, my wife and mistress, my life and passion. Architecture made every girl I'd ever known just a little silly by comparison. Until I met Cordelia and Julia Kirkland.

I met Cordelia first, if only by a few seconds. You should have seen Cordelia at nineteen. She was like a thoroughbred filly, clean-lined, sleek, and high-strung. Her long dark hair swung easily against the beautiful bones of her face. Her dark blue eyes were quick, intelligent, and sardonic. I thought she was the most wonderful girl I'd ever seen. Then Julia stood and joined her at the railing of the deck. I didn't revise my opinion, only doubled it. Julia's face, framed by that mane of honey-colored hair that made me think about tangling my hands in it, was smoother, softer, more sensual. Her eyes, more violet than blue, were provocative rather than inquiring. They seemed to promise a great deal, and absolutely nothing. Her body . . . well, I was a very young man, and Julia Kirkland in a bikini was something I'd only dreamed of. Standing there looking up at the two of them, I thought they were opposite poles of one irresistible magnetic field. I didn't stand a chance.

Of course, Adam was no help. I suppose I fell in love with him that first day too, maybe even before that first day. He was the father I'd always wanted, the mentor I'd never had, the genius I could always look up to, the benchmark I had to surpass. I knew as I stood on the sun-drenched deck that deceptively peaceful July day, my knees weak more from the sight of those two girls than my fall, my head swimming with the scent of their warm skin and the sight of their young bodies and the challenge of Adam's questions, that my life would never be the same again.

I was drawn to Julia first. For one thing, she was more obviously attracted to me. Cordelia made it pretty clear what she thought of me that first day—a hungry young man on the make. For another, Julia was more obviously beautiful. And as long as I thought I had a chance with Julia, I tried to stay away from Cordelia. I swear I did. I don't count that night at Adam's party. I was pretty drunk and damn angry. And anyway nothing happened. As for that day we drove out to the site on Long Island, well, I guess we both forgot ourselves in the shared excitement of the moment. Cordelia and I work well together. We always have. Or almost always. And there's an erotic undercurrent to the creative urge. But I don't want to overanalyze it. We were both young and healthy, and she was so damn beautiful that afternoon. Her color was high, like something in a Fra Angelico painting, and her eyes were as clear and bright as mirrors, and there was nothing I could do but kiss her. Of course, by then things had begun to go bad with Julia, and when she married that son of a bitch Warren, I felt free to go after Cordelia.

Cordelia never believed that, but it was true. I was actually relieved when Julia dumped me. By that time I was pretty fed up with her. And by that time I was already half in love with Cordelia. And once I started seeing Cordelia, certainly once we'd made love, I never gave Julia another thought. I swear to that. (It occurs to me that I keep swearing to things, but, after all, my past behavior doesn't exactly inspire trust.) Anyway, during those first years with Cordelia, I really did forget about Julia, no matter what Cordelia thinks. And I was happier than I'd ever been in my life. I loved my work, and I loved her. I don't mean to sound as if there were no problems. I admit I was jealous of Adam, of Cordelia's adoration of him, but I loved Adam too. And I admit sometimes there were tensions working with Cordelia, competing with Cordelia, worrying that I'd be outstripped by Cordelia, but we always managed to overcome them. To put it in simple terms, we always managed to keep the drafting room and the bedroom separate.

No, that's not true. I remember one night; we'd been married less than a year, and we'd both been working late in the small studio we'd built under the skylight. There was a fire in the grate, and through the windows overhead the stars were as hard and cold as diamonds, and we ended up making love on the rug in front of the hearth. Somewhere along the way we managed to knock over a bottle of ink and ruin one of my sketches.

Afterward Cordelia felt terrible, but neither of us had even noticed at the time. When I remember what her skin looked like in the firelight and the reflection of the flames in her eyes . . . but I'd rather not think about that now.

I loved Cordelia, the way I'd never loved anyone or anything, except maybe my own vision of a building or the feel of stone and steel in my hands. And then everything fell apart.

Cordelia blames it on Julia, and Julia blames it on the competition, but I don't think it was any one thing. Sure, losing the competition to Cordelia hurt. It hurt me, but it didn't break me. I still believed in myself. I still loved her. And things would have been all right if she hadn't spent all that time in Japan. But it wasn't only Japan either. I missed her. I ached for her. And in her absence I started noticing Julia again. In those days Julia was pretty hard to ignore. In the first flush of success she'd blossomed like a lush tropical flower. It was impossible to keep from looking at her. And it was hard, when you looked at her, to keep from touching her. But I never would have, if Cordelia hadn't come home from Japan pledged to Adam's cause and spoiling for a fight with me. It was the first week in March, the week Graham Fowler turned up again, though Fowler didn't have anything to do with it. At least not at that point.

I can forgive Cordelia for a lot that happened that week. I can forgive her for spending most of the ride in from the airport asking me about Adam and the fight over his building. I can forgive her for insisting on going to the office the following morning despite the fact that we hadn't seen each other in weeks. I can forgive her for dragging me out of bed that Sunday to have brunch with Adam and Julia. After all, she wanted to see Adam, and she didn't know that I didn't want to see Julia. Correction: that I was afraid to see Julia, because if I hadn't wanted to see her, I wouldn't have kept turning up, almost against my will, certainly against my better judgment, at the theater. I can forgive Cordelia for all that, but I can't forgive her for expecting me to surrender my intelligence to Adam's, defer my judgment to his, sacrifice my principles to him. Or maybe I simply couldn't forgive her for loving Adam more than she loved me.

It started the night she got home. It was after midnight, and we'd just made love. To be accurate, we'd been making love since five-thirty. As I said, I'd been aching for her. Perhaps that was the problem. I was no longer lonely. Cordelia was by my side, her slender body molded to mine. I knew I still loved her. I knew I no longer had to be afraid of Julia. I had no defenses. And that was when she struck.

We'd opened one of the bottles of wedding champagne, and she poured the last of it into my glass and her own. "You're not really against Papa's building, are you?"

The words should have put me on my guard, but they didn't. Her body beside mine was warm. Her hair lay like a thick cape over my shoulder. "I'm crazy about his building. I just don't like where he's planning to put it."

"The right building in the wrong place at the wrong time." She was the one who first used the phrase that would come back to haunt us all.

I didn't move but the muscles of my body tensed. I felt a similar response in Cordelia. The languor of sweet, soft fulfillment was gone. "As a matter of fact, yes."

She sat up and faced me, and all I could think was that her body was as strong and straight and true as the building she was fighting for. "You can't say that."

I reached for her, but she moved away. "Adam knows how I feel."

"I mean you can't say it in public."

"I don't intend to."

"Of course, you'll come out in support of Papa on the mayor's council."

Perhaps it was the "of course" that did it. "I've resigned from the council."

Her eyes, so soft a moment ago, grew wide with disbelief. "You might as well say you're opposed to the plan."

I put on my glasses. "But I don't want to say I'm opposed to it, so I resigned."

She got up and put on a robe. Watching her fine body disappear into the folds of fabric was like watching a handsome building being defaced by aluminum siding. "Couldn't you just hedge a little? Talk about the superb design."

"You mean couldn't I just lie?"

"My God, Tony, you make it sound like the most important event of the century."

"No, Cordelia, you make it sound that way. You make it so important, you make him so important that everything else, everyone else has to be subordinated."

"It's little enough to ask."

"Adam doesn't think so. He hasn't asked me to lie."

"He has his pride."

"So I'm not supposed to have mine."

271

"But you owe—" She stopped abruptly and turned away from me.

". . . him everything?" I finished for her.

She came and sat on the side of the bed, but we didn't touch. "I didn't mean that."

"Of course you did. Before we were married, Cordelia, you believed in me. Now you doubt me as much as you do yourself. You're not sure of what I've done for myself and what I've done because I'm Adam's son-in-law."

"That's not true." Her voice rang with sincerity, but her eyes gave her away. Doubt crouched in them like a frightened animal.

"It is, and that's one more reason why I can't lie for Adam. Or even for you. Because I still trust my talent, but if I don't stay true to it and myself, if I don't stand up for what I believe, I'll have nothing. Not Adam's respect, not yours, not even my own."

"Are you sure it's your self-respect you're thinking of, or is it your victory? Your victory over Papa. Your chance to show that you're a bigger man than he is."

I knew the answer to that question because I'd been searching my conscience ever since Preston Hunter had posed it, but I also knew from her voice, which had moved from the heat of anger to the chill of disdain, that the question was rhetorical. Cordelia was sure she knew the answer. She was sitting half turned away from me, her back a long stretch of pride and strength. Only the gentle hollow at her waist revealed her vulnerability. I wanted to touch that curve but didn't. "Look, Cordelia, why don't we just forget it? Neither of us is going to make the decision about Adam's building, and you're home for less than a week. Can't we forget it for less than a week?"

She said we could, and perhaps everything would have turned out differently if we had, but the more Cordelia tried not to speak of it, the larger it loomed between us. I could hear it in her voice that afternoon at Adam's when we argued about Graham Fowler's article; I could see it in her eyes every time she looked at me; damn it, I could feel it in her touch that night before she returned to Japan. She couldn't forget Adam, and she couldn't forgive me. After the news services picked up my blunder about the right building in the wrong place at the wrong time, she had to call from Japan to tell me how she couldn't forgive me. I was ruining Adam's life. It never occurred to her what she was doing to ours. She saw everything in black and white.

And then there was Julia, Julia, who recognized the grays, who understood my conflict, who was there in the apartment warm and sympathetic, while Cordelia was halfway around the world, angry and unbending.

I can still see Julia that night. The scenes keep running through my mind like an old movie I ought to forget but can't. The scenes, Julia said later, should have ended up on the cutting room floor, but still I keep running them in the theater of my memory.

She went into the kitchen when Cordelia called, but she must have heard my end of the conversation, because I was angry as well as hurt, and I wasn't exactly whispering. When she came back into the living room carrying the drinks, she was flushed, from embarrassment I think, and she looked more beautiful than ever. Her skin, scrubbed clean of makeup, was smooth and polished as marble, her features so perfect they might have been chiseled. She had a way of moving in her clothes that made you think about how she would look without them. I knew then that I'd lost the struggle.

Maybe that's why I told Julia about Adam's infidelity, though I knew I'd never tell Cordelia. Maybe I was citing precedent. Maybe I wanted to prove to her that if I was no better than Adam, I'd be no worse. Or maybe I just had to keep talking to keep from touching her. But I did touch her. Finally after we'd said all there was to say about Adam and Judith St. John, about the things that had never made sense and the things that were suddenly clear, when we'd circumvented all the things we couldn't or wouldn't say about Cordelia, when she'd put on her coat in a desperate attempt to do the right thing, and I'd helped her with it, still careful not to touch her, when she'd started for the door and I'd felt the loss of her like a dull ache in my stomach, I closed the distance between us and touched her as I'd been wanting to, aching to, forbidding myself to for months. Or maybe it was years. I don't know how to measure the time of my loving Julia. I know only the fact of loving her, and the joy of making love to her. For that's what it was, pure joy. And to this day I can't believe there was any sin in our coming together. There was only love and pleasure, the pleasure of Julia's mouth, the taste of her skin, the thrill of her touch. She was even more beautiful without her clothes. And somehow more real. We moved as if in a dream, but the sensations were real. The sheer, shuddering ecstasy of being with Julia was so real, so vibrant, so vivid that it blotted out everything else. Only later did I think of Cordelia.

So you judge who's at fault. Cordelia for caring too deeply for Adam. Julia for being too desirable. Me for being too much in love with both of them.

I know all this sounds like an excuse, and I've never liked people who make excuses for themselves. So I'll admit it. I'm to blame for wanting them both too much, for wanting, like Adam, everything.

11

I can't recall much about the weeks after Adam's suicide. A memory takes shape, then shatters, re-forms, changes color, shatters again in a kaleidoscope of pain and guilt and bitterness. It was a cruel time, cruelest of all for Cordelia. She'd lost Adam and been betrayed by Julia and me.

Cordelia said that at the moment we came upon Adam's body on the beach and my arms opened to Julia rather than her, she knew what had happened. She knew it at that moment, but she chose not to mention it for more than a week. During those days she walked through life as if she were in a trance, cold to me, aloof from Julia, remote from those who came out of grief or sympathy or curiosity. True to form, Adam had left instructions that he was to be cremated and his ashes scattered over the sea at Windswept. After the memorial service in New York, Cordelia insisted on taking them up to Nantucket herself. She refused to let me go with her, and though she couldn't stop Julia, she succeeded in discouraging her. Julia's grief over Adam was mixed with guilt about Cordelia.

And Adam's letters didn't help. He relinquished his hold over us reluctantly.

Cordelia refused to discuss her letter from Adam. She refused to discuss anything. Julia didn't show me hers, but she said that, among other things, he'd asked her not to turn her back on Cordelia. But he must have known that, under the circumstances, Cordelia would turn her back on Julia.

I didn't open Adam's letter to me until after the memorial service. By then Cordelia had left on her macabre odyssey to Nantucket and Julia had gone to the theater. The show, Cordelia reminded her in a chilly tone, had to go on. The firm had been closed for the day, but I went down to Inter-American House that evening, took the elevator to Adam's office, and closed myself in it with his last words to me. I turned on a single desk lamp. The models glowed eerily in the gloom. I stood before the window, mesmerized by the lights of a living city. How many of those lights were monuments to Adam's genius? I sat behind his desk. I didn't think he'd mind.

My hands trembled as I opened the letter. It was dated the morning of his suicide.

> I have apologized only twice in my life. Once to Judith, and now to you. I apologize for the responsibilities I leave you, and the pain and the chaos. I have tried to tie things up neatly— the firm will go to you and Cordelia, the apartment, the house, and a settlement to Julia; the attorneys know all about that—but I know there will be nothing neat about the aftermath of my death. I regret the anguish I cause you and

my daughters, but I owe this to myself. I owe it to myself to go in my own time and my own way. The time has come. The method is mine.

Over the years I have loved you and I have fought you. In the last battle you won and I lost. I bear no resentment. You were true to your lights, as you saw them. I hope only that those lights don't blind you to your own genius. You sabotaged mine. Don't sabotage your own. Don't squander it in petty concerns and ill-conceived altruism. Build! Build! Build! It's all that matters in the long run. Except love.

I'm leaving Cordelia and Julia in your hands. They're strong women and can take care of themselves. But they're not cold women. Neither of them is meant to be alone. I understand how you love them both. I too loved them both. Why what is permitted me is not permitted you has more to do with the mores of society than the hearts of men. Somehow you and Cordelia and Julia must unravel the tangled skein of your love for each other. You cannot have them both, though I know you will always love them both. Be careful. You can lose them both. I know. I speak from experience.

Be true to them. Be true to your work. The hell with all the rest!

I hadn't cried since I was eight years old, and my father—my biological father, because I'd come to think of Adam as my real father—took a strap to me to teach me some minor lie he regarded as one of life's truths, but that night, confronted with Adam's irrefutable truths, surrounded by the evidence of his genius, grieving for the result of his integrity, I cried.

It was after midnight when I left Adam's office. I went straight to the garage and got out the Maserati I'd splurged on after I'd won my first big commission for the firm. I figured I'd get to Wood's Hole in plenty of time for the first ferry to Nantucket.

I made it with time to spare. Since the season was over, I had no trouble getting the car on the ferry. The day was gray and overcast with a biting wind, but I stayed on deck all the way. I thought of it as penance. I suppose I was bargaining with fate, trading a little self-imposed physical discomfort for Cordelia's forgiveness.

The house was open when I arrived, but Cordelia was not in it. I wandered from room to room. The only signs of Cordelia were an empty mug on the coffee table and her Burberry trench coat, its plaid lining torn where it had been for years, tossed over a chair. The rooms were immaculate, uncluttered, still architecturally thrilling. They conjured up a hundred memories. I recalled a January weekend the first year we were married. Cordelia had said the only way to get away from work was to get away from town. She'd been right. The phone had been disconnected. No one and nothing had intruded. We walked on the beach, joking about frostbite and holding close for warmth and for pleasure. We cooked steaks over an open fire in the hearth. And we made love. In front of the fire, in the narrow bed of her childhood, all over the house, and all through the weekend, we made love.

I remembered another weekend, a few months before Julia married Webster Warren. She'd been in Boston auditioning for a regional theater, and when I'd gone up to see her, she'd suggested we go over to the island for the weekend. I'd been wildly optimistic on the way out, and equally disappointed on the way back. She'd spent a good part of the weekend studying scripts, though she insisted she was only glancing at them at odd moments. We slept in separate rooms. I didn't behave very well, but then I didn't think she had either. I remember calling her a tease. She answered in kind and considerably more coolly. It was not an inspired conversation. It was not a successful weekend.

And I remembered the first time I'd come to the house. I could still picture Cordelia and Julia standing there on the deck, looking down at me, and Adam, imposing, arrogant, the master of it all. It seemed like yesterday. It seemed like a lifetime ago.

I slid open the glass doors to the deck and went out into the chill morning. The beach was half shrouded in mist, but I could make out a figure sitting, knees clutched to her chest, near the water. The curve of her back, the long hair like a dark velvet fringe across her shoulders sent a familiar shiver through me. She was my wife, and I still loved her—despite everything, maybe because of everything.

She didn't hear me approach over the sand, but when I spoke, she neither started nor turned around. "Go away," she said, her voice flat and hard in the soft morning mist. "Go back to Julia."

I was more relieved than surprised. I thought, naively, now that my sins were out in the open, I could begin repenting—and returning. I put my hand on her shoulder. She whirled on me, suddenly on her feet, her face a cold smooth mask of hatred. "Don't touch me! Not now! Not ever!"

"Cordelia." It was a plea.

She started away from me, up the beach, toward the house, hugging her sweater to her. She looked thin and vulnerable. "Don't bother to deny it. I know. I've known ever since we found Papa." She was running along the beach now, and I was running after her. I couldn't see her face, but I could hear the tears in her voice.

"Cordelia, please . . ."

She stopped and turned to me. "Please what?" I could see the tears now as well as hear them. They streamed down her face, and she rubbed them away with the back of her hand. The gesture was childish and touching, and I took a step toward her, but she backed away.

"Please forgive me," I said quietly.

She stopped crying suddenly, and her voice was like a knife. I'd heard that tone before but never from her. It was Adam's tone. "There's nothing to forgive you for. Except marrying me in the first place. You love Julia. You've always loved Julia. I used to know that. It was stupid of me to forget it."

"I love you."

"You have a peculiar way of showing it." Her voice was still Adam's but withering now. Suddenly I was angry.

"As peculiar as your own."

She shivered but that might have been the gust of wind off the water. It blew her hair across her face in long strands, and she didn't bother to push them back. I think she wanted to hide from me.

"You know what kills me, Cordelia? That you

never noticed. Do you know when I first slept with Julia?"

She put her hands over her ears, another childish gesture, but this one was not winning. "I don't want to know!"

"Well, I'm going to tell you," I shouted above her scream. "The night you called from Japan to upbraid me. The night you called from halfway around the world after more than half a year without you to say that I'd betrayed Adam. The night, ironically, after I had tried like hell to defend him, because there was nothing wrong with that building except where he wanted to put it. That was months ago, but you never noticed. I was guilty as sin, so guilty that I wanted to be caught, but you never noticed. You were too wrapped up in Adam to notice. Think of it, Cordelia. Think of when you did notice. Only when Adam was dead. Only then did you have the time or the inclination to notice me again."

Now she pushed her hair out of her face angrily. "I have to give you credit, Tony. You have an affair with Julia, and it ends up being my fault."

"No, it was my fault. I take responsibility for what I did. But for once in your life why don't you take responsibility for what you've done. Because for the last year, you seem to have forgotten one thing—that you were married."

"I'd say you were the one who forgot that. But then Julia always produces a kind of amnesia in you, doesn't she?"

I stood looking at her for a moment, misunderstanding and rage as thick between us as the island fog. "All of a sudden I understand."

"Understand what?"

"You. Us. What happened. You talked about love a lot, Cordelia. And you were convincing. But you never gave a damn about me. You wouldn't have looked at me twice if Julia hadn't first. I was just one more competition with Julia. And after you won that, you went back to the main event. Adam. *Papa*. You grew up competing with Julia for his attention, and you couldn't stop. You still can't. You even fought with her about his ashes. You had to bring them up here alone. And you did. You've won, Cordelia. You've got *Papa* to yourself at last. You and the Atlantic."

"And you've got Julia," she said. "Just as you've always wanted."

Cordelia stayed on the island for a week. By the time she returned, I'd heard from a man named Waters who said he was her attorney. His client, he informed me over the phone, wanted nothing from me but a divorce. I told him she could have it all. I'd be out of the apartment in twenty-four hours. It took me less than one.

The next call came from Adam's lawyer, Albert Fitler. He suggested lunch. We met the following day at the Six Continents. "He lives on," Fitler said, looking around the handsome space.

"He does indeed."

"You know he bequeathed half the firm to you?"

"So he told me in a letter he left."

Curiosity flickered in Fitler's eyes, then disappeared behind the blank professional gaze. "Cordelia wants to buy you out."

I put down my glass, stunned. I hadn't thought about the firm since I'd left the island. I'd thought about work. I'd drowned myself in work. But the firm wasn't work. The firm was a business arrangement.

"I've tried to persuade her not to. For one thing, she can't afford it. For another, the firm will be stronger with both of you. That's the way Adam envisaged it. He said you made a good team."

"We're not a team anymore," I said, regretting the anger that had crept into my voice.

Again curiosity flickered in Fitler's eyes, and again he suppressed it. "So Cordelia told me. I referred her to Waters."

"I'm grateful to you," I said and was immediately ashamed. It wasn't Fitler's fault.

I put down my napkin and stood. I had no more appetite for lunch than I did for this conversation. "Tell Cordelia she doesn't have to buy me out. The firm's hers. She's Adam's daughter. She deserves it."

The professional mask dropped away completely. He couldn't have looked more surprised if his mouth had hung open. "But you can't! Millions of dollars. Don't be hasty." Fitler went on babbling as I left Adam Kirkland's restaurant and Adam Kirkland's building, taking only what I'd entered with years before. My talent, my training, and my two hands.

For the first time in years I had nowhere to go. I couldn't go to the office because it was no longer my office. I couldn't go to my apartment because that too was now Cordelia's. Julia was still in Adam's apartment, and I didn't want to go there. So I walked. A warm rain was falling, and I was glad. It matched my mood. I walked through the rain till my clothes were soaked and my shoes squished with water and I'd lost track of time. I walked up Sixth and down Fifth, cut back and forth between Madison and Park, Lex and Third. I counted the buildings Cordelia and I had loved and the ones we'd hated. I thought of the buildings I would have done with her and the ones I'd still do alone. I wasn't finished, but a part of my life was.

When I got back to the Yale Club where I'd taken a room, there was a message that Cordelia had called. My hand shook as I dialed the number of the apartment that used to be ours. Hope, as the poet says, springs eternal, but her voice managed to stanch the spring.

"That was clever," she said, "but then I always knew you were clever."

"What do you mean?"

"You know I can't take half the firm from you."

"It's yours. You're Adam's daughter."

"He left half of it to you."

"And his wishes must be respected, at all costs."

"I want to buy you out," she said, her voice quick and cutting.

"I want to give you a gift." My tone matched hers.

"I can't take it."

"I won't sell it."

"You're being unfair."

"I think I'm being generous."

"I knew you were ambitious, but I didn't think—"

I hung up the phone. I didn't want to hear what she thought.

I went to the theater that night. When Julia came into her dressing room, her color was high, and her eyes glowed as if a fire burned within her. Applause did that to her. Making love did it too.

"The lawyer came to see me this afternoon," she said.

"Making the rounds of the heirs."

"He said Cordelia wants to buy you out, but you refuse to sell."

"She can have it. I don't want the money."

"I know that," she said impatiently. "Cordelia thinks it's a ploy. They both do."

"I don't give a damn what they think. Do you believe it's a ploy?"

"No. I think it's absolutely in character."

For the next few days Fitler bombarded me with calls. Cordelia increased her offer. She doubled it. She said I could name my price. "You tell her," I told Fitler, "that I don't want her money, but if she keeps this up, I'll give my share to an outsider. Preston Hunter," I added with malicious pleasure.

Fitler called back in minutes. "A brilliant tactic," he congratulated me.

"It wasn't a tactic."

He ignored my denial. "And I must say I'm glad. As I told you that first day, the firm will be much stronger with both of you."

"She expects me to come back?" I asked in amazement.

"Confidentially, I think she needs you back."

I thought of the half-finished plans on my desk, the half-finished buildings around the world. I told him I'd go back.

"I never thought she'd hold out," I told Julia that night.

"You think she's weaker than you are?"

I considered the question for a moment. "No, but I think she hates me that much."

Julia looked at me for a long time before she spoke. "For an intelligent man, Tony, sometimes you say—and do—the stupidest things."

And then Julia and I both did a stupid thing. We made the same mistake men and women have been making for centuries. We assumed that because we were in love we were suited—no, morally obliged—to live together. We were wrong.

12

Julia sold Adam's apartment and bought one almost as large in that bastion of Victorian eclecticism and offbeat affluence, the Dakota. I supposed she felt more comfortable sandwiched between Lauren Bacall and Yoko Ono than she had living among artifacts of Frank Lloyd Wright, Corbusier, and Mies. She filled the apartment with opulent fabrics, Art Deco furniture, and mementos of her own career, Judith's, and even Adam's, though in the negotiations carried on through Fitler—the sisters were not speaking—Cordelia had claimed most of his. Julia made her apartment in her own image—sensuous, sophisticated, and a little erratic. Adam was probably whirling in his grave. I imagined Judith St. John enjoying a sweet vengeance. Cordelia would have hated the apartment. I rather liked it, which was fortunate since I was virtually living there.

By that time I'd gotten a new apartment of my own, but I rarely used it. I spent my nights with Julia, my days beside, if not with, Cordelia. I'd suggested she move into Adam's office. She hadn't hesitated. Neither had she changed anything in it. Each time I entered it from my own adjoining one, it reminded me of a museum. Fortunately, I entered it rarely. We communicated infrequently and only officially. She had her projects, I had mine. She had her life, I had mine.

I can't say it was a bad life. I had my work, more of it than ever. Adam's firm still carried weight. My name was making an impression. So was Cordelia's and with good reason. If the woman had turned out to be less than I'd expected, the talent had turned out to be greater. She was even, though she didn't realize it and I was not about to tell her, beginning to emerge from Adam's influence. The office remained his, but her talent was flowering as her own.

Despite the adjoining offices, we saw little of each other. When she was in New York, I was in Texas. When I was in New York, she was in Montreal. She did several more buildings in Japan, one of them for Graham Fowler. My opinion of Fowler hadn't changed—despite the commissions. I'd disliked him the first time we'd met, and the antipathy had grown with time and contact. He's one of those men who care for nothing but power, who enjoy buying and selling other men—and women—for the sheer pleasure of it. He likes to say that he doesn't know good architecture from bad. Cordelia says that's an act, and in a way it is. Fowler may know a good building when he sees it, but he doesn't care. He'd as soon erect a monstrosity as a masterpiece, if he thought it would make money. Sometimes I think he'd rather erect the monstrosity. He gets a kick out of putting something over on the public, forcing it to live with ugliness, convincing it that it's beauty.

I didn't know what Cordelia saw in him, though I knew she was beginning to see quite a bit of him.

Power, I suppose. Some women are like that, though I never thought she was.

The summer after Adam died, *Eastward* closed, and I took off two weeks to vacation with Julia. She suggested Nantucket, but I said I couldn't handle that. I mentioned Europe, but she muttered something about not wanting to star in a revival of my wedding trip. A friend offered to lend us a house I'd just built for him in that frantic, fad-crazed outpost of Manhattan charading as a summer resort, East Hampton. We accepted. It was a mistake. For two weeks the greats of the American theater, the powers from Hollywood, and the hangers-on who follow both like herds of sheep, drank my gin, clogged the drains of my friend's swimming pool with cigarette butts, and filled our life with inane conversation and incessant name-dropping. And Julia didn't seem to mind a bit. Although to be fair to her, the last weekend when I barred all guests, locked the gates, and told her I wanted her to myself, she didn't mind that either. In fact, she seemed to like it—until Sunday night.

Unable to sleep, I'd gotten out of bed quietly, or so I thought, and come out on the deck. I was sitting there staring out to sea when I heard the boards creak beneath her feet and knew she'd followed me. I don't know what perfume she wore—perhaps it wasn't perfume, only Julia—but the scent was headier than the summer night. She stood behind me, her hands cool on my shoulders. Below us the waves broke quietly, hypnotically on the beach.

"Are you thinking about—"

"No!" I answered before she could finish.

"I was going to ask if you were thinking about Papa."

I was glad she couldn't see my face. "I'm sorry. As a matter of fact, I *was* thinking of Adam."

She moved to the railing of the deck without looking at me and stood gazing out at the undelineated expanse of black sea and sky. The white of her thin caftan glowed against it, and the lines of her body whispered beneath. But when she spoke, her voice was a cry of pain. "Why does everyone I've ever loved leave me?" I was shocked. Julia saved her emotion for the stage and her self-pity for private.

"I won't leave you," I said quietly.

When she didn't answer me, I stood and moved to her side. I took her in my arms then, but we both knew I'd done it too late, if only by a moment. "Don't pay any attention to me." She slipped out of my arms to the other side of the deck as if she were as gossamer as the caftan. "I always go a little mad under a full moon."

"Julia," I said without looking at her, "the divorce will be final in a few months. . . ."

"And you want to make an honest woman of me."

"I'd like to marry you."

She came back across the deck and into my arms. "I think part of you would." She dropped her head back and smiled up at me. "But only part of you. Things are fine as they are, Tony. Let's not ruin them."

"Does that mean you don't want to marry me?"

She was still looking up at me, but she was no longer smiling. "For once in my life I'm doing the sensible thing. I love you, and I believe you love me, but love and marriage aren't necessarily the same thing, despite what the popular songs tell us."

I started to say something, but her mouth on mine stopped me, and her body pressed against mine, warm in the coolness of the summer night, yielding, promising, fulfilling, made me forget all the words.

Julia spent the rest of the summer reading scripts. The bed was littered with them. I had to fight my way through them to find her. When I turned in my sleep, the sound of them hitting the floor awakened me.

In September she went to the Coast to make a movie. I told her I'd miss her and meant it, but the night after she left I stayed late at the office. I was surprised when I looked up from the plans I was working on and saw it was after midnight. I was also relieved that no one had called to interrupt me. When Julia was appearing in a play, she liked to go out after the performance. When she wasn't, she liked to go out.

I worked late most nights that Julia was away—she flew home for two weekends, I flew out for two—and frequently I saw from the sliver of light beneath the door that Cordelia was working late too. But the door between us remained closed, and once, when I heard Graham Fowler's voice in her office, I could have sworn she locked it. I stayed for another hour after that, but accomplished nothing. Sometimes that happens. You go stale after too many hours. Adam used to say you had to know when to quit. I suppose he had.

Julia returned and went immediately into rehearsal for a new play. The shooting schedule for the movie had been killing, she said, and the play wasn't going to be any easier. She wasn't merely the star, she was in every scene. She came home from rehearsals edgy and argumentative. "Maybe you should have taken some time off before you went into rehearsal," I suggested. "You're running yourself ragged."

She whirled from me to the mirror over the elaborately carved mantel and examined her face critically. "Do I look tired?" I told her she looked beautiful, as always. She leaned closer, smoothing the already smooth skin beneath her eyes. "I look like an eighty-year-old woman."

"A-hundred-and-eighty," I corrected. We both laughed, but I was beginning to see it was no laughing matter. I'd thought of Julia's beauty as a gift, but I was learning it came with a price tag. Together we worshiped it like a diocese full of priests, ministered to it like a team of medical specialists, and calculated it like a couple of actuaries.

One night she came home from the lighting rehearsal in a rage. The lighting director, a plain-looking woman with a prodigious lack of talent, Julia reported, was out to sabotage her. "She never heard of fill lighting," Julia wailed. "It's all key. I'm either in the dark or I'm in a spot. And she has a positively ghoulish penchant for greens. You know how I look in green."

"It isn't easy being green," I sang to her.

She laughed, finally, but I noticed it was taking a little longer each time to humor her out of these tirades. Or maybe I simply wasn't trying as hard.

As the opening drew near, Julia became more distracted. Or perhaps I should say more obsessed. She talked of nothing else. When I tried to, a glazed look came into her eyes. The opening was scheduled for a Tuesday. On Sunday she suggested I stay at my own apartment for the next few nights. I didn't argue.

On Monday night, or rather 2 A.M. Tuesday morning, she called and asked me to come over. I staggered into my clothing, a cab, and her apartment.

293

"I can't sleep," she said. "Which means I'm going to look like death tomorrow night."

"Tonight," I corrected her and immediately wished I hadn't. "You'll look fine. You'll be terrific."

"I'll be awful. The play is a disaster. And I'm a disaster in it. A badly lighted, green-tinted disaster."

"Why don't you try to get some sleep?"

"Don't you think I would if I could," she screamed. I wished I'd never picked up the phone.

"Have you taken anything?"

"I can't. If I take a Valium, I'll be like a zombie tomorrow. And if I have anything to drink, I'll look like one."

"Hot milk," I suggested. "My mother used to swear by hot milk."

"Do you want me to throw up—again?"

She went into the bedroom, and I followed her. "Maybe if you hold me." I took off my clothes and got into bed beside her. I knew that she was not thinking of sex, and to be perfectly truthful, I wasn't much interested either. My mind said there was a beautiful woman in my arms, but my instincts recognized a willful child throwing a tantrum. I held her as I would a child I wanted to calm. She dozed off a little after five. I managed an hour and a half of sleep before I crept quietly from her bed.

"You look awful," Cordelia said when she came into my office with some plans that morning. It was the first personal thing she'd said to me in more than a year.

Julia need not have worried. She looked wonderful, as I'd predicted. She was wonderful, as I'd predicted. The audience loved her. At the party afterward the angels and producers and director and cast loved her. And she basked in that love as if in a spotlight.

The party was given by one of the producers. He was powerful in movies as well as the theater, Julia told me, and I believed her. His apartment looked like the set of a soft-core porn movie. There was fur everywhere, on the floor, the walls, the furniture. There were mirrors everywhere, including the ceilings of the bedroom and bath. There was a heart-shaped bed, covered in satin and fur, and a bathtub big enough for four. It was the most grotesque apartment I'd ever seen. I wanted to run screaming from it into the night, but I didn't. I stood in a corner with a drink in my hand and a smile pasted on my face and agreed with the few people who talked to me that Julia had been sensational.

A little after twelve one of the gofers arrived with the morning papers. You could have heard the proverbial pin drop. Then suddenly there was a great deal of screaming and laughing and mutual congratulations. "In a season of grim darkness Julia Kirkland lights up the stage." Her performance was "stunning." She was "dazzling." One critic suggested that she be designated a national treasure. Another warned that if we were to see nothing else this season, we must see her.

An old friend of Julia's, Sean Wellihan, proposed a toast. It was adoring and, I suppose, witty. I wasn't impressed, but then I wasn't much impressed by Wellihan. He was too perfectly handsome and silkily charming to be real. On the other hand, I suppose if he hadn't been both of those things, I would have resented his behavior toward Julia. As it was, I simply chalked it up to a little sexual overcompensation on his part. I wasn't jealous of Wellihan, but I was tired of him. By two o'clock I was tired of the whole bunch of them. The party was still going strong, but after an hour and a half of sleep in the last forty-eight, I was no match for it. I should have left, but it was Julia's night, and I didn't want to ruin it. I didn't want to, but I managed to, or so she told me later.

We got back to her apartment a little after three-thirty, the shank of the evening for theater people, but I was not theater people. I'd never seen Julia so high, though she'd had less to drink than I had. She needed no artificial stimulants that night. All the way home in the taxi, on the way up in the elevator, while she wandered around the bedroom, she kept up a steady stream of conversation. Her thoughts were as disjointed as her actions. She took off one earring, then forgot the other and asked me to unzip her dress. She started an anecdote about one of the actors, then quoted a line from one of the reviews.

"Didn't you love Sean's toast?"

I said I'd loved it.

"I absolutely loved it," she said as if she hadn't heard me. "Sean is absolutely brilliant."

I agreed that he probably was. I was too tired to disagree.

"He's going to write a play for me. Juicy. Like *Anna Christie*."

"Assuming his talent is like Eugene O'Neill's."

Again she seemed not to hear me. "Lots of whoremadonna stuff. Sean says I'm the incarnation, the personification of every man's ambivalence about woman."

I laughed, a little unkindly I suppose, but I was tired and more than a little fed up with Sean Wellihan and the rest of them. She heard the laughter.

"What's so funny?"

"Wellihan and his ambivalence about women." I regretted the words as soon as they were out. I didn't care about Wellihan's sexual preferences, and I don't like the kind of people who do.

"You think Sean's gay? You think just because he's handsome and sensitive and likes me—doesn't just want to sleep with me, but actually likes me—that he's gay?"

"I assume he is. Not that it matters," I added and regretted the self-righteous tone.

"Well, you couldn't be more wrong—not that it matters." She was an excellent mimic. I heard the echo of my own voice perfectly, and something else. I took it to be innuendo.

"I suppose you're speaking from experience."

"Would it bother you if I were?" The statement was a taunt rather than a question, and like all taunts, it brought out the worst in me.

"It sure as hell would."

"The old double standard. You can be married to Cordelia and sleep with me, but I was supposed to spend all those years sitting around chastely waiting for you."

"I never said that."

"But that's what you meant!" she screamed.

"Stop playing to the third balcony. Ellen will hear you."

"Ellen will hear you," she mimicked again. "You think we'll shock her? It's a little late to worry about that, isn't it?"

We went on that way for some time, saying things we didn't mean, arguing about things we didn't understand. There was no issue, no substance, and that only made it worse, because we weren't angry about anything, we were only angry at each other.

We began to spend less time together. Given our different schedules, the change wasn't hard to justify. We justified it to each other, but we both knew the truth. We began to quarrel more often. Sometimes we quarreled about previous quarrels. One night Julia berated me for ruining her opening night with a jealous tirade. "You spoiled the best night of my career!" she screamed. "The best night of my life!"

"*Your* career!" I shouted back. "*Your* life! Don't you ever think about anyone but yourself?" I slammed the door to her apartment on her answer.

The reconciliations were as passionate as the arguments. We each blamed ourselves for every sin in the book. We forgave each other extravagantly. We made love desperately. Life became a roller coaster, thrilling races to the heights followed by terrifying plunges to the earth, followed by another climb to the top. Julia thrived on the excitement, the uncertainty, the drama. I was not so resilient.

The strangest part of it was that the most destructive argument was the least violent. It was a Sunday night, and we'd gone to a cocktail party with seventy-five of Julia's closest friends, all name-dropping, cheek-kissing denizens of the New York–L.A. axis, and on to dinner alone. I was telling her about an important new commission I'd won that week. "The best part of it was that we didn't go after it. A couple of months ago I got a questionnaire from a Fortune 500 company. They'd sent them out to the top ten architectural firms in the country. The idea was that we'd answer the questions—basic stuff on how we'd solve various architectural problems—and they'd score the firms.

Naturally, I threw it away. When they called and said our questionnaire must have been lost in the mail, I told them it was lost in the trash. I also told them we didn't design by the numbers or answer questionnaires. The flunky hung up on me, but a few days later I got a call from the president. They were building a new headquarters. He wanted to know if I had any ideas. I told him if I didn't I was in the wrong business. Well, we had lunch, and this was the upshot." I took a pen from my pocket and began to draw on the expanse of white linen between us. When I looked up, all I could see was the disgust in her eyes.

"Don't you ever think of anything but architecture?" I'd heard her say the same thing dozens of times, to Adam, to Cordelia, to me, to all of us together, but I'd never heard her say it quite that way. Her smile was full of scorn, her voice icy.

I remembered the months Cordelia had been in Japan. "You used to say I was the only one who made architecture as exciting as Adam said it was."

"I used to think that."

We finished dinner in silence. When we reached her apartment, I made no attempt to follow her in, and she didn't ask me to. I was scheduled to fly to Palm Springs the next morning, and Julia knew it. I didn't telephone her before I left for the airport, but then she didn't call me either.

When I returned two days later, I was surprised to find a driver and limo waiting. Julia was in the rear seat. She kissed me hello lightly. I knew Julia's kisses. This one tasted like good-bye.

She asked me if I'd had a good trip. I said I had, but was careful not to elaborate. She indicated the console in front of us and asked if I wanted a drink. Suddenly I did. I poured one for each of us.

"Is this yours?"

"The producers leased it for me for the run of the show."

"Convenient."

"Necessary."

"Now that I won't be around to hail cabs for you?"

"I love you, Tony."

"But?"

"You know the answer."

"It doesn't work?"

"Well, it doesn't."

"Maybe we haven't tried hard enough."

She turned to me, her face serious, her eyes a deep, thoughtful violet. "You don't believe that."

"No, I don't. I think we both tried."

We were silent for the rest of the way into town, but it wasn't an uncomfortable silence. She'd taken off her gloves, and her hand lay in mine trustfully. We weren't angry at each other. In fact, I think for the first time in a long time we knew we genuinely liked each other. Julia must have sensed it too, because when the driver pulled up in front of my apartment house, she turned and smiled at me, not that dazzling public smile, but a private one so intimate it made me want her all over again. But I knew she was right. It was no good.

"We'll still see each other, won't we?" she asked.

"Of course. We're still, as they say, friends." I started to get out, then turned back to her. "No, we're more than friends, Julia. I love you. I always will."

She put her cool fingers against my cheek and kissed

300

me. Again it was light, and again it tasted of good-bye.

"I'll always love you too, darling. And not as a brother."

I never told Cordelia that Julia and I were no longer together—as I said, we talked infrequently and never personally—and she still refused to speak to Julia, but she must have known. In the columns Julia's name was linked with a variety of men. Photographs of her on various tuxedo-clad arms appeared in the papers and magazines. Some of the romances, I felt sure, were trumped up for publicity purposes. Others, I felt equally sure, were more genuine. But the steady stream of names troubled me less than a single one would have. Except when I saw her name linked with Sean Wellihan and remembered the expression on her face when she'd told me I couldn't have been more wrong about his being gay.

Meanwhile Cordelia and I went on working together, Cordelia and Graham Fowler and I. He was putting up a lot of buildings, and we were designing all of them, or rather Cordelia was. I had little to do with him, which was fine with me. I didn't know when the client-architect relationship between them turned to more, and I didn't care. Occasionally I found myself wondering why she didn't marry him. I even broke our rule of impersonality and asked her about it once.

We were in Adam's office, Cordelia's office now. I entered it so rarely that it was still Adam's to me. We'd just finished a meeting with the partner who handled the financial side of the firm. Business was good, our reputation was better than ever, and the ink flowed a reassuring and constant black. Cordelia sat

301

behind the big sleek desk that had been Adam's, looking impossibly smug—and, I admit it, impossibly pretty. I spoke without thinking. "Come on, I'll buy you a drink to celebrate our outrageous success."

She looked startled, but recovered quickly. "I'll buy you one." She nodded toward the bar in the corner. "It's still fully stocked."

I walked to the bar. "Still scotch?" I asked.

"Vodka."

I was willing to bet that Fowler drank vodka but didn't ask.

I handed her a drink and leaned back in one of the client's chairs with my feet on her desk. I knew that annoyed her, but then the thought of Fowler had annoyed me, at least for a split second.

"I remember the first time I ever had a drink in this office."

Again she looked startled, and again she recovered quickly. "We fought then too."

"We're not fighting now, Cordelia."

"I saw your sketches for the Alden house." She became, if not all business, then businesslike. "It's the best thing you've ever done."

"You say that about every new thing I do. Correction: you used to say that about every new thing I did. Except the Japanese competition."

She ignored my comments. "You should do more residential work."

"It doesn't bring in the money the big jobs do."

"The money seems to be taking care of itself."

"Thanks to Graham Fowler."

She ignored that too. "Your use of the waterfall is inspired. The obvious thing would have been to let it cascade through the house in a single plunge. But you've worked it so you meet it in a different setting at each level."

"I thought you'd like that." It was true. For some reason I'd been thinking of Cordelia when I'd come up with the solution to the waterfall problem. "It evolved from a sketch I'd made of that waterfall in the south of France the summer after we were married."

She turned the swivel chair to face the window behind her desk and the panorama of the illuminated skyline, but not before I'd seen that she actually blushed. We'd made love under that waterfall, but then we'd made love everywhere that summer.

When she turned back to me, she was no longer blushing. Her face was serious and, I thought, tense. "How is Julia?"

"I don't see much of Julia these days."

"I gathered that, but you do see her."

"She's out on the Coast for a few months. I had lunch with her on my last trip to L.A. She's fine. Very successful. Turning down scripts right and left."

"She was good in her last movie. Very good."

"You saw it?"

"Of course, I saw it. How is she otherwise?"

"Fairly happy, I think."

"Good."

"What about you, Cordelia? Are you fairly happy?" Her smile was tight. "More than fairly."

"Then why don't you marry Fowler?"

The smile collapsed. "Do you want another drink?"

"You haven't answered my question."

"Maybe he hasn't asked me to."

"I don't believe that."

She looked at her watch and stood. I took the hint.

At the door to my office I stopped and turned back to her. "It was good talking to you, Cordelia."

She looked up from the papers she was stuffing into a Mark Cross briefcase, and her face flushed again. "It was good talking to you too," she answered quietly.

I laughed. "Don't sound so surprised about it."

13

I'd meant what I'd said to Cordelia, and she must have meant it too, because after that our working relationship drifted from correct to cordial to almost friendly. The door between our offices didn't stand open, but it opened more frequently. We traded opinions, sought advice, swapped professional gossip, offered congratulations and even criticism. That was how I got involved in the Fowler Building.

It was an afternoon in October, and I'd just returned from a topping-out party. I was feeling pretty good about myself. There's something about the sight of that flag flying over the completed steel skeleton that has sprung from your own imagination that makes you feel pretty good about yourself. I'd had a beer with the workmen and another with the engineers and had walked the forty-odd blocks back to the office because I was pleased with the crisp autumn day and my building and myself. I was so pleased that I went straight to Cordelia's office.

"How did it go?" she asked.

"Well. The building is nothing less than magnificent—if I do say so myself—we're on schedule, and the construction workers were civil—even though I am a goddamn architect."

"No falling tools or flying bricks?"

"Not during a topping-out party. But a construction worker actually did try to drop a brick on me about a year ago. At that college dorm in Ohio. When I got out there, I found they were using the wrong stone on the facade and made them tear it all out. That was his revenge."

"My God!" She looked horrified. "Were you all right?"

"As you see. I lead a charmed life."

"They've never thrown anything at me, but I hear them making bets on whether and when I'll fall. And their language gets even more foul, if that's possible."

"And what do you do?"

"Depends. I usually play deaf, but occasionally I give them a bit of their own back."

"Do they still make comments about your legs?"

"I'm getting older." She smiled. "And I wear trousers on site inspections. There's nothing very sexy about a woman in trousers and a hard hat."

"I've seen you in trousers and a hard hat," I said and stopped abruptly. We hadn't become that friendly. "What are you working on?" I indicated the plans on her desk.

"Multiuse building for the Broadway renewal project. But I'm not making much progress. Uninspired." She looked from the plans to me with a wicked smile. "It looks like the box that Inter-American House came in."

I moved to the other side of the desk and bent over the plans. My arm brushed her shoulder, but she pretended not to notice. Or perhaps she wasn't pretending.

"It doesn't look like Inter-American House"—I turned from the elevation of the plans—"but you've got a hell of a mess with your kitchen here. It forces you to string out all the restaurants along one axis."

"I know but the client insists on an atrium."

I glanced at the top of the plans. The client was Graham Fowler. I touched her shoulder lightly—camaraderie rather than affection. "I'm sure the client can be convinced of something else." I took a pencil, then hesitated. "Do you mind?"

"Please." She was smiling up at me.

I don't know how long we worked. At one point her secretary buzzed, but Cordelia told her to hold all calls—for both of us. Later she stood and turned on the lights in the office. Later still, I looked up and was surprised to find it was dark out.

We'd turned the building, reduced the atrium, moved the kitchen and restaurants, added three floors to the hotel tower and subtracted one from the residence so that the taller part of the building paid its respects to Broadway and the shorter kept the scale of the cross street.

We were standing side by side behind her desk looking at the plans. I was tired and sensed the exhaustion in Cordelia, but there was a chord of pleasure between us. I felt as if we'd just made love.

"It's good," she breathed.

"It's great," I corrected. "Better than either of us could have done alone."

She looked up at me, and if her eyes weren't exactly trusting, they were no longer wary. There was a pencil smudge on her cheek. I rubbed it away with my thumb. That was a mistake. My watch caught her attention.

"Good Lord, it's after eight!"

I wanted to tell her that business hours were over, but I heard the change in her voice and saw it in her eyes. She'd remembered Fowler and the fact that he was waiting for her somewhere.

I had my own plans that night, though I'd been ready to cancel them. I was going to a dinner party at the house of a client. The husband was extremely rich and frequently absent, and the wife had made it clear some months ago that she believed in a close if not intimate architect-client relationship. I'd managed to keep my distance so far, but I didn't keep my distance that night. The husband was out of town. The wife was attractive in the exquisitely careful and cared for way of women with too much money and time and too few interests. And I was at loose ends. It occurred to me afterward that I was following in Adam's footsteps in more ways than one.

Cordelia came into my office early the next morning. "Graham loved it."

"I'm so glad."

If she heard the irony in my voice, she pretended not to. "He has a few reservations. He wants to see us some time today."

"Not us. You. It's your baby."

She looked at her hands rather than me, and I knew she didn't want this joint meeting anymore than I did. "It's as much your design now as mine."

"And the design's finished. You work with Fowler on the changes. I'm full up today anyway." She returned to her office without an argument.

Fowler was not so reasonable. Two hours later he came striding into my office from Cordelia's. I could tell from the way he did that he was accustomed to bursting into other men's offices unannounced. Cordelia stood behind him in the doorway, looking as if she wished she were somewhere else, but I refused to feel sorry for her. Hell, she'd chosen him.

"I had a few ideas, Tony, and I wanted to know what you thought of them."

He was one of those men who use first names to imply an intimacy that doesn't exist, and it annoyed me. "Sorry, Graham"—I mimicked his style—"but I'm not the designer on this. It's Cordelia's building."

"As I understand it, you both worked on these plans. Cordelia said you solved the restaurant problem and turned the building."

Suddenly I was furious with her, as if she'd told him the intimacies of our lovemaking. "I had a few suggestions. Cordelia's responsible for the plans."

"Of course, she's responsible, but I thought we were all working on this. After all, it's a big project." Fowler was no fool. Without a single personal reference he'd managed to remind me that I was letting personal feelings interfere with business. I took the plans from him and spread them out on my desk. Cordelia looked relieved but not happy.

I listened to his ideas. Though he knew nothing about architecture, he was smart about business. But I still didn't understand what Cordelia saw in him. His mouth was thin, as ungenerous as his manner, and he was damn near bald. I remembered the old adage about bald men and virility and wished I hadn't. To hell with Graham Fowler. To hell with both of them.

"How soon do you think I can see the final plans for approval?" he asked Cordelia. "I'm in a hurry on this one."

"You're in a hurry on every one," she said, then glanced at me nervously.

"We've put the parcel together. Even the last hold-out, the Sarah Siddons. The Shuberts drive a hard bargain, but they finally sold us the theater. Now all we've got to do is demolish it."

I suppose an alarm should have gone off in my head then, but it didn't. Despite Adam's jibes, I'm an architect rather than an historian, and one theater is pretty much like another to me. If I think about them at all, it's in terms of Julia's attributes rather than their own.

Julia returned to New York a few weeks later. She called me occasionally when she was in town, but she didn't this time. I knew she was in only because of the ads announcing her new play—written by Sean Wellihan—and a picture of her in one of the columns—on the arm of Sean Wellihan. Again I remembered the argument we'd had the night of her opening. Apparently, as she'd said, I couldn't have been more wrong about him.

The first time I telephoned Julia's apartment, a man answered. Despite the old caveat, I didn't hang up. He told me Miss Kirkland was not in. He didn't ask my name, and I didn't volunteer it. I was pretty sure it was Sean Wellihan, and pretty sure Wellihan knew it was me. When I called the following day, Ellen answered. Years ago Julia had told me she knew nothing of loyalty, but she'd been wrong. She'd kept Ellen on as her personal maid though she was too old for the job and all the travel. At least Ellen sounded pleased to hear my voice. She asked about me and, at greater length, about Cordelia. Whatever Ellen's view of our triangle, and I had a feeling it contained more than a whiff of fire and brimstone, she kept it to herself.

"How did you know I was in town?" Julia asked.

"It's not exactly the best kept secret. The columns keep tabs on you. And then there was the full page ad in the *Times*."

Her laugh was still deep and throaty, and it still did something peculiar to the back of my neck. "Sean finally wrote me my *Anna Christie*." We arranged to lunch the following week. I'd suggested dinner, but she said lunch was better. I wondered if all her dinners belonged to Wellihan these days.

When she entered the restaurant, every head in the room turned. I told her she was looking more beautiful than ever. I could tell from her glance in the mirror behind the banquet that she didn't believe me or the fifty other pairs of eyes that sent the same message.

We talked about the movie she'd just finished and the play she was rehearsing. She asked what I was doing, and I answered briefly and carefully. I didn't exactly carry a grudge, but I did have a memory.

"And what about Cordelia?" she asked me when the waiter had brought our espresso.

The question caught me off guard. "What do you mean, what about her?"

"Have you patched things up?"

"We're still working together, if that's what you mean."

Though her smile was intimate, it managed to light up the entire room. "That's not what I meant."

"Cordelia sees a lot of Graham Fowler."

"That's bad."

"Fowler's all right."

"Fowler is all right, though you don't think so. He just isn't right for Cordelia."

311

"I don't understand what she sees in him." I regretted the words as soon as they were out.

"Papa," she answered. "She sees Papa in him."

I changed the subject, and Julia didn't return to it until we were outside the restaurant. Her limousine stood at the curb, purring like a fat black cat. The driver held the door open for her, and she started to get in, then turned back to me. "I don't suppose she wants to see me." Julia didn't have to say who *she* was, and I didn't have to ask.

"I think she'd like to, but I don't think she'll let herself."

"Hubris," she said. "Just like Papa." She tried to make a joke of it, but her fine, well-trained voice cracked. She kissed me quickly then and disappeared behind the tinted windows of the limousine that reminded me of nothing so much as a hearse.

Cordelia and I were both tied up in meetings all afternoon, and I didn't get to speak to her alone until after six. When she saw me in the door to her office, she motioned me in though she was on the phone. I heard the change in her voice, as if she were buttoning up an article of clothing, and knew she was talking to Fowler.

"How is our star client?" I asked when she got off the phone.

"Why do you hate Graham?"

"I don't hate him." My voice was elaborately casual.

"You can barely stand to be in the same room with him."

"Okay, you're right. I don't like him. I think he's a cold, unprincipled son of a bitch. No, I take that back. He has one principle: Graham Fowler."

"Isn't that true of most of us?"

I looked at her hard, trying to figure out if she'd changed that much. She seemed the same, a little sleeker, a little cooler, but that might have been the effect of her hair. She was wearing it up again, and it gave her an aloof, untouchable air. Until she bent her head. The line of her neck was unspeakably vulnerable. "No, I don't think it is. Sure, we all run on self-interest, but some of us manage to dilute the fuel a little. Silly as it may sound, some of us still care about other things. About work and beauty and"—I hesitated—"and love."

"And you think Graham doesn't?"

Tired of the discussion, I sat in one of the client's chairs and put my feet on her desk, almost enjoying the frown that flickered across her imperturbable mouth. "Look, I'm sorry I brought the whole thing up. I'm sure Graham is a prince of a guy. And if you're smart enough to see that I don't like him, you're smart enough to know why." Her mouth was not imperturbable now. "Anyway, it wasn't Fowler I wanted to talk to you about." I took a deep breath. "I had lunch with Julia today."

The name seemed to echo through the room during the silence that followed. "How is she?" Cordelia asked finally.

"Fine. A little lonely, I think."

Her smile was tight and ungenerous. It reminded me of Fowler's. "With all her fans and friends—and men."

I wasn't sure whether the last was directed at me. "She'd like to see you."

For a moment I thought Cordelia was going to cry. She rested her head on one hand, her fingers screening her eyes.

313

"Please see her," I said quietly. "For her sake—and your own."

She still didn't answer, and I took a pen and pad, wrote Julia's number on it, and left the office.

Julia telephoned me a few days later. "Thank you." I asked her for what. "Cordelia called me. We're having lunch." Her voice broke in a nervous laugh. "It was quite a logistical problem. She wanted to go to the Six Continents. I held out for Sardi's. We finally agreed on neutral territory: the Palm Court of the Plaza. Where Mother used to take us for tea. But in those days we wore white gloves rather than boxing gloves."

"Oh, to be a fly on the wall," I muttered to myself after I'd hung up.

Lunch was a disaster. I heard Cordelia's side in the office, Julia's over a drink at the Algonquin. The viewpoints varied but not the substance.

"It started off well enough," Cordelia reported.

"We were both nervous as cats," Julia said. "But once we started talking I thought things were going to be all right. The Plaza was a good idea. We started reminiscing about Mother and then Papa. You were not mentioned." She flashed a tantalizing smile. "To tell you the truth, I think we both forgot about you. It was awfully good to see her again."

"It was amazing," Cordelia told me, "how quickly we fell into the old shorthand. You know, one of us would start a story, and the other finish it. I was really glad I'd called her."

"She's still my best audience," Julia said. "Convinced that I'm the greatest actress to hit the boards since Mother."

"We talked about her work for a while," Cordelia

eported. "She still doesn't realize just how good she
s. Then she asked about me."

"I trust you told her about Fowler." I hadn't meant
o interrupt.

"We talked a little about Graham Fowler," Julia
aid. "She's trying to convince herself she's in love
vith him. And about Sean Wellihan." This time her
mile was positively wicked. "Which was odd because
ve both still refused to so much as mention your name."

"And that was when it happened," Cordelia said.
She asked about Graham, and I began to tell her
bout the building. I should have known better. The
ninute I mentioned the location, she went off like a
oman candle. 'But that's the Sarah Siddons!' she said.
Ier voice really is a weapon. She was almost whis-
ering, but every head in the Palm Court turned."

"I didn't think you'd go along with it," Julia said
o me. She was no longer smiling. "I remember how
ou fought to save the library."

"Not exactly fought," I said uncomfortably.

"Cordelia says you're on their side, but I couldn't
elieve it. That's why I wanted to see you. To hear it
irst hand."

"I'm in favor of the building."

"And what about the Sarah Siddons?"

"It's a handsome theater but not a great one. There
re others that are just as good, better architectur-
lly."

"Not to me."

"I'm sorry, Julia. I wish we could put the Fowler
Building somewhere else, but we can't."

"You sound just like Papa. As long as your monument stands, you don't give a damn about anything
else."

315

"It's more Cordelia's building than mine."

She stood and looked down at me, her violet eye
dark with anger. "I'll fight you on this, Tony. You and
Cordelia and Graham Fowler. I'll fight you, and I'll
win." Cordelia was right. Julia's voice was a weapon
She could do anything she wanted with it. And jus
then she'd made it sound exactly like Adam's.

I didn't see Julia after the evening she stormed ou
of the Algonquin lounge, trailing her fur behind her
Even furious, she made a grand exit. It was instinct
I called a few times, but she was never in. Ellen was
so apologetic that I knew she was lying and finally
gave up trying.

"If only I'd kept my mouth shut," Cordelia moaned

"It's not your fault," I told her. "She was bound to
find out sooner or later. You can't raze a theater in
secret."

"You both worry too much," Graham Fowler said
I was sitting with my back to the door of Cordelia's
office and hadn't heard him enter. "I'm just back from
Washington. The Sarah Siddons will not be declared
a landmark."

Cordelia's face lighted up. Whether at Fowler's news
or Fowler's appearance I didn't know. "Are you sure?"

"It helps to have friends in high places, Cordelia
They'll speak to the right people in New York."

I went back to my own office. Fowler had the power,
and Cordelia had the design, and they didn't need me.

Only it turned out, as the battle escalated, that they
needed all the help they could get. Fowler had bought
politicians, but he couldn't buy public opinion, not
when Julia Kirkland set out to mold it. Her name
headed the lists of actors, directors, and playwrights

rallying for the Sarah Siddons. Her signature ran below scores of letters to the editor. Her photograph had always sold papers and magazines, and realizing its value, she'd become more frugal with it over the years, but now pictures of Julia Kirkland on the stage of the Sarah Siddons, in its lobby, beneath its marquee, at a dinner to raise funds to save it, at a rally to incite public opinion in its favor looked out from every newsstand.

The battle raged for more than a year. The wheels of government, as I'd learned in the fight over the library, grind exceeding slow. I saw nothing of Julia during that time, except her photograph, but a great deal of Cordelia. We were field officers in the same army. Fowler was the general. I had to admit he was an excellent tactician. He maneuvered his troops of attorneys, politicians, and public relations people brilliantly. But if Fowler was commanding a professional army, Julia had enlisted the guerrillas. They turned up everywhere, and they were fighting not for money but for a cause.

"He's spending millions," Cordelia said to me at one point.

"He stands to make millions from the Fowler Building," I answered. I'd developed a sneaking admiration for Fowler's abilities as a general, but I still didn't respect him as a man.

The war entered its second year. Julia was still running in Sean Wellihan's play and, from all appearances, with Sean Wellihan. Cordelia took time out from the battle for a week of R and R on an island Fowler had just bought in the Caribbean. According to two of his PR men, he'd bought it as a gift for Cordelia, but she'd refused to accept it. At least I think that was the story. They stopped gossiping as soon as I entered the conference room. All I'd ever offered her was half a firm that was hers by right.

"I told you some people had principles," I said to her a few nights later when we were working late in her office. "Why else would you turn down an island?"

She blushed. "How did you hear about that?"

I shrugged.

"I didn't turn it down entirely." I was irrationally disappointed, and it must have shown on my face. "I mean I didn't accept the island, but I'm going to take the commission. Graham wants to build a huge new resort. Not just a hotel, but a whole village. Houses, condominiums, guest cottages, clubs, shops, everything. It will mean designing an entire town from scratch. You're going to love it."

"Not I. It's your commission."

"It's too big for one designer."

"The hell it is. It's every architect's dream. And you've got dozens of junior designers working for you. Besides, three's a crowd on a desert island. Why don't you put Fowler out of his misery, Cordelia, and marry him?"

"Why don't you mind your own business?" But she laughed when she said it, and for once I knew she didn't mean it.

In March Julia went to jail—for a few hours. When she was arraigned, the judge gave her and the other celebrities suspended sentences. Since they were all gainfully employed, he said, they posed no threat to society. Then came the public hearing.

At first I didn't pay much attention to the announcement of still another hearing on the future of the Sarah Siddons. I'd sat through more than my share of them and had no intention of wasting another morning at this one. Adam had been right. I didn't belong on committees. I had no patience with bureaucracy. But Cordelia was determined to bring me into it. Cordelia and Fowler. I returned from lunch one day to find them in still another of their strategy sessions. I didn't join it though my secretary said they'd asked me to.

Cordelia came into my office later that afternoon. Her dark hair was pulled straight back from her face, accenting the handsome bones. She looked beautiful but severe. Maybe that was the way Fowler liked his women to look. "Didn't you get my message?" she asked.

"I just got back," I lied.

"Graham wanted to see you."

"I doubt that."

She ignored my words. "We were discussing the hearing tomorrow."

"That's public relations not architecture. I've got nothing to do with it."

"He wants me to speak." Her voice was anxious, and her eyes darted to me, then away. She was asking advice, but she was no longer in a position to ask my advice, and I was no longer in a position to give it.

"Are you going to?"

"You know I hate the idea."

I started to say that I didn't know anything about her anymore but caught myself. "Then don't."

"Graham thinks I'm the only one who can carry it off against Julia."

"Graham thinks a lot of you."

Her neck stiffened. "Not that *I* can, that another Kirkland can. That Adam Kirkland's daughter can."

319

"In other words, Fowler wants to stage a three-ring circus with the two of you squaring off in public, and you're going to let him."

"I told you I hated the idea."

"Then why are you going to do it?" I knew now that she was.

"For the building. I'd do a lot more than that for this building."

"Like sleep with the man who's making it possible?" The words were out before I realized it. She turned and walked from my office without a word, as I knew she was.

I felt like a damn fool. She wasn't sleeping with Fowler because of the building. She was sleeping with him because she wanted to. And I no longer had a right to protest or even mind. The divorce courts had seen to that. No, I'd seen to that—almost, if not entirely, on my own.

The following morning I told myself I wasn't going to the hearing. There was no reason for me to attend. There were several reasons for me not to. For one thing, it was scheduled for eleven, and I had an appointment with a client at eleven. At ten-thirty I told my secretary to cancel the appointment. At quarter to eleven I opened the door between Cordelia's office and mine. I suppose I should have knocked. She was in Fowler's arms. I closed the door again. I told myself Cordelia was not my responsibility. And yet I couldn't help worrying about her. In public she was no match for Julia.

Julia had managed to get them to reopen the Sarah Siddons for the hearing. One point for her side before we even began.

I arrived at the theater just as Julia was stepping out of her limo. At first all I saw was a pair of legs, but I knew Julia would follow. I'd know Julia's legs anywhere.

I walked up to her and took her hand, and she wrapped me in her smile as if it were a cloak. "Good luck," I said.

"You're being awfully sporting about this."

Wellihan was behind her by now, leering at me over her shoulder. "The next thing we know you'll be hoping that the best man wins," he said.

"I intend to," I answered.

The theater was almost full. Julia's celebrity had made an obscure preservation issue a cause célèbre. The houselights were up, revealing the Sarah Siddons in all its worn splendor. I was reminded of a beauty who is aging but far from finished. The red plush seats were threadbare, the gold leaf peeling, and the swags musty and faded, but the handsome lines remained, like good bones in an aging beauty's face. The proportions of the theater were intimate and excellent, the proscenium spacious and graceful, the carvings and bas-relief superb remnants of a less hurried age. The chandeliers glowed crystal and gilt, the muses cavorted happily across the proscenium, and the likenesses of Sarah Siddons graced the front of each box. The aging beauty needed new clothes, fresh makeup, maybe even a face-lift, but she was still a beauty.

Cordelia and Fowler were sitting together in the first row. I sat alone halfway down the orchestra. Suddenly I wished Adam were there. I would have liked sitting with Adam during the hearing, and I think he wouldn't have minded sitting with me, despite our disagreement about the architecture and decor. I remembered the letter he'd left me. I'd shown it to neither Cordelia nor Julia, but then they hadn't shown me the letters he'd left them. I suppose we each had our own private Adam that we carried around with us.

Members of various commissions sat at a long table on the stage. I knew most of them. I'd listened to most of them debate for hours and accomplish nothing. I joked with the imaginary Adam at my side. All dozen or so of them weren't worth one of Adam's daughters. Adam's genes and genius and spirit had seen to that. I missed him. And I missed his daughters.

The meeting began slowly. A few of the bureaucrats mumbled through various pros and cons. Then the chairman of the hearing called on Julia. She climbed to the stage with a self-effacing dignity, but it was no good. She might as well have had spotlights focused on her. She was that dazzling.

A lectern stood in front of the long table. She moved to it with her graceful, measured gait. There was nothing cheap or provocative in her walk, but I was sure every man in the theater responded to it. Or was I only remembering the way I did?

She gripped the lectern with her small slim hands as if she were reaching out to every one of us. Her huge violet eyes roamed the audience, and every man in it thought she was looking only at him.

"My name is Julia Kirkland," she began, and a ripple of laughter ran through the audience. "I've come here this morning to speak to you about the Sarah Siddons Theater. The Sarah Siddons is more than a theater to me. It's an old friend, a member of my family. I've played this wonderful theater, and before me my mother, Judith St. John, made history on this stage. She loved it, as I love it, as every serious actor and actress who has ever appeared here does. We love it for its beauty and its technical perfection, for its place in theater history and its potential to keep the American stage alive. But I'm not asking you to save the theater because my colleagues and I love it. I'm asking you to save it because we can't afford not to.

"We Americans are funny people. We have a passion for progress, and that passion has made this country great. We love to build new things. But the other side of that coin is that we tire quickly of the old. We toss away books and clothes and cars. We tear down our houses to build bigger ones. We destroy our theaters and with them part of our tradition. The longest a theater has ever stood in this city is one hundred and three years. The old Bowery Theater was built in 1826 and perished in 1929. Compare us to the rest of the world. In Italy Palladio's Olympic, one of the first roofed theaters, is still in use. In England the old Drury Lane looks much as it did generations ago. But here in New York we do things differently. Here in New York we must destroy to build.

"And what are we going to build here? A multiuse building, Mr. Fowler and his architects tell us, with hotel rooms for those who want to visit New York and its theaters, with living accommodations for artists, with restaurants and bars and meeting rooms, with a spanking new theater. I say bravo! Bravo Mr. Fowler! Bravo the firm of Kirkland and Bain! Bravo to all of it!" She paused for longer than a less accomplished actress would have dared. Her violet eyes swept the audience. "Except the new theater. We don't need a new theater. We have the Sarah Siddons!" Two thirds

323

of the audience erupted in applause. Julia waited for them to finish before she went on.

"The architecture critics tell us the firm of Kirkland and Bain has designed an excellent building. I know something of architecture myself, and I agree. But the firm of Kirkland and Bain has not cornered the market on excellence. There is another kind of excellence. The excellence of sight lines and acoustics so superb that even the most modern technology will never duplicate them." She strode boldly to one side of the stage. "The excellence of being able to walk around a stage freely without a mike taped to your body. The excellence of knowing that the voice you've worked years to train will carry to the second balcony with ease.

"That's all very well, Mr. Fowler and his architects tell us, but we're going to give you not only a better theater but a bigger one. Twenty-two hundred seats, they say. Count them, ladies and gentlemen, they add like barkers in a circus. I say leave the big theaters, the twenty-two-hundred-seat theaters to the circus. Give me these one thousand and sixty-seven seats that you're filling this morning, ladies and gentlemen. Give me a theater intimate enough to let me feel the audience and small enough to fill every night for a serious drama. Give me—no, let me keep—the Sarah Siddons! Let me keep not only a part of the theater's past but the only hope for its future!"

Julia didn't bow though she might as well have. She'd given the performance of her life, only it wasn't a performance. She loved this theater. And the tears that ran down her beautiful face were real.

When the applause finally died after what seemed like an eternity, the head of the commission thanked Miss Kirkland and said that Cordelia Kirkland had also asked to speak. Graham Fowler stood to let Cordelia out of their row. I thought that in his place I would have stopped her.

Cordelia climbed the stairs to the stage and walked to the lectern. She didn't have Julia's magnetic attraction, but she had a certain quiet presence. I like to think that no one else in that theater knew how nervous she was. No one else recognized the telltale tilt to her chin that meant she was steeling herself for combat. No one except Julia.

Cordelia faced the audience. Her eyes, so similar in shape and color to Julia's, didn't sweep the audience. They glanced off mine as a sword might glance off another in a fencing match. They came to rest on Fowler. I suppose all that power gave her strength.

"Like the rest of you, I was deeply moved by Miss Kirkland's words." If she was trying for irony, she'd missed. Her voice, not as well trained as Julia's, not as heart-wrenching, had a disarming intensity nonetheless. "I too am fond of the Sarah Siddons. My mother too scored triumphs on this stage. Judith St. John left us a legacy to beauty and truth. So did her husband, Adam Kirkland. He too believed in excellence. Not only the excellence of the past, a mummified, fixed excellence, but the excellence of the future. He believed in a living, changing city. A city that keeps pace with the growing needs of its citizens. If he were alive today, he would believe in the Fowler Building, which will meet those needs.

"Miss Kirkland admits that the Fowler Building will bring many advantages to an area corrupt with decay. In place of sleazy strip joints and pornography shops, we offer luxury hotel rooms, large meeting spaces, and fine restaurants that will attract income to the city and people to the theater district. In place of cold water flats we offer low-rent housing for performing artists. Miss Kirkland speaks of the rewards of working in an intimate theater, but she says nothing of the joys of living in a closet-sized, rat-and-roach-infested railroad flat.

"And what of the benefits to the rest of the community? Not all of us have Miss Kirkland's prodigious talent. I bow to that talent, but I cower before the high level of unemployment in this city. The Fowler Building will bring twenty-five hundred jobs to New York. True, they are not jobs in the theater or even in the arts, but they are jobs that will allow men and women to earn a living wage, to raise their children with pride, and to live with dignity." I smiled to myself. Adam wouldn't have liked that argument—it was too democratic, and he was too much of an elitist—but he would have used it, just as Cordelia did.

"Miss Kirkland speaks of beauty and excellence as if they were her personal property. They are not. The Fowler Building represents beauty and excellence of another kind. Graham Fowler could erect an ordinary building for less money and still clean up the shame and squalor of Times Square. He could cut corners on materials and methods and still provide twenty-five-hundred new jobs. But Mr. Fowler too believes in beauty and excellence, and that is what his building represents.

"It is true we lose a memory with this building, but we also realize a dream—the dream of a revitalized theater district, the dream of hundreds of young performing artists and thousands of ordinary New Yorkers, the dream of a city that still has the vitality and power and imagination to dream—and to do."

The applause was as loud and as long as it had been for Julia, but unlike Julia, Cordelia was not accustomed to it. She looked surprised. She looked almost frightened. Then she smiled, her fine-boned chin raised not in defiance but in vulnerability, like a child whistling in the dark. As she left the stage, I stood automatically, as if to help her back to her seat. But Graham Fowler was already there, and her place was no longer beside me.

I stayed at the Sarah Siddons for a long time after the public hearing ended. Julia and Cordelia had each left with her own entourage and her own man. I sat in the empty theater, my body slumped in the red plush upholstery, my senses delighting in the fine lines of the house and the handsome if worn decor. It spoke of another era when there was still time and inclination to produce beauty by hand. I understood Julia's feelings all too well, but I understood Cordelia's too. They ran in my blood as they did in hers.

It was after five when I finally got back to Inter-American House. I ran into Cordelia in the hall outside our offices. She was carrying a Gucci overnight bag. In the old days she'd eschewed Gucci, refusing to be a walking advertisement for someone else's initials. Obviously Fowler was corrupting her taste.

"I didn't know you were going away," I said, careful not to sound as if it mattered to me.

"Graham's flying down to Washington. He thinks it would be a good idea, in view of the hearing, if I went along."

I went into my office and spent the better part of an hour looking at plans without seeing them. Then I called Julia. Ellen said she'd already left for the theater and asked if I wanted to leave a message. I couldn't think of one.

I stayed in my office until nine, not because I was working but because it was home. At one point I wandered into Cordelia's. The only changes since Adam's day were the renderings and models of some of the newer buildings. I looked at the model of the Fowler Building. It wasn't as good as Bryant Park Tower which Adam had never built, but it was still pretty good. I was proud and strangely sorry.

I crossed to Cordelia's desk. It was empty except for a telephone, a humicant of pens that had belonged to Adam, and a sketch pad. Even Adam had kept a photograph on his desk, a silver-framed picture of Judith St. John, but Cordelia had dispensed with all personal effects. Neither husband nor lover distracted her from her work.

I glanced at the sketch pad. She'd already gone to work on Fowler's island community. Some of the ideas were good, too good for that philistine to appreciate. I thought without amusement of the irony. Cordelia would go on designing great buildings, and all over the world Fowler's name would come to be associated with excellence, though Fowler himself knew nothing of the trait. I turned out the light over her desk and left the offices of Kirkland and Bain.

The heavy steel letters of my name on the double glass doors of the outer office still gave me pleasure. It was what I'd always wanted, but it was not enough.

I went downstairs to the Six Continents. Julia and Cordelia had left me, but I could still have a drink with Adam's ghost. Though the restaurant was crowded, the maître d' found me a table in a quiet corner of the grillroom. From it I could canvass the entire area and see into the main dining room. Adam's ghost was alive and well.

By the second drink I was almost sure he was there with me. I remembered the letter he'd left me. "Be true to your work. Be true to them. The hell with the rest!" He hadn't mentioned what I should do if they weren't true to me. Yet he must have realized it was a possibility. He'd warned me to be careful. "You can lose them both," he'd written. "I know. I speak from experience." And I had lost them both, as finally and completely as he'd lost Judith St. John in that plane crash.

Adam had known a lot, but he hadn't known enough. He hadn't understood that nothing remains unchanged, neither love nor passion, neither his own unswerving principles of architecture nor the public's view of them and him. He hadn't seen that the people and the theories he'd disdained could prevent him from erecting his last great building.

I was lost in my own thoughts, my eyes blind to the people around me, my senses barely aware of the room Adam had created, my fingers unconsciously busy as they always had to be. Inadvertently I'd twisted the plastic swizzle sticks into a simple structure. The waiter brought me another drink, and I added another support to the arrangement. Then I laughed. It was reminiscent of Adam's design for Bryant Park Tower. My hands had followed my mind. Suddenly I stopped laughing. The solution was so simple I was shocked I hadn't seen it before. But as Adam used to say, the great solutions always were simple—and sudden. The details took time but the concept—if it and you were any good—always struck like lightning, white hot and blindingly illuminating.

We'd use Adam's idea—tall piers and an elaborate truss system—and construct the Fowler Building over the Sarah Siddons Theater. And we could do it more cheaply and more easily than Adam had dreamed. Technology had advanced in the years since his death, and as Adam liked to say, architecture is technology. I downed the last drink, signed the check, and looked at my watch. I hadn't realized how long I'd been sitting there. It was after eleven. Julia might be home from the theater by now.

Julia was home—and so was Sean Wellihan. He opened the door, and when he found me standing there, looked as if he wished he hadn't. Julia followed him into the foyer and stopped when she saw me. She looked surprised, but unlike Wellihan, not displeased. She put her cheek against mine for a moment, a requisite theatrical greeting and not one that could offend Sean, though it seemed to.

She led us into the living room, still cluttered, intimate rather than cozy, and unmistakably Julia. "Sean was just about to get drinks. I won't let Ellen stay up till after the show anymore."

Sean asked what I wanted to drink and disappeared down a long corridor.

"Is he living here now?" I asked, though I knew I had no right to.

Julia laughed. "You're just like Papa. What was it you said about him that time? He wants to design every building, conquer every man, make love to every woman. Yes, Sean is living here now, and don't look that way. You relinquished the role so why should you mind if someone else steps into it?"

"I think you've got things a little mixed up, Julia. I

330

didn't relinquish the role, you replaced me. You're the one who ended things."

"And if I remember correctly, you didn't put up much of a fight then, so let's not fight about it now. Sean is perfect for me. He's in the theater and of the theater, and he understands me."

"Which I never did."

"As a matter of fact, you didn't. But then I wasn't much better for you, was I? Sean is good for me, Tony, and I'm fond of him, but"—she dropped her husky, well-trained voice—"I don't love him the way I love you, so stop making everything more difficult." Her voice broke slightly, and she was so good I couldn't tell whether she was acting. But then for Julia acting was always the ultimate reality.

"If that's true—"

"It's true," she cut me off, "and it doesn't make a damn bit of difference. I don't want to be hurt again."

"I wouldn't—" I began, but Sean's appearance, ice bucket in hand, stopped me. Something in his face made me think that, good playwright that he was, he'd been listening in the wings and timed his entrance. Something in his manner, protective rather than possessive, made me realize that like me, he loved Julia, but unlike me, he accepted her as well. For a moment I almost liked him. I also envied him.

"You gave quite a performance this morning," I said to Julia. "I'm not being sarcastic. It was very moving."

"So did Cordelia. In fact, I have the feeling I was upstaged by an amateur." She laughed her deep throaty laugh. "Though not entirely an amateur. She apprenticed with Judith St. John too."

"She believes everything she said," I insisted.

"You think I don't believe everything I said?" Julia's

voice was cool, Sean's eyes angry. I sensed that he'd like nothing better than to throw me out. I had no intention of giving him the chance.

"I know you did. That's why I'm here."

"You mean I converted you." This time there was disbelief in her laughter.

"What if *I* could convert *you*—to a new plan," I rushed on before she could answer. "After all, preservation doesn't preclude change. What if Cordelia could have her building and you could keep the Sarah Siddons?"

"And you're a magician," Wellihan said, but I could see from the way Julia's eyes opened wider, two huge violet camera lenses letting in the light of my vision, that she'd gussed what I was driving at.

"Papa's monument," she whispered.

"Exactly."

"Look . . ." I took a pen from my pocket and cast around for a piece of paper. She handed me a script, and I turned it over to the blank back. As I began to sketch, she leaned over the coffee table, her head almost touching mine.

"It's a genius stroke," she said, and her breath was warm against my cheek.

"It's so obvious I'm ashamed I didn't see it before."

"You know what Papa used to say." We began to laugh. Both of us knew everything he used to say by heart.

"I wish someone would explain what's going on," Sean said.

We both looked up. I'd forgotten him entirely, and I think Julia had too. She held out a hand to him as if to bring him into our sphere, and I felt another stab of jealousy. "He's going to save the Sarah Siddons," she explained. "He's going to build over and around it." I watched her explaining the sketches to Sean. She was jubilant.

"And Cordelia accepts it?" Her eyes were so full of hope that I hated to answer the question.

"I haven't spoken to Cordelia yet. I came straight here."

Julia dropped the sketches and looked at me. The color of her eyes faded to an icy blue. "Cordelia will never buy it."

"Cordelia," Sean said, "is a bitch."

We both whirled on him. "You don't understand her," we said in unison.

Sean smiled. "My apologies. I seem to have aroused a storm of family feeling."

"She's fighting for what she believes in," Julia said. "And because she believes, she'll never compromise on this." She tapped the sketches with her perfectly manicured index finger. "She's just like Papa that way."

"Only this is based on Adam's plan."

We both knew that fact was the only thing in our favor. But neither of us knew if it was enough.

14

Cordelia returned from Washington the following afternoon. I was waiting with my surprise. I'd kept several draftsmen working all morning, and the plans and rough sketches were ready. But Cordelia had a surprise of her own. It sat on the third finger of her left hand and was big as a headlight and twice as bright. It looked absurdly out of place on her thin hands with the short, carefully trimmed nails and faint ink stains, like a fussy oversized evening gown and smeared makeup on a child playing dress-up.

"Does the island come with it?" I asked. She hadn't shown me the ring, but I could hardly help noticing it. In fact, it was the first thing I saw when I entered her office. It was, I thought, almost as bright as her eyes.

She twisted the ring nervously until the stone was out of sight. "It doesn't mean what you think it means."

I sat in the chair in front of her desk, still holding the new plans, and put my feet up. "Okay, what does it mean?"

She was still toying with the ring. "At least, I don't plan to marry him right away."

"Reservations?"

"Of course not."

"In that case I wouldn't wait too long. He's not getting any younger."

She twisted the ring upright on her finger again. It caught the late afternoon sun streaming through the window, shattered it into a thousand facets, and damn near blinded me. "Did you want to see me about something?" Her voice was as buttoned up and businesslike as the high collared silk blouse and tailored suit. A moment ago all I'd seen was the softness beneath the severe clothes. Now all I saw were the clothes.

"I think I solved our problems." The words startled her. "I didn't mean *our* problems. I meant the Fowler Building." The name tasted like ashes in my mouth. I spread the plans on her desk. She took forever looking at them. I paced the office a few times. I stood at the window and watched the last rays of the sun glinting off the silver and glass spires of the city. I tried not to think about Cordelia sitting behind me and the way the sun had glanced off the stone on the third finger of her left hand.

"I see," she said finally.

I turned back to her. "What do you mean, you see?"

"I see you've been with Julia."

"What's that supposed to mean?"

"She's persuaded you to save the theater." Cordelia stood. "Well, you and Julia are none of my business, but this building is." She tapped the plans with her finger as Julia had. The heavy ring danced clumsily. "I won't let you ruin it."

"I'm not ruining it. If anything, this design is an improvement. The public spaces are more dramatic in a series of levels, we've gained more square feet for

335

Fowler's beloved atrium, and we've saved the Sarah Siddons."

"*You*'ve saved the Sarah Siddons. I'm sure Julia is grateful."

I clenched and unclenched my fists. "She is, but I didn't do it for Julia. At least not only for her. I did it for all of us. No more court battles, no more public relations campaigns, no more delicate negotiations—though I realize you'll miss racing back and forth to Washington in Fowler's private jet." I wished I hadn't said that. She might want to turn this into a personal vendetta, but I was determined to keep it on a professional level. "What I mean is there'll be no more obstacles. We can break ground as soon as the plans are drawn up and approved. Besides," I added, "I think the Sarah Siddons is worth saving."

"Like the library?"

"Aren't you ever going to stop reminding me of that?"

"Some of us don't have to be reminded. Some of us live with the memory every day."

"I'll just bet you do. You live with the memory of *Papa*, and cherish it, and now that you've got Fowler you can go to bed with it!" I stopped abruptly. The only sound in the room was my own short, shallow breathing. "Look, Cordelia," I began more quietly. "Just look at the plans. Calmly and objectively."

"Objectively!" she repeated. "That's a laugh. You couldn't tell if these plans were good, bad, or indifferent. All you know is they're what Julia wants. You designed them for her."

"What if I did design them for her?" My voice drowned out Cordelia's. "What difference does it make to you what I do for Julia? You've got Graham Fowler. Fowler and your island and that goddamn ring! Which

336

is, just for the record, too goddamn big for your goddamn hand!''

Back in my own office, my heart pounding, the air
vibrating from the slammed door, I regretted the words.
They were as silly and vulgar as the ring. I regretted
them, but I wouldn't apologize for them. Anymore
than I'd go back and get the plans I'd left on her desk.

I'm not sure how I spent the next several hours. I
remember stopping downstairs for a drink, perhaps
more than one. I remember walking a lot, looking at
a lot of buildings. I was trying to kill time till ten-
thirty. At ten-thirty I could go to Julia's dressing room.

Time was recalcitrant. It refused to pass. I went to
the theater early and watched Julia play her last scene
from the back of the house. Years ago I'd listened to
her complain about lighting and costumes and direction, but she didn't need any of them. I understood
the mechanics of her beauty, her voice, her move-
ments—I'd watched her hone them—but I couldn't
explain her sheer shimmering presence. It defied analysis. It conquered all resistance. There wasn't an individual in that audience who was immune to it. And
no one succumbed more completely than I. I'd been
a fool to let her go, but I wasn't a fool any longer.

I was waiting in her dressing room when she came
off stage. My mind was made up. My lines were ready:
"Marry me, Julia."

She hadn't looked surprised to see me, but she looked
surprised now and a little wary. "I imagine I owe this
visit and your generous offer to Cordelia."

"Will you?"

"I'm no good at marriage."

"Then live with me. We'll make it work this time. I swear we will."

She turned from the dressing table and looked at me carefully. "It is Cordelia."

"Forget Cordelia!"

"You've got it worse than ever."

"I love you."

"I think you do, Tony. I really think you do, but you love Cordelia more. And you need Cordelia. As much as she needs you. Go back to her. It isn't too late. I don't think it will ever be too late for you two."

I didn't go back to Cordelia, of course. It was too late, no matter what Julia said.

Fowler came to see me the next day. My secretary buzzed and announced him. I told her to find Cordelia. That was when I heard Fowler's voice shouting through the intercom not to be such a damn fool and saw Fowler bursting into my office.

"Don't tell me you're busy. I won't take up much of your time. I saw the new plans. It will be more expensive to build over the Sarah Siddons than to build in place of it."

"Don't talk to me. I'm not the project architect on this."

"You know, Tony, it amazes me that you get any work done at all with that damn chip on your shoulder. I know it's Cordelia's commission, and I know what she thinks of your new plan. I even know why she hates it." He shot me a malicious smile. "Just because you think I'm a philistine about architecture, don't make the mistake of thinking I'm stupid. A lot of men have, and a lot of men have been ruined as a result."

"Is that a threat?"

"How could I ruin you?" His voice was silky now. "Except by taking Cordelia away."

I stood. I'd had enough of Graham Fowler. "All right, you don't want the plans, and you already have Cordelia. Now if you don't mind—"

"I didn't say I wasn't interested in the new plan. I said it would cost more to build. On the other hand, we can start building sooner. When you're paying twenty thousand dollars a day in commitment fees for a loan, every day counts. And costs are going up all the time. When we started, this project was budgeted at a hundred and ninety million. Now the price tag's two hundred and eighty. The sooner we get this show on the road, the better. Besides"—he smiled with genuine pleasure—"I'll get more tax credits for rehabilitating a structure listed in the national register. I'm willing to go along with the alternate plan if ACT is."

"What about Cordelia?"

"What about Cordelia?" His voice was silky again.

"Will she accept the new plans?"

"Oh, I thought you meant something else. Yes, she'll accept the new plans. She doesn't have much choice."

"You mean she's going to be a good little wife."

"I mean she's a smart architect. She knows the plans are good—she has nothing against them, only the fact that you designed them for Julia—and I'm the client. If I'm satisfied, why shouldn't she be?" He started for the door but when he reached it, turned back to me. His smile was no longer smug, and when he spoke, his voice was harsh. For the first time I suspected him of sincerity. "You know, Bain, I don't like you anymore than you like me. But I'll give you one thing."

I was foolish enough to think he was going to give me credit for being a good architect.

"You're the only man I've ever envied." He started to go, then turned back to me a second time. "For Julia. And especially for Cordelia. She's not going to marry me. Having a young wife is dangerous enough. Having a young wife who's in love with another man is suicidal. I gave it my best try—hell, I never offered a woman an island before—but my best try wasn't good enough."

Cordelia didn't come into the office that day, which was unheard of. I wondered if she'd stayed home because of her quarrel with me or her breakup with Fowler. I still didn't trust him. I picked up the phone to call Cordelia, then put it down again. On my way out of the office my secretary reminded me that I had a meeting at four-thirty. I told her to cancel it.

The cleaning woman let me in on her way out. If she was surprised to see me after all this time, she didn't mention it. She told me Mrs. Kirkland—a neat evasion, I thought—was upstairs in the studio and closed the door behind her.

Alone in the living room, I was shocked. Cordelia had changed nothing. The bronzes we'd bought on our wedding trip, the prints she'd brought back from Japan, the pre-Columbian statues I'd found in Mexico stood in the same places. She'd hung three of Adam's sketches—the rest of his collection had gone to the Museum of Modern Art—but everything else remained the same. She'd treated the apartment with the same reverence as Adam's office. Or perhaps she simply didn't care. I wasn't certain, though I did know one thing for sure. There was no trace of Fowler.

340

I climbed to the studio. She heard my footsteps on the stairs. "Did you forget something, Jenny?" she called to the cleaning woman.

She was sitting with her back to the door. Her spine made a smooth arch over the drafting board, more graceful than any man had ever designed. Her hair fell forward, a curtain of dark velvet concealing her face. Her hand, when she reached for another pen, was naked.

I glanced around the room. It too remained unchanged, down to the second drafting table. I couldn't believe it.

"*I* forgot something."

She whirled around on her high stool. Her face registered surprise, then hardened into suspicion. "What are you doing here?" Her voice matched her expression, and I knew this wasn't going to be easy. It might not even be possible.

"Fowler came to see me."

She turned back to her drafting board. "That's right. You won. You and Julia."

"He said some other things—about you and him."

"Did he?" Her voice was flat, without curiosity.

"He said you're not going to marry him."

"More a case of his not marrying me."

"I don't believe that." I was pressing hard, but she refused to be pressed.

"It's true."

The doorbell rang then, as if on cue, and she slipped past me quickly. I think she was afraid I might try to stop her, or worse yet, touch her. I followed her down the stairs and saw Julia come striding into the living room as if she were making a stage entrance. She took command of the scene that completely.

She and Cordelia faced each other. I stood watching them, one vortex of the triangle we formed. "I hope you don't mind my coming here," Julia said. Her wonderful voice was controlled and almost diffident.

"No," Cordelia said quietly.

"Graham Fowler came to see me."

"Fowler's had a busy day," I said. Cordelia glanced from Julia to me, then back to Julia.

"Thank you." Julia's voice trembled with emotion.

"Don't thank me. Thank Graham. Thank Tony," Cordelia added without glancing at me this time. "He saved the Sarah Siddons for you."

"Not for me, Delia. For all of us. For posterity."

"Posterity! You're not on stage now, Julia, so you can skip the melodrama. You got what you wanted. Both of you. I hope you'll be happy."

"Why are you so damned stubborn?" The weapon of Julia's voice sliced through the room. "Why do you refuse to listen to anyone? To see anything but your own narrow vision?"

"I admit it!" Cordelia's voice, not as well trained as Julia's, rasped with anger. "I was blind last time— until Papa died—but I see clearly now."

"You see nothing!"

"I see betrayal. Of me. Of Papa. Of everything he stood for."

"Papa wasn't betrayed. If anything, he—" Julia stopped abruptly. She stood there facing Cordelia across the room, across the chasm of their misunderstanding of each other and their shared past. She stood there on the brink. A few words, a single revelation would sweep away the misunderstanding—and shatter Cordelia's faith. The foundation on which she'd built her life, and destroyed ours, would crumble. Part of me hoped Julia would not speak. Part of me prayed she would.

Julia turned away. My heart sank as if it were a rock she'd tossed into a well.

"If anything, he what?" Cordelia demanded, sure that she knew the truth, and it could not hurt her.

"Nothing," Julia murmured. She was still the older sister, protecting Cordelia from the world, the truth, herself.

"You were going to say something about Papa. Say it."

"Forget it, Cordelia."

"Another family secret? Like Mother's first marriage? Only there's nothing you can tell me about Papa that I don't know, nothing that would matter."

"That's what's so tragic," Julia said sadly.

"That I loved him?"

Julia whirled back to face her sister. "No, Cordelia! I loved him. Mother loved him. You worshiped him."

"He deserved it!"

"He wasn't a god!"

"He was true to his ideals!"

"But not to Mother!"

The words were out, bleak and true and terrible. They hung between them in the awful silence as surely as if Julia had written them in stone.

"I don't believe it," Cordelia said. At her temple a fine vein throbbed with pain.

"It's true." Julia had regained control of her voice. It was soft with kindness—and regret. She knew what she'd done, and she knew that now she had to go on. "Mother wasn't going *to* Hollywood. She was running *away*—away from Papa. Papa and his affair. I've known for years, but I didn't want you to. Neither did Papa."

"I don't believe it!" Cordelia repeated. This time the words exploded among us like a grenade.

"It's true," Julia insisted. "I loved him too, Cordelia, but he was human."

"If you don't see that," I said quietly, "you don't see his real greatness. Not that he was perfect, but that he never stopped striving for perfection."

"You never understood, Cordelia." Julia took a step toward her. I expected Cordelia to back away, but she stood her ground. "You grew up believing in the myth of Papa's perfection and almost ruined your own life maintaining it. You were determined to believe I was perfect—a golden girl, you used to say—but I've got the same fears and doubts you have. I've even suffered the same pain." Julia did not glance at me, but something in her voice made me think she wanted to. "And you were convinced of the perfection of their marriage, but it wasn't perfect. No marriage is perfect. You put a great burden on Papa and on me, Delia, but you put the greatest of all on Tony. You kept measuring him against Papa, but that Papa existed only in your mind. You kept measuring your marriage against Papa's and Mother's, but that was imaginary too. What Tony did . . ." she hesitated, "what Tony and I did was wrong, but then so was what Papa did so many years ago. I like to think that if Mother had lived, she would have forgiven him. I know if you have any sense, you'll forgive Tony."

"And you?" Cordelia's voice was serious but not unkind.

"I'm not asking for perfection. I learned to live with the real world a long time ago—and to escape from it on a stage." Julia turned to me and smiled. I don't think I'll ever forget that smile. There was enough voltage in it to light up an entire theater, but it was meant only for me. "And now if you'll both excuse me, I think I'm what the French call de trop." Her exit was, as always, skillfully timed and beautifully executed.

"Did you know about Papa?"

It was as if Julia had never spoken. Adam was still all she cared about.

"Yes," I said evenly.

"And you never told me."

"Would you have listened?"

Her only answer was to turn away from me. She stood staring up at a framed sketch of Adam's. It was of Windswept, and I was reminded of myself staring up at her that first day. I realized finally that she'd never love anyone the way she'd loved him.

I picked up my coat from the chair where I'd tossed it and started for the door.

"Don't," she said.

"I'm not going to give you the sordid details of Adam's affair, if that's what you mean."

"It isn't. I meant don't go. Please."

I suppose that was my cue to cross the room and take her in my arms, but I didn't. Too much was at stake.

"I was wrong about Papa."

"And now you'll never forgive him." It was not the solution I'd been hoping for. I knew Cordelia and her passions. Love or hatred, it was the same obsession with Adam.

She turned back to me, and I saw the surprise on her face. "I could never turn against Papa. I could never stop loving him. But I guess it's time I stopped worshiping him."

"I'm glad."

"Is that all you can say?"

"Is that all *you* can say?" I repeated. I was still pushing hard, but I had to. I had to get at the truth beneath the words.

She rubbed her finger where Fowler's ring had sat for a day, where the plain gold band I'd given her had rested for years. "I could never stop loving you either. I never have."

Again it was my cue to take her in my arms, and again I resisted it. "You've always said that with such ease. But when it came down to cases . . ." I stopped in midsentence. It was time to let Adam rest in peace.

"It wasn't that I didn't love you, Tony, only that I didn't love myself. And I was sure you couldn't either. I thought you settled for me because you couldn't have Julia. I thought you wanted me because I was Papa's daughter. I thought—"

I didn't have to hear any more. I closed the distance between us in a second. It had been years since I'd held her. It seemed like a lifetime. And it all came back as if it had been only yesterday. The fragrance of her hair, the long slender pride of her body, the softness of her mouth.

"I want *you*, Cordelia. I love *you*." The words had always been true and never more true than they were now. I repeated them to her eyes, her hair, her mouth.

"About the Fowler Building . . ." she murmured.

"To hell with Fowler and his building," I whispered.

"You were right."

"Forget it."

"It's better this . . ."

There was only one way to silence her. "Don't you

346

ever," I murmured, my mouth on hers, "think of anything but architecture?"

She dropped her head back and looked up at me, her eyes as deep blue and life-giving as the sea. Then her mouth on mine gave the wordless answer.

FOWLER BUILDING
REJUVENATES BROADWAY
by Preston Hunter

More than two years ago, after as many years of public protests and legal battles, ground was broken for a vast new multiuse tower to rise over the Sarah Siddons Theater. The design was a compromise worked out between Artists for a Cultural Tradition, who had fought to save the venerable old theater, and Graham Fowler and the firm of Kirkland and Bain.

Compromise is not my favorite architectural style, and I had few expectations and little hope for this building which was going to signal the beginning of the Broadway renewal project. Subsequent sketches and models were somewhat reassuring, but sketches and models, as every architectural critic knows, are as close to the real thing as the description of a great meal is to its eating. Last night I and 999 other guests sat down to that meal at a special gala given by Graham Fowler to celebrate the opening of his building. And if I were Michelin, I would feel obliged in all good conscience to award four stars.

The firm of Kirkland and Bain has designed, simply, one of the best buildings of the last decade, perhaps the last half century. Graham Fowler gave them not only a free hand with the plans, but the extra millions that translate into first-rate materials and superb detailing. And by demanding that the Sarah Siddons be incorporated into the plan, Julia Kirkland and ACT forced the architects to create a building that combines a respect for the past with an inspired view of the future, a building that shows deference to its neighbors and the entire theatrical district, yet points the way to the long overdue revitalization of the Broadway area.

The vigorous facade translates the vitality of the old White Way into a new idiom. The public spaces are dramatic as well as functional. The refurbished Sarah Siddons is nothing less than splendid. And the opulent hotel rooms and comfortable artists' residences are oases of privacy and quiet in the center of this hub of activity and excitement.

The firm of Kirkland and Bain, Miss Julia Kirkland, and Mr. Graham Fowler can all be proud of their achievement. And indeed, all were on hand last night in the grand ballroom of the Fowler Palace Hotel to accept congratulations from the President, the governor, the mayor, and other assembled celebrities. In fact, if any sight rivaled that of this Broadway monument, it was Julia Kirkland, the first lady of the American theater, and Cordelia Kirkland, one half of the firm of Kirkland and Bain, sitting side by side on the dais. It has long been said that, more than any other architect of his time, Adam Kirkland left a legacy of excellence and beauty. Last night his daughters proved that was true.

Sensational Reading from SIGNET

Passionate Historical Romances from SIGNET

(0451)

- [ ] HIGHLAND FLAME by Kathleen Fraser. (131576—$3.50)*
- [ ] MY BRAZEN HEART by Kathleen Fraser. (135164—$3.75)*
- [ ] JOURNEY TO DESIRE by Helene Thornton. (130480—$2.95)*
- [ ] PASSIONATE EXILE by Helene Thornton. (127560—$2.95)*
- [ ] CHEYENNE STAR by Susannah Lehigh. (128591—$2.95)*
- [ ] WINTER MASQUERADE by Kathleen Maxwell. (129547—$2.95)*
- [ ] THE DEVIL'S HEART by Kathleen Maxwell. (124723—$2.95)*
- [ ] DRAGON FLOWER by Alyssa Welks. (128044—$2.95)*
- [ ] CHANDRA by Catherine Coulter. (126726—$2.95)*
- [ ] DEVIL'S EMBRACE by Catherine Coulter. (118537—$2.95)*
- [ ] SWEET SURRENDER by Catherine Coulter. (131916—$3.50)*
- [ ] LOVE'S BLAZING ECSTASY by Kathryn Kramer. (133277—$3.95)*
- [ ] RAGE TO LOVE by Maggie Osborne. (126033—$2.95)*
- [ ] ENCHANTED NIGHTS by Julia Grice. (128974—$2.95)*
- [ ] SEASON OF DESIRE by Julia Grice. (125495—$2.95)*
- [ ] KIMBERLEY FLAME by Julia Grice. (124375—$3.50)*
- [ ] SATIN EMBRACES by Julia Grice. (132424—$3.50)*
- [ ] PASSION'S REBEL by Kay Cameron. (125037—$2.95)*

*Prices slightly higher in Canada

Buy them at your local bookstore or use this convenient coupon for ordering.

NEW AMERICAN LIBRARY,
P.O. Box 999, Bergenfield, New Jersey 07621

Please send me the books I have checked above. I am enclosing $_____
(please add $1.00 to this order to cover postage and handling). Send check
or money order—no cash or C.O.D.'s. Prices and numbers are subject to change
without notice.

Name _____

Address_____

City_____ State_____ Zip Code_____
Allow 4-6 weeks for delivery.
This offer is subject to withdrawal without notice.